DES PLAINES PUBLIC LIBRARY

APR 1997

3 1468 00413 7370

W9-AUK-763

WITHDRAWN

DATE DUE

JUN 2 8 1997	MAY 2 7 1997
JUL 7 1997	
	AUG 4 1997
JUL 2 1 1997	
9/4/97 O.P.	NOV 1 0 1997
12/9/97 AH	
	APR 2 1 1998 ✓
MAR 1 9 1998	
MAY 2 6 1998	AUG 2 7 1998
	NOV 3 0 1998
JUL 2 3 1998	APR 1 3 1999
OCT 0 6 1998	AUG 1 8 1999
MAR 1 5 1999	
	APR 0 2 2000
SEP 3 0 1999	
5-27	
APR 1 8 2003	

GAYLORD   PRINTED IN U.S.A.

TWINS

Katherine Stone

TWINS

DES PLAINES PUBLIC LIBRARY
841 Graceland Avenue
Des Plaines, Illinois 60016

WHEELER
PUBLISHING, INC.
ROCKLAND, MA

★ AN AMERICAN COMPANY ★

Copyright © 1989 by Katherine Stone

All rights reserved.

Published in Large Print by arrangement with
Kensington Publishing Corp. in the United States and Canada.

Wheeler Large Print Book Series.

Set in 16 pt. Plantin.

Library of Congress Cataloging-in-Publication Data

Stone, Katherine, 1949–
   Twins / Katherine Stone.
     p.   cm.
   ISBN 1-56895-428-X
   1. Large type books.   I. Title.
  [PS3569.T64134T85   1997b]
  813'.54—dc21
                                        97-9214
                                           CIP

Prologue

New York City
February 16, 1987

Brooke sat bolt upright. Her heart raced and her breath came in shallow gasps. The dial of the bedside clock glowed ten-thirty. Brooke frowned at the clock. She had only been in bed for fifteen minutes; it was hardly enough time to fall asleep much less to dream! But something—it *must* have been a nightmare—had forced her violently back into wakefulness.

Only later would Brooke recall that she was already reaching for the phone when it rang . . .

"Hello," she breathed uneasily as her mind frantically tried to reassure her anxious heart.

It will be Andrew, Brooke told herself. He will be calling to discuss one final detail, one final *twist,* of the State of New York versus Jeffrey Martin. Andrew was the deputy district attorney. He and Brooke represented the State of New York. Together they planned to put a legal end to the renegade career of Manhattan's most successful cocaine dealer.

Logically, the late-night phone call would be from Andrew. But illogically, and fueled with a knowledge that defied logic, Brooke's heart resolutely pumped dread through her body.

1

"Brooke!" The voice was filled with sheer terror.

"Melanie! What's—"

"He tried to kill me. Brooke, help me!" The terror was strong and pervasive. But the voice wasn't. It was the voice of a body that was badly injured. In shock, maybe dying . . .

It was the voice of Brooke's sister, Brooke's *twin.*

"Melanie," Brooke spoke urgently, "where are you?"

"My apartment," Melanie answered slowly, as if bewildered that something so horrible could have happened in that sanctuary.

"Is he gone?"

"Yes. Brooke it was *him.* The Manhattan . . ."

The Manhattan Ripper. That was the news media's name for the knife-wielding psychopath who had terrorized Manhattan, brutally murdering its young women for the past ten months. The police knew the Ripper was a man because his victims were raped. No one had ever seen him. The Ripper didn't leave witnesses, only victims.

But now Melanie had seen him. And, miraculously, she was alive. *Still.*

"Are you hurt?"

"So much blood," Melanie murmured dreamily. "So much blood."

Melanie was badly hurt. Her voice faded in and out of reality, drifting away. . . .

"Melanie," Brooke spoke sternly She had to make Melanie focus on the present—if it was

2

possible, if Melanie hadn't already lost too much blood.

"Yes, Brooke," Melanie answered in a little-girl voice, surprised that her older sister was talking to her so harshly. What had she done wrong?

"Melanie," Brooke continued softly. There had been so much harshness between them, so much for so long. It hadn't always been that way; it couldn't be that way now. Brooke added gently, her voice choked with emotion, "Mellie."

Mellie . . . It was Brooke's special name for Melanie when they were little girls. *Mellie.* The name recalled such happy memories of laughter and love between sisters—twin sisters—still bound by the unique closeness born in their mother's womb, before the realities of life drove a wedge between them . . .

Brooke shook the memories that flooded her mind. She needed to tell Melanie those lovely memories were with her still, despite the bitter ones. She *would* tell her. But not now. Now she, *they,* had to save Melanie's life.

"Mellie, have you called the police?" Brooke asked, knowing the answer, but hoping.

"I called you!" The voice said clearly, *I called you because you are my sister—my older sister—and I know you will save me.*

"I'm glad you called me, honey. It was the right thing to do. Now listen carefully, Melanie. You have to hang up the phone so I can call the paramedics and the police. As soon as I've done that I will call you right back and we'll talk until they arrive. OK?"

No answer.

"Melanie."

"Uh-huh." The answer came weakly as if from a small child who had answered by nodding her head instead of speaking. Was she getting too weak? Or was she just drifting, too, to the memories of the two happy little girls?

"OK, Mellie. Hang up now. I'll call you right back."

An almost unbearable emptiness swept through Brooke as she heard the phone disconnect. It felt like an end. An ending. The end.

No! Brook shook the thought away angrily as she hurriedly dialed the emergency police number.

"This is," Brooke began urgently, then forced control in her voice and assumed her usual professional tone, "this is assistant district attorney Brooke Chandler. I need a medic unit dispatched to . . ."

Brooke provided the necessary information in a matter of moments. Just before the call ended, she added authoritatively, "Have the police department contact Lieutenant Nick Adrian. He needs to be there."

"Will do, Ms. Chandler," the dispatcher replied with respect. The police, the emergency unit dispatchers, the paramedics, and the district attorney's office were all coconspirators in the war against crime in New York City. They were on the same team. The dispatcher had no idea that the assistant district attorney's call was more than good teamwork. There was nothing in Brooke Chandler's tone that sounded like

4

emotion. "I'll let Lieutenant Adrian know you think he needs to be there."

The Manhattan Ripper case was Nick Adrian's special project, his special nightmare. Nick knew more about the psychopath than anyone else. He had seen every morbid bit of horror the killer left in his wake of death. Nick knew more than anyone else. But Nick knew—and it tormented him night after sleepless night—that despite ten months of searching and four savage murders they still had no idea who the killer was. They were at his mercy, waiting for him to strike again, hoping he would make a mistake and leave even the smallest clue.

Nick needs to be there, Brooke thought as her trembling fingers dialed Melanie's number. He *has* to be. It wasn't because the Manhattan Ripper was Nick's case. Nick needed to be there because he would help Melanie. Melanie . . .

As Brooke listened to Melanie's phone ring, unanswered, her frantic thoughts darted to the other people who needed to know.

Five rings.

Her parents. How could she tell them what horror had befallen their golden angel? Would they blame *her* for allowing this to happen to Melanie? New York was Brooke's city. It was her fault. She should have protected Melanie . . .

Brooke would call her parents from the hospital, as soon as she knew that Melanie was all right.

Ten rings. Pick up the phone, Melanie. Mellie. Please.

Adam Drake needed to know. The society

5

pages of yesterday's—*yesterday's*—Sunday *Times* featured a color photograph of Melanie and Adam taken at *Fashion* magazine's gala Valentine's Day party. Melanie and Adam stood in front of an ice sculpture of Cupid, the perfect backdrop for their fairytale romance. Distinguished elegant Adam and dazzling golden Melanie, smiling, happy, in *love*.

Adam Drake was the reason Melanie left Charles Sinclair. It was so obvious. Why did Melanie deny it? The celebrated breakup of super-model Melanie Chandler and handsome, powerful magazine editor Charles Sinclair occurred months ago, but the emotions lingered. Even at the Valentine's Day party, according to the article that accompanied the photograph, there had been a "scene" between Melanie and Charles. . . .

Charles, Brooke's mind whirled. *How can I tell Charles about this? How can anyone tell him?*

Fifteen rings. Melanie, come *on.*

But Charles needed to know, and Jason needed to know. Charles and Jason, the *other* twins.

Twenty rings. Answer the—

The ringing stopped. So, for a moment, did Brooke's heart. Someone had taken the phone off the hook. Melanie? The Ripper? The paramedics? Nick?

"Melanie?" Brooke whispered.

Silence.

"Mellie, honey," Brooke spoke lovingly to the silence, "I called the paramedics. They'll be there

6

any moment. Hold on, darling. Please. And Nick. He's a police officer. You can trust him, Mellie. He'll take care of you."

Brooke paused, blinking back tears, hoping to hear something, the smallest sound, from her twin. Brooke heard nothing. But she *felt* a presence. Brooke knew Melanie was there, and Melanie would hear her words.

"Mellie. Don't try to talk, just listen. We'll talk when you're better." Tears streamed down Brooke's cheeks. She closed her eyes and saw a little girl with sun-gold hair and bright-blue eyes frolicking on a white sand beach. Brooke could almost hear the laughter. "I love you, Mellie, I always have. We need to talk about the things that have come between us. We *will* talk. Remember the summer we spent at the beach when we were five, Mellie? Remember what fun we had. . . ."

Suddenly there was noise—commotion—at the other end. Brooke held her breath. She heard pounding. It lasted only a few seconds. Then Brooke heard a crash as the door gave way.

"Christ."

Brooke felt the paramedic's horror as he saw her twin sister.

Help her. Please.

"Is she . . . ?" another voice asked.

"I don't know," the voice, now close to the phone, close to Melanie, answered. "Let me find her carotid."

Please. Please. Please.

Depthless, immobilizing fear settled in

Brooke's heart as she silently prayed for the other heart; the other heart that once had been so close.

"OK, Joe, let's get to work," the paramedic breathed finally. "She's still alive. . . ."

Part I

Chapter One

New York City
July 1985

"So it's true."

"Charles," Brooke breathed with surprise. What was Charles Sinclair doing *here?* Why would Charles Sinclair leave the luxurious air-conditioned offices of Sinclair Publishing and journey through the midday heat and humidity and humanity of downtown Manhattan to the district attorney's office? "What—"

"I had to see for myself if Brooke Chandler, attorney extraordinaire, had really forsaken Perkins, Crane, and Marks—not to mention Sinclair Publishing—for . . ." Charles paused. His dark-brown eyes calmly surveyed Brooke's tiny office. The walls wore peeling yellow-gray paint and the linoleum floor was a spiderweb of cracks. A portable fan noisily recirculated the stifling summer heat.

What is he thinking, Brooke wondered.

It was impossible to tell. Whatever Charles *really* thought of her stuffy, dingy office was artfully concealed beneath layers of impeccable manners and aristocratic politeness. At least that was what Brooke chose to believe. But there were other ways to interpret the behavior of the handsome and fashionable editor-in-chief of Sinclair

11

Publishing Company. The polite, pleasant veneer *could* be masking the worst form of arrogant contempt—*indifference.*

Charles's critics proclaimed that the blue blood flowing through his veins, carrying with it a heritage of wealth and power and privilege, was as cold as ice. Witness, they argued, the never-ending series of love affairs begun by Charles and, when he became bored, ended by him. Charles Sinclair's passion was spent on his magazines. There was nothing human . . .

"The glamour of the DA's office?" Brooke finally finished Charles's sentence. "I haven't forsaken Sinclair Publishing. I could still do work for you, assuming—"

"Assuming we would want you? Of course we would. Or, did you mean, assuming you have time? Because—" Charles smiled wryly at the stacks of depositions, police records, and court documents cluttering Brooke's office— "you won't."

"I could make time," Brooke answered swiftly.

Brooke had always planned to work in the district attorney's office after graduation from law school. But during school she clerked for Perkins, Crane, and Marks, the prestigious Manhattan law firm retained by Sinclair Publishing Company. Brooke met Charles and almost changed her plans because of him. She *almost* accepted the position-that-would-lead-to-partnership at Perkins, Crane, and Marks. Because then she would see Charles, work with Charles, be with Charles.

But to what end? Brooke's logical mind finally

12

demanded. There was nothing *personal* between them. There never would be. Brooke Chandler was not Charles Sinclair's type. Brooke was not one of New York's most beautiful, talented, and glamorous women.

It would be easier to stay with the plan to work in the DA's office, Brooke decided. Easier not to see him.

But now Charles was *here,* his brown eyes friendly and polite, and she was telling him she would find time to do legal work for Sinclair Publishing.

"It would keep me sane. A nice clean advertising contract, once in a while, to offset the felonies." Brooke smiled, tilted her head, and added quietly, "I meant, assuming I pass the bar."

"You probably have quite a track record of failing examinations," Charles teased. It had come up once— John Perkins was reciting the accomplishments of his star law clerk—that Brooke graduated summa cum laude from Harvard and was first in her class at Columbia Law School.

Brooke shrugged, her blue eyes frowning for an uncertain moment. She admitted, awkwardly, as if compelled to confess, "I'm a worrier."

"It's probably why you're so good," Charles observed. Then, surprised by the rush of pink that filled Brooke's cheeks, he added, "That's a compliment, Brooke."

"Oh, Brooke, you're back from court. Andrew—" Jean Fletcher, a second-year law student who was clerking at the DA's office, burst into Brooke's office. "Oh! Sorry. I didn't realize."

Jean stopped abruptly and stared with unconcealed amazement at Charles.

"You were saying something about Andrew?" Brooke asked after making introductions.

"Yes." Jean forced her attention away from Charles. "He wants to have a strategy meeting about the Norris case at two."

"Fine." Brooke explained to Charles, "Andrew Parker. He's the deputy DA and a brilliant litigator."

"I've heard of him."

"Oh, Brooke, I almost forgot," Jean interjected. "I was working in your office while you were in court and answered a call on your direct line. It was your sister. She said she told them Yes after all."

"*Yes?*"

"That's what she said." Jean waited a moment, but Brooke was lost in thought. Jean shrugged, cast a final appreciative glance at Charles, and withdrew.

"You have a sister." Charles finally broke the silence that followed Jean's departure.

"Oh. Yes." Brooke frowned slightly. More than a sister, Charles. A *twin*. It was important personal information. Except there was nothing personal. . . . "Melanie. She's a model. Apparently she just agreed to sign with Drake Modelling Agency."

"*Agreed* to? Did she actually consider turning them down?" Drake Modelling Agency handled only top models, only a few, only the *very best*.

14

"I thought she *would* turn them down," Brooke murmured.

"No one says No to Adam Drake," Charles said flatly.

Charles knew Adam well. Drake models appeared frequently in all three of Sinclair Publishing's magazines. Because Drake models were the best. Just as the magazines—*Images, Fashion,* and *Spinnaker*—were the best. Charles Sinclair and Adam Drake were alike, handsome and powerful and wealthy. Both were used to saying No. But neither was used to hearing it.

"You don't know Melanie," Brooke whispered softly.

But Charles *will* know her, Brooke realized.

Melanie would make Charles's spectacular magazines even more magnificent. Brooke could imagine the highgloss photographs of Melanie, elegant and glamorous in designer gowns and glittering jewels, that would appear in *Fashion.* And the natural shots—Melanie's golden hair wind-tossed and her long tanned legs stretched over the varnished decks of a sleek sailboat— perfect for *Spinnaker.* And the soft romantic watercolors visually enhancing the wonderful literature that filled the pages of *Images.*

Photographs of Melanie would appear in Charles's magazines. And Melanie would dazzle and sparkle at the fabulous parties Brooke read about. Melanie would mingle—because she would *belong*—with the powerbrokers and celebrities of fashion and publishing and art and theater. People like Charles.

Melanie was Charles's type. Melanie was like

the beautiful women with whom Charles had affairs.

Except Melanie was more beautiful. And Melanie was *Melanie*. No one said No to Melanie.

"She wasn't sure she wanted to leave California," Brooke continued, trying unsuccessfully to shake the inevitable image of Charles and Melanie together.

"Then why did she contact Drake?" Charles asked. He knew how irritated Adam Drake would be by a fickle model. It surprised Charles that Adam hadn't simply cancelled further negotiations at the first sign of hesitation.

"She didn't. They contacted *her*."

"Oh." Charles wondered if Adam had ever done that before. "Is she an older or younger sister?"

"Younger," Brooke answered carefully. Another confession. "Twenty minutes younger. We're twins . . . too."

"I didn't know that," Charles murmured distantly, frowning briefly. Then, smiling, he asked, "Are you identical?"

Brooke stared at him for a long, bewildered moment. An aristocrat with impeccable manners wouldn't ask such a question. It was worse than indifferent, worse than ice-cold. It was *cruel*.

Brooke's blue eyes flashed hurt, then anger. Charles's eyes answered with surprise and concern.

He couldn't have asked that *seriously*, could he? Brooke's mind whirled as she looked into the serious. concerned brown eyes.

"No," Brooke breathed finally. *Of course not.*

16

"She's blonde, like Jason." Like your golden twin.

"Oh." Charles nodded. Then he glanced at his watch and added, "I had better be going."

"Thanks for stopping by." Why *did you stop by? Will you ever stop by again?"*

"Don't work too hard, Brooke." Charles gave a parting shot to the stacks of work in Brooke's office, smiled at her, and left.

Jean appeared in Brooke's doorway seconds after Charles left.

"That was *Charles Sinclair.*"

"I know. I introduced you."

"How do you know him, Brooke?"

"I don't really know him. I did some work—"

"He just happened to be in the neighborhood? He just *happened* to wander all the way from Park Avenue in the midday heat?" Jean pressed.

"Charles wanders. He works out ideas for the magazines by pacing around Manhattan."

"But you don't know him."

"No," Brooke repeated firmly. It wasn't information Brooke learned from Charles. John Perkins had told her. John described it as a restless prowling, like an animal, driven to search, compelled to keep moving.

"But Charles *is* the creative genius behind *Images,* isn't he?" Jean pushed. "*Images* is his vision—his *fantasy*— isn't it?"

"I think Charles and Jason create *Images* together." Brooke smiled. "You're going to make a good lawyer, Jean."

"It seems impossible that *Images* is a joint effort. Especially between Charles and Jason

Sinclair. They seem so different," Jean mused. "Of course, they *are* twins. One mind, one heart. Or don't you buy that? You should know."

Brooke shrugged, suddenly uneasy. There was a time when she and Melanie communicated in perfect, wordless harmony. There was a time when they knew, instinctively, the other's thoughts and dreams. But that was years and years ago. As they grew, the differences became more important than the closeness.

"Well," Jean continued quickly, sensing Brooke's discomfort, "end of cross-examination. I'll see you at two in Andrew's office."

After Jean left, Brooke sat at her desk and tried to concentrate on the legal brief she was writing. But it was impossible. Charles's visit—now a confusing memory— and the startling news that Melanie was moving to New York haunted her.

Brooke sighed, finally permitting the swirling thoughts and emotions to surface. She had to face them. She had to face the facts.

Charles. Charles was a midday mirage. He would never be a part of her life. She would never really know him. But Melanie would . . .

Melanie. Melanie was moving to New York. Fine. Brooke had her own identity now. She was happy with who she was. She was doing what she wanted to do. Melanie wasn't a threat. That was all ancient history.

Good, Brooke told herself calmly, I can handle it.

Then the emotions took over.

Why was Melanie *really* doing this? She had everything in California. Wasn't it enough?

No. Of course it wasn't enough. Having everything had never been enough for Melanie. . . .

A continent away Melanie grabbed her car keys and dashed out of her Westwood apartment into the warmth of the perfect California summer day.

She drove the pale-blue Mercedes sports coupe west along San Vicente Boulevard to the ocean. The traffic heading east toward the maze of freeways was heavy. *They* were going inland to the smog and heat and stagnation. *She* was going to the beach.

Melanie hummed softly to the music on the radio, her fingers tapping rhythmically to the beat, and smiled contentedly as the fresh ocean breeze swirled her long golden hair.

Will I miss this? she wondered. The California lifestyle with its easy sunny freedom and the year-round songs of summer was all she had known for twenty-five years. The warm sparkling sunshine and limitless blue Pacific and gentle ocean breezes still made her tingle with joy. Her body was sleek and healthy and golden, and her spirit was joyous and free.

Melanie was like what Southern California used to be, before the crowds and the smog and the too fast pace and the drugs and the crime and the glitter that was false. Before all that there was *real* glitter, the natural glitter of a golden sun smiling on the endless pristine seascape and luxuriant tropical foliage. Melanie flourished in Southern California. This was *her* lush green land, *her* vibrant exciting town, *her* sapphire-blue ocean, *her* snow-white beach. Life was easy. Melanie was in control and unafraid.

What would it be like to live on the East Coast? Would she fit in? Would she feel comfortable? Brooke had moved to the East Coast right after high school and never returned. She lived in Boston, attending Harvard University, for four years. Then she moved to New York City— to *Manhattan*—for law school.

If Brooke can do it, so can I, Melanie told herself with bravado. She knew it wasn't true.

She *couldn't* do what Brooke could do. Brooke earned her many successes through hard work. If Brooke put her bright, logical, disciplined mind to something—anything—she could achieve it.

Melanie's successes were *handed* to her. All she had to do was smile and dazzle and *perform*. She just had to be what everyone *expected* Melanie to be: beautiful and happy and charming and slender and sexy and fashionable and radiant.

It was so easy.

And it was so hard.

Melanie sighed softly as she eased the Mercedes sports coupe into an oceanside parking space. She tossed her car keys under the front seat, shed her light cotton windbreaker and her sunglasses, and scampered gracefully down the narrow gravel path to the beach.

Usually when Melanie jogged she could down-shift her mind into neutral. Usually she could breathe the salt air and feel her strong, athletic body pumping against the wind and the sand. Usually she didn't think, she just *felt*.

But not today. Not since she said Yes to Adam

Drake. Ever since then a constant taunting dialogue echoed in her brain.

Why are you moving to New York? You have everything you want right here. Isn't it enough?

Yes, of course.

So, why are you moving, Melanie? To impress Brooke?

No.

Good. Because Brooke won't be impressed even if you are the top model in the world. It's just too easy.

Maybe I want to be friends with Brooke.

You think that's possible? After all these years?

Yes. Sure. It has to be.

So you're moving to New York to be friends with Brooke? It has nothing to do with the fact that Drake is the best agency—

Of course that matters. I love modelling. If I really want to make the most of my career I have to move to New York.

It really might show Brooke if you become the best in the world. It's hard to stop competing after all these years. . . .

I don't want to compete with Brooke anymore.

Oh?

I feel empty. Part of me is empty.

The twin thing.

Some*thing.*

So, move.

I am.

But, remember, Brooke may not feel the same way. Why should she?

I know.

Melanie stopped, panting, at the end of the beach. The jog had turned into a full run. Every-

21

thing ached. Her arms, her legs, her rib cage, her *lungs.*

But there was a deeper ache, a painful clue to how empty she would feel if she moved to New York and she and Brooke grew even further apart. It was fear of that pain that almost made her say No to Adam Drake.

Brooke doesn't really like you, remember?

I remember. But she doesn't know me. It's been so many years.

It's a very big risk.

Yes. But I have to try.

Chapter Two

Pasadena, California
September 1963

"What have we here?" The preschool teacher eagerly hurried across the classroom toward Ellen Chandler and her identically dressed four-year-old daughters. *"Twins."*

By the time the teacher reached them, Melanie and Brooke had removed their matching blue-hooded jackets, revealing Melanie's straight sun-gold locks and Brooke's dark-brown curls.

"Oh!" the teacher exclaimed. A little disappointed she added, "They aren't identical."

"No," Ellen murmured, almost apologetically.

"Well, it actually makes it easier for us if they aren't." The teacher recovered quickly. "We can tell them apart. And they can't play as many tricks on us."

The teacher looked down at the two sets of blue eyes—one dark, one light—that gazed earnestly in return. She smiled a knowing smile. "I bet you two have your share of tricks." Then she looked at Ellen and added, as if Melanie and Brooke weren't there, "I don't envy you having twins. Twice the work. I'm sure you're just as glad it's time for them to start school."

Ellen frowned, lifted her chin, and said firmly, "I think it will be good for them to meet other children. But I will miss them very much."

Ellen knelt down in front of her daughters, wrapped an arm around each one and pulled them close. "Be good, my little ladies."

"We will, Mommy," Brooke and Melanie answered in unison.

That night, in the bedroom they shared even though they could each have had their own, Melanie and Brooke talked about the events of their first day of school.

"We were the only twins." Melanie frowned. "Everyone else was alone."

"We're lucky."

"But, Brooke, what if . . ."

"What if what?"

"What if," Melanie whispered, "what if everyone starts out as twins and one twin always dies?"

"*Mellie.*"

"What if that's the way it's supposed to be?"

"It's not."

"How do you know?"

"I know."

Melanie was silent for a moment. Then she said urgently, "Brooke, promise me if I die I can be your shadow."

"I'm not going to talk to you if you say things like that."

"Promise me."

"I promise."

They chewed thoughtfully on chocolate-chip cookies for several minutes. Then, at the same instant they had the same worry, another troublesome memory from this baffling, disruptive day. Brooke started the question and Melanie finished it.

"Do you think Mommy . . ."

" . . . wishes she didn't have us?"

"Twice the work."

"But we *help* her."

"Maybe we should help more."

"We should."

"We will," they agreed together, nodding solemnly.

After several moments, Melanie asked, "Brooke, what's identical?"

"Mommy says it means exactly alike."

"But the teacher said we *weren't* identical. And we are," Melanie said firmly.

Brooke and Melanie didn't look in mirrors. For the first four years of their lives, and the nine months before they were born, the other was always there. The same size. The same shape. With the same thoughts and ideas. They brushed each other's hair and stared in each other's eyes and *assumed* they were looking at reflections of themselves.

Brooke had made the discovery they didn't look exactly alike six months before, staring in disbelief at the very different little girls she saw reflected in a plate-glass window. It worried and upset her. But she didn't tell Melanie, because she knew it would upset Melanie, too.

"No. We are exactly alike *inside*," Brooke explained earnestly. "But we look different. That way people can tell us apart."

Melanie followed Brooke skeptically toward the full-length mirror in their parents' bedroom.

"See?" Brooke asked when they stood in front of the mirror. "Your hair is yellow and mine is brown."

Melanie shrugged. "But that's all."

"Your eyes are a different color blue," Brooke persisted. She had suffered alone with this for six months. It was a relief, finally, to share it with Melanie.

Melanie stared in the mirror at her own pale-blue eyes. They were the color of a summer day sky. Melanie had never seen these eyes before. The eyes she knew so well, Brooke's eyes, *were* different. Brooke's eyes were deep dark blue— ocean blue, not sky blue. Melanie stared, mesmerized by her own eyes, half hating them, half intrigued by the pretty color. The more she stared, the more Melanie liked the soft pale blue that stared back at her. And the halo of gold that framed her face.

Finally Melanie said, a pronouncement, "Maybe it's better not to be identical after all."

As little girls, Brooke and Melanie were The Twins. The similarities were more important than the differences. Melanie and Brooke had a combined identity—the Chandler Twins—not two distinct ones. They were inseparable and indivisible.

As they grew, their unique identities emerged. But, because they were twins, they couldn't be simply Brooke and Melanie. The twin unit still existed. Instead of being indivisible, each formed a complementary and opposite half of the whole. They were the *golden* twin and the *dark* twin, the *smart* twin and the *athletic* twin, the *fun* twin and the *compulsive* twin, the *happy* twin and the *serious* twin, the *beautiful* twin. . . .

The labels—assigned carelessly and even whimsically—came from teachers and friends and family. Throughout grade school, Melanie and Brooke paid little attention to the labels. They knew they were identical *inside*. They shared everything, understood each other perfectly and wordlessly, and were best friends.

Then, one day, in sixth grade, Melanie didn't select Brooke to be on her hopscotch team.

"Melanie, why didn't you choose me?" Brooke's deep-blue eyes glistened with tears.

"You aren't any good at hopscotch. You're not *athletic*" Melanie answered simply, amazed by Brooke's reaction.

"But, I'm . . . we're . . . *twins,*" Brooke sputtered.

"Brooke, you're being silly. If you were captain of the spelling team, would you choose *me?*"

"Yes! Of course!"

"That would be *stupid,* Brooke," Melanie insisted flatly. "You wouldn't win if you picked me."

"*Still.*"

"It would be stupid. And you're not stupid."

As tears spilled onto Brooke's cheeks, Melanie's eyes flooded with tears, too; because then, still, they shared everything. Then, still, the other's sadness made her twin ache.

"Brooke!" Melanie cried, throwing her arms around her sister and holding tight. "Please don't cry. I'm sorry. Let's go do something else. I don't feel like playing hopscotch anyway—it's a dumb game!"

During the summer of their thirteenth year, something happened that neither girl could change or control or stop or alter. It was a label that couldn't be ignored, and it drove them apart.

That thirteenth summer Melanie became beautiful. Her little-girl golden prettiness transformed into breathtaking, heart-stopping, head-spinning beauty. Heads spun when they—until Brooke could no longer stand being the ugly companion—walked by, and mouths murmured *oohs* and *aahs* and smiled appreciative, dazzled smiles.

Melanie smiled a flawless, happy, radiant smile in return. This was *fun!* Why was Brooke being such a sad sack? Brooke, smile!

But Brooke couldn't smile. It hurt too much.

Sometimes Melanie's admirers had cameras and they not so graciously asked Brooke if she would step aside, out of the picture. . . .

Brooke stepped aside and completely out of the picture. She retreated into *her* labels—bright, scholarly, capable, competent, serious, compulsive Brooke—and shunned all that was Melanie. Melanie, momentarily surprised and hurt that Brooke abandoned her, rebounded quickly, finding solace in the wonderful *high* of being the stunningly beautiful, happy, *popular* twin.

Brooke and Melanie were no longer a unit and they were no longer two halves of a whole. Now they were sisters and siblings competing as sibs and sisters did. But their competition was all the worse because there were important yet-to-be-assigned labels. The *best* twin, the *favorite* twin. . . .

Ellen and Douglas Chandler watched their twin daughters grow with a mixture of pride and wonder and concern. Each girl was so *special;* each had her own unique talents and personality. But the twin bond was special, too. The twins' parents marvelled at their perfect communication; words and giggles and ideas would begin in one and finish, without dropping a beat, in the other. Brooke and Melanie's unspoken communication was free-flowing and effortless and wondrous.

Ellen and Douglas's wonder shifted to helpless concern as they watched their teenage daughters emphatically deny the bond. Each twin tried desperately and forcefully to prove that she was no part of the other. There were *no* similarities, *nothing* in common. They shared no friends, no hobbies, no laughter. They didn't even celebrate their birthday together anymore.

As her daughters transformed from little girls to little women, Ellen wondered if she knew them at all. What kind of women would they be? *Controlled* women, Ellen decided. *Controlled, driven, private* women.

Ellen's heart ached as she watched Brooke struggle with Melanie's sudden beauty. At first, Brooke sought comfort in food. Her dark lovely face and slender young body became heavy, ugly symbols of her great unhappiness and pain. Eventually, Brooke reversed it all. She stopped eating and became thin, even thinner than Melanie. Rigidly and with unfailing resolve, Brooke discovered the self-discipline and control that would enable her to survive any pain and achieve any goal. After that, Brooke escaped into her goals and her achievements.

"Honey," Ellen lovingly stroked Brooke's short-cropped dark-brown hair, the antithesis of Melanie's long flowing gold, "when you are older, in college, you will be very beautiful."

Ellen knew it was true. Brooke would mature into a dark, seductive, sultry beauty. It would happen whether Brooke *allowed* it or not. Right now, at age fifteen, Brooke denied herself any attention to her appearance. Her clothes— somber blues and browns and grays—and her looks were neat and orderly and functional. But Brooke *would* be beautiful.

"It's not *important*, Mother," Brooke answered sternly, pulling away.

Oh, my darling, Ellen thought. I wish I could help you.

But Ellen couldn't. Brooke wouldn't talk about her pain; it was private.

In Melanie, in her golden daughter, hidden deep beneath the sunny surface, Ellen saw the same control and drive and privacy. Melanie radiated pure sunshine; the sun never went behind a cloud, and it never set. But *that* was Melanie's control. Melanie might suffer and struggle and hurt and ache. But it would be private; she would never let it show.

Melanie had to be all and always happy and shining just as much as Brooke had to be all and always serious and competent. Each girl demanded it of herself, because *they*—the twins who vehemently denied their relationship—demanded it of each other.

And all Douglas and Ellen could do was hope it would pass. The vigorous denial of the twin bond gave their daughters almost limitless energy; it was much stronger than the gentle, loving advice of a mother or father. . . .

During high school, on the rare occasions when the family ate dinner together, the conversation rapidly degenerated into a litany of each twin's accomplishments, designed as a challenge to the other to push even harder and achieve even more. Brooke and Melanie shared nothing but the all-consuming desire to be the best. Or, at least, to be better than the other. Each excelled in her own sphere, and each belittled what her twin considered to be important.

"Debating is just arguing for argument's sake, isn't it?" Melanie asked one evening. Brooke captained the school's debate team and won local, state, and national competitions. Melanie tossed her golden hair as she dismissed the value of Brooke's achievements. "It seems so pointless."

"But not *mindless,*" Brooke countered with contempt. Melanie was the head cheerleader and had just won the lead in the school play. Brooke's blue eyes icily reminded Melanie what she thought of cheerleading and acting.

Brooke studied constantly, won top honors, had few friends, and didn't date. Melanie studied when necessary, earned all B's, and was constantly surrounded by an admiring entourage of friends of both sexes.

Brooke spent her free time curled on her uncluttered bed in her perfectly ordered, silent bedroom, reading books on law and writing essays in her journal. Melanie never had a moment of free time. Her life was a golden collage of dances and parties and music and laughter. Her graceful, sleek body frolicked in the sapphire ocean and galloped horses bareback on the white sand beach and sent seductive, tantalizing messages of vitality and joy.

Brooke's favorite classes were history and English. Melanie's favorite classes were home economics and study hall. During study hall, Melanie eagerly sketched designs for clothes, and during home economics she sewed them. The clothes Melanie wore—her own designs—were daring and vivid and innovative.

Melanie enjoyed designing outfits for herself, but her favorite activity was creating new "looks" for her friends. They flocked to her bedroom— a colorful clutter of clothes and fabric tossed carelessly amid books and shoes and scarves and ribbons—and emerged, giggling and thrilled, as vivid, sexy "fashion statements."

Melanie's eye for color and design and fashion and style was instinctive. And it was more than an *eye;* it was a talent.

"Melanie, I can't wear bright red with my coloring!" a friend protested.

"Oh, but you can," Melanie countered confidently as she expertly cuffed the bright red sleeves, knotted the shirttails, and stood back to admire the surprising stylish effect.

"I can," the friend breathed. "Wow."

Brooke steadfastly ignored the laughter and music and gaiety that flowed from her sister's bedroom-boutique and rigidly battled the uneasy thoughts that plagued her.

Why can't I look like Melanie? Brooke's heart cried. Why can't I *be* like Melanie? I want—

No you *don't,* Brooke reminded herself sternly, as she fastened her neatly pleated navy-blue skirt and buttoned her wrinkle-free white blouse.

If only Brooke would let me help her with her clothes, Melanie thought wistfully a thousand times. Then Melanie would remember the haughty disdain in Brooke's cold blue eyes and low deep, somber voice. Brooke doesn't like me. I will never be good enough for Brooke. Why should I care if she looks drab and dowdy? I shouldn't care. I *don't*.

At the end of their senior year in high school, Brooke, the class valedictorian, was voted Most Likely To Be President. Melanie, the prom queen all three years for a prom to which her twin was never invited, was chosen Most Likely To Be Miss America.

Brooke won a full scholarship to Harvard. She moved to Boston a week after graduation from high school. Melanie enrolled at UCLA and worked at a florist in Westwood to help offset the cost of her education.

Divided by a continent and away from the expectations of the other, Brooke and Melanie began to make discoveries about themselves. Brooke's dormitory room, adjacent to Harvard Square, was a maze of unfolded clothes and scattered record albums and term papers in progress and unshelved romance novels. During her freshman year, Brooke added tweeds to her wardrobe of brown and navy and gray. By her sophomore year—after months of secretly and eagerly trying different combinations in the privacy of her room—Brooke started to wear colorful sweaters and embroidered blouses and bell-bottom jeans. She let her hair grow and casually gathered the unruly brown curls in brightly colored scarves and ribbons.

Brooke and her girlfriends danced to Beach Boys music and talked about the "men" who asked her—*her*—for dates. Those "men" gazed into Brooke's deep blue eyes and whispered hoarsely how pretty she was and how much they wanted to hold her and kiss her and . . .

Brooke returned their gazes in wide-eyed disbelief. But they showed her they meant it, and Brooke stayed out long past curfew, giggling breathless explanations to the dormitory supervisor about why she was so late.

Brooke's life suddenly overflowed with laughter and friendship and joy. She discovered a happy, warm, lively, loving Brooke. But what about the other Brooke, the self-disciplined, driven Brooke? Where was she? Still there, Brooke realized. That Brooke was part of who she really was, too. The new, happy Brooke was still going to graduate at the top of her class at Harvard and attend Columbia Law School. She was still going to be the best lawyer she could be.

Melanie's dormitory room, overlooking the tennis courts and Pauley Pavilion, was impeccably neat and ordered. Her books were shelved alphabetically and her clothes were carefully folded. Melanie studied diligently and earned A's. Late at night, in the peaceful privacy of her tidy room, Melanie sat cross-legged on the floor in her baggy gray sweats and sketched designs for beautiful clothes.

In college, with Brooke no longer watching, Melanie shed her colorful plumage and her entourage of admirers. She wore bland, colorless clothes, little makeup, and unadorned hair; but still she was not anonymous. It was impossible to shed the conversation-halting-I-don't-care-if-it's-rude-to- stare beauty. By the end of her freshman year everyone knew Melanie Chandler, the stunningly beautiful but aloof coed who preferred studying to dating. She must have a boyfriend somewhere else. . . .

Melanie studied and sketched and sewed. Every morning, at dawn, she jogged along San Vicente Boulevard to the beach at Santa Monica. She loved the feel of the soft white sand and the gentle lapping sound of the ocean and the graceful freedom of the seagulls and the taste of the cool salt air. Her sky-blue eyes marvelled at the pale-yellow dawn and she felt great peace.

In her junior year, the term project for Melanie's class in fashion design was to design and sew three outfits. Each student was to submit the completed designs. Melanie did even more; she included photographs of herself modelling her outfits.

A week after the term project was submitted, Melanie's instructor stopped her before class.

"I showed the photographs to a friend who works for Malibu Sportswear and he showed them to the owner." The teacher smiled. "Who would like to see you."

"*Really?*" Melanie couldn't believe it! It was her dream—her private, secret dream—to be a designer. . . .

But when Melanie met with Grant O'Connell, she learned that it was *her* beauty, not her beautiful innovative designs, that Grant wanted.

"You have the look we want, Melanie. Healthy California, natural and athletic. You are an athlete, aren't you?"

The *athletic* twin. Melanie didn't participate in team sports at UCLA. But she kept fit, running

35

on the beach, horseback riding, surfing . . . private sports.

"I guess." *What did you think of my designs? Did you even look at them?*

"We'll need to do a formal photo session, of course. Swimsuits, shorts, sundresses—the entire Malibu Sportswear line. But I think you're exactly the model we've been searching for."

Malibu Sportswear *had* been searching. They had received hundreds of applications, but none had been quite right. Until Melanie Chandler. And she hadn't even applied.

"Model," Melanie murmured. I *want to design clothes for models to wear. I don't want to* be *a model.*

But Melanie loved modelling. She loved the beautiful clothes. She loved the photographs they took of her. She didn't dwell on the fact that the beautiful woman in the photographs was *her.* Her artistic, fashion-conscious eye simply appreciated the beauty.

Melanie didn't forget her dream to be a designer—someday. For now, modelling was fun and exciting. And it was something she could do well.

With modelling, and her instant success, came celebrity. Melanie was in the limelight again. But this time she was doing it for herself, not Brooke. She could set her own limits. This time she could, *would,* protect the private, peaceful, quiet moments of her life that meant so much to her.

On the rare but necessary occasions—Christmas, holidays, their parents' twenty-fifth wedding anniversary—when Brooke and Melanie saw each other during college, they lapsed into the uncomfortable long-since-abandoned labels. Melanie glittered and dazzled. Brooke retrieved her old navy skirts from the back of her closet, forsook her colorful ribbons, and forced a now unfamiliar somberness on her lips. Both hated the charade and were grateful when the visits were over.

Between the requisite family visits, Brooke and Melanie had no contact. Then, one spring day during their senior year, Melanie impulsively reached for the black rotary phone in her dorm room, called Directory Assistance in Cambridge, Massachusetts, and moments later dialed Brooke's number.

Brooke lifted the receiver of her peacock-blue Princess phone on the first ring.

"Hello."

"Brooke?"

"*Melanie.* I can't believe it."

"Can't believe what?"

"I was just about to call you."

"Really. Why?"

"I have no idea. I just . . ."

". . . wanted to talk to you."

"Yes."

They wanted to talk. But they couldn't. The painfully awkward attempt at conversation sputtered and finally died. Stupid. Dumb. What made them think they had anything to say to each other?

They lapsed into silence for another three years.

Until one day, seven years after Brooke left Pasadena to get away from her twin and find herself, Melanie called to tell Brooke that Adam

37

Drake had flown to California because he wanted Melanie to move to New York. . . .

Chapter Three

New York City
July 1985

"Margot, you look very happy," Charles observed as Margot Harper, fiction editor of *Images,* walked into his office.

"I have the five finalists for the fiction contest."

"And?"

"They are all very good." Margot stopped abruptly.

"But? But one is sensational?" Charles guessed.

"One is sensational."

"You all *agree?*"

Usually Margot and the other editors were not unanimous in their decision of the winner of the *Images* fiction contest. The annual contest was so important to the winner. It frequently launched a career for an unknown-but-destined-to-be-great writer. The editors were supposed to select on the merit of the story. But in the back of their minds they were making a prediction about the future success of the author. Usually it was a difficult decision; the *Images* fiction contest always attracted entries of exceptional quality.

"Is it because the others weren't good?" Charles asked.

"No. Any might have won another year. Of course—" Margot shrugged— "you may not agree with our choice."

As editor-in-chief it was ultimately Charles's decision. But he valued the judgment and opinions of his editors. Of the hundreds of entries, Charles only read the five selected by the editors. Charles smiled. "You're not going to give me any clues, are you?"

"No," Margot said firmly as she handed him the stack of manuscripts. "Here they are. In alphabetical order."

Margot hesitated. Charles eyed her quizzically "Yes?"

"One was handwritten. We had it typed. But we gave you the original also."

"Handwritten?"

"The author lives in Africa. I don't think she had access to a typewriter."

Margot tried to say it casually; but, of course, it was a dead giveaway. Charles knew instantly that the handwritten story by the writer who lived in Africa must be his editors' unanimous choice. Charles smiled reassuringly at Margot. It didn't matter that he knew. It wouldn't influence him. He would choose the story he thought was best.

That night, in the elegantly and expensively decorated pastel-and-cream living room of his penthouse overlooking Central Park, Charles read the stories. He read them slowly and carefully and in alphabetical order. The handwritten one was the fourth. Charles almost decided to read it last. No, he could be objective.

Charles looked at the handwritten copy. It was quite legible, written with a dark blue fountain pen in elegant script. He decided to read the original. His eyes drifted from the title, "Emerald," to the author's name: Galen Elizabeth Spencer.

"Galen," he whispered. *"Galen."*

As Charles stared at the pages of notebook paper he held in his hands, he remembered a lovely, innocent fifteen-year-old girl writing in a crimson notebook in the dim light of a kerosene lamp. It was a foggy, dreamy memory of red-gold hair and huge green eyes that shyly and bravely told him, No, Charles, you can't read what I'm writing.

Finally I get to read those precious secret words, Galen.

Charles's hands trembled slightly as he turned to the first page . . .

. . . by the time he finished Galen's story, Charles's heart was pounding with quick, uneasy energy. Charles paced around his penthouse trying to subdue his heart and focus his thoughts. He swallowed a glass of bourbon—his mouth was so dry—and stood for timeless minutes gazing at the sparkling glitter of the Manhattan skyline.

Finally he dialed the number to Jason's apartment on Riverside Drive. The phone rang, unanswered, twenty times. Charles glanced impatiently at the Tiffany chime clock on the white marble mantel. It was eleven o'clock on Friday night. Jason could be anywhere.

Charles put down the receiver. Then, without thinking, without specifically trying to recall the number he had not dialed for over eleven years, Charles's fingers pushed the sequence of buttons that would connect him to the estate in Southampton. Charles guessed that Jason spent time there. But they never discussed it.

As Charles listened to the distinctive ring of the Southampton exchange, uneasy feelings flooded him; ancient painful feelings that reminded him of a part of his life that was over but would be with him always.

Answer the phone, Jason, goddammit.

Jason stared for a moment at the always-silent phone. How could it be ringing? No one had the number, not even any one of the many caretakers or gardeners or housekeepers. Jason needed the phone to *make* calls. But it hadn't rung, literally, for years.

Jason laid down his paintbrush and wiped the paint from his hands with a turpentine-soaked rag as he moved slowly toward the phone.

"Hello?"

"Jason," Charles breathed. He had almost hung up. He had almost needed to stop hearing that ring. "Am I interrupting—"

"No, Charles," Jason answered swiftly. Of course Charles had the number. It had been his home, his telephone number, once. *Too.* "Is something . . . ?"

"Everything is fine. I just finished reading the entries for the fiction contest." Charles stopped abruptly. He realized then that he had never even read the fifth story. He *would* read it. But it wouldn't make a difference.

"Oh?"

"There's one, Jason," Charles began, his voice gaining pace and energy and enthusiasm as he spoke. "It's so good. I've never read anything like it. It's romance and adventure and passion and strength and beauty."

Charles took a breath. After a moment he continued, his voice low and soft, "And with the art, Jason . . . it's our vision of what *Images* should be."

Our vision, Jason mused. It was true. *Images* was their creation. Together they had transformed *Images* into Elliott's dream for his beloved magazine—a harmonious, sensual, graceful blend of art and literature. Charles and Jason created each splendid issue together, but only Charles knew if the final product met their vision. Only Charles could read the words.

Charles and Jason together wove the art and literature in *Images* into a beautiful, intricate, compelling tapestry. Charles spent long, patient hours telling Jason about the words. Jason listened carefully and translated the passion and emotion of the words into art.

And either Charles told him perfectly or Jason understood perfectly, because the art and the words always blended. *Perfectly. As* if a single heart and mind had carefully and lovingly chosen both.

"Tell me about 'Emerald,' Charles."

As Jason listened to the story of Emerald—the captivating love story of a naive young girl and a

42

dashing, experienced adventurer set in turn-of-the-century Africa—his mind formed clear, vivid images of the scenes Charles described. And of the beautiful, innocent, passionate heroine.

"So?" Charles asked when he was through. Charles didn't say, because he never would, *If you could read it, Jason! It reads like poetry.*

"More than one picture." Jason was thinking out loud. "Probably three. Watercolors, I think. The mood needs to be soft and romantic."

"Yes," Charles agreed. "Even though 'Emerald' has danger and adventure in it, it is, above all, a love story."

"I think Fran should be the model for the art," Jason continued seriously. "Fran should be Emerald."

Even if Charles and Jason were in the habit of friendly, brotherly, *twin* teases and taunts, Charles would not have observed lightly that Fran just happened to be Jason's lover. Because Jason's decision was a professional one. And it was the right one. Fran Jeffries would make a perfect Emerald.

"I'll speak with Adam on Monday," Charles said. Fran was a Drake model. "Jason, I think we should offer her—Galen—a contract for four stories to be published over the next year."

"*Really?*" Jason's surprise was obvious. There were a few authors, *established* authors, whose work was published repeatedly in *Images*. But never an unknown. And never four times in a year.

"It's that good."

"All right."

43

Jason's permission was necessary. *Images* was Jason's magazine. Just as *Fashion* and *Spinnaker*—all of Sinclair Publishing—belonged to Jason, not Charles. Jason's signature would secure the four-story contract with Galen Elizabeth Spencer. Jason's signature. Jason's money. Jason's profit.

But *their* vision.

After he hung up, Charles realized he hadn't told Jason that he knew Galen; or had known, barely, a teenage girl named Galen in Kenya. Maybe Galen wouldn't even remember. His name on the letter he would send her—congratulating her and inviting her, as all winners were invited, to spend a week at Sinclair's expense in New York City—would mean nothing to her. She had known him only as Charles, the Peace Corps worker with malaria who wanted to read her stories.

"God, she is beautiful," Steve Barnes whistled under his breath as he sifted through the photographs of Melanie Chandler modelling Malibu Sportswear. It was because Adam Drake had seen *these* photographs that he decided to fly to Los Angeles to see *her*.

"These don't begin to do her justice. They were taken to sell the clothes—which they did—not Melanie. But you"—Adam levelled his blue-gray eyes at the man he considered the best fashion photographer in the business—"you will be able to make her the top model in, I would guess, under six months."

"Is she a bitch?" Steve asked, tossing the photographs onto Adam's carved oak desk.

Adam grimaced slightly. Steve's contempt for the models annoyed Adam. But Steve was the best and Adam had never heard a word of complaint.

"She's lovely," Adam answered firmly, remembering the sky-blue eyes and sensuous lips that smiled coyly, disbelieving, when he told her how much money he would give her just to sign a contract with Drake. And when he told her how much money—it was a conservative estimate— she would make in the first year, Melanie tossed her sun-gold hair and laughed merrily. As if she didn't *care*. As if it didn't *matter*.

But something did matter to those sparkling eyes and beckoning lips. They became serious and thoughtful as she told him honestly how much she loved her life in California. She would have to think about it. She would have to *think* about moving to New York and becoming the top model in the world.

It just might not be that important.

A week later Melanie called and told him, Yes, she would come. And there was something in the soft, sexy voice that made Adam decide *some* part of it was very important after all.

"She's unspoiled," Adam continued, his eyes sending a message to Steve: *Be gentle with her.* "Natural. Unpretentious—"

"It will be interesting to see what fame and fortune do to that," Steve suggested knowingly. He knew what would happen. He spent his life dealing with vain, selfish, beautiful women.

45

"I hope," Adam murmured, "that it does nothing."

Steve shrugged and turned to leave.

"Oh," Adam said. "I almost forgot. Charles Sinclair called. They want Fran to model for the art for the *Images* fiction winner. December issue. Something set in Africa. I'll have Alice schedule an appointment with Charles and Jason to see what they have in mind."

"Like taking the shots in Africa?"

Adam smiled. Charles and Jason might want that. The cost never mattered, only the quality.

"Fran, huh?"

"They need dark brown eyes and hair."

"She's Jason Sinclair's, uh, *girlfriend.*"

"I know. And *you* know that Fran doesn't need connections to get jobs," Adam added hotly.

Fran's silky brown hair blew into Jason's face as she curled against him. Jason cradled her in one arm and steered the sailboat with the other. The late-afternoon summer breeze glided the sailboat briskly and silently across the white-capped waters of Peconic Bay.

"This is heaven," Fran purred against Jason's strong neck.

"I love it." Jason tilted his head skyward toward the lingering warmth of the afternoon sun. He closed his light-blue eyes and felt the wind, strong and powerful, caress his cheeks. He inhaled the clean salt air and sighed. He loved to sail. He loved the energy and the silence and the peace. It was a passion he had shared with Elliott, a passion they still shared. Part of Elliott was always with him when he sailed.

"You sail with your eyes closed?"

Jason smiled. He opened his eyes and gazed into the lovely brown ones.

"I could sail Peconic Bay with my eyes closed. If there were no other boats. . . ."

"Did you live near here when you were a boy?"

Jason nodded. He narrowed his eyes against the setting sun and looked toward shore. In the distance he could see the perfectly manicured emerald-green lawns of Windermere sweeping from the red-brick Georgian mansion to the white sand beach. Windermere was Jason's boyhood home and his home, his private retreat away from Manhattan, *still*.

Jason loved Windermere, despite the bittersweet memories and the haunting, unanswered secrets. Jason wondered—a tormented, helpless wonder—if some of the answers lay in Elliott's journals. Was there something there—emotions and secrets of his beloved father—that Jason should know? Or never know?

Jason sighed heavily. The journals were in Elliott's desk, as they had been since the day Elliott had died. But Jason couldn't read the words. And there was no one Jason could trust to read them to him. . . .

"Jason?" Fran touched her slender ivory finger to his cheek.

Jason caught her hand and pulled it to his lips.

"Yes." He pressed his lips against her hand and smiled gently into her soft fawn eyes. Fran, I don't know if I will ever be able to share Windermere with you, Jason thought. What we have is wonderful. You make me feel wonderful. But . . . maybe it's just too soon for me to be certain. And I have to be certain. So certain. "I grew up in Southampton. Charles and I grew up here."

Chapter Four

Southampton, New York
August 1952

". . . *tomorrow they would greet the dawn together.*" Elliott Sinclair stopped reading and gazed at his beautiful, pregnant wife. Meredith was lost some-where—in the story he had just read to her, in the picture she was painting, in gentle dreams of their unborn child. Elliott waited in silence. He was in no hurry to interrupt this moment. He could spend his life watching Meredith.

Finally she turned toward him, her pale-blue eyes shining. "That was lovely. A beautiful story. If . . ."

"If?"

"If there could be art to go with it," she said softly.

At her request—a shy, quiet request—Elliott had read every word of the latest issue of *Images* to her while she painted.

"There *is* art in *Images.*"

"I know. But it's separate from the literature.

If the words and art could blend, so that together they created an image . . ."

Elliott considered Meredith's suggestion. Her idea was innovative and exciting. Done right, with great care and thought and painstaking, loving attention to detail, every issue of *Images* could be a work of art.

"Yes," Elliott whispered finally. *"Yes."*

Meredith smiled, but her lips trembled slightly, uncertain and hesitant. His thoughtful, sensitive wife had more to say. Elliott urged gently, "What else, Merry?"

"Images should be for everyone, not just the wealthy."

Elliott smiled at the pale-blue eyes he loved so much. *Tell me, Meredith.*

"You already have two magazines for the aristocracy. *Fashion* is for elegant, bejewelled, glamorous women and *Spinnaker* is for their yacht-loving husbands."

"His-and-her magazines?" Elliott laughed softly.

"Yes. His-and-her magazines for your friends." Meredith shrugged. "Which is fine. The magazines are magnificent."

"But?"

"But *Images* should be for everyone. I don't mean the price. People are willing to pay for quality. I mean the *vision.* Poetry and literature and art should be for everyone. Like sunsets and roses and . . ."

Meredith shrugged again.

"Your nose is red," Elliott said softly, moving toward her.

"I'm a little embarrassed. I mean, you do have a magazine empire. You know what—"

"It's fuschia, actually." Elliott wiped the smudge of paint from her nose, then kissed the spot where the paint had been. "I love you, Meredith. And you're right about *Images*. And sunsets. And roses. If you help me, if you remind me of the vision, if we do it together . . ."

"You and I and Charles," Meredith murmured, gently touching the bulge under her painter's smock. In three months she would have Elliott's child. It filled her with such joy. *Charles* was Elliott's choice for a boy's name.

"You and I and Jason," Elliott countered lightly with Meredith's choice.

"Jason, if he's blond like me. But Charles, if he's dark like you. And Rebecca, if she's a she." It was what they had agreed.

"And you and I and Jason or Charles or Rebecca will make *Images* a thing of beauty for everyone." Elliott wrapped his arms around her.

"Yes, darling, we will."

Meredith went into labor at six A.M. on November eleventh, twelve hours before she gave birth to a healthy golden-haired baby boy with pale-blue eyes. It was all easy. Elliott was with her—touching her, stroking her damp blond hair—the entire time. Thirty minutes after the delivery Meredith was back in her hospital room holding her beautiful baby, herself cradled in her husband's arms.

"He looks just like you," Elliott whispered lovingly.

"All babies . . . No, you're right. He *does* look like me," Meredith said, smiling, nuzzling the brand-new silky blond hair. "I guess he's Jason."

"He's Jason."

"Our next son will be Charles, all right? No matter what or who he looks like."

"Our next son? Are you ready to do this again?" Elliott teased.

Meredith didn't answer in words, but she pressed closer and nodded her head against his lips.

"I love you, Meredith."

"I love you, Elliott."

Elliott held her and their son for several silent, tender moments. Suddenly, abruptly, Meredith pulled away and searched for Elliott's eyes.

"Meredith?" Elliott saw fear in her pale-blue eyes. *Why fear? "Merry?"*

"Promise me something, Elliott." Her voice was urgent.

"Anything darling." *What was wrong?*

"Promise me that you will love him, cherish him, protect him. *Always.*"

"Of course I promise that. But we will do that together. *Forever.*"

"But if anything ever happens to me," Meredith persisted as tears spilled inexplicably onto her cheeks.

"Nothing is ever going to happen to you," Elliott said firmly, trying to conceal the worry in his voice. "Meredith, what's wrong?"

"I don't know," she answered truthfully, forcing a smile. Her lips trembled. "Just emotions catching up with me, I guess. Seeing our precious baby, our precious Jason.''

But it was *more*. A deep sense of dread and emptiness pulsed through her. Something was terribly wrong.

Elliott pulled her close again, kissing her and the baby, feeling her tremble.

Then the pain came. Cramping, tearing, excruciating pain that caught her breath and held it.

"Elliott," she gasped. "Get the doctor, *please."*

As Elliott rushed out of the room he saw the blood that had already begun to seep through the bedding. Meredith closed her arms around Jason and pressed her lips against his warm soft forehead, trying to find strength, trying to breathe.

Elliott returned almost immediately with two doctors and a nurse.

Meredith smiled at him, a distant, dreamy, loving smile. She handed Jason to him and said, "Love him always, Elliott. And know that I love you. Always."

It wasn't possible to control the bleeding in time to save Meredith's life. As the doctors battled frantically but futilely to save her, they discovered the cause of Meredith's bleeding. Retained products of conception . . . a second placenta . . . another life.

The second baby, the twin, was tiny and undernourished. Surely he was too weak, too tiny, to survive. Still, he was breathing. And his heart pounded. They moved him quickly into an incubator in the newborn nursery.

★　★　★

"Doctor, have you spoken to him?" The head nurse of the newborn nursery glanced meaningfully at the incubator labelled *Baby Boy Sinclair.* "It's been almost two weeks."

"I know." The doctor grimaced.

"Maybe it's hard for him to come back here, because of his wife. But that's his *son* fighting for his life!"

"I *know.*"

The doctor moved beside the Baby Boy Sinclair incubator and looked at the tiny, fragile infant. He was so small, so helpless, so alone. His little perfect arms and legs struggled against the air. Or maybe they were reaching, desperately trying to find some sign of life and warmth in his cold, lonely world.

The doctor put his finger into the incubator beside the small hand. The reaction was instant and instinctive. The tiny fingers wrapped around his, holding tight, unwilling to release the grasp.

The doctor blinked back tears. Who is going to love you, little man? Who is going to care for you the way your mother would have?

Not your father, the doctor thought angrily. Could Elliott Sinclair actually blame this helpless baby for his wife's death? The doctor was afraid that that was exactly what Elliott was doing. It was just grief. Surely it would pass.

But the doctor wondered, his jaw muscles rippling as he recalled the conversation with Elliott, once Elliott had finally agreed to speak with him. The doctor eagerly told him of the remarkable progress his son was making, what a *fighter* he was. He asked Elliott what he wanted to name him. And all Elliott said was, *If he lives, call him Charles.*

Charles Sinclair was released from the hospital when he was two months old. A nursery, away from Elliott's bedroom where Jason slept, had been prepared, and the nurses, nannies, and staff of housekeepers had been notified that there would be another infant at Windermere.

When Charles arrived home, in the arms of the chauffeur, Jason was playing with Elliott in the great room. The chauffeur had been instructed to take Charles to his room, away from Elliott and Jason. But the moment Charles entered the house, Jason became distracted, frowning, anxious. He wriggled in Elliott's arms in the direction of the entry hall.

Elliott spoke to him lovingly, but Jason's restlessness increased and tears threatened. Elliott carried him to the window, to the panoramic view of the gray-green wintry Atlantic Ocean. Usually Jason loved that, as if he *felt* the beauty even though his young eyes couldn't really see the vastness. But not today. Today Jason just kept turning, now almost frantically, toward the entry hall.

Finally, reluctantly, Elliott gave in to Jason's urgent demands. The chauffeur and Charles's nurse were preparing to take Charles upstairs to his remote isolated nursery. Even before Elliott and Jason appeared, Charles became animated, his thin, quiet body suddenly energized and eager.

And when Charles saw his twin, the first smile of his short lonely life erupted on his face and the first sound he ever uttered flowed—a squeal of joy—from his frail lips. Jason squealed in return. And smiled and giggled and wriggled, commanding Elliott to carry him even closer.

Finally the twins were close enough to touch, again, as they had for nine months of their lives. Jason's plump, soft, dimpled hands grasped Charles's lean, undernourished arms. Small fingers explored eyes and noses and mouths. And all the time they were talking—a language of coos and gurgles—and laughing.

Charles and Jason spent the afternoon, the afternoon of their reunion, playing on a soft blue blanket on the floor of the great room. Elliott watched with amazement and concern. His happy, charming, beloved Jason was even happier now.

Jason wants to be with Charles, Elliott thought as he gazed at his sleeping sons, curled together, each sucking his twin's thumb as if it were his own, a portrait of peace and harmony. I can't separate them if Jason wants to be with Charles.

Elliott couldn't separate Charles and Jason. But *he* could ignore Charles. When Elliott returned late at night from work he would go to their crib, his voice gentle and loving as he spoke Jason's name. Elliott would lift his golden-haired son from the crib and leave the room, taking Jason with him and leaving Charles, his small arms stretching frantically toward the loving voice of his father as it faded in the darkness.

Charles was left alone for endless hours in the dark silence. And as he grew, Charles understood that even though he and Jason were close, and even though he *wanted* his father's love as much as Jason did, Jason was the only one who would be loved.

There was something wonderful about Jason. Something that made Jason loved.

And there was something wrong with Charles. Something that made him *not* loved.

Charles's happy times were with Jason. They had a hundred games—a *thousand*. They shifted from one game to the next without pause, one moment patiently taking turns filling a red plastic bucket with sand, the next moment impatiently chasing each other on the grass, the next moment pulling each other's hair and laughing.

One afternoon, when they were two, Elliott witnessed the twins' game of tug-of-war. Standing on sturdy two-year-old legs that had just learned to walk with some degree of confidence, each had hold of a corner of a silk pillow. This day it was Charles who let go first. Jason, the would-be victor, toppled backward clutching the pillow. His head hit the floor with a thud, and in the stunned moment in which Jason had to decide if he should laugh because he won the game or cry because the thud surprised him, Elliott rushed beside him to make sure he was all right.

That wasn't part of the game. And it got worse. As soon as Elliott was certain that Jason was all right, he lunged at Charles, grabbing him violently.

"You are a bad, bad boy," Elliott scolded as he spanked Charles over and over, harder and harder. "A horrible boy."

"Do, do, do!" Jason screamed his version of *no*. He toddled toward Elliott, his small arms flailing. When he reached Elliott his pale-blue eyes were flooded with tears, and his face twisted with horror as he saw what his father was doing to Charles. Jason's small hands wrapped around Elliott's strong forearm. *"Do!"*

Elliott stopped spanking Charles the instant he saw the look in Jason's eyes. It was as if Elliott was punishing *Jason*, not Charles. As if hurting Charles caused pain to Jason.

"Jason, don't cry," Elliott whispered, releasing his rough grasp on Charles and scooping Jason into his arms. Charles fell to the ground, sobbing large gulps of pain and sadness as Elliott held Jason, talking softly to him, reassuring him.

The spanking was the first and only time Elliott Sinclair ever touched Charles. He didn't scold Charles again—he only neglected him—until Charles and Jason were four and a half. That June, while Jason was taking a sailing class for children at the Peconic Bay Yacht Club, Elliott called Charles into his study.

"The language between you and Jason has to stop." Elliott glowered at Charles.

"Sir?"

"Jason doesn't speak English. Not one word. And it's your fault."

Charles blinked back tears. It was true that Jason didn't speak a language anyone but Charles could understand. He and Jason had their own private language. As Charles learned the language of their nannies and their books and their *father*, Jason fidgeted and seemed disinterested. Jason understood English. But he didn't speak it. He seemed quite content to have Charles translate for him.

Father, it is not *my* fault that Jason doesn't speak. Please don't blame me.

"As long as you and Jason continue your own silly language, Jason will never learn to speak properly. If you don't stop it at once I will send you away. You are a bad influence on Jason. He would be better off without you."

"No, please, Father." Charles felt the darkness and silence closing in. His heart pounded with panic. He sputtered, "I'll make sure that Jason learns to speak."

It was a painful, emotional struggle. Jason didn't understand. He felt betrayed. Why didn't Charles want them to be special anymore?

"Charles, tell me why," Jason pleaded in *their* special twin language.

Charles ignored him, his heart aching, drenched in fear. What if Jason couldn't speak any other language? What if Father sent him away? *Try, Jason, please try.*

Jason did try. By their fifth birthday Jason was speaking fluently, if reluctantly. Charles taught him the meaning of all the words he knew. He taught his twin how to speak perfectly. It took great effort and care and patience.

But no amount of effort and care and patience could teach Jason how to read.

"Your son has a form—a severe and somewhat atypical form—of what is called dyslexia," the specialist told Elliott a year later. He added, unnecessarily, because it was the reason that Elliott had sought help, "He can't read."

"Atypical?" Elliott asked hopefully. Maybe that was good. Although the specialist had said *severe*.

"He is quiet, not terribly verbal. But unlike most dyslexics who are reluctant to speak, Jason *can* speak fluently. Perfect syntax. His vocabulary is truly exceptional for a six-year-old. You have done very well—"

"Can he be taught to read?" Elliott interjected, realizing that it was *Charles* who had done very well, *Charles* who had taught Jason to speak. Against all odds.

"I really don't know. His block is very severe. We can try, of course. It will be a frustrating and difficult struggle for him. And it may never work."

"Never?"

"It doesn't mean that Jason can't learn. He retains and assimilates the spoken word beautifully. I wonder if we should just focus on that and work *around* the dyslexia." The specialist was thinking out loud. He continued, "Jason has the verbal equivalent of a photographic memory. It's really quite remarkable. He is very bright. There is nothing he can't learn. He just has to hear it, not read it. Of course your other son is also very bright. His ability to read and write is way beyond that of a six-year—"

"We're talking about Jason," Elliott interrupted impatiently. He didn't want to hear about Charles's brilliance.

"Yes, well, there are special schools. Not many,

admittedly. There is one in California. Or you could hire tutors. Jason can be told—and will remember—everything another child would learn through formal schooling. He could probably even attend a regular school if someone read the assignments to him and if he could take oral examinations."

"I'll hire tutors," Elliott decided without hesitation.

Elliott didn't want Jason to go away to school. He loved him too much to be apart from him. Jason was so much like Meredith. He was so generous, so loving, so kind, so happy. Even the dyslexia, Elliott realized, was like Meredith. Meredith *could* read, but she rarely did. In the evenings, she would paint and Elliott would read aloud to her. Elliot couldn't remember seeing Meredith read a book or even a newspaper. But he remembered vividly the way her soft blue eyes concentrated as he read to her or as she listened to the news on the radio.

Meredith had dyslexia, too. It hadn't been as severe for her as it was for Jason. But it was one more thing that his beloved son had inherited from his beloved Meredith. It made Elliott love Jason even more.

Elliott hired the best tutors. Until they were twelve, Charles and Jason both had all their schooling at Windermere. Charles was Jason's best and most devoted tutor. Charles read to him and told him stories. Jason listened eagerly as Charles told him about Robin Hood and Tom Sawyer and Huckleberry Finn.

Sometimes they would pretend the dense wood

surrounding Windermere was Sherwood Forest or the Atlantic Ocean was really the mighty Mississippi. Charles and Jason enjoyed living the fictional adventures Charles read about, but, even more, they loved to create their own stories, imagining scenes together, sharing visions. . . .

Charles read about twins. He told Jason some of the stories, but not others. Charles didn't tell Jason about the biblical twins, Esau and Jacob, who tricked and connived and competed for their birthright. And he didn't tell Jason about Romulus and Remus, the twin sons of Mars whose bitter quarrel over the location for their city on the Tiber River ended in Remus' death at the hands of his twin.

Charles chose not to tell Jason about Esau or Jacob or Romulus or Remus. But Charles told Jason—and they shared the story again and again as they sat on the beach and searched for *their* constellation in the star-glittered sky—about Castor and Pollux, the Gemini.

"Castor and Pollux were the twin sons of Zeus and Leda. They loved each other . . ." Charles began.

". . . and Neptune rewarded their brotherly love by giving them power over the wind and waves," Jason continued enthusiastically. He especially loved the story because already he shared Elliott's passion for sailing and Castor and Pollux were the special guardians of all seafarers. "And he gave them St. Elmo's Fire, the mysterious light that guides lost sailors to safety."

"When Castor died in battle," Charles spoke

quietly, "Pollux was so upset that he begged Zeus to allow him to join his twin."

"Zeus said Yes and they became the Gemini," Jason finished the story solemnly.

The pattern of Charles's life established before his birth continued throughout his childhood. The lovely, warm, secure moments—his mother's womb, curled against Jason in their crib, laughing and playing with Jason—were so fragile. Without warning, the happy moment would suddenly be disrupted and he would be alone again. It happened whenever Elliott came home.

At first, when he was old enough to follow, Charles would go with Elliott and Jason. But it soon became too painful to be with Elliott and Jason, watching their love and being *excluded* from it. So whenever Jason was with Elliott, Charles retreated to the wood-panelled library at Windermere and read. Eventually he read every book in the vast library.

Charles read every book in Elliott's library, and he read every issue of *Images, Fashion,* and *Spin-naker.* Charles dreamed of being an editor and publisher like Elliott. He would make Elliott so proud of him! Someday, Elliott would love him, too.

When Charles was twelve, the terrible loneliness and isolation that had punctuated his boyhood became permanent. Without warning or explanation, Charles was sent to Morehead, an expensive, exclusive boys' school in Pennsylvania. The cost didn't matter to Elliott. He just wanted Charles away from Jason, away from Windermere, and away from *him.*

Jason stayed at Windermere, surrounded by a constant stream of well-paid and enthusiastic tutors who taught him English and history and mathematics and science and geography and literature and current events. The tutors weren't told that Jason had dyslexia. Elliott *implied* there was something wrong with the beautiful pale-blue eyes that watched them so attentively and were so appreciative of *their* hard work for him. Jason's eagerness to learn seemed tireless. And his tutors matched his energy and enthusiasm with their own. They all cared about the happy, charming boy with the white-blond hair and rosy cheeks and ready smile. He was so special.

Jason didn't understand why Charles had gone away. But Jason guessed it was because Charles was so bright. Charles needed to get away. It held him back, encumbered his learning, to be at Windermere with Jason who could learn nothing on his own. It was *nice* that Charles had been willing to stay for twelve years. He might have left sooner. Jason missed Charles so much! Even with his father, and all the tutors, Jason felt terribly lonely. But he would never tell Charles. He would never make Charles feel guilty for having finally left. . . .

Without Jason, without the hope of wonderful moments to offset the lonely, isolated ones, Charles somberly accepted his fate. He was meant to be alone and unloved. There was something about him—something wrong with him—that made a solitary life his destiny. In a small corner of his heart he felt relief to be away from Elliott and the constant reminder that his father didn't love him.

In broad daylight, in the middle of his English class, Charles accepted the realization calmly. But at night, tossing and turning in his bed in his dormitory room, Charles dreamed of a day when Elliott *would* love him, when the nightmare would end and he and Elliott and Jason would be a family.

Charles's dreams gave him hope. He wrote long, loving letters to Jason and Elliott. Charles mailed the letters to Jason in care of Elliott. Elliott could read them to Jason.

Charles wrote to Jason about his life at Morehead. Charles made it sound like a wonderful, exciting adventure he wanted to share with his twin through his letters. Charles didn't tell Jason the truth—how sad and lonely he was—because he didn't want to make Jason sad. But sometimes, because he couldn't help it, because he hurt so much, Charles told Jason how desperately he missed him.

I want to be like you, Father, Charles wrote bravely to Elliott. He would never have had the courage to *tell* Elliott. But he could write it. And Elliott could see how hard he was trying to achieve his dream. . . .

Charles's grades were the highest in his class. An essay he had written had been entered in a national contest, and the short story he sent to Elliott would be published in the town paper, and he was elected to the editorial board of Morehead's literary magazine even though it was only his first year and . . .

Charles's letters to Jason and Elliott were never acknowledged, much less answered. Jason could call, couldn't he? Couldn't he have one of the tutors dial the number for him? And Elliott . . .

But Charles heard nothing. Still, he eagerly awaited the Thanksgiving break, forgetting his destiny, forgetting that Windermere was not his home.

No one came to get him. At eight o'clock on the Wednesday night before Thanksgiving Day, the headmaster at Morehead placed a call to Windermere.

"Mr. Sinclair is away for the holiday," the chauffeur explained.

"What about his son?" the headmaster demanded, relieved he had told Charles to wait *outside* his office.

"His son is with him."

"His *other* son."

"Oh." The chauffeur's voice softened. It was *he* who had brought the tiny, frail two-month-old Charles home from the hospital twelve years before. The chauffeur knew, he had seen it, the silent agony of the serious, unloved little boy. "Oh, dear. May I speak with him?"

"Hello?" Charles asked eagerly moments later. Jason's voice. *Elliott's* voice.

"They are away, Charles. Sailing in the Islands. I will get in the car right now to come fetch you."

"Oh. No, thank you. I have schoolwork to do." Charles blinked back tears. And the familiar aching.

"Yes, well." Then the chauffeur asked quietly, vowing to himself that he would be responsible, "When does Christmas break begin?"

For the next six years, whenever Charles returned home he felt like a visitor. He felt like a friend of Jason who was spending the holidays with Jason's family. A *friend*. It was an awkward friendship at best. Jason never mentioned the letters Charles wrote to him, although he always seemed happy to see Charles.

During summers and holidays Charles and Jason tried without success to re-capture the familiar closeness. They were both changing so quickly. They were boys becoming young men, making discoveries, learning, wondering. The brief moments together weren't enough. Too much happened during the long, silent gaps between visits. They drifted apart, friendly and polite, but separate.

Most of the time Elliott paid little attention to Charles. But sometimes—a few horrible times that Charles would never forget—he caught his father staring at him. And what Charles saw then, in the dark eyes of the man whose love he wanted so desperately, was hatred.

"I want to go to college, Father," Jason told Elliott a week after Charles returned to Morehead for his senior year.

"Where?" Elliott asked cautiously. Charles had decided on Princeton, Elliott's *alma mater*. What if . . .

Jason shrugged. He didn't know much about colleges. It would be nice to be at Princeton with

66

Charles. But that wouldn't be fair to Charles. Charles would worry about him, wondering if Jason could survive outside the protected, cloistered world of Windermere, assuming the burden if Jason *couldn't*. Jason said quietly, "Not Princeton."

Relief pulsed through Elliott. *Good.*

"I should be on my own," Jason continued tentatively. He thought about it all the time. It scared him and excited him. He had to *try*.

Elliott smiled at the earnest pale-blue eyes of his beloved son. Then he tousled the white-blond hair and said gently, his voice begrudging but full of love, "All right. But don't go so far away that you can't come home for the regattas."

"No," Jason agreed. "I won't."

Elliott and Jason decided on Harvard. Elliott made a few calls. It was easier to grant Elliott Sinclair's son an interview than to explain why Jason was not really a suitable applicant. . . .

The admissions interviewers were instantly charmed by the quiet, intelligent boy with the pale-blue eyes—he had an eye problem?—and gentle, polite manner. They decided to give him the SAT examination orally. Jason answered question after question, effortlessly and accurately.

Charles had told him how easy the SAT examination was, but that was *Charles*. Still, the examination was easy for him, too! Jason wanted desperately to tell Charles, but Jason didn't know how to use a phone.

Harvard University was pleased to offer Jason Sinclair a place in the entering freshman class of

1970. The dean of students agreed to serve as the liaison with faculty and tutors. With Jason's remarkable memory he could major in any subject. Did he have any idea what he wanted to do?

Jason had a precise idea of what he wanted to do, even though he had never articulated it. What was the point? What he wanted was impossible. Jason wanted to be able to read. He wanted to be like Elliott and Charles. He wanted to be able to run Sinclair Publishing the way Elliott did. He wanted those impossible things.

And he wanted something else. He wanted to be independent, to find something that was his, to learn how to survive without help.

When the dean of students asked Jason to declare a major, Jason answered swiftly and confidently, even though he had never thought about it before, "Art history."

Chapter Five

During spring semester of his senior year at Morehead, Charles made an important decision. This summer he would find the courage to ask Elliott if he could spend time with him at Sinclair Publishing. Nothing was more important to Charles. He would happily abandon the carefree summertime activities of Southampton—flirting with girls at the pool at Shinnecock and playing tennis and swimming—in favor of working with Elliott in Manhattan.

Charles knew that Elliott was grooming Jason, the beloved son, to run the company. That was fair. Jason was the eldest. But Jason couldn't read and Charles *loved* to. Surely there would be room for both sons in the company. . . .

This summer Charles would tell Elliott how much he wanted to be a part—however small—of Sinclair Publishing. Did he need to reassure Elliott that he wouldn't compete with Jason for control of the company? Charles would never compete with Jason. But Jason would need help. Jason would need someone to do what he, Jason, could never do.

Charles would do that willingly, *eagerly*. It was what he dreamed about. Jason could have the control and the power. All Charles wanted was a chance do what he loved to do and *could* do. . . .

Elliott telephoned Charles's dormitory room at Morehead two days before graduation.

"Father?" Charles's heart leapt. Maybe Elliott had decided to come to the graduation ceremony to watch Charles receive top honors after all!

"I need to discuss some business matters with you, Charles," Elliott said flatly.

"When?"

"When will you be done with school?"

I'm done now. I graduate day after tomorrow. Why don't you come?

"The day after tomorrow."

"When are you planning to come here?" Elliott asked. He did not ask, When are you planning to come home?

"By midafternoon Saturday." Charles's heart ached. His father sounded so serious and distant. What was happening?

"All right. We'll meet here at three on Saturday," Elliott said.

An appointment with his father? In his own home?

Charles felt his dreams begin to die.

"You're disowning me," Charles whispered in disbelief after he listened to his father's words. They were in the great room in the mansion at Windermere. Charles sat facing the tall French doors that opened onto the colorful rose gardens already magnificent in early June.

"I am providing you with a substantial trust fund. A lot of money, Charles. You will never have to work. And I am giving you a penthouse on Central Park West." Elliott firmly reiterated what he had already told Charles.

"But I have no part of Sinclair Publishing," Charles said quietly. "I never will have."

"No."

"You're disowning me," Charles repeated.

Elliott shrugged.

"Why?" Charles asked. He wasn't thinking clearly. But how could he? He needed to know what he had done wrong. He needed to understand.

Elliott looked at him. And the look, a little surprised, full of hatred, asked, Don't you know?

"Your things have been moved to the penthouse," Elliott continued, ignoring Charles's question and avoiding his son's hurt bewildered brown eyes. "You can go there now. On Monday you will meet with the attorneys. There are some papers to sign."

"Guaranteeing that I will never fight this?" Charles asked. Some things were clear. Even in the midst of this unreal nightmare, the message from his father, the bottom line, was clear.

Charles was no longer part of the Sinclair family.

"What about Jason? Can I say good-bye to my own brother?" My own twin?

"Jason is sailing. He won't be back for hours."

"Am I permitted to see him or to speak to him? Or do I sign something about that, too?"

"Of course you can," Elliott answered easily.

Charles and Jason's closeness had suffered from disuse and separation over the past six years. This would separate them further. Jason's love for his father was strong and unshakable. Just like the unfailing, unwavering love Elliott felt for Jason.

Charles decided he would call Jason in a day or two. He knew Jason wouldn't call him. Someone—Elliott—would have to dial the number for him. Charles wondered how Elliott would explain this to Jason. Maybe Jason knew the reason. Maybe Jason *agreed* with Elliott.

Maybe Charles wouldn't call Jason after all.

Charles drove down the long gravel drive, away from the house that had never been his home, his eyes stinging with tears. He felt the empty loneliness that had been woven through the happy moments of his life now settling firmly and irrevocably in his heart. It was part of him. It was who he was and who he would always be.

John Perkins stared with amazement at Charles Sinclair. As he and Elliott had drawn up the legal papers over the past few months, John assumed Elliott must have a compelling reason to disown his son, however generously. John expected a rebel. He expected long hair, drug-glazed eyes, obvious contempt for the life and dreams of his father, *something*.

But all John Perkins saw two days after Elliott banished Charles from Windermere was a polite, bewildered, sensitive young man who appeared, in every way, to be a young version of the father who was washing his hands of him. The physical resemblance between Charles and Elliott was striking—dark, handsome aristocracy laced with a slightly mean, slightly threatening sensuality. The resemblance between father and son ran far deeper than looks. In both men John Perkins saw great pain; a somber, persistent grief for a loss of immeasurable magnitude.

Why? John wondered. He realized that the young, dark eyes staring at him, as if *he* were the executioner, were asking the same question.

"I don't know, Charles." John answered the unspoken query. He had to clear the air before he offered the next, "But if I can help."

"Your firm could manage the . . ." Charles didn't even know the words. Trusts? Assets? Funds? All he knew was that his father had given him millions of dollars to be rid of him forever.

"Everything. If you want us to." At least until

Elliott comes to his senses and takes you back. But Elliott won't do that, John realized sadly.

"Yes. Thank you."

Six months later, in a luxury apartment on Fifth Avenue, a beautiful young woman watched as Elliott dressed in the darkness. It was three in the morning and he was leaving her, as he always did, to return to his apartment on Park Avenue or to make the long drive to his forbidden-to-her retreat on Long Island. Now, fortified by champagne and an unusually passionate evening of lovemaking, she urged herself to ask the question she had never before had the courage to ask.

She had never asked before because there was something a little frightening about Elliott Sinclair. And she had never asked before because she knew, if the well-publicized history of the past fifteen years of Elliott Sinclair's love life meant anything, that she was just the latest in an endless series of meaningless affairs.

But could he make love like that and not really care? Wasn't she, finally, the special woman in Elliott Sinclair's life?

"Elliott? What am I to you?"

"What?" His voice was harsh.

"You have been with me for almost six months." Even though you have never spent the night with me. She shook the thought. "We see each other almost every night." Except when your precious son is home from Harvard.

"You're my mistress," Elliott answered impatiently

"How can I be your *mistress?* You don't even have a wife!"

In the dark shadows she saw the anger in Elliott's eyes. She shivered involuntarily, suddenly afraid he might harm her. But Elliott didn't move toward her. He did just the opposite. In a silent rage, he finished dressing and left.

She knew that she would never see him again.

Sixty miles away, in Princeton . . .

"Do you want some more dope?" The pretty coed with strawberry-blond curls held a half-smoked joint to Charles's mouth.

"Mmm." Charles inhaled slowly, expertly filling his lungs with the smoky heat and holding his breath.

"Do you want some more of me?" she cooed, pressing her soft nakedness against him and slowly curling her fingers in his shoulder-length brown hair.

"I have to go," Charles said as he exhaled.

"You always leave, Charles. Why don't you spend the night?"

Charles didn't answer. Instead, he stood up from the bed, his handsome, naked body silhouetted by candlelight, and pulled on his faded jeans.

"Don't you like making love with me?"

"Yes," Charles answered truthfully. "We just did it. *Twice.*"

"But you never hold me afterward. And you don't stay." She pouted and whispered carefully, "Sometimes I think you don't care, Charles. Sometimes I think you don't love me."

Of course I don't *care*, Charles thought as he smiled a seductive smile. And I don't *love*.

Charles left Princeton two weeks before the end of his freshman year. By spring he had become restless with the drug-blur of his life. In fall and winter the drugs and the girls had provided a warm, seductive, foggy escape from his shattered dreams. He missed class after class in favor of the endless, purposeless pleasure of drugs and sex. He convinced himself that the dreams didn't matter anymore. Nothing mattered, not literature or reading or writing or . . .

But Charles bought every issue of *Images*. And he imagined wonderful conversations with Elliott. He would tell Elliott what was wrong with *Images* and Elliott would listen carefully and his dark eyes would glisten proudly at his son.

If there could be art to go with the literature, Father.
What do you mean?
If the words and art could blend, so that together they created an image. . . .
Yes. What else?
Images should be for everyone, not just the wealthy.
You're right, Charles, Elliott would say. Then smiling, he would urge, *Come back, son. Come help me make* Images *all it can be.*

"It's not going to happen, you idiot!" Charles yelled aloud in his dormitory room one spring evening. *"Face* it."

It took all of April for Charles to wean himself off the mind-numbing drugs and to force himself back into the painful reality of his life. On May first he dialed the Madison Avenue law offices of Perkins, Crane, and Marks.

"Mr. Perkins, this is Charles Sinclair."

"Yes, Charles. How is Princeton?" Charles sounded fine. John imagined a robust, handsome Ivy League look. In fact, Charles now looked the way John had expected the disowned son of Elliott Sinclair to look last summer. Charles's body was thin and sallow, his hair was long and tousled, and his dark eyes were vacant and glassy.

"Fine, sir. But I have decided to take some time away."

"Oh?"

"Yes. I have joined the Peace Corps. I'll be leaving for Kenya in a week?"

"And returning?"

"It will be at least two years. I wanted to give you my address."

"Good idea. We will undoubtedly need to reach you about some of the investments."

"Oh. That doesn't matter. Do whatever you think is best," Charles murmured. "I just wanted you to know where I will be."

In case something happens to Jason or Elliott.

"You're early." Jason was already smiling as he responded to the light knock on his dormitory-room door. The confident, charming smile for his date dissolved into a thoughtful, tentative one for his twin. *"Charles."*

"You're expecting someone."

"In a while."

Charles and Jason hadn't seen each other or

76

spoken to each other in over a year, not since *before* Charles had left Windermere forever. Charles had never made the call to say good-bye.

"How are you, Jason?"

"Fine."

Jason looked fine, as if the new environment—Cambridge, Harvard, the stately red-brick dormitory—suited him more than terrified him. Charles had worried that it would be overwhelming for Jason. But the pale-blue eyes were relaxed. Jason wore a cream-colored sweater with a crimson H—a letterman's sweater.

"What's that for?" Charles asked, gesturing toward the letter, wondering if Jason had any idea what the crimson shape meant.

"Yachting?" Jason looked at Charles, and a thousand questions bombarded his mind. What's wrong, Charles? Why did you leave? What happened between you and Father? Why didn't you even say good-bye? Why are your eyes so empty?

Jason started to speak, but stopped. As carefully and patiently and lovingly as Charles and Elliott and all the tutors taught him how to speak, the language was still foreign. He couldn't use it to express his feelings or emotions. It didn't belong to him. It wasn't part of him.

Their language—the private, special language he and Charles had shared until Charles wouldn't share it anymore—had been different. How he wished he could tell Charles, in their special language, how he felt.

Instead he asked politely, "How are you, Charles?"

"I'm good. I guess I need a haircut. I'm going away for a while. I wanted you to know. . . ."

In Kenya, Charles learned to be comfortable with his isolation and solitude. The physical exhaustion of his daily work—construction work under the blazing equatorial sun—numbed his mind without clouding it. He found peace in the wild, vast beauty of Africa. The haunting pain that had driven him into hedonistic hiding during his year at Princeton subsided, and he could be alone without feeling the empty ache of loneliness.

Charles kept a polite, acceptable distance from the other volunteers. He worked beside them during the day, but withdrew in the evening, preferring a solitary walk on the savanna to fireside reminiscences of home and college and family.

At the end of the second year in Kenya, Charles and his team were joined by an anthropologist.

"Are you here to study *us?*" Charles asked one evening when he unexpectedly found the man on *his* grassy knoll.

"Spectacular sunset, isn't it? Please sit down. What did you ask? . . . Oh, yes. . . . No, although studying Peace Corps communities might be interesting. Actually, I'm studying beliefs and customs about twins in different parts of Africa. I'm just using this as base camp for a few weeks."

"Twins?"

"Yes. Of course the highest twinning rate in the world is in Nigeria. I have been there for the past year."

"What sort of beliefs and customs are there about twins?"

"Basically whether the tribe fears or reveres them. Some tribes welcome twins, celebrating them as symbols of fertility and good harvest. Other tribes reject—and even kill—them."

"Kill? *Why?*"

"Animals, not *humans,* typically have multiple offspring. So, for some tribes, a human twin birth means that the mother consorted with evil spirits. In other tribes, two children equal two fathers. Thus, the twins are a symbol of the mother's infidelity. Sometimes the mother *and* the twins are killed."

A pang of sadness and loss swept through Charles for the mother he had never known. He knew so little about her; Elliott never told them, *him* anyway, about her. *Meredith Sinclair.* Her signature was on the beautiful paintings at Windermere. But who was Meredith Sinclair? All Charles knew was that his mother was a wonderful, talented artist. . . .

"Awful."

"It's natural to fear something so different. Actually, most tribes revere twins."

"I'm a twin," Charles admitted slowly. "I have a brother. We're not identical."

"Really? So you must already know all this."

"No. I know about the mythological twins like Castor and Pollux. . . ."

"The belief that twins have supernatural power—good and bad—over weather is quite universal. Twins have been credited with both horrible droughts and desperately needed rainfall. Some mythical twins ascend to earth on lightning bolts and argue in claps of thunder." The anthropologist smiled. He asked lightly, "Do you and your brother have much control over weather?"

Charles laughed softly and shook his head. "I'm afraid not."

"Being a twin is such a unique experience," the anthropologist continued seriously. "To be that close, that much a part of another human . . . I've really become intrigued since doing this study. Do you mind if I pry?"

Charles shrugged.

"Do you know each other's thoughts?"

"No," Charles answered swiftly. After a moment he added, "When we were very young, we did. We had our own language."

"Are you terribly competitive?"

"No. Not at all. We've never competed." The only prize was Elliott's love. And that belonged to Jason. It always had and always would.

"That's unusual."

"We haven't really been together for nine years."

"Who is the firstborn? Not that that is a big issue in American culture. Critical in the Bible, of course, and in the royal families. The heir apparent and so on."

"He is?" Jason, firstborn and heir to the empire.

"In parts of Africa," the anthropologist explained, "the secondborn is the important twin. He is the eldest and strongest and heir. He sends his younger brother into the world to

80

announce his impending birth and to make certain the world is a fit place for him."

That night Charles sat awake in his tent and carefully transcribed what the anthropologist had told him into his journal. Someday, Charles hoped, he would share what he had learned with Jason.

During the middle of his third year in Kenya. Charles acquired malaria. He was transported, with high fever and delirium, to a small clinic sixty miles away.

"You need to stay with him, Galen"' Elise Spencer told her daughter. "I have to attend a delivery in the village."

"Yes, Mummy," Galen answered uneasily. She knew there was no choice. Her father was away for three weeks, providing much-needed medical care to the most remote villages. Sometimes Galen accompanied him, but this trip she stayed behind to help her mother at the clinic. To *help* but now she was being left alone! And the new patient looked so sick, so pale. She asked weakly, "What does he have?"

"It's *Falciparum* malaria, dear, so he's going to be delirious. I've given him his first dose of chloroquine." Elise smiled at her shy fifteen-year-old daughter. "You just need to make sure he doesn't crawl off the cot in his delirium. If he gets too hot, sponge him down. And, Galen?"

"Yes?"

"If he goes into coma . . ."

Galen looked at her sick charge. Underneath the pallor of sickness lay strong sinewy muscles and youth and health. "He *won't.*"

81

At first she was part of his dreams, a lovely vision with red-gold hair and green eyes who blended with images of Jason and Elliott. But as his mind cleared, as he remembered what was *real* about Elliott and Jason, she was still there, smiling at him, whispering softly to him.

"You'll be all right, Charles," the British accent reassured, over and over. "You're getting better, stronger."

"Who are you?" he asked one day Her words were becoming a reality. He *was* getting better and stronger.

"Galen. Galen Elizabeth Spencer. Mummy and Daddy are doctors for the clinic here."

"And you're a nurse?" Charles asked the wide young green eyes. "And a writer?"

"No." Her cheeks flushed pink. *"No."*

"No? You're not just writing my vital signs in those notebooks, are you?" Charles gestured toward the crimson notebook in her lap. As he gestured, lifting his arm from the cot, Charles realized how weak he still was. He had been just about to ask her to take a walk with him along the river. But it was much too soon.

"No," she admitted.

"Then what?"

"Just stories." Her voice was barely audible, and she tilted her head, throwing a curtain of red-gold between herself and Charles.

"Let me read one."

"No."

"Tell me then."

"No, Charles. I can't do that, either."

"OK, scaredy cat. Then tell me about Galen Elizabeth Spencer."

"I'll tell you about the places I've lived. Would that be OK?"

"That would be very OK."

Charles remained at the clinic for two weeks. By the end of the first week, he was strong enough to take slow walks along the riverbank and on the savanna. Galen accompanied him when she could. The hours they spent together were mostly silent, but they were *together*, sharing the magnificence of a brilliant purple-pink sunset or the splendor of a gazelle bounding across the high grass or the peaceful, melodic chirping of the spectacular tropical birds.

Four days before Charles was scheduled to leave, Elise Spencer announced that she needed to go to Nairobi. The clinic supplies had dwindled and had to be replenished. Elise had hoped to wait until her husband returned, but she couldn't. And now was a good time to be away. There were no patients lying in the cots in the makeshift hospital and no babies were due. The sickest patient, Charles, was virtually well.

Charles, Elise mused. The strong, silent Peace Corps worker made her timid daughter feel safe and confident. It would be best to take the necessary trip before Charles was gone.

Three hours after Elise left for Nairobi, a pregnant woman who was visiting from a distant village went into labor. The woman's frantic sister found Galen and Charles sitting by the river's edge, watching a baby hippo's clumsy antics in the warm, muddy water.

"No," Galen told the woman, "she's in Nairobi, but—"

"But Galen's here," Charles finished confidently. "And I'm here to help her. Please tell your sister that we're on the way. We just have to pick up, uh, the medical bag."

"Charles," Galen whispered as the woman left. The fear in her emerald eyes matched the panic in her voice. "Do you know how to deliver a baby?"

"No." He smiled at her. "But you do. You told me you've watched."

"Yes, I've watched!" Galen paused, catching her breath, searching her memory for deliveries she had witnessed. "Sometimes, there is almost nothing to do, because everything is fine. But, Charles, there can be complications, horrible ones. Mummy needs to be here. We have to go after her!"

Charles saw the fear in Galen's eyes and knew it was rational fear based on knowledge. Galen knew what could go wrong. She had seen it. As an ice-cold shiver of terror pulsed through him, Charles realized that he had knowledge about childbirth, too. He had never watched a baby being born, but he knew about a woman who had died giving birth to her twin sons. . . .

Still, they had no choice.

"Galen." Charles was amazed that his voice could sound so strong and calm. "We can send someone after your mother, but it can't be you. You know how to deliver babies. I'll help you. Tell me what we need to do."

84

Galen frowned briefly, then her eyes met his and she smiled a shy, brave smile.

"All right." Her voice still trembled, but the pace of her words was slow and controlled. "We need to stop by the clinic and get Mummy's medical bag and sterile forceps and a scalpel and string."

Galen calmly spoke the medical terms, but could she *really* apply forceps to a tiny, fragile skull?

Charles saw the doubt and panic begin to return to her eyes and said quickly, refocusing her on the mechanics, "The scalpel and string are for an, uh . . ."

"Episiotomy," Galen supplied the correct term. "No. We'd need a suture set for that." Galen frowned. She *couldn't* perform an episiotomy, even though she had seen it done. *No.* She forced her thoughts away from that worry and told Charles something she could do, would *have* to do, "That scalpel and string are for tying the umbilical cord."

"Oh." Charles looked surprised.

"It *does* happen naturally, of course. The vessels clamp down on their own. But if you tie it off, you can separate the baby, and hold it and care for it, immediately."

"I see. How do you do it?"

"You tie the cord in two places and cut in the middle. You just have to be sure," Galen continued, giving firm instructions to herself, "that the string nearest the baby is tied very tight."

"Uh-huh," Charles agreed uneasily.

As Galen spoke, the reality of what he was about to witness and the horrible knowledge that his own mother had died giving birth increased Charles's sense of dread. But as Charles's inner terror crescendoed, Galen became visibly calm. By the time they reached the small mud hut in the village, Galen had vanquished, or banished for the time being, her fears.

As Galen entered the hut, she transformed into her mother, mimicking the calm, reassuring manner she knew so well. Galen had seen Elise deliver many babies. Galen had heard the words and the tone and had seen the soft, caring, compassionate smile on her mother's lips.

"How are you?" Galen took the woman's clammy hand and squeezed gently. "This is Charles. He's here to help. Not that we will need much help." Galen smiled comfortingly. "Babies deliver themselves, you know."

The woman shook her head vehemently.

"Yes," Galen spoke softly. "Yes they do. Let me see."

Galen walked to the foot of the cot and lifted the woven blankets that covered the woman's legs and abdomen. Charles stood motionless near the doorway of the small hut, watching Galen, waiting for her instructions, hoping, hoping . . .

Charles watched her suppress a gasp, then her emerald-green eyes, glistening with tears, found his.

"It's almost born," she whispered. "Charles, I need the clean towels and the string and scalpel, please."

Charles moved beside her and watched in

speechless wonder as Galen gently, but confidently, eased the baby, a little girl, from the birth canal. Charles's hands trembled as he cut two twelve-inch pieces of string, and Galen's hands trembled as she tied the string around the umbilical cord.

"Do you think it's tight enough?" she asked in a whisper.

Charles didn't know. It looked tight. He whispered back, "I think so."

Slowly, carefully, breath held, Galen cut the umbilical cord. The knots were tight enough! She hesitated for a moment, then wrapped the now squirming baby in a clean towel and carried the precious bundle to her mother.

"You should rest," Galen told the new mother. "We've sent for Mummy. She'll check on you as soon as she returns."

The woman nodded as grateful tears spilled down her cheeks.

The moment Galen said "Mummy," the moment the ordeal was over, her braveness vanished and she was a shy fifteen-year-old girl again. Charles took her hand and led her out of the hut and away from the village. When he stopped, finally, and turned to face her, Charles saw liquid, astonished eyes and trembling lips.

"Hey." Charles touched her cheek gently. "You were terrific."

Galen couldn't speak. Her words were blocked by a sob.

"Galen." Charles wrapped his strong arms around her shaking body and held her tight. "Galen."

After many moments Galen finally spoke. She buried her red-gold head into Charles's chest and whispered, "It was a miracle, Charles . . . a miracle."

Four days later, Charles returned to the Peace Corps village.

"Good luck with your writing, Galen," he teased carefully.

"Good luck with your buildings, Charles," she teased in return.

Galen realized, as Charles left, how much she knew about *what* he was—kind and gentle and sensitive—and how little she knew about *who* he was. Charles told her he did construction work for the Peace Corps and that he was American. Charles never told Galen his last name. And the other names—Jason and Father—that he called desperately when he was delirious he never mentioned at all when he was well.

A week before the end of his third year in Kenya, Charles felt a sudden, urgent need to return home. *Home?* Where was that? The posh penthouse on Central Park West? The dorm room at Princeton that probably still smelled of marijuana? Certainly not to Windermere . . .

Charles didn't know, but the feeling was strong. It had something to do with Jason. Jason needed him. Jason was in trouble. Charles had to go *now*.

A week later Charles sat in his elegant penthouse overlooking Central Park immersed in culture shock hut feeling inexplicably *comfortable*. The urgency had dissipated. *This* was where he was supposed to be, at this moment, as the dark, ominous storm clouds gathered to the northeast over the Atlantic Ocean and moved swiftly toward Long Island.

Chapter Six

Southampton, Long Island
June 1974

Jason completed his studies at Harvard two weeks before the other graduating seniors. At the end of his courses he was given oral examinations. As Jason made the trip from Cambridge to Southampton, already a Harvard graduate, his classmates were just beginning Reading Week.

The route from Jason's dormitory at Harvard to the mansion at Windermere was a now familiar one. The most direct way, which Elliott taught Jason during his freshman year, was to take a taxi to Logan Airport, a plane to La Guardia, and a limousine to Windermere. Jason needed only to pay the taxi driver, find his way to the appropriate departure gate at the airport, and provide the limousine driver in New York with the Sinclair Publishing Company account number.

Paying the taxi driver was easy. With Elliott's help, Jason memorized the faces on bills—Washington, Lincoln, Hamilton, Jackson, and Grant—and the monetary value assigned to each face. Since Jason had no trouble doing mathematics in his head, determining appropriate cab fare, plus tip, was simple.

Negotiating Logan Airport was trickier. Elliott made certain that Jason had an ample supply of prepurchased airline tickets. Jason always flew on the same carrier and quickly became familiar with the terminal and the usual departure gate. When the departure gate changed, Jason would have to ask directions, his pale-blue eyes offering sincere apologies for being a bother to his fellow travelers and airport personnel.

Once Jason was on the plane, heading for La Guardia, he was home free. He could always get a limousine, even if it meant a wait, and he never faltered as he recited the perfectly memorized Sinclair Publishing Company account number to the driver.

Jason was almost home now, and he couldn't wait. He had such wonderful, exciting news to share with Elliott!

I'm an *artist,* Father. Look at my paintings. Do you like them? I think the style is like my mother's. . . .

Jason loved the wonderful, vivid pictures, painted by Meredith, that adorned the walls of the mansion. He had no idea he had inherited her marvelous talent. What if his art appreciation course at Harvard hadn't included studio time? What if he hadn't been forced to put a paintbrush in the hands that hadn't held a pen or a pencil in eighteen years?

But it *did* and he *had* and he might tell Elliott how his painting made him feel—Father, it makes me feel so free!—or he might keep that small part private.

In his art, in his own remarkable talent, Jason found a release for the turbulent feelings that churned beneath the always calm, always cheerful exterior. For twenty-two years Jason felt like a puppet, a charming, intelligent creation of a hundred dedicated tutors. Jason was *grateful* to all of them. The tutors didn't treat him like a machine, but that was how he felt. He was so dependent on them all.

Before his painting, there was nothing that was uniquely Jason; there was nothing private or personal. Jason was everyone else's creation and he was a masterpiece. But who was *he?*

With the discovery that he was an artist, Jason discovered himself. At last he was more than a bright, pleasant, meticulously trained and impeccably educated *specimen*. At last it really *didn't* matter whether he could read or write. That wasn't what Jason Sinclair was meant to do. He was meant to translate emotion and passion into rich, beautiful images.

Jason's art professor at Harvard tried to convince him to stay at Harvard for an additional year for formal training. The professor was confident that Jason's talent was marketable; Jason could be a *major* artist. His work—even in its embryonic, untrained form—was vital and powerful and unique.

But Jason didn't care about sharing his talent with the world. Jason didn't care about fame or success. It was enough that he had found something that gave him such peace and joy. Jason didn't need to make a career of his art. His career was with Sinclair Publishing. And even that—something he wanted to do because of Elliott but feared because how could it ever be *his* if he couldn't read?—suddenly became less frightening. Jason's talent made him believe in himself.

It was raining hard as the limousine pulled into the long drive at Windermere. A sudden June storm had brought cold rain and strong gusts of wind. Before the limousine pulled away, the driver helped Jason carry his luggage and his paintings, curled dry and secure in a black plastic tube, to the marbled foyer inside the mansion.

Father isn't here, Jason realized, a little disappointed.

Of course, Elliott wasn't expecting him home so soon. It was all part of Jason's surprise for Elliott; the paintings *and* his early arrival home.

It would be a wonderful summer. On weekdays, he and Elliott would live and work in town. They would spend the weekends in Southampton, sailing, playing tennis, dining at Shinnecock Golf Club, and enjoying the peace and quiet of Windermere. While Elliott read manuscripts Jason would paint. There was so much Jason wanted to paint. He would continue what Meredith had begun—the permanent commemoration of their magnificent home.

It would be a perfect summer. Perfect, except that, for the fourth summer in a row, Charles would not be there.

Jason had no idea what happened between Charles and Elliott four years before. When he arrived home from sailing the day Charles moved out, Elliott unemotionally told him that Charles was gone and that it was for the best. And when Charles came to his dormitory at Harvard a year later, Charles didn't mention it at all.

It angered Jason that neither Elliott nor Charles offered an explanation. But Jason didn't let his anger show. Charles and Elliott had always protected him, as if his inability to read was an *illness*. As if, despite how bright he was, there were things he couldn't understand.

Jason didn't push. Because then, before he discovered that he could paint and that it didn't matter that he would never be able to critically review a manuscript, a large tormented part of Jason believed that there *was* something wrong with him. Not an illness, but something that didn't give him the right to push Elliott or Charles on issues they didn't choose to share with him.

Last Christmas, when Elliott had told him that Charles would never inherit any part of Sinclair Publishing and wanted Jason to agree that he would never give any of his shares to Charles, Jason didn't ask his father *why*.

But now life was different. Jason had something that Elliott and Charles didn't have. It gave him power and confidence. This summer he would find out what had happened between Elliott and Charles.

By five-thirty in the afternoon Elliott still had not returned and the storm had worsened. The gray-green water of the Atlantic Ocean swirled angrily in the distance, meeting the torrents of rain with its own windswept salty spray. It was a dramatic scene, almost colorless, a picture in a hundred shades of gray. On another day Jason would have found great peace in sitting at his easel and translating this powerful rage of nature onto canvas.

But today Jason was too restless, too anxious. Where was Elliott? He was in Southampton, somewhere, because the house had been opened for the weekend and a used coffee mug sat on the kitchen counter. But where? Elliott usually preferred to stay at Windermere. He only left to go to the club to play tennis or to dine.

Or to sail. But Elliott wouldn't be sailing today, as much as he enjoyed the challenge, because today there was no challenge, only danger. No one would sail today. But what if Elliott had left before the storm hit? What if, before it was a true storm, it had been a gusty, exhilarating day? A perfect day for sailing. . .

Jason didn't know how or when the storm began. The weather had been clear until they reached Long Island.

Jason wanted to call the Peconic Bay Yacht Club and the club house at Shinnecock and even Elliott's office in Manhattan, in case, discouraged by the inclement weather, Elliott had returned to work. But Jason couldn't read a telephone book. He had no idea how to use a telephone. His remarkable memory enabled him to easily and accurately memorize a sequence of numbers, but could he match the symbols on the phone with the numbers in his mind?

Jason believed he could. In the past few months, perhaps bolstered by the confidence his painting gave him, Jason began to notice numbers—on the money he carried, on signs along the road, over the departure gates at the airport, on cash registers and receipts—and the numbers made sense! Jason needed someone to check him, to make sure he was right. Elliott would help him. This summer, he would learn to use numbers, to dial a telephone. . . .

If only I could drive, Jason thought. I would drive to the yacht club *and* Shinnecock *and* Manhattan, and I would find him.

Jason couldn't drive, but it was another plan for this summer. If he could read numbers, he could read the speed limit signs and the car speedometer. And he had already learned the meaning, by observation, of a red octagonal sign and a yellow triangular one and . . . if someone read him the rules, and if he was allowed to take an oral examination, he could drive, *couldn't* he?

This summer, maybe, but not today, not *now*. Now, Jason couldn't dial a phone, and he couldn't drive. He could only wait—desperate and frustrated and trapped— miserably consumed by the familiar feelings of helplessness and dependence.

Jason heard the sound of sirens in the distance. He opened the front door of the mansion. His heart pounded uneasily. As he walked down the brick stairs Jason saw the police cars. The sirens hadn't been distant at all; they had been on the private drive leading from the entrance of Windermere to the mansion. The whistling of the wind and the pelting of the rain and the roar of his own blood pulsing in his head had merely muffled the sound.

There was no need for sirens, no need to rush. The news was forever. The sirens simply matched the harsh turbulence of the day, strident and punishing. The sirens were a warning and a signal.

A warning of something unspeakable.

A signal that something wonderful was over.

The officers had sounded their sirens in angry protest against the raging storm and what it had done to a man they all knew and respected; a man whose life had not been entirely happy and whose greatest happiness after the tragic loss of his beautiful wife was his beloved son Jason.

Jason was away at college. He wouldn't be at home. He would not hear the sirens. He *should* not hear the sirens.

But Jason was there. And the officers told him, in the rain, their own tears mixing with the cold raindrops, that his father was dead. Elliott had been sailing and was caught by the unexpected storm. He drowned in the violent sea. They had just recovered the body. Elliott had been wearing a life preserver.

"If he was wearing a life preserver," Jason protested swiftly.

"He was probably hit in the head and thrown from the boat," the officer explained gently. He knew it was true. He had seen the body. And the head injury.

Jason stared at them all for many moments, his eyes registering disbelief and terror. They stood facing each other, the officers, the bearers of the horrible tragic news, and Jason, the beloved son, the innocent victim. The *other* innocent victim of the punishing storm. As they stood, immobile, silent, the rain fell even harder, drenching them, chilling them with an outer coldness that matched the chill within.

As Charles drove through the walls of rain toward Windermere, he forced his concentration on the dangerous rain-slick winding road and didn't think about why he was in Southampton. Charles didn't *know* why. The same urgent feeling that made him leave Kenya dragged him from the warm luxury of his Manhattan penthouse into the violent summer storm and forced him to drive *too fast* toward Windermere and Elliott and Jason. . . .

Charles saw the nest of Southampton police cars as he approached the brick pillars at the entrance of Windermere. He parked his car at a distance and darted into the woods, running along the now overgrown paths where he and Jason spent wonderful hours sharing make-believe adventures. By the time Charles emerged from the woods onto the emerald green lawn his clothes were rain-soaked and branch-torn and his face and hands were scratched.

Charles narrowed his eyes against the pelting rain and looked across the expanse of manicured lawn toward the Georgian mansion. There were more police cars in the drive in front of the mansion. Standing on the porch in the rain, in the middle of a huddle of police officers, was Jason.

"Son." The officer touched Jason on the

shoulder. "Let's go inside. There must be someone we should call . . ."

"My brother is in Africa," Jason murmured numbly.

Oh, yes, the officer remembered, there *was* another son. But *that* son, the dark twin, had vanished from Windermere. No one in Southampton knew why, but there was speculation that Charles must have done something terrible.

The officer looked at Jason, the beloved son. Jason was in shock, and the only family he had left in the world was in Africa. The officer tried to guide Jason into the mansion. But Jason resisted, spinning free, and inexplicably faced the woods. In the distance, blurred by sheets of rain . . .

"Charles," Jason whispered.

"We'll try to reach him, son," the officer said sympathetically. "It may take a few days."

"Charles." Jason ran to meet the approaching figure. The officer followed.

"Jason," Charles panted when they met at the edge of the red brick drive. "What happened?"

"It's Father . . ."

"What?"

"He's dead, Charles."

"No. God, no."

The police officer watched with interest, his well-trained mind entertaining a series of questions and theories. Wasn't it peculiar that the estranged son miraculously appeared—from *Africa*—moments after Elliott's death? Why were Charles's clothes drenched and torn? Why were there scratches on his face? Why did he come through the woods? Where had he been earlier in the afternoon, say, for example, at the moment of the lethal blow to Elliott Sinclair's head?

Charles's shock looked genuine, and his horror matched that of his twin. Still, they would have to check. They could begin checking this afternoon. In a day or two, if necessary, they would ask the questions of Charles. For now, until there was reason to suspect guilt, Charles was an innocent young man grieving the tragic death of his father.

Charles and Jason went inside the mansion, and the police retreated to the pillared entrance of Windermere to protect the bereaved twins from the inevitable onslaught of the press. It was the least they could do.

Charles and Jason sat in numb silence at opposite ends of the sofa in the great room. Twilight fell, shrouding the mansion in darkness.

"Why did you come here today?" Jason's voice finally broke the silence.

"I don't know." I *had a feeling you needed me.* "I just had to."

"But did you know about . . . did you know what happened before you arrived?"

"No."

The darkness cast shadows across their faces, hiding their eyes.

Jason's blurred, grief-stricken mind whirled. He didn't know his twin anymore. They hadn't been close for so many years. And now, in this intimate, tragic, private moment, Charles had miraculously reappeared. Why? Why had Charles left? Why had he returned? Jason needed to know.

"What happened between you and Father?" Jason asked quietly.

"When?"

Four hours ago, Jason thought and shuddered. *No,* I can't even think that.

"When you left, four years ago."

"Nothing. I don't know why he made me leave."

"Father wouldn't have *made* you leave!" Jason protested. Don't lie to me, Charles, *please.*

"Nothing *happened,* Jason."

Jason heard the edge in Charles's voice, but he couldn't see his face. Was Charles angry because Jason had struck a nerve? Or was he angry, as Jason was angry, at the nonsensical tragedy of Elliott's death? Or was Charles angry because Jason was taunting him instead of trying to find the closeness they needed now, so desperately?

I have to trust him, Jason thought. Even though he won't tell me why Father disowned him or why he is here today. I *will* trust him.

"Why did he have to die, Charles?" Jason's voice broke.

Charles didn't answer, but the words of the anthropologist he met in Kenya swirled uneasily in his mind: *Twins have supernatural power—good and bad—over weather. Do you and your brother . . .*

"Where was St. Elmo's fire?" Jason demanded bitterly, his thoughts drifting with his twin's to the fabled Gemini, guardians of all sailors. Why wasn't Elliott guided to safety in the storm?

"*Myth,*" Charles hissed hoarsely. He added softly, "It's just a myth, Jason."

Charles started to shiver, chilled from his rain-soaked clothes and the icy horror of Elliott's death.

"We should get changed and eat something," Charles murmured between clenched teeth.

"What about the magazines?" Jason's voice was shaky, too, quivering from cold and emotion and panic. What about Elliott's beloved company and his wonderful magazines?

"What about them?"

"Father said he gave you your entire inheritance four years ago and that you would never own any part of Sinclair Publishing."

"Unless I buy it."

"He told me," Jason said slowly, "that I was never to give or sell you any part of Sinclair Publishing."

Charles drew a breath. Why did Elliott hate him so much? In Kenya Charles had found peace with his solitude. But now, being in this house where he couldn't be loved, the depthless pain rushed back, reminding him that there was something terribly wrong with him.

"I guess I'm going to inherit the entire company," Jason continued carefully.

"I guess so."

"I can't run the company without someone I trust, someone who knows about *me*, someone who has Father's instincts as editor-in-chief."

"No, of course you can't. But Sinclair Publishing has the best editors in the business. There are probably three or four who could step into that position tomorrow . . ."

A long silence followed. Finally Charles stood up.

"Could you do it?" Jason asked quietly in the darkness.

"Do what?"

"Be editor-in-chief."

"Me?"

"I thought that was what you wanted to do."

"Yes. Someday." It was his dream, *still*. After Elliott had disowned *him*, Charles tried desperately to disown the *dream*. But he couldn't. It was who he was.

"Could you do it now?"

"Are you asking me to?" Sudden warmth pulsed through Charles's shivering body.

"Yes. I need your help." Jason spoke confidently, but fear seized him. Could he really trust Charles? Jason didn't know, but he had no choice. It was the only way he could save Elliott's dreams.

"Then, yes," Charles whispered, "I'll do it."

Six months after Elliott's death, Jason knocked on the door of Charles's adjoining office at Sinclair Publishing.

"Come in. Oh, Jason, hello."

Charles forced a smile for his twin. Charles was exhausted. Running Sinclair Publishing Company had been a monumental task for *Elliott*, despite his uncanny business instincts, years of experience, and respect of the entire publishing world. And now he, Charles, inexperienced and with unproven instincts, was trying to take Elliott's place. The powerbrokers of publishing and the press and the fashion barons hovered like skeptical, hungry vultures, waiting for the estranged son—how dare he?—to fail.

The support within the company was strong; but it was support for Elliott's memory and for Jason, the loved son. Charles had no idea how long the support would last or if there would ever be support for *him*. He was just a visitor, as he always had been, but the future of Sinclair Publishing Company was riding on his shoulders.

Charles owned no part of the company. He could have been an employee—Jason told him to name his salary— but Charles would accept no money. Sinclair Publishing was his heritage and his dream. . . .

"You need help, Charles." Jason looked apologetically at his tired, overworked twin.

Charles shrugged. He couldn't ask for help. Everyone was watching, and there was the secret—Jason's dyslexia—to protect.

"I think I can help. I majored in art history at Harvard. I have an eye for color and design." Jason paused. He could tell Charles he was a talented artist, but he didn't. "Would it help if I handled the art for the magazines?"

"*Yes.* It's the biggest struggle for me," Charles admitted gratefully. If Jason could really do this . . .

"Good. Then, that's settled." Jason hesitated. The next was personal. It was so important to him—it would give him such a feeling of independence—but he had to be certain he was right. Someone, *Charles,* had to tell him. Jason sighed softly, then continued, his voice tentative, "There's something . . . I need your help."

"Yes?"

"You know I can do mathematics in my head."

Charles nodded. He knew that. He discussed all of the Company's financial issues with Jason, and Jason understood perfectly.

"Well, I *think* I can read and write numbers."

"*Really?*"

"I need to have you check me to be sure."

"Of course." Charles paused. He asked carefully, "Is it happening with letters also?"

"No." Jason smiled wryly. "And I don't think anything's *happening*. I think I always could have done numbers."

By the first anniversary of Elliott Sinclair's death, it was obvious that Sinclair Publishing Company wasn't going to fail. *Fashion* and *Images* and *Spinnaker* flourished, rejuvenated by the energy and talent and vision of the Sinclair twins.

"I want to make changes in *Images*," Charles told Jason fourteen months after Elliott died.

"What changes?" Jason asked swiftly, worried. *Images* was Elliott's legacy.

"I would like the art and literature in *Images* to blend, so that together they create an image."

Jason listened to Charles in stunned silence. Charles was describing Elliott's dream! It was a dream Elliott had shared with Jason a hundred times. It had seemed so private, something just between them. Now Jason heard the words, the same words, from his twin.

"Did you and Father discuss this?" Jason asked finally.

"No." Only in my fantasy conversations. Charles added wistfully, "We never talked about the magazines."

"It's what Father dreamed *Images* would be."

"Then we'll do it? Together? I'll tell you the stories . . ."

Jason nodded solemnly. *Spinnaker* will be mine, *Fashion* will be yours, and *Images* will be ours.

As *Spinnaker, Fashion,* and *Images*—the new *Images*— soared in popularity and prestige, the world wanted to know all about the handsome, powerful, and wealthy Sinclair twins. The press obliged willingly, and Charles and Jason cooperated politely and easily, as if there was nothing to hide.

Jason and Charles Sinclair made such good copy! Charming, pleasant, golden Jason, and dark, seductive, restless Charles.

Jason was an expert yachtsman, preferring the vast, wind-tossed sea to the glitter and glamour of Manhattan. Jason's love affairs lasted months or years, and they were *almost* private. Someday Jason would find the right woman and they would have happy, golden, beautiful children. Everyone would celebrate the day he found his true love, because everyone wished happiness for Jason Sinclair.

Charles was like Manhattan: fast-paced, energetic, dazzling, and a little menacing. Did Charles Sinclair ever sleep? His seductive elegance graced all the important parties—they would be devastated if Charles Sinclair didn't appear—and all the major fashion shows in New York and Europe. Charles's love affairs with New York's most glamorous women were high profile, well publicized, and short-lived. Charles Sinclair would probably never marry or have children, and that was almost certainly for the best.

The press and public were happy with their profiles of the Sinclair twins. Jason was the perfect symbol of *his* magazine, *Spinnaker:* healthy and natural and pure. And Charles was the perfect symbol of *Fashion:* sexy and risky and elegant. But which twin was responsible for Sinclair Publishing's greatest triumph, *Images?*

No one knew Charles and Jason created each issue of *Images* together. No one knew, because no one asked. Charles and Jason would willingly have told them. It wasn't a secret, they would say, smiling, as if there were no secrets.

But, of course, there *was* that one astounding secret: the terribly interesting and potentially devastating fact that Charles Sinclair, editor-in-chief of Sinclair Publishing, worked for no money to help his dyslexic twin run the company his father had vowed he would never own . . .

Chapter Seven

New York City
September 1985

"Brooke, it's for you, line three. It's about the Cassandra case."

"Thanks." Brooke depressed the blinking button. "This is Brooke Chandler."

"This is Nick Adrian, NYPD."

"Yes?"

"I hear the DA's office is dropping half the charges against Cassandra before you even go to trial. Do you know anything about that?"

Of course Brooke knew about Cassandra. The case had monopolized her summer. It virtually prohibited her from studying for the Bar. And now, finally, the trial was scheduled to begin— *tomorrow*—the day Melanie was moving to New York. Of course she knew about Cassandra.

"Yes, I know about that." It was so hot in her office! Mid-September and still humid.

"Tell me why."

"Because we don't have enough evidence to convict on all the counts."

"We *sent* you enough evidence. Did you lose it? The DA's office has been known to misplace evidence before. Especially if it's too much of a nuisance to prosecute." The voice was deep and cool.

Who the hell did he think he was? How dare he say that about the DA's office?

"We weren't too happy with the way NYPD collected the evidence."

"Want to spell that out?" The voice turned to ice.

"I don't really have time." Brooke's iciness matched his. He was wasting her time.

"Well, you've told me enough. For example, if I were Cassandra's attorney I would be one happy man right about now."

"Oh, my God," Brooke whispered. What had she done? She held her breath.

107

"I'm not," Nick said after a long silence. "I'm who I said I was. Let me tell you who you are. You're a recent law school graduate. You probably made *Law Review*. You took the Bar four weeks ago and are on pins and needles waiting to hear if you passed. During law school you clerked at a prestigious law firm with a Madison Avenue address. Then, in the eleventh hour, you felt a pang of guilt, an urge to serve the people, so you signed up with the DA's office. How am I doing?"

"I always planned to do trials," Brooke interjected defiantly. But it was a weak protest. Except for her motives for joining the DA's office, his description of her was entirely accurate.

"Well, that's a little original. I like it when attorneys don't even *pretend* to be altruistic."

"Who are you? Why are you doing this?"

"I told you who I am. I really called to find out why the hell the charges were dropped. But, 'tis the season."

"Meaning?"

"There's a new kid, like you, every year. They don't stay— you won't—because there are greener, cushier pastures in, say, Westchester County."

"I'm going to stay."

"If you stay will you promise to stop ignoring the evidence we so carefully and *legally* collect?"

"Sure," she breathed.

"Good. It was nice talking to you, Brooke."

Brooke listened to the dead line and tried to regain her composure. She had almost made a critical mistake. She *had* made a critical mistake, but fortunately it was to someone who was on the same side of the law. Even though he wasn't on her side. Or was he? What he'd done was a cheap lesson for her. Dirt cheap. All it cost her was a little pride.

"Who in the world is Nick Adrian?" Brooke asked as she walked into the open office.

She got a few confounding answers.

"He's the best narcotics detective in the city."

"He's an arrogant sonofabitch."

"He is absolutely gorgeous."

"Probably impotent."

"I don't think so."

"Sounds like you know."

"I hear he's being transferred to Homicide."

"Is that a demotion?" Brooke asked hopefully.

"No way. Brooke, the guy is the best. What did he do to you anyway?"

What did Nick Adrian do? He probably saved her career in the DA's office. Brooke would have to thank him if they ever met. Maybe they wouldn't.

"Nothing," she said.

Of course they would meet. She was planning to stay.

Nick returned to his small apartment at eleven P.M. The heat of the day still hung over Manhattan, heavy and suffocating and oppressive. Nick collected his mail as he passed through the foyer. There were two pieces: the electricity bill—he would open that tomorrow or the next day—and *The New Yorker,* badly damaged from being unceremoniously wedged into the too-small mailbox.

Nick swore under his breath and frowned at the torn and wrinkled magazine. Wanton destruction annoyed him. More than *annoyed*, it enraged him. Maybe that was why his war against crime was so impassioned. That was what crime was—wanton, senseless, careless destruction of property and lives and minds and hope.

Nick glowered at the mutilated magazine and admitted the other reason he felt so emotional about *The New Yorker*. It had been a month since he submitted his short story, "Manhattan Beat," to the magazine. He hadn't heard back. Nick wondered what it meant. It could be a *good* sign—they were considering accepting it. Or a *neutral* sign—no one had even looked at it. Or a *bad* sign—it lay in the Reject pile awaiting return to its presumptuous author when time permitted. Returning rejected material could not be a top priority, could it?

Nick had been away from his apartment—tying the "red-tape" around a perfectly orchestrated midnight drug bust—for almost twenty-four hours. In his absence the apartment had accumulated all the day's heat and allowed none to escape. Nick's first breath drew in a moist warmth which settled, heavy and tenacious, in his chest. Nick opened the windows even though he knew there was no breeze. He turned on the portable fan—unopened electricity bill be damned—poured himself a glass of Scotch, and filled his bathtub with cold water.

Nick felt the tension drain out of his body as

the cool water drenched his tired muscles, and the warmth of the Scotch drenched his exhausted mind. His thoughts drifted to the events of the past twenty-four hours—the late-night phone call, the textbook drug bust, the meeting with the Chief of Police about his transfer to Homicide as soon as he finished his testimony in the Cassandra case. . . .

The Cassandra case. This time they ought to stop Cassandra once and for all.

Except the DA's office was waffling, playing it safe. The DA's office . . . Brooke Chandler. What does she look like, Nick mused as the last swallow of Scotch took hold. She *sounded* efficient and haughty and ice-cold.

Ice-cold, with a soft, sexy voice.

Charles and Jason stood in the Concorde reception area. Galen's flight from Paris's Charles de Gaulle Airport had just arrived. The passengers were clearing customs.

"Do you think she'll recognize you?" Jason asked.

"I don't know," Charles answered distantly. There was nothing in the correspondence with Galen over the past two months to suggest she knew that Charles Sinclair, editor-in-chief of *Images,* and Charles, the Peace Corps volunteer stricken with malaria, were the same. "Probably not."

Charles and Jason watched as the Concorde passengers, the ritual of customs and immigration behind them, rushed through the exit door into the bustling international terminal at JFK toward

111

their waiting limousines. These were purposeful, important, wealthy men and women who commuted across the Atlantic as routinely as they crossed town. It was many moments after the transatlantic powerbrokers vanished from the reception area that Galen emerged.

She wore an old-fashioned—*tattered*—floor-length pink-and-purple gingham dress with a crocheted white shawl draped over her shoulders. She clutched a bright red duffle bag to her chest. Neither perfectly tailored twin noticed Galen's archaic clothes or the clash of the torn duffle bag. What caught their attention were her astonished green eyes squinting against the brilliance of New York, as if she were Dorothy arriving at the Emerald City of Oz.

"Galen?" Charles spoke gently.

Charles and Jason walked toward her, as if drawn by instinct to protect her. Protect her from what? From the startling foreign glamour of which the Sinclair twins were the most dazzling symbols?

"Charles?" Galen whispered. As she stared into his brown eyes, her full lips spread slowly into a shy smile. "Charles without a beard."

"I wasn't sure you would remember. That's why I didn't tell you in the letters."

The green eyes flickered amazement. Not remember? Galen started to answer, but she couldn't find the words and simply shook her head, frowning slightly.

"Galen," Charles rescued her quickly, "this is—"

"Jason," Galen said quietly. She found a shy smile for Charles's golden twin.

"Did I . . .?" Charles began. He didn't remember telling Galen about Jason. But of course she knew the name of the owner and publisher of *Images*. . . .

"You called his name when you were delirious." Galen's eyes held Charles's for a moment, sealing the memory. Of course I remember.

"Let me take this," Jason interjected, reaching for the bulging red duffle bag. It dropped slightly—it was heavier than he expected—as he took it. Jason recovered instantly, swinging it effortlessly over his shoulder.

"My stories," Galen explained apologetically to Jason. Turning to Charles she added, "You wrote that you might want to publish more, so I brought them with me."

"Good. Let's get you to your hotel. You must be exhausted."

"Your letter said something about dinner tonight?"

"Jason and I would like to take you to dinner at Le Cirque. It's—" Charles was stopped by the sudden look of apprehension. Galen Elizabeth Spencer did not want to have dinner at one of Manhattan's trendiest restaurants.

"I brought stories instead of clothes," she mumbled, gesturing weakly at the red duffle bag.

Charles started to offer to buy her a dress—*ten* dresses, a hundred—but he thought better of it. He didn't want to embarrass her. He suggested gently, "Why don't we just have a casual dinner at my place tonight?"

113

Charles arched an eyebrow at Jason, who nodded agreement.

"Perhaps Fran could join us?" Charles suggested to Jason.

"She's in Bermuda."

Charles and Jason silently searched their respective lists of female friends, silently rejecting one after another as too stunning, too self-absorbed, too glamorous. . . .

"How about Brooke?"

Jason nodded and added confidently, smiling at the green eyes he had just met, "You'll like Brooke, Galen. She's very nice."

"Brooke, Charles Sinclair called," her secretary told her when she returned from court.

"Charles Sinclair?" Brooke repeated quietly.

"Yes. There was no message, except to have you call him."

"All right." Brooke's heart set a new pace. Why was Charles calling? It couldn't be that he had legal work he wanted her to do. Despite her offer, Brooke knew Charles would never ask her to moonlight for Sinclair Publishing.

"This is Brooke Chandler returning Charles Sinclair's call."

"Oh, yes. He is in a meeting. But he asked that you speak with Jason Sinclair."

"Fine." Maybe it *was* work for Sinclair Publishing, Brooke thought, a little deflated.

"Brooke?"

"Hi, Jason. Charles—"

"Brooke, Charles and I are having a very small, very informal, very last-minute dinner party

114

tonight. It's in honor of Galen Spencer, this year's winner of the fiction contest. We hoped you could join us."

"How nice," Brooke answered mechanically, wondering why *her*, why at the last minute. Brooke suddenly remembered why she couldn't. "But, my sister is arriving this evening."

"Melanie?"

"Yes, how . . . ?"

"Fran mentioned it. In fact—" Jason laughed easily— "she mentions it constantly. Your sister is *the* topic of conversation among Drake models. Something about their jobs."

They're afraid that once Melanie arrives their modelling careers may be in jeopardy, Brooke mused.

"Oh, well." Brooke fumbled awkwardly. She couldn't tell Jason it was a silly worry.

"Is she an older or younger sister?" Jason asked the same question Charles had asked two months before. Apparently Charles hadn't told *his* twin about the Chandler twins.

"We're twins. Not, of course, identical. We're golden and dark, like you and Charles." Golden and dark. Sunny and stormy. Open and secretive.

After a moment's silence Jason said, "Melanie is invited to the dinner party, too. We would love to have both of you."

Brooke spent the afternoon in court. She listened attentively to Cassandra's attorney's opening statements and nodded at Andrew Parker as he jotted down precedents raised by opposing counsel that she would need to check.

Brooke forced thoughts of Melanie's arrival and the dinner with Charles and Jason to the back of her mind. It took great discipline, but that was her specialty.

At the end of the day, as Brooke rushed from the courthouse to her tiny apartment on West Fifty-seventh Street to dress for the evening, the carefully suppressed worries, now unrestrained, flooded her mind. She was anxious *enough* about seeing Melanie. And now she would be seeing Charles, introducing Melanie to Charles. . . .

Brooke scowled at the dresses in her closet. They were all so soft and colorful and pretty and feminine! Brooke didn't wear plain, drab, dowdy clothes anymore. That wasn't who she was *now*. She had long since left the vestiges of high school behind her. The new Brooke, the real Brooke, was happy and stylish. The new Brooke liked her silky chestnut curls and deep-blue eyes and full sensuous lips. . . .

But next to Melanie, she would always be plain and drab, wouldn't she?

Brooke sighed. Then, with firm resolve, she chose her most feminine dress, swept her curls softly off her face, and artfully accented her huge blue eyes with shadow and mascara.

This is it, Brooke thought, critically examining the finished product. This is who I am.

Brooke arrived at La Guardia by taxi ten minutes before Melanie's flight landed.

"Brooke!" Melanie touched her cheek briefly, awkwardly, to Brooke's. "You look terrific."

"So do you."

Melanie looked fresh and *refreshed* from the

transcontinental flight. In sharp contrast to her fellow travelers, Melanie appeared rested and wrinkle-free and cool and full of energy. It was all illusion, all part of the perfect golden image. Melanie had spent the flight—stomach knotted and fists clenched—wondering why she had made this foolish decision and if it was too late to turn back. *Mr. Drake, I'm sorry. I wasn't thinking clearly. I don't belong in New York. You see, I have a twin sister and we've been apart for so long and I thought . . .*

"Charles and Jason Sinclair invited us to dinner tonight. I said Yes. I hope that's OK."

"Charles and Jason Sinclair? As in *Images*?"

"Yes." It surprised Brooke that Melanie made the association with *Images* rather than *Fashion*.

"It's fine, *wonderful*," Melanie lied graciously. She had mentally prepared herself for a quiet dinner with Brooke; that would be hard enough. But this . . . she would have to dig deep to find the energy.

"I thought you'd like to drop your luggage off at your apartment."

"And change."

"You look fine." Melanie wore a straight white linen skirt—miraculously unwrinkled—with front and back slits tastefully exposing her long tanned legs, a turquoise cotton blouse, and a simple gold necklace. She was the picture of understated elegance. "It's casual."

"I'd feel better if I changed. I *am* eager to see the apartment."

A luxury, decorator-furnished, all-expenses-paid apartment on Central Park East was included in Melanie's contract with Drake Modelling Agency.

"This is nice," Brooke said forty-five minutes later as they walked from room to room of Melanie's apartment.

"It is," Melanie breathed with relief. It *was* nice. It felt peaceful and quiet and she had a lovely view of the park.

"Charles, I'm sorry we're late," Brooke said apologetically when they finally arrived at Charles's penthouse.

"You're not. Jason and Galen aren't here yet. Come in."

"Oh. Good. Thank you." Brooke took a deep breath. Then, with a calm that amazed her, she said, "Charles, this is Melanie."

"Welcome to New York, Melanie." Charles's dark eyes smiled at the magnificent sky-blue ones. *At,* not into. Melanie's eyes resisted penetration; like perfect tranquil ponds they reflected the world but revealed nothing of the pale-blue depths.

So handsome, Melanie mused as she smiled at Charles. "Charles, what a wonderful place!"

Adam Drake has discovered pure gold, Charles thought as he watched Melanie flow gracefully into his tasteful, elegant living room. Melanie nodded appreciatively, as if *her* approval of his taste would somehow make him happy. Pure, egocentric, impossible gold.

"Charles," Melanie purred, "I love this Monet. I can't believe it isn't hanging in the Louvre."

"You mean the Jeu de Paume." Charles quietly reminded her that the major Impressionist works were housed in the Jeu de Paume, not the Louvre. "It used to be."

"The Jeu de Paume." Melanie's eyes sparkled, acknowledging Charles's victory. Touché, Charles. What fun it will be to spar with you! But I have to be on my toes, don't I? "Of course. Silly of me."

Undaunted, Melanie swept across the living room to the window overlooking Central Park. Her apartment was almost directly across from his, on a lower floor, blocked from view by the trees.

"Lovely," she murmured. When she turned away from the spectacular view, her eyes fell on an Orrefors crystal vase of roses standing beside the marble fireplace. "Oh!"

Melanie moved to the vase of roses and gently traced the delicate lavender petals with her finger.

"Sterling Silver," she spoke to the prize-winning rose by name.

"That's very good," Charles observed. How the hell did *she* know the species of that rose?

Melanie smiled a proud, dazzling, defiant smile. Take that, Charles Sinclair.

The sound of quiet conversation in the marbled foyer signalled the arrival of Galen and Jason. Charles's attention shifted from roses and Melanie to Galen. Melanie and Jason introduced themselves as Charles protectively shepherded Galen toward Brooke.

"Hello, Galen. Welcome." Brooke smiled warmly. She looks like a small, frightened bird,

119

Brooke thought, desperate to fly away and be free. Don't worry, Galen, no one here will hurt you.

"Hello Brooke." She's so beautiful, Galen thought. She seems nice. "Thank you."

"And this," Charles said as Jason and Melanie, now introduced, joined them, "is Melanie."

Prepare yourself, Galen, Charles thought.

"Hello Galen." Melanie smiled. Then she tilted her head, narrowed her pale-blue eyes and added quietly, "You have the most beautiful hair I have ever seen."

Melanie emphasized the sincerity of her words by impatiently running her long fingers through her own spun-gold locks, as if the shiny gold had suddenly turned to gilt.

Galen frowned slightly at the earnest sky-blue eyes. Then she touched a strand of the waist-length red-gold silk that was as much a part of her as her shyness or her need to write or her old tattered clothes and whispered, "No."

"Yes!" Melanie countered emphatically. It was not a debatable point. "Have you ever twisted it in coils and piled it on top of your head? Stuck a few wild flowers in it?"

"No." A soft laugh.

"*No?* Galen, I'll have to show you how to do that. How long will you be in New York?"

"For a while," Galen answered quietly. She spoke to Melanie, but her eyes drifted for a questioning moment to Charles and for a brief flicker to Jason. "I thought it might be good for me, for my career, to live in New York for a while."

"Then you and I have moved here on the same

day for the same reason." Melanie smiled conspiratorially at Galen. Now they had something much more important in common than long beautiful hair.

"This calls for a toast," Jason said. He helped Charles pour chilled champagne into crystal glasses.

"To successful careers in New York." Charles raised his glass to Galen and Melanie. Then, turning to Brooke, he added, "To all of you."

The evening flowed easily and effortlessly. Melanie's energy kept the conversation light and flowing, and she filled the rare silences with her happy, golden laughter.

Melanie is making it fun and easy for everyone, Brooke thought, marvelling at Melanie's confidence and energy. Melanie, the *fun* twin. It wouldn't have been the same evening without Melanie. *She* could never have made Galen feel so comfortable.

What does Charles think of Melanie? Brooke wondered. But she knew the answer. Charles was charmed and enchanted by Melanie, just like everyone was. How could he not be?

"Tell us about your stories, Galen," Melanie urged during dinner.

"They're just stories about Africa."

"*Just,*" Charles teased gently.

"What are they about? Galen? Charles? *Jason?*" Melanie pushed.

Melanie looked to the golden, sunny Sinclair twin for an answer. But, for a fleeting moment, the sun had gone behind a cloud. Doesn't Jason like Galen's writing? Melanie wondered.

"They—'Emerald,' at least, Galen hasn't shown me any others yet—are wonderful literary journeys into love." Charles spoke, rescuing Jason. Charles's voice softened as he said *love*.

The conversation halted for a moment.

Why did you frown when Melanie asked *you* about my story, Jason? Galen wondered.

Love, Brooke mused. The way Charles said it . . .

I haven't read it, Galen. I can't. I'm so *sorry.*

Fabulous theatrics, Charles, Melanie thought. The inflection on "love" was perfect—*so* seductive. Charles Sinclair, the great lover. Melanie wondered if he was. Probably. She guessed Charles did everything spectacularly well.

" 'Emerald,' " Melanie mused, looking at Galen's eyes. "Is it autobiographical?"

"No." Galen blushed.

"Emerald, the heroine, has dark-brown eyes and hair," Jason explained. See, Galen, I know *that* about your story.

"Are all your stories love stories?" Brooke asked.

"No. Only four are. The others are about life in Kenya."

"So, you're the Isak Dinesen of the nineteen eighties," Melanie suggested.

Charles arched an eyebrow at Melanie. Then he remembered. There had just been a movie about Isak Dinesen. Charles was a little surprised Melanie hadn't said Galen was the *Meryl Streep.* . . .

"She's one of my favorite authors," Melanie

continued, staring defiantly at Charles. You are so handsome, Charles, but so arrogant.

"Mine, too," Galen agreed.

Mine, too, Brooke thought. But when had *Melanie* read Isak Dinesen?

"Are you planning to publish all your stories, Galen?"

"If they're publishable. Charles wrote something about—"

"They'll be publishable," Charles predicted confidently. It was a safe prediction, if "Emerald" was any indication of Galen's talent. "Maybe we could publish all four love stories in *Images* and arrange a book deal for the others."

"A book?" Galen whispered.

"Sure. We don't do book publishing, but I can make some phone calls to people who do."

"Really?"

"Of course."

"It sounds like you may need an attorney to look at some contracts, Galen. My fee is an autographed copy of your first book," Brooke offered.

"Thank you, Brooke."

"All your stories are set in Africa?" Jason asked. He wanted the emerald eyes to know he was interested in her work.

"Most of them. I have a few about India. We lived there when I was young." Galen paused. Then she added, hoping it would please these four magnificent people who were being so kind to her, "Beginning tomorrow I'll write about Manhattan. I would like to do a collection of stories about twins."

123

The reaction was immediate. They all spoke at once.

"You wouldn't want to do that."

"There's nothing special, *really.*"

"Better to stick with love stories."

"It's too confusing."

Galen drew a sharp breath. They weren't pleased. The emotion, the common thread that suddenly bound the two sets of twins, was fear.

Chapter Eight

New York City
October 1985

At nine-thirty in the morning on the second Tuesday in October, Andrew Parker queried the group of lawyers in the DA's office.

"Does it surprise anyone here that Brooke Chandler passed the Bar?"

"*What?*" Brooke asked.

"It doesn't surprise me," someone said.

"No, not a bit," another added.

"How . . . ?" Brooke whispered weakly.

"I have my spies at the courthouse." Andrew flashed his confident, charming, I-rest-my-case smile. "The list was posted at nine A.M."

"Are you sure?" Brooke had been planning to go to the courthouse at noon. The results were always posted a day or two before the notice arrived by mail.

"Of course I'm sure. But I had him jot down your candidate number, just in case there is *another* Brooke Chandler." Andrew handed her a scrap of paper with a number, *her* number, on it.

"There isn't another Brooke Chandler. There never could be," someone added amiably.

"But how does he know I passed?"

"They don't post the names of the losers, Brooke. So, what does everyone think, a celebration lunch for Brooke?"

"Sure, where?"

"Somewhere near the courthouse, I'm afraid. I think *Ms.* Chandler wants to see the fine print herself. Am I right, Brooke?" Andrew teased.

Brooke nodded sheepishly. She wanted to see her name on the list. But it would be there. She had done it. She had passed the Bar!

Not that there should have been any doubt. Brooke passed—more than *passed*—every exam she had ever taken. But she worried about them all, especially the important ones. What if . . .

Relief pulsed through her, relief and elation.

"Brooke, sorry to interrupt, you have a call on line three."

"Oh. Thank you. Ill take it in my office."

Twenty seconds later she spoke into the phone, "This is Brooke Chandler."

"Congratulations, counselor."

"Who . . ." Brooke began. The voice was vaguely familiar. It was a pleasant, seductive, easy voice. But the memory it evoked wasn't pleasant; she had heard the pleasantness turn to ice. "Lieutenant Adrian."

"Very good."

"I don't deserve the congratulations, *you* do," Brooke said lightly.

"What?" How did she know?

"I heard it was your testimony that really sealed the verdict on Cassandra."

"Oh," Nick said. Oh, *that.* "You weren't there?"

Nick had decided, as he was giving his testimony, that Brooke Chandler was not there. There was no face in the DA's entourage that could possibly match the voice.

"No. I missed it. I was in the library researching a very old precedent." Brooke was sorry that she had missed Nick's testimony. Everyone said he was so good—so *cool*—on the stand. "I don't really deserve any congratulations for what happened to Cassandra."

"That wasn't what I was calling about."

"Oh?"

"I heard you passed the Bar."

"That's *very* recent information."

"I'm a very good detective. So, now you can start looking for a million-dollar practice in Westchester."

"No way, Lieutenant Adrian."

"No? All maybe I'll see you then. Maybe we'll do a homicide case together sometime."

"I'm looking forward to it," Brooke answered gaily. Maybe it wouldn't be so hard to thank him after all, if she ever saw him.

After Nick hung up he wondered, what would Brooke Chandler think if she knew "Manhattan Beat" was going to be published in *The New*

Yorker? That was *his* exciting news. It had come in yesterday's mail. Nick hadn't told anyone, but he had almost told Brooke Chandler. Whoever she was.

"Galen." The voice—one of her housemates—called through the door of her room. "You have a phone call."

"Yes?" Galen rushed to the door. "Who is it?"

"Some man. He said his name, but I didn't catch it."

Charles. It had to be Charles. She'd been waiting to hear from him. She had given him her duffle bag of stories. He told her he would call after he finished reading them all.

Galen's hands trembled as she lifted the receiver of the communal phone on the battered wooden table in the entry hall of the brownstone on Spring Street in Greenwich Village. Her housemates, like her co-workers at the Champs-Elysées coffee house on Washington Square, were aspiring actors and actresses, dancers and musicians, poets and writers, artists and comedians. The phone was the link to their dreams. It had brought luck recently; last week a housemate made the chorus line of *Cats*. . . .

"Hello? Charles?"

"They're all sensational, Galen."

"Really?"

"Really." Sensational was an understatement. "You want to publish them?"

"*Yes.* Galen, I'd love to publish every one, one at a time, for the next few years. But it's better for you to publish a book."

"I thought you wanted to publish 'Emerald' and three others." Galen spoke quietly. Charles didn't really like them after all! He was her friend, and he was being kind; but his kindness didn't extend to publishing her stories in *Images* in the name of friendship. . . .

"I do. I would like to publish 'Emerald' in December, as scheduled. Then 'Sapphire' in March and 'Jade' in June and 'Garnet' in September. If that's not too tight a schedule for you."

"For *me?* The stories are already written."

"But the revisions."

"Revisions?"

"Minor fine-tuning. The sort of changes you made yourself along the way."

"I didn't make changes."

"From draft to draft." Somehow they weren't communicating.

"There weren't drafts. I just wrote them."

In the silence that followed, Charles remembered the teenage girl beside his cot, staring in the distance, focused on something only she could see, mesmerized. Occasionally she would smile, fill her blue-ink fountain pen and write in slow, confident strokes, perfectly translating the image of her mind's eye into words.

One draft, the way she wanted it.

"Galen," Charles continued patiently "Your stories are sensational, but they can be *better.*"

"How?"

Charles heard skepticism mixed with fear.

"I've written some suggestions. You don't *have*

to follow them. I will publish your stories as is if you insist."

"I insist," she told him bravely.

"Galen." Charles's patience was faltering. "Most writers welcome feedback from editors. Don't take this personally."

"How do you *expect* me to take it, Charles?"

Charles sighed. He answered flatly, "Professionally."

"Oh," she breathed. *Oh.* Her stomach churned.

"Why don't we get together tonight and discuss—"

"I'm working."

"I will send my suggestions to you by courier, then."

At midnight the following night, Galen dialed the unlisted telephone number Charles had given her to his penthouse.

"Charles, you were right," she began as soon as he answered.

"Galen?"

"Your suggestions, Charles. My stories can, will, be better. Thank you."

"It's what editors do."

"Yes, but—"

"It's my job, Galen."

"Still . . . these were so sensitive, so . . . ."

"Good." Charles laughed softly, then, changing the subject, said, "I am glad you called. I've found three major book publishers who are very interested in publishing the collection of African stories."

A long silence followed.

"Galen?"

"Why are you doing this, Charles?" she asked quietly.

Charles didn't answer. He didn't *have* an answer.

"Happy Birthday, Brooke! Trick or treat?"

"Likewise, Melanie. Treat. Come in."

Halloween babies *and* twins. For the first twelve years it had been so much fun. They celebrated their Halloween birthdays by dressing up in wonderful costumes, sometimes identical, sometimes complementary. They hadn't celebrated a birthday together since seventh grade. It was Melanie's suggestion, just as window-shopping along Fifth Avenue or brunch at the Tavern on the Green or seeing the sights of New York, together, was initiated by Melanie.

Brooke accepted Melanie's suggestion of birthday dinner politely, as she accepted all of Melanie's ideas, and even offered her apartment. In the six weeks since Melanie had moved to New York, she had never been in Brooke's apartment. Always before they met in public, amid the amusing distractions of Manhattan. Sometimes Galen joined them.

But tonight, on their twenty-sixth birthday, Brooke and Melanie were alone and private. They sat in Brooke's small, immaculate living room thoughtfully eating carrot sticks and searching their minds for safe neutral topics. Noticing the recent issues of *Images* and *Fashion* neatly arranged on the dust-free coffee table,

Melanie offered eagerly, "I can't wait to read Galen's story."

"The December issue, isn't it?" Brooke asked, then blushed. It was a stupid question, fueled by nervousness and the desperate desire to keep the conversation alive. They both knew "Emerald" would appear in the December issue. Galen was their friend and *she* was Galen's attorney. Brooke knew the precise date of publication of all Galen's stories in *Images*.

"Her next one, 'Sapphire,' will be published in the March issue," Brooke continued quickly, providing new information. "And Charles has spoken with several book publishers who want to publish her stories about Africa. Galen and I are meeting with them to discuss terms next week. It's so nice of Charles—"

"Good old Charles." The cynicism in Melanie's voice was lost in the crunch of a carrot stick.

"Do you see him much?" Brooke asked carefully.

"All the time. He's at the fashion shows, of course. And we seem to be on all the same guest lists."

"How is he?" Brooke hadn't seen Charles since the dinner for Galen at his penthouse, but she had discussed the details of Galen's contracts with him over the phone.

"Fine, I suppose."

Even though Melanie *saw* Charles frequently, they didn't speak. After the first few parties, after awkward attempts at light banter deteriorated quickly into unveiled taunts, Charles and

Melanie avoided each other. Melanie didn't *like* Charles. It was an easy decision to defend. Charles Sinclair viewed the world with such arrogance and disdain!

But it bothered Melanie that Charles didn't like *her*. She wasn't used to being disliked; only in high school, only Brooke . . . Melanie shook the painful memory. Charles didn't even know her. It was more proof that there was something wrong with *him*. Melanie added wryly, "Vintage Charles Sinclair."

The timer on the oven sounded with a startling buzz.

"Time to make the sauce." Brooke stood up.

"Can I help?"

"No. Thanks. The kitchen's too small. It will just be a few minutes." Brooke added gaily, "Make yourself at home!"

Left alone, Melanie's nervous energy drove her to pace in the tiny living room, and that done in a matter of moments and taking Brooke literally, she explored the rest of her sister's apartment.

There wasn't much to explore—only two closed doors. The first was a small bathroom with ancient wallpaper and a chipped mirror. Behind the second door was Brooke's bedroom. Melanie opened the door and gasped.

"Brooke!" she shrieked. "Come *quickly!*"

"Melanie? What's wrong?"

"Brooke," Melanie exclaimed in mock horror as Brooke rushed into the bedroom. "Your room is a *mess!* The bed is barely made. There are mounds of clothes and piles of books and . . ."

Melanie suppressed a giggle with great effort

and found a stern face. "Brooke. This is serious. You are the *neat* twin. Someone has been in your bedroom and almost destroyed it!"

Melanie couldn't contain herself any longer and the giggles won out and were contagious, and in moments Brooke and Melanie, weak with laughter, flopped helplessly onto Brooke's haphazardly made bed.

"I can't believe it, Brooke." Melanie tossed a pair of jeans that lay on the bed onto an already clothes-cluttered chair.

"So they were wrong." Brooke shrugged. "We're both messy."

"No. I'm *neat.* I," Melanie hesitated. She continued slowly, suddenly serious, "I hated living in a messy room all those years."

Melanie lay on her twin's bed and stared at the ceiling, avoiding Brooke's eyes; Melanie felt as if she had made a monumental confession. It was monumental, or *could* be. It *could* be the beginning of telling each other the truth.

"And I," Brooke whispered, staring at her own piece of cracked plaster ceiling, "hated wearing all those drab clothes."

Melanie sat up and turned to look at Brooke. "Bright colors really do suit you. Which reminds me, I got you something."

Melanie left the room.

"Here." Melanie handed the gift-wrapped package to Brooke when she returned. They hadn't given each other presents for years. The package was small. It fit, completely hidden, in her purse. She could have left with it, if it hadn't felt right to give Brooke a present. Melanie added awkwardly, "Happy Halloween."

"Thank you." Brooke opened the package and withdrew a beautiful silk scarf. "Oh, Melanie."

"There's one shade of blue . . . here"— Melanie pointed to a dark-blue piece of the silk— "I thought it exactly matched your eyes. Let's see."

Melanie turned and led the way to the bathroom.

"It *does,*" Brooke agreed moments later as they stood side by side in front of the mirror. "Exactly."

"Your eyes, Brooke. I remember . . ." Melanie frowned.

"What?"

"I remember when I learned we weren't identical." Melanie spoke to Brooke's image in the mirror. "I remember looking in the mirror and thinking how pretty *my* blue eyes were. Like the sky."

"They are." Brooke answered Melanie in the mirror.

"But your eyes are so dark. So interesting."

Brooke and Melanie watched the faces in the mirror for a long silent moment. As they watched, the faces became solemn and thoughtful, transformed by bittersweet memories and worrisome questions. What *else* did you hate? What else of mine did you want?

"If only you had my eyes, Melanie Chandler," Brooke's tease had an uneasy twist, "you *might* have a shot at a really big modelling career."

★ ★ ★

"Eyes half closed, Melanie. The breeze is stroking you and it feels so good." Steve's voice was low and seductive and mean. He crouched in front of her, taking shot after shot, moving around her, making her move, coaxing her. . . .

Melanie arched her neck and breathed the forced air from the portable fan. The photo session was in one of the studios at Drake, but Melanie could pretend the hot lights were the warm California sun and the fan-fueled air was a fresh sea breeze. That wonderful memory made her smile. She didn't need Steve's vulgar words. . . .

"Spread your legs, Melanie. Wider. *Wider.* Open your mouth. Wet your lips. Now think about my cock. It's big and hard. Think about where you want it. Your mouth."

Melanie froze. Her pale blue eyes flashed with anger. "How *dare* you?"

"How dare I what?"

"Speak to me like that."

"Like what? Like you're a whore? It's what you are, you know," Steve snarled.

"How can you say that?"

"You sell your body, Melanie. You *sell* sex. Just because no one touches you doesn't mean—" Steve's voice was ugly. "What do you think men do when they see your pictures? How do you think they *use* your pictures?"

"You have a filthy mind," Melanie hissed.

"I'm just being honest with you."

"The truth is," Melanie said icily, her body trembling with rage and fear, "my pictures sell beautiful clothes and beautiful jewels and—"

135

"The truth is you're a whore."

"*No.*"

Melanie rushed out of the studio and into the dressing room. Once inside the door she drew deep breaths. It didn't help. She couldn't breathe, the knot in her stomach tightened, and her body trembled.

"Melanie?"

"Fran."

"Melanie, sit down." As Fran spoke she put her hands on Melanie's quivering shoulders and pushed her firmly onto a hard wooden chair in front of a makeup mirror. "What happened?"

"Steve," Melanie squeezed her eyes shut against the memory.

"Oh."

"*Oh?*"

"He made some suggestive comments to you during a session?" Fran guessed.

"Yes," Melanie breathed. At least she could breathe now. "And he said that I was a whore, selling my body."

"That sounds like Steve," Fran murmured. "I don't think he's too fond of women, at least not beautiful ones."

"He's done this to you?"

"To everyone."

"Has anyone told Mr. Drake?"

"Are you kidding?"

"Adam Drake is a fine man. He would fire Steve instantly if he knew."

"Melanie, let's do a little reality testing. Steve is probably the best fashion photographer in the world. He may hate us, but he makes us look

136

wonderful. And we all— you, me, Steve, Mr. Drake—make a lot of money."

"The pimps and the whores," Melanie whispered.

"I don't believe that and neither do you," Fran countered impatiently.

"No," Melanie agreed quietly, frowning slightly. "But I think Mr. Drake—"

"Melanie, ten years from now, when you and I are *history* in the modelling business, Steve will still be the top photographer around and Drake will still be the number-one agency. We are commodities with short shelf lives—"

"What a happy thought!" Melanie laughed, tossing her golden hair and with it the unpleasantness with Steve. She wasn't going to let Steve Barnes ruin this for her. She could tolerate his vulgarity if she had to. "Ten years?"

"If we're lucky. Maybe only five." Fran looked at their reflections under the harsh lights of the makeup mirrors. Flawless beauty now, but it wouldn't last. "What are you going to do after our fling with fame is over, Melanie? Where will you be in ten years?"

"In ten years," Melanie mused distantly, "I'll be living with my husband and children in Malibu. We'll have horses and a white sand beach and rose gardens. In my spare time, when the children are in school, I'll design clothes."

"Oh, my God."

"What?"

"I kind of imagined that *you* of all the models in the history of Drake would be the one to end up with Adam. But that would put you in a penthouse in Manhattan for life. And he *had* his children two marriages ago."

"He probably has no intention of remarrying anyway."

"He almost got married last summer. To Dr. Jane Tucker, a neurosurgeon who works at Cornell. I met her once. She was very impressive. So, anyway, how many children?"

"Two, I think." Melanie frowned briefly What if she had twins? "How about you ten years from now?"

"In ten years—hopefully long before that—I will be Mrs. Jason Sinclair."

"Really?"

"It's all I want." Fran sighed. She glanced at her watch and added, "In fact, I am on my way to see him now to cancel our lunch date because of the Tiffany shoot. See you later, Melanie, you homebody whore."

Fran cast a playful smile at Melanie as she left.

Melanie sat in the silence of the dressing room for a long time, staring at herself in the mirror and thinking. Finally she walked down the hall to the studio. Steve was preparing for another session.

"If you treat me like that again," Melanie began solemnly. . . . She saw Steve's back stiffen in response to her words. "I will tell Mr. Drake."

"*Mr.* Drake?" Steve taunted. "*Adam* will laugh at you. He might even fire you."

"I don't care," Melanie answered calmly, truthfully. It was what she had decided. She loved modelling because it was so beautiful. But Steve

138

was tainting it. She would rather give it up than have it tainted. "But, Steve, he might fire *you*."

"No."

"There's an easy way to find out." Melanie's voice was strong and confident. She believed she *would* win. Adam Drake loved beauty, too.

"You wouldn't tell him." It sounded like a threat. Steve spun and faced her. His dark eyes were hidden in shadows, but Melanie still saw the rage. And the fear.

Steve was afraid.

"Try me."

Chapter Nine

Galen left Charles's office just as Jason emerged from his.

"Galen! Hello."

"Hello, Jason." She blushed.

"How are you?"

"Fine." Give me a minute, Jason. I have to think what to say. . . . She felt him pulling away. The words burst out, awkward and unrehearsed. "Charles just showed me the art for 'Emerald.' He said you chose it. It's . . . Jason . . . so beautiful. Perfect."

"I'm glad you like it. If you have a moment there's someone in my office you might enjoy meeting."

Galen followed Jason into his office. A woman

stood by the picture window overlooking Manhattan.

"Fran." Jason's voice drew her attention away from the gray-black clouds that threatened to drench all of Manhattan.

Fran turned gracefully and elegantly and smiled a beautiful smile.

"Galen, this is Fran Jeffries. Fran was the model for 'Emerald.' "

Galen stared at the lovely brown eyes and rich dark hair and breathtaking beauty. The art Galen had just seen in Charles's office captured the innocence of the character Galen had created. But this woman was so confident, so experienced, so beguiling. She wasn't Emerald, was she? Galen didn't know and it confused her. Galen knew Emerald so well. So much of Emerald *was* Galen. So much of what was inside.

Galen smiled politely at Fran and wondered if she and Fran had anything in common. There was certainly nothing on the surface, and probably nothing inside. Fran. Emerald. Galen. What was real and what was art?

"It's nice to meet you, Fran."

"It's nice to meet you. I can't wait to read your story. Jason keeps raving about it."

Really? Galen looked shyly to Jason for confirmation—a smile, a nod—but Jason's pale-blue eyes avoided hers.

"Jason, I have to go," Fran said. "I'm sorry about lunch, but Tiffany calls. See you tonight. Good-bye, Galen."

Galen moved to the window as Fran and Jason

kissed good-bye. It was a brief kiss, nothing more. But it was enough, too much.

"She's very beautiful," Galen said after Fran left. She spoke to the thunderclouds.

"You look hungry." Jason ignored Galen's comment about Fran. Maybe he hadn't heard it.

"What?" Galen spun to look at him, to see if his pale-blue eyes were serious. They were.

"You look like you've lost weight."

Embarrassed, Galen folded her arms around her thin body. It was true. She *had* lost weight. Sometimes she got so involved in her writing she forgot to eat. She was thin to begin with and now Jason—*Jason*—noticed that she looked even thinner, even gawkier. Galen reached for her handwoven cloth purse. "I'd better go."

"Have lunch with me." Jason blocked her exit. "Fran just cancelled and I have reservations for two at La Lumière. Will you join me?"

La Lumière. Galen had heard of it. It was expensive, exclusive, and elegant. Most people couldn't even *get* reservations. One had to be *known.*

"I'm not dressed . . ." Galen looked at the utilitarian wool coat she had bought—second-hand—when the Indian summer suddenly gave way to an early frost. Underneath she wore an old cotton dress. She didn't own any clothes suitable for lunch at La Lumière.

"Who cares?" Jason asked.

You care, Jason. I'm sure you care. You're just much too polite, much too well bred, to let it show.

★　★　★

141

Later that night, as Galen thought about the lunch at La Lumière with Jason, she couldn't remember if she even touched her gourmet meal. And she couldn't remember if there was anyone else in the restaurant, or the color of the table-cloth, or the name of the waiter, or the kind of flowers on the tables, or the art that hung on the walls. Galen couldn't remember any of the things that everyone else considered so memorable about the restaurant.

All Galen could remember was the way he made her feel, the way he laughed, the way his eyes looked at her, the way he leaned toward her until they almost touched.

And when Jason thought about it later that night, before he and Fran made love, and after, and even during, he wondered if it had all been a dream. Surely it had been just an illusion, just a moment of fiction wedged between the realities of life.

Because for two and a half hours there had been magic. Jason had never felt such joy and enchantment, never before in his life, not even for a minute.

It wasn't real. It *couldn't* be.

Galen waited—restless, anxious, eager, waiting—for one week.

Maybe Jason doesn't know how to reach me, her heart suggested with each passing day.

Of course he does, her mind answered. He just isn't calling. He isn't going to. Why would he? He has Fran . . . Emerald. . . .

At the end of the week, Galen decided to send

him a thank-you note. It was appropriate, wasn't it? *Polite.*

A busboy at the Champs-Elysées agreed to hand-deliver it for Galen at noon. Galen wrote Jason's name and the word *Personal* on the envelope.

The busboy reported that Jason's secretary was at lunch. He asked the receptionist to put it on Jason's desk.

Jason noticed the pale-pink envelope on his desk the instant he entered his office. It was so out of place. Jason's office was cluttered with photographs and sketches and layouts and designs. But not *words*. There were no letters or memos or appointment calendars or manuscripts or telephone directories in Jason Sinclair's office.

Jason gazed at the pale-pink envelope and the beautiful design drawn in blue fountain pen. Jason's artistic eye recognized the lovely, delicate design, and knew who drew it, but he couldn't know its meaning.

Jason closed his eyes. Feelings of helplessness flooded him, bringing with them ancient anguish. He was *dependent* again, destined to know only what someone else chose to share with him, unable to know it on his own. As the horrible memory of the day of Elliott's death—the day of his greatest helplessness—began to surface, Jason quickly opened his eyes.

Jason put the unopened envelope in his suit pocket and walked, coatless and desperate, into the winter chill.

Why didn't he just ask Charles to read it to

him? Charles did all the reading for the Sinclair twins.

Because this was different. *Private.* Charles didn't need to know.

I don't *want* Charles to know, Jason realized as he walked along Park Avenue, his cheeks numbing quickly in the icy November wind. There was so much Charles had never shared with him.

Despite the bitter cold, Jason wasn't alone. The streets of Manhattan were crowded with purposeful people rushing swiftly to warm destinations. Jason was surrounded by humanity, *literate* humanity. He was surrounded by people who could read the precious note in his pocket. But Jason was recognizable. He had to be careful who he asked.

After several blocks, Jason turned off Park Avenue onto a side street and headed east. The humanity changed: less purposeful, even colder, and without warm destinations. These people wouldn't recognize him. The first two people Jason spoke to were like him—they couldn't read.

Three blocks east of Park Avenue the street ended in a schoolyard. Groups of teenagers huddled in defiant celebration of recess despite the winter cold. Jason approached a boy who huddled by himself.

"Can you read?"

"What d'ya mean?"

"Can you read?" Jason repeated.

" 'Course I can."

Jason wondered if it was bravado.

"Would you read this for me?" Jason took the

envelope from his pocket. "I'll give you twenty dollars."

The boy eyed him skeptically.

"Twenty-five," Jason offered. Or fifty. Or a hundred. Or a *million.*

"Somethin' wrong with your eyes, mister?"

Jason shrugged. "OK?"

The boy nodded, eagerly shoved the money into his jeans pocket, and took the note.

"OK. This here says," he began, scowling at the envelope, *"Jason.* And *Per . . . son . . . al. Personal.* You want me to read what's inside?"

"Yes. Please." No. But do I have a choice?

"Dear Jason. Thank you for lunch. No, it's more." The boy frowned, struggling. *"Lunch . . . eee . . . on."*

"Luncheon," Jason breathed. Very British. Very Galen. "Go on."

"Luncheon last week. It was . . . lovely. I have thought of little else." The boy stopped. "There's one more word. It's strange. I'll spell it to you."

Jason listened to the letters that had no meaning.

"Could the word be *Galen?"*

The boy wrinkled his nose, studied the pink notepaper, and nodded energetically. "Yup. That's what it is. *Galen.* Funny. Is it a name?"

"Oh, yes," Jason retrieved the notepaper from the boy's hand. "Thank you."

"Sure."

Jason hesitated. "You probably won't believe this, but, it's so important. You should learn to read as well as you possibly can."

"Sure." The boy shrugged. "I will."

I have thought of little else. The words echoed in Jason's mind. Neither have I, Galen. But it wasn't real. It was just a lovely fantasy. If we see each other again it will only be disappointing, won't it?

Still, as Jason thought about her, the magical feelings swirled inside him. He walked faster and faster in the bitter cold, beyond Park Avenue toward Greenwich Village and Galen.

By the time Jason reached the Champs-Elysées coffee house his lips were blue with cold and his cheeks had faded from rosy red to ashen. As soon as he saw her, Jason tried to turn his numb lips into a smile for her. It must have worked, or Galen just smiled anyway, and in moments Jason's cold body was pulsing with a magical warmth that was Galen.

"Jason."

"Hi."

"Hi."

"I got . . . Thank you . . . it was nice. . . ."

"Oh." She blushed. "Yes . . . it was nice."

They stood in the entrance of the Champs-Elysées fumbling to find words, but eloquently communicating with their eyes and their smiles. Galen was an artist with words, but her art was in writing not speaking. Her emotions and feelings flowed articulately from her heart to paper. But speaking the words—*saying* what was important—was foreign to her.

Saying what was important was as foreign to Jason as it was to Galen. Jason spoke the language that Charles, Elliott, and the tutors taught him— their language, not his—because he had to. But

146

the words weren't his. Jason couldn't use them to express his feelings. Jason painted his feelings, and he shared his paintings with no one.

Until now he had never wanted to.

"When do you. . ."

"In an hour."

"Are you free?"

"Yes."

Jason and Galen spent the next two weeks falling quietly and confidently in love. They dined in Greenwich Village, in dark secluded restaurants where no one recognized *him* and where *she* felt at home in her long calico dresses. Jason felt at home in the Village, too. He loved the music and the theater and the art and the people. They were people like him: quiet, talented, passionate artists.

Jason belonged in the Village and he belonged with Galen. He smiled at her and held her hand and desperately hoped that she knew. Galen smiled back with glistening emerald eyes and hoped that he knew, too.

Late at night, after Jason left her at the door of the dilapidated brownstone on Spring Street, Galen lighted her hyacinth-scented candles, drew ink into her fountain pen, and wrote letters to him telling him how she felt.

At the end of the second week Jason suggested they spend Thanksgiving weekend in Southampton at Windermere.

"Will Charles be there?" Galen asked.

"No. Charles doesn't live there. No one else would be there. We would be alone." The sizable staff required to maintain Windermere did their work on weekdays and vanished on weekends when Jason was in residence. It had been that way ever since Elliott's death.

Jason watched her struggling, searching for words, her lovely eyes flickering with worry.

"Don't you want to be alone with me?" he asked gently, bewildered.

"*Yes.*"

"No?"

"Yes. It's just," Galen faltered. Then she remembered. She had written it all down already. When she told him he would understand. Her eyes met his bravely, "You read 'Emerald,' Jason. That's who I am."

Jason shrugged slightly, unable to hold her gaze. Of course he knew the story. He sensed the mood and passion from what Charles told him. But Jason didn't *know* Emerald; he didn't know that when Emerald fell in love, when she gave herself to love, it was forever.

Jason doesn't feel the same way, Galen realized. She had exposed herself entirely by telling him about Emerald. And now Jason was telling her he couldn't promise anything.

"I haven't—" Jason gazed into her tear-damp emerald eyes and he knew he had to tell her—"I haven't read 'Emerald.' "

"Why not?" Galen's voice trembled. Foolish, innocent, silly Emerald. Silly *Galen.*

"Because," Jason spoke hesitantly. He had never told anyone before. Only Charles knew. Jason reached for her hand. "Because I can't read."

"Can't read?"

Jason told her. Jason told her in the language that had never been his; it was a story without emotion. Jason didn't tell Galen about the anger and frustration and helplessness. He didn't know how to.

"Is it dyslexia?" Galen asked when the pause was so long that she decided he had finished.

"I guess so."

"There's so much work with that now. Have you—"

"I'm adjusted. I almost forget about it until there's a story I want to read or until I get a note on pale-pink stationery."

"Who read it to you?" Galen asked. "Charles?"

"No one who knows you or me."

"Oh."

"Galen? What's wrong?"

"Writing. It's how I communicate."

"Not the only way."

"I've written you a letter every night."

"You have? Will you read them to me?"

Galen started to shake her head, but Jason seemed so pleased about the letters. Maybe she *could* read them to him—this weekend, at Windermere, when they were alone.

"Jason, I . . . Emerald . . . I am inexperienced."

"There's no hurry, Galen. About anything." *We have forever.*

"Jason," Galen breathed as they walked, hand in hand, through the mansion at Windermere.

"I love it here." I love sharing Windermere with you.

"Does your art ever appear in *Images?*" Galen asked.

"What?"

"Your paintings, Jason. They're magnificent."

What Galen had been noticing and admiring and loving, even more than the panoramic views of the sea or the rich splendor of the mansion, were Jason's wonderful paintings. Jason had never told Galen about his painting, but she didn't seem surprised. It was just one more marvelous discovery about the man she loved.

"Some are my mother's."

"Yes." Galen hesitated. "The signatures . . ."

"Oh." Jason smiled. "Of course."

"Hers are wonderful, too," Galen added quickly.

"The style is similar."

"Yes. But yours are stronger and more vivid." More emotional. "Have you ever done a show?"

"No." Jason's painting was for him and for Windermere; and, now, for Galen. He continued gently, "I would love to do a painting of you."

"Oh, I wouldn't be a very good model." Galen's cheeks flushed pale pink.

Jason touched her warm cheeks and smiled into her eyes.

"You are beautiful, Galen, so beautiful."

Jason kissed her full, soft lips. He felt her tremble.

"Galen?"

"I've never . . ." She looked down, too shy to meet his eyes.

"Made love. I know. Galen, I won't push you. Kissing doesn't mean—"

"I've never *kissed*. . . ."

"No?" His voice was so gentle. "Do you want to?"

"Yes, Jason. I just . . . if I do something wrong."

"You can't do anything wrong. Nothing is wrong. We'll do this together, learn together. OK?"

Galen answered him with her lips, kissing his cheek, then finding his lips. Jason held her face in his hands and laced his strong fingers through her fine shiny hair.

How long had it been since he had just kissed someone? *Just,* Jason mused as the thrill of kissing her, the wonder of sharing that warmth and closeness with her pulsed through him, filling him with joy and desire. *Just,* he thought, as she opened her mouth, inviting him, wanting more of him, more closeness, more warmth, more discovery.

We'll learn together. Jason was learning that he could do this—kiss his beloved Galen—forever. He could spend forever in the tangle of red-gold silk that covered them both as the passion of their kisses grew. They kissed for a half an hour, then an hour, then two as the great room fell dark and cold in the early winter twilight.

Between kisses they gazed at each other, smiling, tracing gentle lines around the other's eyes and lips and face and neck. They kissed lips and mouths and cheeks and eyes and necks and hair and hands. Again and again.

Sometimes the kiss was a long, slow, leisurely

dream. And sometimes it was deep and urgent and eager.

That night Jason and Galen walked hand in hand to her cheerful pink-and-cream bedroom overlooking the courtyard and rose gardens. Jason kissed her good night in the hallway.

"Sleep well, Galen."

An hour later Jason heard a soft knock on his door. He was awake, lying in the darkness, thinking about her, unable to sleep.

Galen stood in the hallway, barefooted, wearing a tattered paisley bathrobe over a modest flannel nightgown.

"I couldn't sleep."

"Me neither."

Jason waited. He needed to know what she wanted. There weren't any rules. They were learning together. But this had to be her decision. He smiled at her, encouraging her to tell him.

Galen smiled in response to his smile, then frowned.

"What, Galen?"

"Do you think we could sleep together? I mean, literally, sleep. It's too soon, but . . . being this near you without being with you. Would that be unfair to you? Would it be wrong?"

"Nothing is wrong." Jason led her by the hand to his bed.

Galen took off her robe and crawled in beside him. Jason wrapped his arms around her and held her close. Within moments they were both asleep, their restlessness vanquished by the peace and joy of being together.

Chapter Ten

"How's the law-and-order business?" He leaned against the doorjamb of her office just as he had six months before. Then, the sweltering heat of summer collected in her office. Now, two days before Christmas, she kept herself warm with endless mugs of overbrewed coffee.

"Charles." Brooke smiled. She tilted her head to the pages and pages of legal briefs stacked in precarious piles on the floor and table and said, "Disorderly. But legal."

"It was nice of you to make time to help Galen."

"She's my friend."

"You negotiated quite a deal for her." Galen had told Charles the details of the two-book contract. She would be well paid for her stories about Africa *and* for another yet-to-be-written collection.

"It was fair. Who is it that says, Quality is always worth the price?"

Charles looked embarrassed for a fleeting moment. He recovered quickly, guessing lightly, "Brooke Chandler?"

"Charles Sinclair."

The conversation came to a shuddering halt. The realization that she had been teasing Charles caught up with her. Who did she think she was? Melanie?

"I sent 'Sapphire' to Mitchell Altman in Holly-wood." Charles's voice was suddenly all business. "He's interested in making a movie from the story. He'll fly out in mid-January to meet with Galen and her attorney to talk about the rights, who'll do the screenplay, that sort of thing."

"Is Sinclair Publishing becoming Sinclair Productions?"

"Jason and I will be the executive producers."

"Sounds like fun."

"Do you really have time?" Charles gestured to the mounds of work in her office.

"Yes," Brooke answered truthfully. Nights. Weekends. Every night. Every weekend. She wasn't dating. She had offers, but she said No. There was no one. Brooke added another truth, "I enjoy it."

"Maybe enough to someday give up the life of crime and come to work at Sinclair?"

"Maybe." Brooke smiled. Maybe.

The five beats of silence that followed felt to Brooke and her pounding heart like a hundred.

"Are you going away for the holidays?" Charles asked finally.

"Yes, to see my parents in California. Melanie can't go. Adam wants her here for his New Year's Eve party. Something about her celebrity image and keeping a high profile at the right events."

Charles nodded. "Very effective marketing. Adam's New Year's Eve party is the grand finale of the season."

"I was invited," Brooke said carefully. What if an unguarded look of horror crossed his hand-some face at the news? Brooke, you don't

154

understand, Adam Drake's party is for the Beautiful People. Brooke explained quickly, "Actually, Andrew Parker was invited. He's married, of course, but his wife will be away. Andrew thought I should go." Brooke smiled. "Effective marketing for the DA's office, I guess."

"But you won't be back in time?"

"No."

"That's too bad." The dark eyes were serious.

"I'm really sorry I can't go to the party," Brooke told Andrew that evening. She added hopefully, "Maybe your wife will return in time."

They were at Giorgio's on Fifth Avenue, sipping hot buttered rum as frenzied, last-minute, holiday shoppers rushed past on the street outside. Brooke had accepted Andrew's invitation a holiday drink after work—reluctantly. Andrew was her mentor, her role model, the kind of brilliant, insightful, articulate trial attorney she wanted to be. Brooke was in awe of Andrew. Going for a drink with him . . .

But the hot buttered rum and spirited holiday crowds and glitter of Fifth Avenue made her feel warm and festive and confident.

"Allison won't return in time." Andrew's voice was low. He sighed and explained, "She's in an institution, Brooke."

"An institution?" Brooke could barely hear her own words above the laughter and gaiety of the crowd at Giorgio's.

"She's ill. It's a kind of depression." Andrew's

155

dark eyes stared thoughtfully at his gold wedding band and then at Brooke.

"Andrew, I'm so sorry." Brooke had an image of Andrew's wife—strong and beautiful and talented—a perfect match for confident, handsome, brilliant Andrew. Andrew hid the sadness so well. Brooke's deep-blue eyes told him, again, how sorry she was.

"Brooke, I'm all right," Andrew reassured her swiftly. "I shouldn't have mentioned it."

"Yes, you should have," Brooke spoke softly.

Andrew smiled a half-smile. "There are times— months—when Allison is fine. Then, without warning . . ."

"It must be very difficult." All the more difficult, Brooke realized, because Andrew loves her so much.

Andrew nodded briefly. Then, purposefully shifting the topic and the mood, he urged, "Tell me about California, Brooke. What will you do while you're home?"

What you should be doing, Andrew, Brooke thought sadly, celebrating the holidays with people I love.

"You see before you an unemployed waitress." Galen laughed softly. "They found a replacement today."

"You're probably the first employee in the history of the Champs-Elysées to give notice."

"They've been so nice to me. It's the least I could do."

"Let's go to Windermere now and stay through New Year's Day," Jason suggested.

"You have the Drake party."

Jason had planned to make a brief, dutiful appearance at Adam Drake's New Year's Eve party while Galen was working. Now she was free. They could go to the party together, but Jason knew it would overwhelm her.

"Not anymore."

"Shouldn't—?"

"No." I should be with you and we should be at Windermere.

Jason and Galen arrived at Windermere just as the first snowflake fell from the wintry gray sky. Jason built a fire in the great room and they settled into their peaceful ritual, Jason painting, Galen writing, both pausing as if by a silent signal to gaze together at the spectacular views of the winter sea.

"What are you reading?" Jason asked when he looked up from his easel.

Usually Galen wrote, curled in the huge sofa, surrounded by candles scented with lilac and wild rose and hyacinth and French vanilla, her fountain pen resting between her lips while she planned the next sentence, word perfect, before writing it down. Jason loved watching her write, absorbed, thoughtful, sometimes smiling, sometimes frowning, *living* the moments with her characters.

But today Galen was reading. And her concentration was intense.

"It's a book about dyslexia." Galen watched Jason carefully as she spoke. She didn't want to make him angry. If Jason could *be* angry.

He smiled.

"So, do I have it?" he asked idly.

"Well, you're male and you told me that your mother may have been dyslexic. That fits."

"Really?" Galen had his attention.

"You don't know much about it, do you?"

Only how it feels, Jason thought.

"No. Tell me." Jason put down his paintbrush.

"It was first recognized in the late eighteen hundreds. It was called word blindness."

"That's apt," Jason murmured. He added thoughtfully, "I see the letters, but I am blind to the words they form."

Galen waited a moment before continuing. "In some people it's just words. In others it's words and numbers."

"I learned mathematics in my head. It wasn't until . . ." Jason paused, his eyes narrowing as he recalled his helplessness that horrible stormy afternoon. He blinked, clearing the pain, and continued. "It wasn't until after my father died that I discovered I could read and write numbers."

That discovery had given him such freedom!

"And you can write your name," Galen reminded him carefully. Surely he could read and write letters, too. It might be a struggle, but . . . "Your signature is on your paintings and on contracts. . . ."

"My art teacher at Harvard taught me. It's really his signature. I see it as a design, not a sequence of letters. I don't know where *Jason* ends and *Sinclair* begins."

"Oh." Galen was beginning to appreciate the magnitude of Jason's dyslexia and how frustrating it must be. She continued, changing direction, "The experts used to be divided about whether dyslexics could be artists."

"Why?"

"Because sometimes they have difficulty with spatial relationships."

"We do?" Jason asked, for the first time in his life identifying himself with all the others who were like him. He wondered who they were, how they had adapted to their lives, if they were as lucky as he. He looked at Galen and felt so lucky.

"Sometimes. But there have been talented artists. Even before you," Galen added lovingly. "Artists and engineers and architects and doctors and lawyers and poets and writers and—"

"Writers?"

"It is believed that Hans Christian Andersen was dyslexic. They've analyzed the original copies of his work, the way he wrote and spelled. . . ."

"He must have been able to write well enough. It must not have been so severe."

Galen was silent for a long moment. Then she began quietly, "There are ways, Jason, to teach—"

"Galen," Jason sighed. That was where this was leading. She wanted him to try. "Oh, Galen. I would give anything to be able to read. But I can't. I can't even read a stop sign. I've tried, honey. After I discovered I could read numbers I had such hope. But . . ."

Jason shrugged.

Galen had read the horrible case studies of people with dyslexia who died because they couldn't read warning signs: *Stop; Railroad*

Crossing; Danger; High Voltage. She shuddered. She also had learned that even when people with dyslexia were taught to read so that they could function safely and independently, they rarely read for pleasure. It was always a struggle.

Galen remembered then, for the first time *feeling* what it must be like for Jason, the terror she herself had felt as a little girl in a remote part of India. The written language bore no resemblance—because the symbols weren't letters, they were uninterpretable, nonsensical lines and curls—to anything she knew. She remembered spending fruitless hours staring at the signs on street corners and in the markets, trying to make sense of them, but unable to.

She was so *afraid* of getting lost and being unable to find her way back to her parents! Galen remembered the horrible frustration and isolation and fear.

"I'm sorry, Jason," she whispered.

"Don't be." Jason moved beside her because it had been too long, an hour, since he had kissed her.

When they awakened the next morning their entire world, the magnificent acres of Windermere, was white and pristine and pure. Virginal.

"Jason," Galen breathed as they gazed out Jason's bedroom window across the soft white blanket and delicately snow-etched trees toward the gray-green sea. "Will you paint this?"

Jason stood behind her, his arms wrapped around her over the modest flannel nightgown.

"If you want me to." He kissed the top of her head, nuzzling his lips in the red-gold tangle.

Galen was still for a moment. Then she turned in his arms and softly touched his handsome cheeks with her slender white fingers.

"I want . . ."

Jason waited. Her eyes told him she wanted much more than a painting of Windermere in snowy splendor.

"Make love to me, Jason."

Jason didn't ask her if she was sure. If she wasn't, if he sensed uncertainty as he was loving her, he would stop. If he could. Could he? He wanted her so much. Holding her warm, lovely softness against him night after night had been such pleasure. And such torment.

Could he stop? *Yes.* If he had to. If her eyes or her body sent a message of doubt he would stop. His love for her would stop him.

But all the green eyes told him was that they wanted him. It was time. And all the softness underneath the flannel nightgown told him, as she pressed against him, moving in a rhythm of passion and desire, was to hurry please, and to be gentle.

"I love you, Galen," Jason whispered as his lips found hers.

They kissed in front of the window in the pale morning light as the snow fell silently outside. Finally Galen eased away, and, her eyes searching his and finding love, she lifted her nightgown over her head.

Jason had never seen her naked. He knew her lovely round cream-colored breasts from feel and taste, but not from sight. And he had imagined the rest.

But she was even more beautiful than he had imagined. Her round, soft womanliness was modestly draped by her long red-gold hair. Jason thought of Botticelli's "The Birth of Venus." It was a distant image, because his mind and his senses were consumed by his desire for her.

Jason removed his pajamas and they stood gazing at each other, not touching or speaking or moving. Then, at the same instant, they smiled, gentle, loving, knowing smiles.

Jason lowered her onto the bed and their naked bodies met in joyous discovery.

She was so soft and warm and lovely!

Oh, Jason, *Jason.*

I want you, Galen. All of you.

Jason searched her eyes as he loved her, searching for doubt and finding none as he touched her breasts, her hips, her thighs . . .

"Galen," he whispered hoarsely, when he could barely wait a moment longer and he thought it was time for her, too.

"Jason." Her eyes glowed, welcoming and confident, as she moved her hips under him.

Her smile didn't waver and her eyes squeezed tight—it hurt a little—for only a moment. Then they were together. They paused for a moment, acknowledging the wonder of the union with loving smiles and shining eyes. Then Jason had to move again, quickly, and their lips kissed and their eyes closed and their arms and legs held tight and the rhythm of their loving was *I love you, I love you, I love you.*

Chapter Eleven

"Hello, Charles." Melanie smiled a beautiful, sexy smile. It was almost midnight, almost time to greet the New Year.

"Hello Melanie." Charles smiled in return, matching Melanie's smile in sexiness and adding a curve of danger.

Viveca Sanders, New Orleans belle turned Rona Barrett of Manhattan, stood nearby watching the exchange between Melanie and Charles with great interest. Viveca's nightly television show, *Viveca's View*, entertained its faithful fans with intimate details and tantalizing gossip about New York City's Beautiful People.

That's right, Viveca, Melanie mused, casting a conspiratorial smile her way. You just witnessed the first conversation between Charles Sinclair and Melanie Chandler in almost three months.

It *had* become conspicuous. Charles saw Melanie at all the fashion shows. Charles watched from a seat of honor—reserved for him as editor-in-chief of *Fashion*—at the end of the runway as Melanie modelled the stunning, elegant, avant garde, and chic-collections of Lauren and Blass and Ellis and Miller and Klein. Charles saw Melanie at the shows, and he saw her at the fabulous lavish parties attended by New York's most famous and wealthy and powerful.

Melanie Chandler's meteoric rise in the world

of fashion *should* have at least piqued the interest of Charles Sinclair. Yet he seemed singularly unintrigued by the newest and most glamorous star in the galaxy of Manhattan celebrities.

And now Charles and Melanie were talking and smiling and everyone was watching.

"This month's *Images* was wonderful," Melanie purred honestly. It was true. Of course, she was complimenting the wrong twin. *Images* was pure Jason—passionate, sensitive, imaginative—it *had* to be.

"Did you like 'Emerald'?"

Wonderful performance, Charles, Melanie thought. You actually seem interested in what I thought of the story.

"Galen is very talented, isn't she?"

"Very. Wait until you read 'Sapphire.' " Charles hesitated a moment, frowned slightly, then asked, "Do you think you could sit on a horse in Central Park in mid-January and pretend it was equatorial Africa?"

The dark eyes were serious. What was he asking? Did he want her to model for the art for one of Galen's stories? The watercolors of Fran for "Emerald" had been breathtaking.

"Yes," Melanie answered quietly. She completely forgot about their audience. "I know I could."

Maybe Jason is right, Charles mused, as he looked at Melanie and tried to be objective. Jason wanted Melanie to model for the art for "Sapphire." It was Jason's decision, but he had sensed Charles's reluctance and they hadn't yet arranged it with Adam.

Jason *is* right, Charles decided. She may be blinded by her own brilliance, but her beauty is flawless. Melanie will make a perfect Sapphire; the artist won't capture her personality.

"OK."

"What does that mean?" Melanie pushed. The dark eyes became aloof, impenetrable walls. Charles was dismissing her.

"I will speak with Adam."

"Speak with *me.*"

Before Charles could reply, cheers of "Happy New Year" and strains of "Auld Lang Syne" flooded the room. Adam Drake's rich and famous guests were greeting the New Year with kisses and hugs all around. No one was watching Charles and Melanie anymore.

"Happy New Year, Melanie."

Melanie's sky-blue eyes met his and beckoned, taunting but intrigued. Charles Sinclair was going to kiss her. He *had* to, it was the New Year. The idea was a little exciting. Melanie lifted her chin slightly, tilted her head, and smiled.

Charles returned the smile, but he didn't kiss her. Instead, he turned and kissed someone else, *anyone else.*

"You bastard," Melanie hissed.

She watched his back stiffen. A deep instinct warned her too late that it might be dangerous to anger Charles Sinclair.

Charles turned to face her. His dark brown eyes sent an ice-cold message of arrogant contempt. Even though Charles didn't move toward her, even though there was no physical threat, Melanie stepped back. Charles watched with astonishment. She was afraid of him. *Why?*

Charles started to follow her, but Melanie was already in the embrace of Russ Collins, Publisher of *Style* magazine, and Viveca Sanders's mauve sunset lips had found Charles's, and the New Year had begun.

"Maybe I shouldn't go."

"Yes, you should, darling." Galen kissed the frown away from his handsome forehead. She continued gently. "And if they want you to crew for the Cup, you should do that, too."

They *did* want Jason to crew for the America's Cup. Last week, the captains of both *Shooting Star* and *Westwind* had asked him. Two months ago, when he was with Fran, Jason would have accepted eagerly. He had always dreamed of racing in the America's Cup.

But now . . . Jason couldn't imagine being away from Galen. Even if she was with him in Australia for the six months, he would see very little of her. Just being away for a week, as he was planning to now, seemed too long. But Alan Forrest wanted Jason's advice about a new rigging for *Shooting Star,* and Alan was an old friend.

"I'm not going to crew."

"But if Dennis Conner wants you to crew for *Stars and Stripes,* Jason . . ."

"No. I do plan to be in Fremantle next January to watch Dennis bring the Cup back home. That is, if you'll come with me?"

"Oh, yes."

"This is such a bad time for me to be away."

Jason's frown returned. "I should be at Melanie's photo session *and* at the meeting with Mitchell Altman."

"Adam knows what you want," Galen reassured him. "And Charles will be there."

Yes, Jason thought, Charles will be there, helping and protecting Galen. For the hundredth time Jason almost decided not to go.

"And the *author* will be there," Jason added lovingly. "But will she tell them if they're doing it wrong?"

"Of course," Galen answered bravely. She was brave with Jason; his love gave her courage and confidence. "It will be good practice for the movie."

"I'm going to miss you." Jason wrapped his arms around her.

"And I will miss you." Galen sighed. "But I'm going to get a lot of work done. I *have* to start on the revisions for 'Jade.' And I'm having dinner with Brooke and Melanie Friday night."

"That's nice."

"Yes. I haven't really seen them since . . . since you."

"Since *us*," Jason corrected quietly. "Since us."

"Galen, it's wonderful to see you. You look," Brooke hesitated, searching for the right word. Beautiful? Yes. Radiant? Yes. *Womanly*. Brooke needed to fill the pause that was becoming awkward . . . "Terrific."

"Thanks, so do you."

"Hi, Galen." Melanie joined them. "You know Fran Jeffries, don't you?"

"Fran, yes, how are you?" Galen managed to keep strength in her voice.

What was Fran doing here? Galen's pounding heart demanded. Fran was a logical guest, she realized, forcing calm. Fran and Melanie worked together. They were friends. And Fran was free on Friday nights now that her boyfriend—make yourself say it, Galen, her *lover*— had found someone new.

"I'm fine," Fran responded mechanically, but the flatness in her voice betrayed her. She hadn't been fine since Jason left her.

"Galen," Melanie began eagerly. "Are you ready for tomorrow's shoot? You know, if I freeze to death in the name of art . . ."

"Melanie, you shouldn't do this if—" Galen interjected, worried.

"I'm teasing. I can't wait."

"It's going to be an *event*, Galen." Brooke smiled, but she fought uneasy memories of Melanie in her favorite role as center of attention. She continued, "Quite an audience. Adam, Charles, you, me. Even Mitchell Altman has decided to watch. Fran, would you like to come along?"

"Jason won't be there." Fran's tone made it clear that Jason's presence—or absence—was all that mattered.

How does Fran know that? Galen's mind whirled.

"Oh?" Melanie asked.

"I spoke with him yesterday." Fran's voice

brightened slightly as she remembered. They had talked for ten minutes. Jason's voice was kind and gentle. Even if his words—what they meant —were not. "He's sailing for a week, checking out the rigging for one of the America's Cup entries."

"Fran and Jason used to be together," Melanie explained to Galen.

I know, Melanie. I *know*. But why did Fran and Jason talk *yesterday?*

"Fran and Jason are *still* together," Fran corrected swiftly. "He'll get over her, whoever the hell she is. He'll realize how special what we had really was."

No, Fran, *no*.

"You don't know who she is?" Brooke asked.

"No. No one seems to. Jason never liked the parties, but he—we—went to the few really important ones." Fran sighed. "This year he even missed Adam's New Year's Eve party."

"Maybe the woman is married," Brooke offered.

"Maybe he's ashamed of her." Fran smiled hopefully.

"Maybe, since we have the author of the most romantic stories ever written right here, we should ask Galen." Melanie's wasn't a serious suggestion. She merely made it to shift away from her one friend's relentless preoccupation with Jason and to include her ever-shy *other* friend.

But Galen had retreated, a little frightened bird, to a far corner of the living room.

★   ★   ★

169

The hair stylist swirled Melanie's silky golden hair into soft curls on top of her head and wove blue satin ribbons into the gold. The dresser adjusted the one-of-a-kind Miguel Cruz ivory lace wedding dress while the makeup artist put the finishing touches on the *look*. Melanie entered the trailer in Central Park wearing high-heeled leather boots, skintight designer jeans with matching denim jacket, and a mink Cossack hat. An hour later she emerged, a breathtaking ethereal portrait of femininity and innocence and grace.

"What, no sidesaddle?" Melanie teased gaily as she climbed a small step ladder to mount the prize-winning palomino. Once settled into the English saddle she smiled radiantly at her audience as the dresser and Steve's assistant adjusted the layers of lace. Melanie held the reins loosely as the trainer led the horse.

Brooke and Galen and Charles and Adam and Mitchell Altman watched in silence as Steve, expert and professional, and Melanie, expert and professional, created and photographed perfect pose after perfect pose. During the necessary breaks, when Melanie's muscles finally protested or she began to shake from the winter wind or the horse became restless, Melanie didn't speak. She was an actress still in character.

"I think that's plenty," Steve announced finally. He smiled at Melanie as if they were dear friends instead of the bitter enemies they had become since Melanie declared war that day last October. When he was alone with her, Steve did nothing to conceal his animosity; but the vulgar remarks ended. In public, he and Melanie were exemplary professionals, working together harmoniously and artistically to create the beautiful pictures that made both of them so rich and famous.

"OK." Melanie smiled in return. "Thanks, Steve."

As the trainer started to lead Melanie back toward the step ladder, she collected the reins and pulled the horse's head away from him.

"Galen, is this"—Melanie gestured to herself and the exquisite look of fragile feminity—"really Sapphire? Or is Sapphire like Emerald? Strong and passionate."

"She's like Emerald," Galen answered quietly.

It bothered her from the moment Melanie emerged from the trailer. If only Jason were here. Why didn't Charles say something? Charles knew Sapphire. Galen looked to Charles, but he was strangely detached, barely watching the photo session, speaking occasionally to Adam or Mitchell.

"All right, Steve?" Melanie asked sweetly. Dear friend? "Would you mind taking just a few more shots?"

Melanie swung her right leg over the front of the saddle and slid to the ground. She took the saddle off the horse and instructed the trainer to change the expensive silver-and-leather bridle to the hemp halter. She slipped off her white satin slippers and stood barefooted on the frozen grass until the trainer made a stirrup with his hands and helped her onto the bareback palomino.

Melanie had everyone's attention now,

including Charles's. Her eyes met his, seducing him, daring him to watch as she loosened the curls, and her long beautiful hair fell in ropes of golden silk and pale-blue satin.

"I won't charge you for this, Charles." Not money anyway. But there's a price—your arrogance. I can make you want me. And when you do, when you want me desperately, I'll show how I really feel.

Melanie took the hemp rope, pulled the horse's head, pressed her bare feet into its belly and galloped away.

"Brooke," Galen whispered anxiously.

Brooke had been watching Charles. Melanie was doing this for Charles, flirting with him, teasing him, making him want her. *And it wasn't working.*

He's not impressed, Melanie, Brooke realized with amazement. Adam was impressed. And the trainer. And the hair stylist and dresser and makeup artist and Galen and Mitchell And even Steve, as he unpacked his camera and prepared to take the best shots of the day.

Everyone was impressed. Except Charles.

"Don't worry, Galen," Brooke answered. "Melanie knows what she's doing."

Melanie knows what she's doing, and it's not working.

"She's very good," Galen murmured.

"She's sensational," Adam agreed. Then he teased his friend, "Come on, Charles, *smile.* Apparently I'm not charging you."

"If she lames the horse on this damned frozen ground," Charles growled.

"She won't, Charles," Brooke assured him. A deep instinct told Brooke confidently that Melanie would never harm an animal. A human being, yes—a sister, *yes*—but not an animal.

As if sensing Charles's concern, or her twin's confidence, Melanie slowed the gait to a gentle rocking canter. She circled the field twice, then loped back toward the group. She pulled up near Steve, her chest heaving from the exercise, her cheeks flushed, her hair a wild damp tangle of gold.

"Now," she whispered to Steve as she caught her breath. Her eyes swept toward Charles for a moment, but he had turned away, bored and uninterested in *her*, to talk to Mitchell.

You bastard, Melanie thought.

"You're glowering, Melanie," Steve observed cheerfully, looking at her through the lens of his camera. "Give me one of your Good-Day Sunshine looks, please."

"Do you think she can act?" Mitchell asked Charles and Adam after the photo session was over.

"Sure," Adam answered confidently.

"Why?" Charles asked quickly.

"Because she's perfect. I'm not a big believer in models becoming actresses. Usually they're stiff or their voices aren't good. But Melanie's flawless."

Flawless, Charles mused. That had been his initial impression of her, too.

"I wonder how easy it would be to direct her," Charles said.

173

"Easy," Adam assured him. "She's not temperamental. She's tireless, energetic, professional. . . ."

"What do you think, Charles? This is really your decision. You and Jason *are* the executive producers."

"What am I deciding?"

"Whether to ask Melanie if she's interested in playing Sapphire in the movie. It's not really much of a risk. Melanie Chandler will be big box office, even if she can't act. My bet is she'll be sensational."

"Brooke and Galen and Mitchell and I are dining at La Côte tonight, Adam," Charles answered without answering. "Why don't you and Melanie join us?"

Of course I can act, Melanie thought later that evening when Mitchell posed the question to her. I've been acting all my life. What did you think of my performance with Steve today? Or with Charles? Or even now . . .

"It would be fun to try," Melanie purred prettily.

Why the false modesty, Brooke wondered. Melanie played the lead in all the productions in high school, and she was very good.

"So you'll do it?" Galen asked. Melanie had made Sapphire come alive today. Working with Melanie would be so comfortable and so much fun!

"It's up to Charles, isn't it?" Melanie tilted her head and threw a pale-blue dare: Tell me I can't have the role, Charles. Tell me in front of all of them.

"It's up to Charles and Jason," Charles responded evenly. "And then there's the contract. You might not like the terms."

"Which are . . . ?"

"We'll draw it up. I've just made the decision for Jason." Charles smiled a handsome, aristocratic smile at Melanie. Then he turned to Brooke and the smile became human. "You should go over it with a good attorney."

Quality is always worth the price. That was Charles Sinclair's motto. I don't want to know the price you put on my twin, Charles, Brooke thought. I don't want to know how much you're willing to pay for a few months of Melanie Chandler's golden life.

Brooke thought those troublesome thoughts, but her blue eyes sparkled at Charles.

Brooke actually likes him, Melanie realized with amazement. So does Galen. Don't they see it? Don't they see that the only person Charles Sinclair cares about is Charles Sinclair?

But it's not *true, a* renegade part of her mind argued. Charles does care about Brooke and Galen. He asks Brooke's opinion and listens carefully and thoughtfully to what she says. Charles respects Brooke, and he is helping Galen realize her dreams.

Charles just doesn't care about *you,* Melanie.

"What's the time frame?" Adam asked.

"Galen," Mitchell's voice softened, as all voices softened when they looked into the timid-trying-to-be-brave emerald eyes, "says she'll have the screenplay done by May. The plot and chronology can go as is. It's just a matter of translating the emotion and romance of the prose into dialogue. The characters need to speak their feelings instead of thinking them."

Just, Galen trembled at the word. That's *just* exactly what I've never been able to do. But with Jason's help, and Charles's . . .

"And then revisions in June and July," Galen added boldly. *Revisions* was a word she could say now. The *revised* version of "Sapphire" was better than the original. "So, in August or September we go to Kenya."

"Oh-oh." Melanie looked at Adam.

"We've already made commitments to the major couturiers and jewelers in France and Italy for August and September."

"You'll be in Europe for two months?"

"That's what the boss tells me." When Adam told her about it a week ago, Melanie was thrilled. She and four other models would spend two months showing the fabulous clothes and jewels of Dior, Lacroix, Van Cleef and Arpels, Chanel, Gucci, Saint Laurent, de la Renta, Tiel . . .

Between the photo sessions and shows they would explore Paris and Cannes and Monte Carlo and Rome and Milan and Naples and Florence.

"How about mid-October to mid-December?" Mitchell suggested.

"Fine with me." Melanie smiled amiably.

"And me," Galen agreed. "Charles?"

"I guess. I'm trying to remember when Jason will be away for the America's Cup trials."

He won't be, Galen thought.

"Jason will want to be there, too?" Mitchell asked.

"Yes," Charles answered. "We'll both want to go."

"Who will run Sinclair Publishing?" Brooke teased.

"Is that an offer, Brooke? Because if it is you've got it."

Brooke blushed, laughed softly, and shook her dark brown curls.

"Mitchell," Melanie's voice was low and seductive, "have you thought about who you will cast as Jeremy?"

Jeremy was Sapphire's roguish, sexy, daring lover; the man who unleashed her hidden passion.

"I don't know, Melanie." Anyone you want.

Chapter Twelve

New York City
February 1986

"It will take me all night to finish the revisions for 'Jade.' I promised I would have them to Charles before he leaves for Paris."

"And you will."

"If I work all night. I feel guilty that I didn't get them to him sooner. But," Galen's voice softened lovingly, "that's your fault."

177

"It's your fault for making me need you every minute. Can't you finish them over here?" Jason was in his apartment on Riverside Drive. Galen was in her tiny room in the brownstone in Greenwich Village.

"Not if you're there."

"I won't bother you."

"I would want you to."

"Come over when you're done. Whenever."

"It will take me all night."

"I won't throw the dead bolt, just in case."

"Jason."

"You're really not coming over?"

"No," she sighed wistfully. "I'm really not."

When his doorbell rang at eleven o'clock that night, Jason assumed it would be Galen. She had her own key, but maybe her arms were full of a not-quite-revised manuscript, hyacinth-scented candles, and fountain pens. Jason was already smiling as he opened the door.

"Fran." The smile faded quickly.

"Is she here?"

"No."

"May I come in?"

Jason frowned. "Fran . . ."

"Jason, please, just for a minute." The dark-brown eyes were liquid and her lips trembled.

Reluctantly, Jason opened the door wide and stood aside as she entered. This was pointless and painful, but she was so upset.

"Who is she, Jason? I have a right to know."

"It doesn't matter who she is," Jason said firmly. No one knew. Galen and Jason hadn't even told Charles, yet. It was still too precious to share.

"It matters to me."

"Fran, we've gone over this."

Jason told Fran in November, the day after Galen sent the pale-pink note, that he couldn't see her anymore. It was difficult for both of them; they were good together. Jason had almost decided he was in love with her.

But that was because Jason didn't know what love was. He didn't know until Galen.

"You're still seeing her, aren't you?"

"Yes."

Jason told Fran his new love was forever when she called him in early December. And he told her again when she called in January.

"You're going to marry her?"

"Yes." Jason and Galen had never talked about marriage, but he knew. They both knew.

Fran began to cry.

"I'm sorry, Jason," she whispered, impatiently wiping tears that wouldn't stop. "I miss you so much. I really thought what we had was good."

"It *was* good," Jason said gently. He cared about Fran. He was sorry he hurt her. It was an honest mistake. If he had known there could be magic, he would never have gotten so involved with Fran. But he hadn't known.

"Hold me, Jason," she pleaded.

Jason moved beside her and wrapped his arms around the lovely body he had known so intimately. Jason felt no rush of desire; he only felt sorry that Fran had been hurt.

After a few minutes she pulled free.

"Will you just talk to me for a while, Jason? Not about her or us."

They sat in the living room and drank bourbon and talked about safe, neutral topics that had nothing to do with either of them. Fran inadvertently stumbled onto the most personal topic of all.

" 'Emerald' was wonderful. Galen's next story will appear in the March issue, is that right?"

"Yes," Jason replied evenly. He didn't want Fran to know about Galen. He could imagine Fran confronting Galen, trying to convince her, as Fran had tried to convince him in December and January, that she and Jason belonged together.

"When I first read about naive, innocent, trusting Emerald, I wondered how you could have chosen me for the art—*You* of all people." Fran's provocative brown eyes reminded him of their not-so-innocent lovemaking until Jason's eyes reminded her that it was over. She sighed and continued thoughtfully, "Sorry. Anyway, I was like Emerald, once upon a time. Maybe there's a part of Emerald in everyone."

"Maybe."

"I had dinner with Galen—and Brooke and Melanie—last month. Galen is so quiet. I guess the passion is deep inside her."

"I guess so." Jason's mind spun. Why hadn't Galen told him about dinner with Fran? It must have bothered her. Why hadn't she shared it with him?

"So," Fran began carefully. She didn't want

to make Jason angry. "It's two in the morning. You're not spending the night with her tonight whoever she—"

"No."

"Let me stay, Jason."

"No."

"Just let me fall asleep in your arms one last time. I don't want you to make love with me. Just hold me."

"No."

"It won't hurt you," Fran pleaded as tears filled her eyes. "And it will help me."

"How?"

"It will make it seem more real. Taking to you has helped. You don't look at me the way you used to." Her voice was so sad. "And being in bed with you without making love to you . . . well, that never would have happened, would it?"

"It's not going to happen."

"I know. I won't try to seduce you. It would be too humiliating."

Jason shook his head slightly and sighed. Fran was unhappy and exhausted and it was late. She'd had too much to drink. If it would help her, he could let her fall asleep in his arms.

Jason took her hand and led her into the bedroom. He didn't bother to clear the empty crystal glasses from the table. And he didn't remember to throw the dead bolt.

Charles is going to like this, Galen decided as she read the final page of her revised version of "Jade."

It was five A.M. Galen looked out her small

window into the predawn darkness of the cold February morning. She wanted to be with Jason. She reached for the phone to tell him to release the dead bolt, but she didn't dial.

Jason had probably forgotten to throw it anyway. He usually forgot. Jason didn't worry about the daily robberies that plagued the wealthy inhabitants of Manhattan. Maybe he didn't even know about them. Jason couldn't read the newspaper, and that sort of crime rarely made the television or radio news. There were worse crimes to report in Manhattan.

Galen smiled. She would surprise him, awakening him with gentle kisses . . .

Galen let herself in with her key. The hall light was on. Funny. Jason usually turned it off. Maybe he was expecting her.

Galen pulled up abruptly when she saw a coat, a woman's coat, on the chair. As she noticed the two empty highball glasses on the table a sense of dread washed through her.

No. It isn't possible. It can't be.

Galen's heart pounded and her stomach churned as she forced herself to walk toward Jason's bedroom. She didn't want to know, but she had to.

The bedroom door was open. The soft light from the hall illuminated the room. Galen only looked for an instant, but her mind made a memory she would never forget, its every detail perfectly and indelibly preserved.

Fran's clothes were tossed carelessly—because their passion couldn't wait?—on the floor. She wore Jason's pajamas; at least, his pajama *top*.

Fran's arms draped across Jason's chest and her head lay in the crook of his arm. The rest of her body was hidden beneath the covers with his. Jason slept peacefully, his strong arms casually encircling her. His tousled golden hair glowed in the darkness.

It was a beautiful tranquil picture—the perfect portrait of lovers satiated from a night of passion.

I hate you, Jason, Galen's heart screamed as she ran through the dark, cold, dangerous streets of Manhattan. I will always hate you. I hate you for doing this to us. I hate you for doing this to love.

I hate you for doing this to Emerald . . .

Emerald. Jason lay in bed with Fran, the woman whose lovely image appeared next to her words; the real Emerald. The Emerald Jason *really* loved.

Galen telephoned Charles at ten.

"I'll send the revisions over by courier this morning."

"Fine. Are you happy with them?"

Happy? Galen mused.

"Yes. Of course. Have a nice trip, Charles."

Galen hung up before Charles could answer.

Charles waited ten minutes before calling her back. Maybe she was just exhausted; emotionally exhausted from immersing herself in her story and physically exhausted from staying up all night.

But Galen's voice hadn't sounded like exhaustion. It had sounded like despair.

"What's wrong?" Charles asked directly when she answered the phone.

183

"I—" Her voice broke. "I can't talk about it."

Charles waited without speaking for several moments.

"Why don't I come over?" he suggested finally.

"No, Charles, thank you. I'll be fine, really. I just need some time." Time. How much time? Would any amount of time lessen the pain? Galen added flatly, "I just need to grow up."

But it had nothing to do with growing up, Galen realized. It had to do with abandoning everything she believed. She had always believed—it was simply faith until she met Jason—in love. She believed in it with all her being. Her stories celebrated the wonder and magic of love.

Now she knew the truth. It was all a myth.

"I'm available, Galen. At least, until about two."

"Then off to Paris."

"You can reach me there, too. My secretary has my itinerary. Galen?"

"Yes. Thank you, Charles. I'm all right. Really. Good-bye."

Five minutes after Charles's second conversation with Galen, Jason appeared at his door.

"Good morning."

"Jason."

"Did Galen get the revisions for 'Jade' to you?" Jason asked casually. He had expected to hear from her by now. He didn't want to waken her if she was asleep.

"She called. She's sending them over."

"Oh." Jason concealed his disappointment. He hoped she would bring them over herself. He wanted to see her. He wanted her in his arms. Nothing had happened with Fran, *of course,* but it felt so wrong. There was only one woman who belonged in his arms or in his bed or in his life.

Galen was probably asleep now. He would wait until early afternoon before calling.

The revisions for "Jade" arrived by courier at eleven-thirty. As Charles put them in his briefcase, he thought about his trip to Paris and about Galen. The trip to Paris was business. It was part of his responsibility, as editor-in-chief of *Fashion,* to view the spring collections of the major couturiers of Europe. It was a responsibility Charles enjoyed. The fashion shows were exciting, and there were other pleasures, like Monique.

But the hedonistic pleasures were easily expendable if Galen needed him . . .

"Galen?"

"Charles. They should be there any minute." The lifeless voice spoke with great effort.

"They're here. That's not why I'm calling."

"Oh."

"Have you ever been to Paris, not counting the airport?"

"No."

"Why don't you come with me? It sounds like you need to get away."

"Run away," Galen breathed. She was suddenly tempted, *so* tempted.

No, Charles thought. Paris is getting away. St. Barts is running away. . . . In three months, in May, he would run away—for a while—to St. Barts.

"I'll be at the shows all day. You could join

185

me or wander around Paris or stay in the hotel and work on your screenplay or take luxurious bubble baths . . ."

Charles thought he heard a soft laugh. *I'm your friend, Galen, let me help you.*

"I wouldn't be very good company."

"I'm not looking for company, Galen." *I wasn't very good company for you once, either, when I was delirious, but you never left my side. And that was* before *we were friends.*

Jason telephoned Galen at one-thirty. He had waited long enough.

"Hi." He was relieved to hear her voice. "Were you sleeping?"

"No," she answered flatly, her heart pounding.

Galen didn't want to talk to Jason, but she had to. It had to be behind her. She hadn't decided by the time Jason called if she would tell him she had seen him with Fran. What if he tried to make an excuse or offer an explanation? It would be so humiliating.

No excuses or explanations, Galen decided impulsively. *And I don't have to explain, either.*

"I'm not sleeping. I'm packing. I'm going on a trip."

"*What?*" The sound of her flat, lifeless voice worried him as much as her words.

"I'm going to Paris with Charles."

"Charles," Jason breathed in disbelief.

"Charles sensed I needed to get away. He offered to take me with him."

"Why do you need to get away?" Jason asked

carefully. She must know about Fran. *Somehow.* I have to explain.

"I just do."

"I didn't throw the dead bolt last night. I thought you might come over.

"I told you I wouldn't."

"And you didn't?"

"I told you I wouldn't," Galen repeated. "Why?"

"Because I want to be certain we don't have our signals crossed." Jason was going to tell her, when his arms were around her, about the *nothing* that had happened with Fran and how *terrible* it made him feel. He wouldn't tell her now, over the phone, unless the flatness in her voice was because of Fran.

But it wasn't because of Fran. Galen hadn't come over. So what had happened? It had to be Charles. . . .

"I don't think we have our signals crossed, Jason."

"Then what has changed since last night?"

The tears came then, washing away the anger and the control, drenching her in sadness. She couldn't speak. She didn't want him to hear the tears. She didn't want him to know how much he had hurt her.

"Galen?" His voice was so gentle.

Galen forced herself to remember what she had seen in his bedroom. With the vivid, painful memory came the emotion: I hate you.

"It's over."

"Over? How can it be over"

187

"You know about love, Jason, it's all a fiction anyway."

"I *don't* know that."

Well, I do, thanks to you.

"I have to go. Good-bye, Jason."

Jason held the receiver in his hand long after the line had disconnected.

Charles. He had always been there, part of Galen's life. Maybe Charles and Galen had loved each other, years before, in Africa. Maybe they found that love again. In spite of what Galen felt for Jason, her feelings for his twin were stronger. It explained why Galen wanted to keep *their* love private, hidden from the world and from Charles. All this time, Galen had been struggling to make a choice. And now she had made it.

It isn't possible, Jason's mind screamed. But it was. Galen was going away with Charles. She had chosen Charles.

Jason walked out of his office and into his brother's. He needed to know.

I need to know if Charles has taken away someone *else* I love. Jason shuddered at the unsummoned thought and the hatred that churned inside him.

Charles wasn't in his office. He had already left.

Jason took a taxi to the brownstone on Spring Street. The young bearded man who answered the door told him that Galen had gone on a trip. She would be away for one week.

Chapter Thirteen

She is devastated, Charles thought. Whatever it is, it's tearing her apart.

Galen didn't speak during the taxi ride from Spring Street to JFK, except to acknowledge Charles and his kindness—briefly and awkwardly—with a trembling smile and eyes that threatened to cry, *again.*

When Charles handed the first-class tickets to the agent, Galen murmured, almost to herself, "I don't have money with me. I'll have to pay you back."

Galen had money in the bank. She had been paid substantial advances for the four short stories that would appear in *Images,* for her book, *Songs of the Savanna,* and the screenplay for "Sapphire." The advances were payments for *promises;* Galen wondered now if they were promises she could keep. Her mind was so foggy and her heart ached. What if she had lost the clarity and peace so necessary to her writing?

Charles got the boarding passes and touched her briefly on the shoulder, indicating the way toward the first-class lounge on the concourse. Before they reached the lounge, when they were away from the crush of passengers in the main terminal, he stopped and faced her.

"It's on me."

"What?"

"You're not paying for any of this. You're my guest."

"Charles, I . . ." Tears spilled down her cheeks. "Thank you."

She was so raw and so fragile. Whatever it was, *whomever* it was had taken her life and smashed it into a thousand pieces. If he could undo it for her, he would.

But he couldn't. He could only be her friend.

Charles put his arm around her small, thin shoulders. So fragile . . .

They stayed in adjacent suites in the Hotel Meurice on the Place Vendôme. The first night, during a gourmet dinner Galen barely touched, Charles tried to pique her interest in the City of Light.

"The Meurice is centrally located. You can walk, safely, to the Louvre, the Jeu de Paume, the Rodin Museum, Sainte-Chapelle, Notre-Dame, and the Left Bank. It's a long but interesting walk along the Champs-Elysées to the Arc de Triomphe. You should probably take the Métro—it's very easy, Galen—if you want to go to the Eiffel Tower or Montmartre. Of course, you're welcome to come see the collections with me. Tomorrow morning I'll be at Chanel." Charles looked at the sad distant eyes glistening in candlelight and asked gently, "Galen?"

"Yes?" She almost jumped. Her mind had been so far away. "Charles, I'm sorry. Not very good company . . ."

"It's OK, honey."

"You're so nice to me."

That evening, before saying good night and

withdrawing to their separate suites, Charles and Galen made arrangements to meet for lunch at Charles's favorite sidewalk cafe in the Latin Quarter. Charles circled the location on the pocket map of Paris he bought for her.

The next day, after viewing the fabulous Chanel spring collection and murmuring apologies to Monique, France's most glamorous model, Charles rushed to the Latin Quarter. He arrived ten minutes late. It didn't matter; Galen wasn't there. Charles waited for two hours, until it was time, past time, for him to be at Yves St. Laurent.

Where the hell was she?

Probably blissfully lost in the wonders of the Louvre, Charles tried to reassure himself. It happened to him in the Louvre or in front of the rose window in Saint-Chapelle or gazing across the Seine at the flying buttresses of Notre-Dame. Charles often lost track of time in Paris.

But Galen wasn't a happy tourist discovering the limitless joys of Paris. She was despondent and distracted. What if she wandered in front of a speeding car, or into the Seine . . .

As the magnificent St. Laurent spring collection paraded past on some of the world's most breathtaking models, Charles's anxiety increased.

You should be out looking for her. You shouldn't have left her alone. You shouldn't have brought her with you if you couldn't take care of her.

Charles wanted to leave, but he couldn't. It would be impossible—physically *or* politely—to extricate himself from his chair of honor at the end of the runway.

Finally, mercifully, it was over.

Charles checked for messages with the concierge in the mirror and marble lobby of the Meurice. There were none. But there was a note on the door to his suite: *Charles, I'm sorry, Galen.*

Charles knocked on the door of her suite.

"Galen?" Please be all right.

The door opened slowly. Her pale, drawn face and her dark-circled emerald eyes told him it had been a sleepless night and a tormented day.

Galen hadn't been blissfully lost in the treasures of the Louvre.

"Are you all right?"

"I forgot about our lunch, Charles. I'm sorry."

"You've been here all day, haven't you?"

She nodded, head bent.

"Come here." Charles guided her gently to the silk chaise lounge near the window that overlooked the Tuileries and the Seine. Charles sat beside her, holding her hands. "Look at me, Galen."

The red-gold head lifted slowly.

"Tell me."

"Charles, no, I can't."

Her head started to drop again, but he caught her chin, lifting it, making her eyes meet his.

"Tell me."

Galen's eyes filled with tears and she tried to look away. But he wouldn't let her.

"Galen."

"I . . . I loved him so much, Charles," she whispered through the tears.

"What happened?"

"He never loved me." That was all Galen could say that night. The tears came and she didn't have the energy to fight them.

Charles held her against him until her silent sobs subsided, finally vanquished by exhaustion. He carried her into the bedroom, gently tucked her into bed, and stayed until she fell asleep.

Galen spent the following day at the Louvre. That night Charles dined at the Tour d'Argent with the *joailliers* from Van Cleef and Arpels. Galen remained at the Meurice and went to bed early. The next evening Charles made reservations for them at *Taillevent,* but, at the last minute, he and Galen decided to dine in his suite.

"I think I'll go to Versailles the day after tomorrow. Could you join me?"

"No." Charles watched her reaction. She was going to go anyway. *Good.* "I wish I could. Be sure to walk to Le Petit Trianon."

"Marie Antoinette's hunting lodge? I will." Galen tilted her head and gazed at him thoughtfully. "You think I'll survive this?"

"You already are."

"Not really. You're protecting me."

"I'm not."

Galen smiled a soft, wistful smile. Yes, you are.

"I've always had someone protecting me. Until I moved to New York, it was my parents. Then it was you. Then it was—"

"Him."

"Him," Galen repeated quietly. Your brother. Your twin.

"And you were in love with him," Charles said

carefully. Galen had told him nothing more since the night she cried in his arms.

"Love." Galen's voice was distant, because love was a distant memory, a blurry dream. "Do you believe in love, Charles?"

"For some people, yes. For people like you, people like Jason—"

"But not for you?" Galen asked swiftly. Her mind reeled at Jason's name. No, Charles, love *isn't* for people like Jason.

"No," Charles answered easily. It *was* easy if he didn't think about the reason—the inexplicable, impenetrable hatred of the father whose love he wanted so desperately. "I'm not meant to love." *Or to be loved.*

"What about Viveca?"

"*Viveca?*" Charles's surprise was genuine. He and Viveca had been "dating" since early January. Charles liked Viveca. He liked the sultry, inquisitive sensuality that smoldered beneath the frilly Southern belle fluff. But *love?*

"Yes. You—" Galen blushed.

She is so naive and innocent, Charles thought, suddenly feeling great anger toward the unknown man who had hurt her so deeply.

"You sleep with her, don't you, Charles?" Galen asked bravely. See I'm not so naive or innocent any more.

"It may be my fate not to love, but I'm not doomed to loneliness." Charles smiled as he spoke, but his words made her sad eyes even sadder. "Galen?"

"I want you to be happy, Charles."

"Galen, I *am* happy. I'm living my life exactly

the way I want to," Charles told her truthfully. I am living my dream. "Even if there isn't love, there are wonderful, warm moments to share."

"Sharing warm, wonderful moments," Galen mused. "That's far better than living the illusion of love."

"Did it feel like an illusion when you were with him, Galen?"

"No," she sighed softly. "But he—"

"He made a big mistake."

"Make love to me, Charles."

It was their final night in Paris. They were in Charles's suite, drinking champagne. The golden lights of Paris twinkled below.

"Galen."

"Share a warm, wonderful moment with me."

"Honey, this isn't the answer." Charles spoke gently to the lovely emerald eyes.

"I'm not looking for answers."

"You are looking for ways to be strong and independent."

"This is a way." I need to know how it feels to make love with someone I don't love. I need to know how it felt for Jason every time he made love with me. That knowledge will give me strength.

"No." Charles touched her hot, flushed cheek with his strong cool fingers.

"Don't you like me, Charles?"

"You know I do." I like you too much to do this, even though I want to. . . .

"Charles."

Galen's soft lips, tentative and trembling, found his.

"Galen," Charles whispered. His lips brushed lightly against hers. Then he wrapped his strong arms around her and drew her close.

Galen's kiss became confident and demanding. She opened her soft mouth to welcome him. Charles responded; his deep, intimate kiss betrayed his desire and passion. Galen's mind spun. The tender lips that kissed her, the gentle, experienced hands that explored her, the sensual, sleek body that wanted her didn't belong to an unknown lover. They belonged to Charles, her dear friend with the dark seductive eyes and hidden passions and lips that . . .

Lips that were kissing her naked breasts and making her tremble with deep, warm, tingling sensations.

You don't need to be so careful, Charles! I'm not that fragile. I know how to do this. I *want* to do this with you.

Galen awakened at eight A.M. She was alone in the bed, Charles's bed. She closed her eyes briefly, remembering the tenderness of the night. He had been so gentle! They had shared a warm, wonderful moment of their lives. It hadn't felt awkward or wrong, and she had learned what she needed to know. It was possible to make love without being *in* love. Jason had made love with her even though he was in love with Fran. And she had made love with Charles even though she was in love with . . .

She had proven it. The knowledge gave her

strength, even though it was more proof—devastating proof—of her own foolish naiveté.

As Galen lay in Charles's bed, remembering the tender intimacy of their loving, a wave of panic swept through her. How could she face him? What did Charles think of her? Galen didn't have answers, but she knew that she couldn't put it off. She had to see him, face him, and leave.

Galen frowned, sighed, and got out of bed. Her hands trembled as she dressed and hurriedly brushed her red-blond tangles. She took a deep breath and opened the bedroom door. Charles sat in the living room, fully dressed, reading the *International Tribune*. He stood up when she appeared.

"Good morning."

Galen couldn't meet his inquisitive, probing eyes. She had *made love* with him! And she felt naked still.

"I have to go," Galen whispered.

"Go?"

"Go pack. When is our plane . . . ?"

"We leave the hotel at noon."

"All right." Galen started to move toward the door. Charles caught up with her and blocked her path.

"Galen, what we did last night was nice. I don't know if we'll ever do it again—we both have to think about it—but it was *nice*. It didn't hurt us and it didn't hurt our friendship." Charles made her look at him. "Did it?"

"No." Galen smiled a shy smile. She added courageously, "And it was nice."

"Good. Then how about some tea and croissants?"

"No, thank you. I really do have to pack." And I have to think about what happened last night. And, Galen realized with dread, I have to prepare to return to New York and my life without Jason.

Galen spent the next two weeks in her tiny room on Spring Street. She made a few false starts toward the outside world, but they always ended just inside the front door of the brownstone. She couldn't go outside. Jason was out there, somewhere, and he was with Fran.

Galen needed to write. She had promised the screenplay of "Sapphire" by May and the revisions for "Garnet" by June. But now that she knew the truth, how could she perpetuate the myth? She couldn't write about love anymore. Love—the wonderful, magical love of Emerald and Sapphire and Jade and Garnet—didn't exist.

Galen couldn't write about the fantasy, and she couldn't write about the *reality;* the shattered dream was too close and too painful. And who would want to read about it anyway?

Night after sleepless night, in darkness illuminated by her candles and warmly scented with French vanilla and hyacinth and lilac, Galen grieved for what she had lost. She grieved for the dream, and for the man.

She missed Jason so much!

Galen missed Jason, and she missed Charles. She wanted to talk to Charles, but she couldn't find the energy to call him.

Two weeks after she and Charles returned from Paris a package arrived in the afternoon mail.

"Oh," Galen breathed as she carefully removed the lilac silk and ivory lace dress from the neatly folded tissue paper. It was so beautiful. Beneath the dress were two gold barrettes and a small cream-colored envelope. Galen opened the envelope slowly. What if it was from Jason? What would she do?

The card read, *Galen, this seemed like you. Melanie.*

"This is Melanie." Melanie answered her call in the models' dressing room.

"Melanie, it's Galen. Am I interrupting?"

"No. They're setting up the studio for the next session.

"Thank you so much."

"Oh, it arrived already?"

"Yes. It's lovely. I've never . . ." I've never seen such a beautiful dress.

"Worn lilac? But does it work? I thought *that* shade, and *your* hair, might."

Galen hadn't thought about how the dress would look on *her*. She would never wear something so beautiful. But now, in response to Melanie's question, Galen stood in front of the cracked mirror on the wall and held the dress against her. Strands of her red-gold hair fell across the fabric. The effect was stunning.

"It's perfect," Galen whispered truthfully.

"And it fits all right?"

"Oh." She should have tried it on before calling, but it hadn't occurred to her. "Yes."

"Good. I have an image of you wearing it with your hair in swirls dotted with small sprays of pink and white lilacs." It was more than an image;

199

it was how Melanie sketched it when she designed the dress for Galen.

"Sounds lovely."

"However, failing lilacs, I included those gold barrettes. I thought if you swept your hair off your face—a soft sweep, the way Brooke does her hair—it would look nice."

"Oh, yes, I see," Galen murmured.

"Are you OK, Galen? You sound—"

"I'm fine, Melanie. I'm just overwhelmed. It's so beautiful."

"I'm glad you like it. Oh-oh. They're calling for me. I have to go. Galen, let's get together soon, all right?"

"Yes, sure, I'd like that."

After Melanie hung up, Galen tried on the dress. It fit perfectly. The soft hues of the dress and her hair and her eyes blended into a harmonious bouquet of color. It was as if the lilac-and-ivory dress had been made especially for her. Galen wondered where Melanie found it. There was no label.

Her spirits lifted by the beautiful dress and Melanie's thoughtfulness, Galen impulsively dialed the number to the private line in Charles's office.

"Hello."

"Hello." Charles was relieved to hear her voice. He knew she needed time and she would call when she was ready, but still he worried. "How are you?"

"Not making great strides."

"I would try for baby steps. Are you writing?"

"Can't."

"I'm not a big believer in writer's block."

"I'm too unfocused."

"Maybe writing would help you focus."

"Maybe. You're not really a very sympathetic sort, are you?" Her voice had a slight lilt, a little tease. She knew Charles was her friend. She knew, too, that sometimes he helped her most by pushing her.

"I don't think you need sympathy. You probably need dinner, though, knowing the way you tend not to eat. How about tomorrow night? La Lumière?"

La Lumière. She and Jason—*she*—had fallen in love at La Lumière. She couldn't go back there; but she *had* to. La Lumière was exactly where she needed to go. She even had a beautiful dress to wear.

"That would be nice." Nice. Making love had been *nice*. But she couldn't do that again, not now, not yet, maybe not ever. "Charles?"

"Just dinner?"

"Is that OK?"

"Of course. I told you it was something we would have to think about." Charles added easily, "And you have."

But what about you, Galen wondered. Have you thought about it? What do you want?

"I'll be by at eight," Charles said.

"Why don't I just meet you at the restaurant? I know where it is."

All right, Charles thought. If it makes you feel strong and independent.

★　★　★

"Galen."

"Hello, Charles." She blushed. "New dress."

Before Charles could reply, Henri, the maitre d', offered to seat them. Henri was not in the habit of keeping the Sinclairs waiting. Henri looked at Galen and silently admired Charles's taste, as he always did. All of Charles Sinclair's women were magnificent, but this woman was so different from Charles's usual companions. Hers was a serene, timeless beauty, not a confident, glamorous, contemporary one. Henri approved, and so did Charles.

"I like your hair that way," Charles told Galen after they were seated and had ordered champagne cocktails. "Melanie said I should make swirls of hair and lilacs. This is a compromise."

"Melanie? Did she help you find the dress?"

"She sent it to me."

"Out of the blue?"

"Yes. When I called to thank her she made it sound like nothing."

It wasn't *nothing*, Charles knew. The dress— a terribly expensive original design—looked as if it had been made especially for Galen. To have seen the dress and known how perfect it would be for Galen took a very special eye, not to mention time and effort and care.

Melanie?

"Did she say where she got it?" Charles couldn't guess at the label. He knew the work of the major designers; it wasn't one of them. It was a new, innovative talent, someone whose designs would become familiar to him and who he might someday feature in the pages of *Fashion*.

"No, but I wonder." Galen shook her head. It seemed impossible. But . . . there was no label, so much had been sewn by hand, and it was exactly the right size. Clothes were never the right size for her; she always had to make alterations.

"What?"

"I wonder if Melanie made it."

"No," Charles said definitively. "No."

Jason entered the restaurant just as Charles and Galen were leaving. He was alone. Jason's motive for dining at La Lumière was the same as Galen's; it was part of saying good-bye to the dream.

"Galen!"

"*Jason.*"

"Hello, Jason." Charles smiled at his twin. The smile was untainted, neither apology nor gloat.

Jason had seen very little of Charles in the past two weeks; he hadn't wanted to. He realized now, as his eyes met his twin's, that Charles had no idea that he and Galen had ever been together.

Galen never told Charles about us, Jason thought sadly. *We weren't that important to her. All that mattered—her top priority—was that she didn't hurt the only man she really loved, Charles.*

Jason didn't want to look at her, but he couldn't help it. How she had blossomed—proud and beautiful—nurtured by Charles's love!

Galen didn't want to look at Jason; but she couldn't help it, either. She made herself think about Fran as her eyes met his.

I am going to survive this, Jason.

Part II

Chapter Fourteen

New York City
March 1986

It was dark, and he was warm and strong, and
his lips were soft and gentle, and he wanted her.
The demanding sensations swirling inside her
wanted her to let him love her. It would be so
easy. He wanted her so much and her mind was
playing wonderful tricks, pretending he was
Charles . . .

Brooke pulled away.

"Andrew."

"Brooke?" Andrew had dark, seductive eyes,
like Charles.

"I can't. This is wrong. Your wife . . ."

Allison Parker had been home and "normal"
since early January. But last night, Andrew told
Brooke over cocktails at the Hunt Club, he had
to face the agony of taking Allison back to the
sanitarium. Andrew spoke softly, sensitively, and
the intimacy of the conversation flowed so easily
into the intimacy of the kiss . . .

"Let me worry about Allison."

But you love her, Andrew, Brooke thought.
Not that what drove Brooke and Andrew into
each other's arms was *love*. It was much simpler
than that—just unfulfilled sexual desire and loneliness.

"I can't anyway, Andrew." Even though it would be so easy.

Andrew touched Brooke's flushed cheek gently and smiled.

"Friends?"

"Of course."

Their hands touched the book at exactly the same moment.

"Oh!" she exclaimed, looking up into the face. It was a strong, handsome face, framed in dark black curls and highlighted, a subtle, understated highlight, with steel gray-eyes.

"Sorry." He took his hand from the book. "Ladies first."

"What about tie goes to the runner?"

"I think 'ladies first' wins over everything."

"Well," she said hopefully, but unconvincingly, "there must be another copy."

"There will be on Monday."

It was Saturday. The book, a collection of short stories entitled *Reflections* was released on Thursday and sold quickly. More copies, hastily reordered, would arrive on Monday. At that moment she held the only unsold copy in Manhattan.

"Were you planning your weekend around this book?" she asked. *She* had been. She was going to hide in her apartment, away from the late-winter snow, and escape into the book the critics hailed as the best collection of short stories in a decade.

"It was going to be my Saturday night," he answered. "I have to work this afternoon."

"Well,"—she had a briefcase of work—"I don't *have* to have it this evening. I can read it this afternoon and you can have it tonight."

"Really?"

"Sure," she agreed as they walked to the cash register. He started to withdraw some bills from his wallet, but she held up her hand. "I'll buy it. Ladies first."

They walked into the cold March morning. The snow was falling lightly adding a clean fresh layer to the foot that already blanketed the city.

"I should have written my address for you while we were still inside." Her "loveless hands started to search in her purse for a pen and paper.

"Just tell it to me."

He listened, nodding slightly when she finished.

"And what's your name?"

"Brooke."

His lips curved into a slow, knowing smile and his gray eyes twinkled.

"Why? What's yours?"

"Nick." He watched her ocean-blue eyes widen.

"Lieutenant." She laughed softly, extended a cold hand to him, and felt the warmth and strength of his handshake.

"Counselor. At last we meet."

"Yes," she murmured. The thank-you that she had been dreading for seven months suddenly seemed easy. "What you did last September . . . It was a gentle way for me to learn a hard lesson. Thank you."

Nick shrugged. "So, when shall I come by to

get the book? What time you leaving for the evening?"

"I'm not leaving. Any time is fine."

"You don't have plans?"

"No."

"How about seven?"

"That's fine."

"I'll see you then, Brooke."

"I'm sorry," Nick apologized as soon as Brooke opened the door. He was an hour late. "We were interviewing a suspect. I couldn't even get away to call."

"It's no problem. *Interviewing?*"

"Interrogating." Nick grinned.

"Someone I know?"

"Someone you may get to know. We need a little more evidence before we can make a charge that will stick."

"And you know how *we* are about evidence!"

"Indeed."

"Anyway, you couldn't have called to let me know. My telephone number is unlisted."

"You don't think that's really an obstacle, do you?" Nick teased. He could get any number for any address in the city in a matter of minutes, for police business. But this—Brooke—was personal.

"Oh." Her cheeks pinkened slightly. Another just-out-of-law-school remark. Brooke had been with the DA's office for nine months. She was beginning to feel comfortable, but there was something about Nick's casual confidence that

210

made her uncertain about herself and all the things she didn't know.

"How is the book?"

"Wonderful. I haven't—"

"Finished? That's good. At least I hope it means each story is so good that you want to linger over it—live with it—for a while before going on to the next."

"That's what it means." Brooke handed him the book.

"Well, don't worry. I'll return it to you bright and early tomorrow morning."

"That's OK. I can linger over the ones I've read until Monday."

"That good?"

"Yes."

They stood in the entry area of her small apartment. Nick's hand still rested on the doorknob, poised to leave as soon as he got the book. Now he had it, but he hesitated. Brooke said she didn't have plans. What the hell . . .

"Have you eaten?"

"No. I've been reading and lingering."

"And I've been interrogating since noon. Would you like to go somewhere?"

It was Brooke's turn to hesitate.

"No?" he asked pleasantly.

"I don't know." She had taken the afternoon off to read *Reflections*. She had planned to spend the evening with the contents of her bulging briefcase.

"When do you think you'll know?" Nick asked easily. "I'm famished."

"I know now." Brooke decided impulsively. "Sure, I'd like to."

They walked to an Italian restaurant nearby and ordered pizza.

"Are you Italian?"

"Nikolai Adriani?"

"Greek."

"Abbreviated Greek. Born in Brooklyn." Nick thought, And raised on street fights and poverty in the deadly shadow of crime.

"Did you always want to be a cop?"

"Did you always want to be a lawyer?"

"Who do you think is the better, er, interviewer?"

"Do you want to try to find out?"

"No!" Brooke exclaimed. You would win, her sparkling blue eyes told the calm gray ones. She added seriously, "I would like to know why you always wanted to be a cop, if you did."

Nick started to counter, to continue the playful banter, but he stopped. He would tell her. What the hell . . .

"I did. Something about believing the streets should be safe for children and that innocent people should be free from harm." Nick spoke quietly.

Brooke wondered if Nick had been harmed, or if someone he loved had been. Was Nick's a personal vendetta against crime? Or did he just, simply, *care?* Brooke couldn't tell, but, whatever the reason, it was very important to him.

"That's," Brooke searched for the right word. *Wonderful? Impressive? Moving? Inspirational?* She finished weakly, "Nice."

"It's just the way it is. You probably wonder why I didn't go to law school."

Brooke thought for a moment before answering.

"I guess that being a lawyer would be too removed for you. I think you want to catch the criminals *in flag*—" Brooke stopped abruptly It was a legal term.

"In flagrante delicto?" Nick smiled.

"Yes." In the very act of committing the offense.

"There *is* something clean about catching someone with two hundred thousand dollars worth of coke he's trying to sell to an undercover agent."

"Until we muddy it up with technicalities? I bet you're not very tolerant of mistakes," Brooke mused. Why would she say that? There was nothing in the tranquil gray eyes to suggest intolerance. But Nick was good. He did his job well and he cared. And if you were good and cared, you didn't tolerate mistakes; not from yourself or from others.

"I bet you're not, either."

They ate pizza in silence for several bites. Then Nick said, "I'm a little surprised you don't have a boyfriend."

"Lieutenant Adrian, you are making deductions without enough facts." Why wasn't she offended by his remark? Of course he was right. . . .

I *could* have a lover, Lieutenant, Brooke mused. Yes, you know him. You may even know the tragic story about his wife.

"Ah-ha," Nick continued. "He does exist, but for some reason he is unavailable on Saturday night. Let's see, he flies the Concorde and is at this moment touching down in Paris."

"No."

"He's a doctor on duty for the night. Or he's starring in an off-Broadway show and you're going to meet him later. But why wouldn't you be at the theater, admiring him? Or he's married. No, that doesn't seem like you."

No, it doesn't seem like me; and it isn't happening.

"Maybe he's a cop on an all-night stakeout," Brooke suggested, swiftly shifting away from the married man guess.

"That doesn't seem like you, either," Nick said evenly "I give up."

"You were right to begin with. No boyfriend."

"Don't tell me you're married to your career. . . ."

"Would that be so bad?" She was, and it wasn't so bad, for now, until . . .

Nick didn't answer.

"Do you mind if we stop?" Nick asked as they passed a newsstand on the way back to Brooke's apartment. "I want to buy the new issue of *Images.*"

"Here it is, sir." The vendor handed the magazine to Nick. "March issue. Hot off the press."

"I used to subscribe," Nick explained to Brooke as they continued the short walk back to her apartment. "But my mailbox is too small. Magazines get damaged. So, I pay newsstand prices. More profit for the Sinclair twins."

"I'm sure if Charles and Jason knew they would make some arrangement. . . ."

"Charles and Jason? You know them?"

"Yes. Not *well*. Through legal work."

Brooke invited Nick into her apartment for coffee. She had an ulterior motive; she wanted to see the art for "Sapphire."

"May I? Galen Spencer has a story in this month's issue. I've read it, but I just want to see how the art turned out."

"You've read it?" Nick wanted to see the art, too. Like everyone in New York, Nick knew who had been the model for Galen Spencer's latest romantic heroine.

"She's a friend." Brooke smiled a wry smile. "And client."

"Any more surprises?"

The smile faded as Brooke reached for the magazine—just that one *other* surprise. "I have a subscription, but it always arrives about three days after everyone else's in town."

"You should really talk to Charles and Jason about that."

"Cute."

Nick noticed the recent issue of *Fashion* on Brooke's coffee table and leafed through it while Brooke looked at *Images*. Nick had never opened an issue of *Fashion* before. Why would he? But, as he turned page after page, his interest increased. *Fashion* was more than a random series of high fashion photographs. Like *Images*, it was a carefully, lovingly crafted work of art.

Nick and Brooke sat across from each other engrossed in the magazines. Finally Nick looked

215

up, expecting to attract Brooke's attention with his eyes, but unable to. She was totally absorbed.

Nick watched, captivated and intrigued. There was something in the photographs that evoked in Brooke a bittersweet mixture of pride and pain. Her head tilted thoughtfully, her lips smiled a soft smile, but her lovely dark blue eyes were stormy.

"She's your sister, isn't she?" Nick spoke quietly. In the hushed silence of the tiny apartment his voice sounded loud.

Brooke looked up at him. "What did you say?"

"Melanie Chandler is your sister." Nick changed his question to a statement.

"Yes," Brooke whispered. Not that it was a secret, but, so far, it had escaped even the watchful ever-curious eye of Viveca Sanders. It would not have been big news; just a small, embarrassing item: *Model Melanie's Mousy Twin.* "Very good detective work."

"I'm a very good detective."

"How did you know?"

Nick shrugged. It had something to do with the eyes that gazed—sky blue or ocean blue—at the world with such determination.

"We're twins."

"That's interesting." Nick meant it. It was *very* interesting. He realized too late he shouldn't have told Brooke.

"It is?" Brooke's voice was icy.

Nick walked across to her and retrieved his issue of *Images*.

"If you point me in the direction of the coffee,

I'll make it." Nick's smiling gray eyes finally defrosted the dark-blue ones.

Chapter Fifteen

Galen tried to write. She put words on paper, but they didn't make sense. Always before the words had flowed, clear and sure, like a crystal-blue river flowing from a pure mountain lake. But now the words and ideas and feelings came from different directions, forming tortuous, criss-crossing paths that started nowhere and travelled aimlessly.

For a solid month, urged by Charles through careful phone calls and occasional necessary meals, Galen tried to write. But what once had been so easy, and had given such pleasure, was impossible. Every day brought more anger, frustration, and exhaustion.

Finally, she made herself sick.

Galen couldn't eat, even though something inside told her she must. The same *something* told her she needed to see a doctor.

Eight weeks after she and Charles returned from Paris, Galen waited in the cheerful office of Sara Rockwell, M.D. Dr. Rockwell specialized in obstetrics and gynecology. Galen made an appointment with Dr. Rockwell because *that* was what worried her the most. Other potential causes of her symptoms—leukemia, tuberculosis, kala-azar—seemed less urgent than the one Dr. Rockwell was trained to diagnose.

Galen decided to wait for the test the doctor said would only take an hour.

"The test is positive. You're pregnant." Sara Rockwell smiled.

And Galen sighed. Dr. Rockwell had already told her, during the pelvic examination, that if she was pregnant it was very early. Her uterus was small. She was eight, nine, maybe ten weeks along. It was difficult to be more precise than that on physical examination, especially this early. As Galen waited, knowing the test would be positive, she thought, Eight weeks means it's Charles's baby; nine or ten weeks means it's Jason's.

"I can't have the baby," Galen told Dr. Rockwell.

"Oh?"

"No. I guess I need to have an abortion," she whispered in a voice that wasn't hers. Someone else was speaking, someone who had slept with two men— *brothers*—and was pregnant by one of them. She added, "I don't have a choice."

"You do have a choice, Galen," Sara countered swiftly. "That's the whole point. You can choose not to have the baby. Or you can choose to *have* it."

Galen stared at her. "You don't understand."

"Tell me what I don't understand," Sara urged gently, warning herself, Stay neutral.

"I don't know who the father is," Galen confessed quietly, embarrassed.

"I guess that's important if you think the potential father might have a genetic disorder that

218

should be screened prenatally," Sara offered, chiding herself a little. She knew about Galen Elizabeth Spencer. Sara had read "Emerald" and "Sapphire." She knew Galen could care for her child, would love her child, and might never forgive herself for making an impulsive emotional decision.

It was the same approach Sara took with all her patients, not just the Galen Spencers of the world. She wanted her patients to make the right choice, whatever it was. It had to be carefully considered.

"There's nothing genetically wrong with the father. It's one of two men," Galen admitted a little defiantly. If Sara Rockwell was surprised or shocked at Galen's admission—she was neither—it didn't show. "They both are healthy."

"And you are healthy."

"Yes." I am carrying a healthy, genetically sound baby.

"Why do you want an abortion, Galen?"

"I'm unmarried. I don't know who the father is. Not that it matters anyway," Galen started to explain, then stopped. It was true. It wasn't relevant. If she knew Jason was the baby's father, would she tell him? No. And if Charles was the father? Maybe . . .

"So, its socially a little awkward . . ."

Galen frowned at Sara.

"I'm not trying to make your decision for you, Galen. I just want to be sure that you really consider it. Just because the procedure is small doesn't mean the decision is."

"You think I should keep the baby?"

"I can't possibly make that decision for you, but I can provide you with literature and telephone numbers. As I'm sure you are aware, abortion is an emotionally charged issue on both sides."

"How soon do I need to decide?"

"You have time. Weeks. The risk goes up with time, so it's a balance between having enough time to be certain and not waiting too long."

Galen nodded.

"Shall I get the literature and phone numbers for you?"

"No. The only one I need to talk to is myself. I'll let you know."

"That's fine. And if you have any questions, please call."

Galen called Sara the following day.

"I'm going to have the baby."

"OK." *Good.*

"I need to ask you some questions."

"Go ahead."

"Well, due to the social, uh, awkwardness of this," Galen began, trying to sound confident, "I need to move away."

"I'll be happy to refer you to another obstetrician. Do you know where you are going?"

"I'm not sure, but I need to move before I begin to show. When will that be?"

"It varies. Certainly by the fifth month. In the meantime I should see you soon. We need to talk about diet and nutrition. I want you to start gaining weight. You seem a little frail."

"No, I'm strong," Galen said bravely. Strong and independent. "I always have been thin. Is that a problem?"

"You just don't have any reserves for yourself, much less for the baby. Are you eating?"

"I'm quite nauseated. Not just in the morning."

"You need to force yourself to eat."

"OK," Galen agreed vaguely. She had more questions, pressing questions. "Will there ever be a way to know who the father is?"

"Probably not before the baby is born, not by uterine size anyway. A two-week difference in gestational age can be subtle."

"And you can't guess when it would have been possible for me to get pregnant?"

"Not with your history of irregular cycles."

"And after the baby is born?"

"Blood-typing might help. It doesn't prove paternity, but it can exclude it. But that all depends on their blood types and yours."

"I'm type B. One of them is type O." Galen knew that Jason was type O because she had read the contents of his wallet, including his blood donor card, to him one day. "I don't know about the other, but they are twins."

"Twins?" Then Sara made an educated guess about the identity of the potential fathers. Sara hadn't even told Galen that she knew who *she* was. It wasn't pertinent. Now Galen had unwittingly told her that Jason or Charles Sinclair had fathered her child. *That* wasn't pertinent, either, except to the unborn child who was heir to an enormous publishing empire.

"Not identical."

"Then the other's blood type could be any of the four, depending on what his parents were. Obviously if he's O, like his brother, or B, like you, it won't help. But if he's A or AB . . ."

"A or AB," Galen repeated.

"*And* the baby is A," Sara added. She continued, "Beyond simple blood typing there are more sophisticated genetic tests. With twins—even fraternal—there might be such genetic similarity that it would be impossible to be certain. Those tests would require carefully collected samples of the father's blood.

"It's probably better not to know," Galen murmured.

But three nights later when Charles called, because he hadn't heard from her for almost ten days, Galen asked him.

"What's your blood type?" Galen made the question sound impulsive. In fact, she had been waiting for most of the conversation, hoping to make it seem like an unimportant afterthought.

"Why? Don't tell me you're shifting to murder mysteries."

"No, I just read an article about the percentages of each type in the population. I'm B, which is a little unusual."

"I'm O. Very mundane."

"Oh. O," Galen repeated. Then I'll never know. . . .

"You sound disappointed."

"No. Just in search of an A, I guess."

"So, are you writing?" Charles asked after a brief silence.

"Yes." Galen was forcing herself to write. She needed money, and a career, to support her unborn child. "I should finish the revisions of 'Garnet' by next week."

"That's ahead of schedule. How's the screenplay?" It was due in three weeks.

Galen sighed. She had rehearsed this. She was going to call *him* when she had her speech exactly right. But now he was asking.

"I'd like to postpone filming the movie until next spring." Galen held her breath.

"Why?" Charles asked evenly.

"I'm having trouble writing about love." It was true, even if it wasn't the *real* reason. But she couldn't tell Charles why she couldn't be in Kenya with him and Jason in the fall. She couldn't tell him that her baby— her baby and his or his twin's—was due in early November. "My rose-colored glasses are shattered."

"I thought you were fixing them."

"I need time, Charles." The truth. "I'm sure that Melanie—"

"Melanie is hired help."

"Charles, please."

"Galen, you signed a contract."

"I can't do it, Charles." Tears filled her eyes and her voice broke. Since the night she found Jason with Fran, Galen's emotions had been only skin deep. Now, with her pregnancy, they were right at the surface, raw and exposed and fragile.

"Yes you can."

"You won't let me change the contract?"

Galen felt betrayed. *Charles, you're my friend, please.*

"It's not my decision." Charles and Jason were executive producers, but . . . "The signatures on the contract are yours and Jason's. You can ask him."

No I can't.

Five days later Galen awoke with lower abdominal cramps. It felt like the beginning of a menstrual period.

But I shouldn't be having a period!

Galen lay quietly, willing the cramps away. After several minutes they were gone, an uneasy early-morning memory. Galen waited for fifteen minutes, thinking about her baby—happy thoughts—before getting up.

As she finished dressing the pain came again. This time it was so severe that it knotted her stomach and paralyzed her lungs. And this time the pain was accompanied by a hot dampness on her thighs.

Blood. No.

Doubled over with pain and fear Galen staggered to the phone in her room. Galen had gotten the private phone, because of Jason. She had been meaning to have it disconnected. With trembling fingers she dialed the number to Dr. Rockwell's office.

"Galen. Take a few deep breaths. Calm down."

"What is happening?"

"I can't be certain over the phone, but I can

get an idea. I need to ask you some questions. All right?"

"Yes." Galen straightened slightly. She wasn't more calm, but the pain had eased a little.

"Is there a lot of blood?"

A lot? There shouldn't be *any*, should there? Any amount is too much.

"No."

"Have you passed clots or tissue?"

"Tissue? No. Just red blood."

"Is the pain in the middle or on the side?" Sara was asking questions that would help her decide whether Galen could come to the office or needed to go directly, possibly by ambulance, to the emergency room. Now she was asking about a possible ectopic—tubal— pregnancy. Ectopic pregnancies were life-threatening.

From everything Sara knew about Galen, it was unlikely that she would have an ectopic pregnancy. Galen had only been sexually active since late December. She—they—had used no birth control. Sara remembered the surprise in Galen's eyes when she asked the question. Of course they used no birth control. They were in love—always and forever—and if she got pregnant it would be wonderful. The look of surprise, and the brief memory of the lovely dream, had faded quickly, dissolving into what looked like despair.

Galen was a low risk for ectopic pregnancy— virtual monogamy, no history of pelvic inflammatory disease, no previous pregnancies, no known tubal damage—but Sara had to exclude it.

"The pain is in the middle. Like a period. Only worse."

"How does it feel now?"

"The pain is less—it did that earlier, too—and the bleeding has slowed," Galen answered hopefully. Maybe she was overreacting.

"Call a cab and come, now, to my office. If it gets worse on the way over, go to . . ." Sara gave Galen the name of two hospitals. "OK?"

"Yes. Am I losing the baby?"

"Not necessarily, Galen. I'll know more when I see you."

"The internal cervical os is closed," Sara told Galen after she completed the examination forty-five minutes later. "And you haven't passed tissue. That means you're having what is called a threatened abortion."

"*Threatened?*"

"That's what it's called."

"What does it mean?"

"It means that you haven't lost the baby," Sara explained carefully.

"But I may."

"Yes. We'll know in the next few days. The pain and bleeding may stop and everything may be fine. Or it may increase and you may miscarry."

"What can I do?"

"First, you can understand that none of this is your fault. Many women miscarry in the first trimester. Often it is because there is something wrong with the fetus. Even the things I am going to tell you to do now don't necessarily change the outcome. But I want you to do them because they are safe and sensible for you and the baby. OK?"

Galen nodded.

"Strict bed rest." Sara hesitated. Then she continued, even though it didn't seem applicable, but was a usual recommendation, "Pelvic rest."

"What?"

"No intercourse."

"Oh."

"How's your weight?"

"I've gained a pound!"

"That's not much."

"I've really been trying." Tears threatened. It was a struggle for Galen not to lose weight. To have *gained* a pound, despite the nausea, was a major accomplishment. But it hadn't been enough! What if that was why she was losing the baby?

"Babies are very tough," Sara said, correctly reading Galen's self-recrimination. "You must know that from all the time you've spent in underdeveloped countries."

Galen did know that. She had seen it.

"You know who I am."

"Of course. What I don't know is whether you have a living situation that can ensure strict bed rest and nutritious food and someone who can watch you for the next few days." In other words, what I don't know is, Do you have a friend?

Galen thought about her living situation in the brownstone. Her third-floor room, the main-floor kitchen, and the housemates who changed too frequently to become friends did not meet Dr.

Rockwell's requirements. Galen had friends—Charles and Brooke and Melanie—but none of them could know about her pregnancy.

"Not really."

"I think it would be best to put you in the hospital. We don't usually do that for threatened abortions, but . . ." Sara paused, thinking, But most women have husbands or lovers or families or friends or *someone*. Most women, but not Galen. Sara continued, "But given your weight, a few days of enforced nutrition seems sensible. Is that all right?"

"Whatever is best for my baby."

Chapter Sixteen

Galen was hospitalized in a small community hospital north of New York City. The pain and bleeding subsided after four days, but she remained hospitalized for three more days, to be safe, to be *sure*. They made great progress with her nutrition. She gained weight and the anemia improved with iron and her electrolytes were back to normal. Even her cheeks had a soft pink glow of health.

"You look good," Sara told Galen on the morning of her release from the hospital.

"I feel good. Happy. Lucky."

"Ease back into things slowly. . . ."

"I thought we were out of danger."

"I believe you are, from the standpoint of the

threatened abortion. I think the baby plans to go the whole nine months." Sara smiled. "I'm more worried about you—your strength—than the baby. So take it easy. Eat."

"I will. I promise. I really feel better than I have in a long time."

It was true. Galen felt better physically and better emotionally. During the week in the hospital, during the long hours of waiting and hoping and praying the baby would survive, the blur of the past two and a half months came into clear, sharp focus. She had to take charge of her life. She had to make decisions for herself and her baby.

First and foremost, Galen had to sever all ties—personal and professional—with the Sinclair twins. The tie with Jason was already broken—everywhere but in your *heart,* a voice taunted—because he betrayed her and them and everything she believed in.

And Charles, her dear friend . . .

Galen didn't dwell on whether it was *fair.* None of it was fair to any of them.

"Brooke? It's Galen, are you busy?"

"Galen. Where are you?"

"At the brownstone." She had been back, home from the hospital, for an hour. "Why?"

"I tried to reach you all last week."

"Oh. I was away. Was there something?"

"No." *Yes.* Charles had called because he was worried about Galen. He wondered if Brooke had heard from her. "I just called to say hi. Are you all right?"

"Yes. Fine." Galen wished she could tell Brooke. It would help explain the question she was about to ask. But no one could know. Galen sighed and continued, "Brooke, how difficult would it be for me to get out of the contract for the screenplay?"

Charles had asked the same question! Brooke told Galen what she had told Charles three days before.

"It wouldn't be difficult at all, *legally.*"

"Really?"

"No. I wrote it that way. You would have to refund the advance."

"Of course."

"Galen, what about *Songs of the Savanna* and *Spring Street Stories?*" Brooke had negotiated a two-book contract for Galen. The completed manuscript for *Songs of the Savanna*—the stories about Kenya—had been promised for September. *Spring Street Stories*—stories about life and people in Greenwich Village—was due next spring.

"I will complete them as scheduled." Galen paused. She asked quietly, "Brooke, could you just send something in writing cancelling the screenplay contract?"

"I *could* Galen, but . . ."

"I have to tell them myself, don't I?" She would have to see Jason and Charles one last time.

"Galen, let's have lunch," Brooke suggested. "Are you free today?"

"No, not today. But we will, Brooke, before I leave."

"Leave?"

"I'll explain later. I have to go now. Thank you, Brooke."

Galen's next call was, to the executive offices of Sinclair Publishing Company. She scheduled an appointment with Charles and Jason at ten the following morning. That done, she sat on the lumpy mattress in her room and gazed at herself in the mirror.

Hopelessly out of date and naive, she thought as she looked critically at her waist-length red-gold hair and her unstylish clothes. I can't look like this anymore. It isn't how I feel inside. I'm not a wide-eyed virgin full of hope and dreams. I'm a twenty-six-year-old woman who is about to have a child. I *know* what's on the other side of the dream. I've been there. It's where I'm going to live.

Time to step into the eighties, Galen Elizabeth Spencer. Not with wide eyes . . . but with your eyes wide open.

It didn't scare her. Nothing was as frightening as learning that everything you believed in was just a mirage. And she was beyond that now; she had faced it and accepted it. Galen wasn't afraid anymore. She wasn't afraid and she wasn't alone. There was a new life—a life that wanted to live—growing inside her. How she would love that precious little life! She already did. Despite everything, Galen still believed in her own ability to love, deeply, unselfishly, and forever.

"Cut it all off," Galen told the hair stylist two hours later.

"Are you sure? This is the most beautiful hair. . . ."

"I'm sure."

"Do you want us to make a fall for you?"

"No. Do you want to buy it from me?" Galen suggested, remembering "The Gift of the Magi." But that was a different century. Maybe they didn't buy hair, real hair, in the nineteen eighties.

But they did. Galen and the owner of the salon settled on a price that included the haircut *and* styling *and* cash.

"We're going to cut it pretty short," he warned. "On the other hand, that's the style—*a* style— and with your eyes . . ."

The result was dramatic. Galen's remarkable emerald eyes, no longer hidden by the red-gold veil, commanded attention. The lovely eyes attracted the attention, but they were only part of the effect; the fine, straight nose, the healthy pink cheeks, the full, sensuous lips. . . .

Galen wasn't old-fashioned pretty any longer. Now she was modern and stunning and beautiful.

Beautiful, Galen mused as she sat in her room that evening, hemming, de-smocking, and modernizing one of her dresses. *You are so beautiful, Galen.* Jason's words, whispered gently, as he kissed her and made love . . .

Galen pricked her finger with the sewing needle, distracted by the memory of Jason. Go away, *dream,* she told herself with annoyance, Go *away.*

Charles noticed Galen's name in his appointment book with a combination of relief and apprehension. She was *back* from wherever it was she had been for the past week. Good. But why had she scheduled an appointment? Why did she want to meet with him and Jason together? Was it just about delaying the filming of "Sapphire"?

Galen appeared in Jason's office at precisely ten A.M. Charles and Jason were already there. They stood up and drew silent breaths when they saw her. She looked so different! Her hair, her eyes, her face, her dress—somehow vaguely familiar—radiated confidence.

Strong and beautiful and independent, Charles thought, relieved. Good for her.

But as he watched Galen closely, as she smiled, as she extended her hand first to Jason and then to him, he saw her lips tremble slightly and her eyes flicker with uncertainty.

She's trying so hard, Charles realized. And she'll make it. We'll help her.

Darling Galen, Jason's heart cried. He wanted her missed her, so much. He wanted the old Galen or the new one, it didn't matter. He had never really known her anyway. What he thought they had—a love forever—never existed. The "love" vanished overnight, but still Jason wanted her.

Jason wondered why Charles looked so surprised by Galen's appearance. It was as if Charles and Galen hadn't seen each other for a while, as if something had happened between them in the weeks since Jason had seen them at La Lumière. Was it already over between Charles and Galen? Was Galen just another of Charles's women?

"You look wonderful, Galen." Charles smiled, encouraging her.

"I needed a change." Galen looked at her hands for a moment, collecting her thoughts and calming her racing heart. Then she raised her proud head and added, "I need some other changes, too."

"Yes?"

"Ten days ago, I spoke with Charles about delaying the deadline for the screenplay." Galen paused. "Well, I've changed my mind."

"Good," Charles said, but the look in her eyes worried him.

"I've decided to cancel the contract," Galen continued bravely. "I'm not going to write the screenplay at all. I've brought a check in the amount of the advance."

"You want someone else to write it?"

"No. I hold the copyright. I don't want a movie made from 'Sapphire'. Ever."

"Why not, Galen?" Charles demanded, suddenly angry. He was worried about her tears—she was so fragile—but he couldn't let her get away with this. It made absolutely no sense.

"You know why." Her glistening emerald eyes met his for a moment.

"Galen, you had a love affair that didn't work out the way you wanted. It happens." Charles forced gentleness into his voice. "But you go on. You don't run away, especially not from *us.*"

As Charles spoke the last words, he saw what looked like hatred in her lovely eyes.

Charles drew a sharp breath. What have I ever done but care about you, Galen?

Jason watched and listened. A *love affair that didn't work out the way you wanted.* Galen loved Charles, but Charles didn't love her. It was over with Charles, and still Galen hadn't come back to *him.*

She was leaving both of them because it was too painful to be near Charles. . . .

What had happened between Galen and Charles to make her want him out of her life forever? What had happened between Elliott and Charles to make Elliott want Charles out of *his* life forever?

"Keep the advance," Jason whispered.

"Jesus Christ!" Charles hissed as he stormed out of Jason's office.

"I'm sorry that something happened to hurt you this much," Jason told Galen after Charles was gone. His voice was so gentle, so loving.

Galen couldn't speak. Her astonished emerald eyes met his for a bewildered moment before she left.

"She asked me if she could break the contract. I told her yes." Just like I told you when you asked, Brooke thought.

"Why the hell did you write that escape clause into the contract?"

"Because I always try to do what's best for my client," Brooke spoke quietly into the phone. He sounded so angry, and he was blaming *her.* "Don't you think, no matter what . . . you couldn't force her to write it."

Brooke wondered if Charles was still there. She wondered if the polite aristocratic eyes matched the icy voice. "And she didn't give you any reason?" Charles finally broke the silence.

"No," Brooke whispered.

"It doesn't make any sense."

"I know. I'm sorry, Charles."

"For what?" A slight tease, a little softness. "For being such a damned good attorney?"

"Is Melanie Chandler available? I'm a friend." Galen had remembered her friend, and the fabulous leading role that would never happen, in the middle of the night. As soon as the ordeal of telling Charles and Jason was over, Galen walked along Park Avenue to Drake Modelling Agency. Galen wondered if Melanie would be as angry as Charles had been; Melanie had every right to be.

The receptionist at Drake assumed Galen was herself a model and directed her to the models' dressing room. The dressing room door opened before Galen had a chance to knock.

"Fran."

Fran looked at her quizzically and without recognition.

"I'm Galen Spencer. We met . . ." In Jason's office and at Brooke's apartment. And I saw you—you were asleep—in Jason's arms. Don't you know me? I'm the mystery woman who wasn't really a threat to your love after all.

"Galen. I didn't recognize you."

"Galen?" Melanie overheard the conversation and joined them. "Wow."

Galen shrugged. "A new look."

"Sensational," Fran murmured. "I have to go. It was nice seeing you again, Galen."

Galen nodded politely. It wasn't so nice. . . .

"How are you, Galen?" Melanie asked cheerfully. She wanted to *demand* of the troubled emerald eyes, Tell me what is wrong.

"Fine." Galen frowned. "Melanie, I've decided I don't want a movie to be made from 'Sapphire' after all."

"Oh?" Why did Galen look so worried? Because of *her*, "That's OK, at least with me."

"Really?"

"*Really*. It's probably best for me not to take a break from my modelling career anyway." Melanie waved it away with her long, graceful hands. She hadn't really been looking forward to spending two months in Kenya with Charles Sinclair. "No big deal."

Relief flickered across Galen's face, but a deeper sadness lingered.

"What's wrong, Galen?" Melanie asked gently.

"I'll be all right."

"Don't you want to talk about it?" Galen *hadn't* wanted to talk about it, Melanie realized. That was why for the past two months Galen had graciously, but firmly, declined Brooke and Melanie's invitations to get together. Maybe now . . .

Yes, Melanie, but I can't.

"No."

"Maybe in a week or two?"

"I'm leaving New York."

"Where are you going?"

"I'm not sure. I'll let you know." Galen moved to the door to leave. "Thank you for not being angry about the movie, Melanie."

Galen didn't know where she would go when she left New York. It would be easy—safe and easy and her parents would protect her and her baby—to go back to Kenya. But that would be going *back,* and she had to move ahead. At the beauty salon she had browsed through the current issue of *Unique Homes;* there was a photograph of a charming stone-and-cedar gatehouse in Lake Forest, Illinois.

Galen dialed the number of the real estate agency listed in *Unique Homes* underneath the photo ad for the gatehouse in Lake Forest. The gatehouse, situated on two acres of parklike property, had a view of Lake Michigan, a private inner courtyard surrounded by a six-foot brick wall, two fireplaces, a wood-panelled study, a country kitchen. . . .

The pace of the agent's voice increased as she described the property. Did Galen know Lake Forest? No? Well, it was one of Chicago's most prestigious north shore suburbs—old money and elegance and privacy and charm. The asking price was a little high, the agent admitted, but Galen could probably get it for right at half a million.

"Are you interested?" the agent asked.

"It sounds lovely," Galen murmured, reeling at the price, wondering if she should just apologize and hang up. "Perfect. Do you think they would consider renting it?"

There was a long silence.

"Renting?" It was almost a gasp. Homes in Lake Forest weren't usually rented. The agent sputtered finally, "I don't know."

"Do you think they might be?"

The agent hesitated. They *might* be. The owners lived in the mansion on the property. They didn't really like the idea of subdividing the property—it had been in the family forever—but they didn't like the gatehouse sitting vacant, either. One would never list a house in Lake Forest as a rental. Still . . . the agent wondered about the woman with the soft British accent from New York. The owners might rent to the right person.

"Why don't you give me your name and number and I'll get back to you?"

Charles called her at ten that night.

"Why, Galen?" he demanded as soon as she answered.

"I had to."

"Really. *Why?*"

"I just did. You're the one who kept telling me to resolve the past and get on with my life."

"I didn't expect you to do something crazy like tossing away everything and everyone that happened to be around during the great tragedy of your unsuccessful love affair."

"I wish you could just believe that I know what I'm doing. I wish you could understand how I feel."

"Let me tell you how I feel, Galen. I feel betrayed."

"Betrayed," Galen breathed. *She* felt betrayed. "If the movie had done well . . ."

"Do you think I'm talking about *money?*"

"No," she admitted softly. I know the kind of betrayal you mean. I know about the betrayal of love and friendship.

A long silence followed.

"I thought we were friends," Charles began again finally. His voice was gentle. He wanted to understand. "I thought we talked to each other and told each other the truth."

Tears filled her eyes. She wished she could lessen the hurt in Charles's voice. But what could she say? If she even hinted that there was something more, something that didn't make what she was doing seem so crazy, Charles would push until he found out.

"Was it because we made love? Did that really change everything after all?"

It wasn't because we made love, Charles. That was lovely, but. . . . If Charles knew I was carrying his baby he would probably want to marry me, Galen realized suddenly. She allowed herself to think about it for a moment, and the vision was pleasant. She and Charles cared about each other. They could make a gentle, loving life together with their child.

But Galen didn't *know* the baby was his.

And Charles was Jason's brother. She couldn't spend the rest of her life seeing Jason, she with Charles and Jason with Fran. Galen could never see Jason again. Seeing him today hurt too much, because, today, more of her wanted him than hated him.

"No. It wasn't because we made love," Galen answered finally, part truth, part lie. She added sadly, she would miss him, it wasn't fair, "It just has to end. That's all."

Good-bye, Charles.

Chapter Seventeen

New York City
May 1986

Melanie stood at the edge of a rose garden in Central Park, her arm stretched toward the rain-wet petals of a pale-pink rose. It was six-thirty in the morning. The spring dawn was soft yellow and the air was clean and fresh following the midnight rain.

A restlessness had driven Melanie from her warm bed into the cold, still dawn. Restlessness for what? Melanie didn't know. Now, as she touched the velvety petals, warm tears spilled inexplicably onto her cold cheeks. What was *wrong?* Why was she crying?

The sound of approaching footsteps pulled her from her thoughts. The menacing intruder hovered close behind.

Please go away. Melanie's body stiffened with fear. *Please.*

"Melanie?"

Melanie spun and looked through a blur of tears at familiar brown eyes. But not so familiar, because now they weren't taunting; now they looked concerned.

"Are you all right?" He had never seen her like this. She wore a pale-gray sweat suit, bland, baggy, colorless, and no makeup. She was unadorned, and her eyes glistened with tears, but she was so beautiful. And so sad.

"Yes. I'm fine. Thank you, Charles. Just looking at the roses." Melanie impatiently wiped the tears from her cheeks. But then there were new tears; they wouldn't stop. *Why?*

"Here." Charles withdrew a monogrammed handkerchief from his pocket.

"Thank you." Melanie accepted the offered handkerchief mechanically and held it in her hand, staring at it, as if its use was unknown to her.

"Speaking of raindrops on roses," Charles murmured as he retrieved the handkerchief and gently dried her tear-damp cheeks. She watched him with startled blue eyes which, for the moment, had stopped weeping.

"So. What's wrong?" The dark-brown eyes wanted to know.

"I don't know. These lovely roses remind me of—" Melanie stopped, suddenly confused. It was her heart speaking to Charles Sinclair.

"Of home? Are you homesick?" Charles asked gently. He knew about homesickness. He had been homesick all his life. He had never had a home.

"Maybe, except we didn't have roses." She smiled distantly. The roses didn't remind her of home. They reminded her of her dreams. In the life she would have someday, there were gardens and gardens of roses. "Sometimes I feel like a withered leaf. Every time I try to pause for even a moment a gust of wind comes and whirls me away."

"The price of success and celebrity. You have no privacy, and there's nothing constant but whim and change. That's why I escape to St. Barts—" Charles stopped abruptly. He was telling Melanie Chandler something private and important. Of course St. Barts was on his mind, he was going there in less than a week, but still. . . .

"I haven't taken a vacation," Melanie mused. Not a vacation or a holiday or even a moment to breathe since September. Without looking back, without skipping a beat, she had arrived in New York and soared right to the top. "Do you suppose a vacation would help?"

"Maybe. But maybe it's more. You need to decide if this is what you really want. It's a roller coaster, Melanie, and you haven't even gotten to the steep part." It might have been a warning except his voice was soft.

"Why are you so wise?"

"I'm not. And you are not a withered leaf. You have a good shot at becoming an icicle, however. Do you want my coat?"

Melanie realized then that Charles was dressed in a three-quarter-length camel's hair coat over his perfectly tailored suit. It was six-thirty in the morning' and Charles Sinclair—Manhattan's dashing and dapper playboy—was on his way to work.

"No. I'm fine." *Better* thanks to you. Melanie

took the handkerchief from his hand. "I'll return this to you."

"OK."

"I'd better go. Thanks."

"I like your jogging outfit."

Melanie felt a rush of adrenaline pump through her, and suddenly she was a soldier preparing for battle. It was going to end badly with Charles Sinclair after all. He couldn't resist the one final taunt, the few words that would prove all the other words had been false. Melanie's eyes narrowed as they met his.

But the dark-brown eyes weren't taunting. They were telling the truth. He liked her drab, baggy gray sweats.

"So do I," she whispered.

Melanie watched the honey-colored drops splash into the pool of champagne at the base of the ice sculpture fountain. She smiled slightly as she tried to remember *which* extravaganza this was. Let's see, if it's Friday it must be the *Cosmo* party. The dazzling, glamorous parties were part of the whirring blur of her life. The gowns and coiffures and jewels and partners varied from night to night, but the ice sculptures and champagne fountains and gourmet hors d'oeuvres and mountains of caviar and beautiful and handsome faces were the same.

And the conversation was the same.

"Melanie, the cover of *Vogue*. Really the best cover in years."

"Melanie, twelve pages of Dior's spring collection, *all* modelled by you. Unbelievable."

"Melanie Chandler, probably the sexiest voice in television commercials *ever*. X-rated, really."

"You must be terribly disappointed about 'Sapphire'."

And Melanie smiled her flawless smile, her sky-blue eyes sparkling, as her sexy voice answered softly, "It was a lucky shot."

"Dior designed a long blond look this season. It just worked out."

"Not that sexy."

"No. I'm sure Galen made the right decision."

Melanie gazed into the golden pond of champagne. Her reflection glittered back at her in soft honey ripples. Her reflection and another.

"Do you know the legend of Narcissus?"

It was a taunt, a not-so-subtle reminder of her own vanity. Those kind, gentle, early-morning moments in the park were a mirage.

"I'm not admiring myself."

"Neither was Narcissus. He was a twin. He and his sister looked very much alike. When she died he spent endless hours gazing at his reflection because it reminded him of her."

"I always thought . . . something about a wood nymph named Echo . . ." Melanie narrowed her eyes, trying to remember.

"There are two versions of the myth. The mythologists are divided to this day." Charles smiled.

"Poor Narcissus. What a bad rap. Hard enough to be a twin," Melanie mused. Then blushed. She was telling Charles Sinclair the truth again.

"Hard enough," he agreed.

Melanie reached into her Gucci evening bag and retrieved Charles's washed, ironed, and carefully folded handkerchief. "I thought I might see you tonight."

"Thank you." Charles raised the handkerchief to his nose. *"First.* What you always wear."

"I guess the scent is in my evening bag," Melanie apologized, embarrassed, shaken. She always did wear First. It was her favorite perfume. Charles had noticed. "I could wash it—"

"I like it."

"Charles." Viveca Sanders joined them and slipped her perfectly manicured fingers around Charles's arm. She flashed a well-trained—trained not to use the muscles that would lead too soon to wrinkles—television camera smile at Melanie. "Melanie, I just saw the Tiffany ad. I never gave a hoot about diamonds until now. When are you coming on my show?"

"Viveca, always working," Charles teased lightly.

But they were all working. That was why they were here.

"Sometime, Viveca," Melanie promised gaily. She would have to appear on *Viveca's View.* It was part of her job, part of the celebrity expectations. She would put it off until Adam told her that she *had* to.

"I love these firm commitments." Viveca turned her attention to Charles, her fingers squeezing possessively. She spoke softly, "Charles, I have to find out why George Phelps is here alone. I'll be back."

Viveca cast a seductive glance at Charles and a territorial one at Melanie.

Don't *worry*, Viveca.

"Would you like to dance?" Charles asked as Viveca disappeared among the forest of designer dresses and silk tuxedos.

Melanie nodded without looking at him and turned toward the dance floor. Charles guided her through the crowd, his hand strong and warm on her bare back. Melanie paused when they reached the edge of the dance floor. Charles took her hand and led her to a dark, secluded corner.

They began to dance, awkwardly assuming the formal ballroom position. They danced that way—stiff and distant—for a few moments.

Then Charles laughed softly, and in one fluid motion lifted both her arms around his neck and wrapped his arms, strong and gentle, around her back and waist.

"Melanie," he whispered, pulling her close.

She rested her forehead gently against his chest and shook her head, unable to speak, suddenly overwhelmed. The closeness felt so wonderful, and the soft, seductive way he spoke her name . . .

"What?" Charles asked quietly, lifting her chin, gazing into her eyes.

"You," she breathed.

"You," he whispered in return.

Take me away, Charles. Take me to a private place where we can dance forever.

"What are you doing later tonight?" The sensuous brown eyes wondered.

Making love with you. Melanie's mind spun.

Somewhere in the spinning images she saw Russ Collins, who she had met at Adam's New Year's Eve party and had been dating since March. Russ was probably looking for her. Russ knew how Melanie felt about Charles; he would be surprised to find them dancing together. Russ would be even more surprised to learn that Melanie wanted Charles, desperately.

"Seeing you." Melanie heard a voice, her voice, answer.

"One o'clock?"

She nodded.

"Tell me where you live."

One. One-fifteen. One-thirty. One *forty-five*.

As the minutes passed, slow, heavy minutes, the eager anticipation that had carried her through the rest of the evening vanished. In its place was a deep aching fear that this was what Charles Sinclair had planned all along. He wanted to show her her own foolishness. She didn't really believe he wanted her, did she? She couldn't really think that after all the animosity everything would magically change, could she?

Months before Melanie had laid—tried to— the same trap for him. But Charles hadn't taken the bait. Now the tables were turned, and she had fallen for the ruse.

Damn you, Charles. *Damn* you.

Numbly, Melanie removed the strand of flawless diamonds from around her neck and replaced it, to be returned Monday, in the peacock-blue box labelled Tiffany and Co. Then she replaced the diamond-and-sapphire earrings and the diamond bracelet . . .

The buzzer sounded. Melanie's heart pounded with renewed energy and excitement; anticipation flooded through her in warm, tingling, frightening waves.

"Yes?" she spoke into the intercom linking her apartment to the building's main entrance.

"I'm sorry."

Melanie pressed the button to release the front-door lock. It would take him two minutes to reach her apartment. As Melanie paced impatiently, she caught her reflection in the hall mirror. I look naked without the jewels, she mused, gazing at her bare arms and long, graceful neck. That's OK, isn't it? Isn't that what this is all about? *Is* it? Damn you, Charles. It was almost easier when I thought you weren't going to come. Easier to hate you . . .

The doorbell rang.

"Hi."

"Hi."

His just-washed dark hair was still slightly damp. His silk tuxedo had been exchanged for khaki slacks, an oxford shirt, and a cashmere V-neck sweater.

He went home to change, Melanie realized. After he took Viveca home. After he. . . . What if Charles had made love to Viveca before coming here? What if that was why he was so late?

Charles touched her face with his hands and Melanie stopped thinking. He held her face as his lips hungrily explored hers. Melanie returned his deep, searching kisses and her hands found his damp, strong back beneath the cashmere and cotton. Charles pulled her close, wrapping his arms around her, enveloping her in warmth and strength and desire.

But the breathless embrace and the warm deep kisses weren't enough. Their bodies urgently demanded more; they had to be even closer, *now*.

"Where is the bedroom?"

Melanie's blue eyes told him to follow her.

They undressed each other quickly There was nothing gentle or leisurely, no pretense of wondrous discovery, no careful, lingering kisses, no slow exploration in search of pleasure. . . .

As soon as they were naked Charles was inside her; it was what they both wanted and needed. They shared the urgency, and now, as their strong, healthy bodies moved together—consumed with desire and passion—they shared the ecstasy.

Afterward, they held each other tight and close, unwilling to let distance intrude again. This was how they wanted to be, this close, *joined*. At first, even though they lay very still, there wasn't silence. Their hearts—each heard both hearts—pounded noisily and their lungs recovered in gasps from the breathless moments of their loving.

Finally there was only the soft rhythm of quiet breathing and the strong, slow beats of their athletic hearts and the wonderful warmth of their still-joined bodies.

"You," Charles whispered.

"You," Melanie breathed into his chest.

She lifted her chin and found his lips. Charles took her lower lip gently in his teeth.

"Is it possible to do that again?" she asked between kisses.

"Possible?" Charles laughed softly. "Yes."

"Now?" Melanie knew the answer. It was already happening.

"Maybe more slowly this time," Charles spoke into her mouth. "I needed you so much."

I still do, he thought, as he felt the same urgent need and desire. He couldn't control it.

"Maybe more slowly next time." I need you, Charles, just the same way, *please.* "The time *after* this time."

"I should go."

"Go?"

"It's five-thirty," Charles answered simply. But he didn't move. Melanie felt his hesitation.

Tell him not to go, Melanie. But what if he *wants* to? Then you'll be humiliated. Then you'll know.

"You're welcome to stay." Forever.

Charles stayed. They slept in each other's arms and were awakened by desire—their bodies already moving in a rhythm of love—once in the morning and once in the afternoon. Twelve hours after he said it the first time, Charles said it again.

"Now I really should go."

"There *is* food here." Melanie smiled. "Well, there's lettuce and lemon juice and sprouts."

"Aren't you going to the Tony Awards?" Charles asked. "I can't imagine Russ would miss them."

Russ. Russ was before *you.* Last night I said good-bye to Russ, because of you . . .

"Melanie?"

"Russ is going. I'm not." She forced gaiety in her voice. She added firmly, as if it was her first choice, "I need a quiet night."

It *was* quiet in Melanie's apartment that night, but it wasn't the peaceful quiet she treasured. Tonight the quiet wasn't interrupted by the soft, comforting swishing of pencils as she sketched. Tonight the silence was absolute; except for the strident thoughts that echoed and reechoed in her brain.

What a fool she was! Charles Sinclair had promised nothing. They spent a night and a day of passion. That was all. She had shared meaningless moments of pleasure before, but last night with Charles felt so different. Even before it happened she knew it would be different; that was why she told Russ Collins good-bye.

"I think we should stop seeing each other, Russ," she had purred, her blue eyes sorrowful.

"What? Melanie, *why?*"

"It's me, Russ, not you. I'm not really a very nice person. I'm self-centered and petulant. You're better off without me."

These words had worked in high school and college and even after. Melanie delivered them with great sincerity when she felt, as she inevitably did, suffocated by a relationship. They were her escape when she was tired of being coddled and admired, and when she yearned for her precious privacy

"Melanie, that's nonsense," Russ replied calmly. "Tell me the real reason."

Russ had almost startled her into telling the truth; but, fortunately, she hadn't. After their secret night and day of passion, Charles returned to Viveca, to be with Viveca under the bright lights and watchful eye of Manhattan. And Melanie sat in her twilight-darkened apartment and felt as if her heart had been torn from her.

Charles called at ten. Melanie answered the phone in the darkness.

"I couldn't cancel this evening with Viveca. Not the Tonys. It was too important to her."

"Charles."

"Yes. Do you understand that, Melanie?"

"Yes." Maybe.

"May I come over later?"

"Charles, I . . ." Yes. *Please.* Oh, later? You mean after you've tucked Viveca into bed? "No."

"How about tomorrow? We could go riding in the park."

"You ride?"

"Just a little better than you."

"Oh?"

"I'll show you."

"Brooke and I are going to Boston tomorrow." It was Brooke's idea. She offered to show Melanie the historical, charming city where she had spent four years of her life. Melanie was thrilled at Brooke's suggestion because, mostly, still, when she and Brooke got together, it was *her* idea.

Melanie wanted to be with Charles, but it was

important—too important—to spend time with Brooke.

"For the day?" Charles asked.

"Uh-huh."

"How about Monday evening?"

"Adam wants me to . . ."

"Do you want to see me again, Melanie?"

"Yes," she breathed. Come over tonight, Charles, even if you've been with Viveca, even if we only have an hour or two before I leave for Boston. "Very much."

Charles hesitated. He *had* to see her. It had only been five hours since he left her and already he ached for her.

"Come to St. Barts with me then. We leave Tuesday morning and return Sunday."

We. Charles and Melanie.

"I have sessions booked all week." But I don't care. I could just cancel them, couldn't I?

"You were talking about a vacation." If you can't come with me, I'll stay here, to be with you.

"Yes, but, Adam . . ."

"I'll talk to him. He's here tonight."

"No. I'll talk—*tell*—him."

"So, yes? We're going?"

"We're going."

Brooke and Melanie walked along the Freedom Trail, ate clam chowder in a restaurant overlooking Boston Harbor, toured Harvard and Bunker Hill and Faneuil Hall, and strolled among the picnickers in the Commons. Next trip, they decided, exhausted but excited by their fascinating journey into history, they would go to Concord and Lexington.

It was a wonderful day. Brooke and Melanie could have fun as long as the history and lives they explored belonged to someone else. They could be amiable, easy companions as long as the topics were neutral and impersonal.

At least we're not enemies, Melanie thought, searching for a glimmer of hope in the slow, difficult struggle to become Brooke's friend.

The animosity, the contempt for all that the other held important, had vanished. Of course, by unspoken mutual truce, Brooke and Melanie had long since stopped taunting each other with their accomplishments. Melanie didn't tell Brooke that she was already among the highest paid models in the world, and Brooke didn't tell Melanie that she was about to be appointed the youngest assistant district attorney in the country.

Brooke and Melanie didn't talk about their work, and they didn't talk about their personal lives. On that Sunday afternoon in Boston, Melanie didn't tell Brooke about Charles or the trip she was going take with him to St. Barts.

Chapter Eighteen

Melanie finally gave up on sleep at four Tuesday morning. The mental pacing that kept her awake all night became physical as she nervously and aimlessly moved from room to room in her apartment.

What was she doing? She didn't even know him. Until recently she had disliked him as intensely as she had ever disliked anyone. What would she *say* to him? The taunts had come easily, fueled by contempt, but now . . .

Brooke was able to talk to him. Brooke and Charles talked about business and law and contracts and stories. Charles *listened* to Brooke, respected Brooke's opinion, valued her intelligence. Brooke could talk to Charles and hold his interest, but could *she?*

Melanie sighed as she inspected the contents of her neatly packed suitcase for the fifth time. It was a colorful collage of shorts and halter tops and sundresses and swimsuits. On the top lay her sketchpad and her plastic box of colored pencils. Melanie's hand rested for a thoughtful moment on the sketchpad. Then she removed it and the pencils and returned them to their place in her sewing room. She wouldn't sketch in front of Charles; it was much too silly and trivial.

But wasn't *she* too silly and trivial for Charles? What did she have to offer?

The answer came with a hard, painful jolt.

What do you *think* you have to offer? Your flawless, perfect, beautiful body and your flawless, perfect, beautiful face. Charles Sinclair may be terribly scholarly and intelligent, but he is also a sexual, passionate man. When it comes to you, Melanie Chandler, Charles doesn't *care* about the story, just the art.

★   ★   ★

Charles arrived at seven.

"Hi. All set? Do you have your passport?"

"Hi. Yes." Melanie's answer sounded like, *Yes, of course,* even though she had only remembered the passport at six-thirty.

The limousine glided away from Manhattan and the already heavy crush of early-morning traffic.

"How was Boston?" Charles asked when they reached the bridge.

"Wonderful. Such history. Everything is so old."

"Spoken like a true Californian." Charles smiled.

Melanie returned the smile, but her stomach ached. Brooke would never have said something so silly. Brooke would have told Charles—and he would have listened with such interest—the intriguing details of the Boston Tea Party.

"Have you been to Europe?" Charles asked.

Melanie shook her head. Her passport was only two weeks old. "But I'll be there in August and September."

"I know."

Of course Charles knew. Melanie remembered his unconcealed annoyance when they had to delay the filming schedule of "Sapphire" until October because of her trip to Europe. But that was a different Charles Sinclair, wasn't it? This one was smiling at her and his eyes were gentle.

"I've never been out of the country before," Melanie admitted softly. So if you want the limousine to turn around and take me back. . . . Even the cover is a fake, Charles. I'm not really the worldly, sophisticated woman pictured in my photographs. It's only an illusion, just trick photography.

Charles answered the worry in her eyes by reaching for her hand.

Charles kept hold of her hand, releasing for the brief necessary moments of check-in and security clearance, until they settled into their seats in the first-class cabin.

"No breakfast?" Charles asked when Melanie shook her head in response to the stewardess's request for entrée selection.

"This," Melanie answered lifting the glass of champagne, "is plenty."

"You probably don't eat much."

"Not much." *That's why I have the perfect, beautiful, flawless body you want. . . .*

Their conversation was interrupted by a communication from the pilot describing the flight plan. By the time the pilot's message was over, Melanie had taken a thick paperback book from her purse and finished the glass of champagne. Charles retrieved a manuscript from his briefcase, accepted an offer of more champagne for both of them, and began to read.

Melanie stared at the page of her book, but she couldn't read. Shouldn't they be talking and laughing and getting to know one another in a way other than *that?* The champagne made her warm, but it didn't give her the courage to talk to him. Where was the endless, effortless stream of gay flirtation that was her trademark? Where was the Melanie Chandler *charm?*

"That must be quite a passage," Charles

observed thirty minutes later. In those thirty minutes Melanie hadn't turned a page.

"Riveting."

"Why don't you read this?" Charles handed her the manuscript he had been reading—"Garnet" by Galen Elizabeth Spencer.

"Oh. The final gem."

Charles smiled. If anyone could tease Galen about the names of her stories, and their heroines, it would be Melanie. Perhaps Galen had told Melanie something about why she left.

"It arrived yesterday. The return address is a post office box in Lake Forest, Illinois."

Melanie nodded. She knew where Galen was. She also knew the address and telephone number of the gatehouse on Mayflower Lane. Apparently Galen didn't want Charles to know; maybe Charles was part of the mystery Galen steadfastly refused to reveal.

"You knew she was in Lake Forest?"

"Yes. Brooke and I saw her off at the train station when she left."

"Train?"

"Galen said she wanted to see the countryside." Melanie frowned briefly. "But I also think she didn't want to fly."

"Do you . . ."

Know why she left? Know why she cancelled "Sapphire?"

Melanie looked into his serious brown eyes and shook her head.

"I have no idea, Charles. *Something* happened, but she never told me what it was. I thought you would know. You and Galen seemed so close."

"I know that she was in love and it ended badly. But . . ."

"It doesn't really explain everything."

"No."

Melanie read "Garnet" twice, losing herself in it, forgetting, for a moment, that she was flying to St. Barts with Charles.

"What did you think?" he asked when Melanie finished reading.

"Wonderful."

"Like the other gems."

Melanie frowned slightly.

"What?" he urged.

"It's not as hopeful or joyous as the others."

"No."

"It's a little sad and wistful, like . . ."

"Like?"

"Like Galen was when she left."

Melanie chewed thoughtfully on her lower lip.

"I do think it's wonderful, Charles. It's bittersweet, but that's more realistic, more the way love really is." Melanie blushed. She was telling Charles Sinclair, editor-in-chief of *Images,* about the quality of a short story; and she was telling Charles Sinclair, the man, about love.

"You're right, Melanie." His voice was gentle and seductive.

Right about *what?*

An hour after their jet landed in Martinique, Charles and Melanie boarded the Windward Air nineteen-passenger Twin Otter STOL that would take them to St. Barts. Melanie gazed out the window during the fifteen-minute flight mesmerized by the sparkling blue Caribbean. As the small plane swooped through a narrow passage that miraculously appeared in the volcanic terrain and came to a sudden stop a few feet short of the white-capped sea, Melanie gasped and clutched Charles's arm. Her pale-blue eyes shimmered with fear.

Charles curled his strong, confident hand over her cool anxious one.

"Melanie, I'm sorry. I should have warned you."

Charles didn't even think about it anymore. The tourist books and travel magazines made much of the precipitous descent into St. Barts: *Not for the weak at heart!* But for Charles it was all so familiar; it was all part of the wonderful feeling of being on St. Barts.

Charles had discovered St. Barts two years after Elliott's death. Since then he returned as often as he could.

St. Barts was peace and paradise and privacy.

Charles drove the rented Mini-Moke along the narrow, winding road from Baie de St. Jean east toward Lorient. At every turn they were greeted by a breathtaking vista of turquoise water and snow white sand and lush tropical foliage and azure sky.

"Lovely," Melanie whispered into the warm, fragrant breeze that welcomed her to the tropics.

"We're staying at a villa," Charles explained when they reached the Anse de Cayes.

Melanie nodded into the wind. She hadn't known that. She had imagined a hotel.

"Have you stayed there before?" Charles seemed to know where he was going.

"Yes. It's my favorite."

It would be my favorite, too, Melanie thought when they reached the villa. It was perched on a cliff above the Anse and hidden in a bountiful bouquet of apricot and pink and violet bougainvillea. Walls of flowers provided impenetrable privacy for the pool and veranda. No one could see them, but they could see a sparkling blue forever of sea and sky.

"Oh," Melanie breathed appreciatively as she followed Charles through the beautifully decorated interior to the veranda. When she saw the view and the white sand beach below, she whispered again, *"Oh."*

"The villa has its own beach." Charles gestured to the gate in the forest-green wrought-iron fence surrounding the veranda. The gate opened to a white gravel path. "This is the only way to get there, except by boat."

"Lovely." Melanie turned to the dark, handsome stranger who had brought her to paradise.

"Come here." The seductive eyes wanted her. Melanie obeyed their command. "Did I tell you how glad I am that you're here?"

"No." Tell me. No, she thought as rushes of desire pulsed through her, *show* me.

Charles made love to her on the veranda in the fading golden rays of the tropical sun. The soft fragrant breeze caressed their naked flesh and the seagulls cooed and the ocean hummed.

Their lovemaking could have followed the

leisurely rhythm of the tropics. It could have been slow and soft and lingering.

But it wasn't; they needed each other too much.

"I was wrong about you." Melanie lay beside him on the sand in the secluded cove carved out of volcanic cliffs.

"Oh?"

"I thought"—Melanie gently kissed his lips between words—"you were so arrogant."

"But I'm not?" Charles returned her kisses.

"No." Not at all.

"Neither are you. I was wrong, too."

Charles kissed a gentle path from her lovely warm mouth to her soft, round breasts. Melanie didn't wear a bathing suit top. There was no need. No one could see her but Charles. Her perfect breasts belonged to him. All of her, every inch of her golden body, belonged to Charles. Charles wanted her and she gave him all that she could give.

Charles and Melanie spent most of their idyllic week on St. Barts in the intimate privacy of the villa. They made brief excursions to shop in the charming villages and to dine at the island's gourmet French restaurants. They saw familiar faces—wealthy, famous, celebrity faces like theirs—but acknowledged them only with silent, knowing nods. Respect for privacy; that was the rule on St. Barts. That was why the rich and famous escaped there to mourn losses, rediscover themselves, and fall in love.

"One more fabric shop." Melanie's sky-blue eyes sparkled as she tugged playfully at his hand. This would be the fourth fabric shop they had visited. Melanie didn't explain her fascination with the shops, and Charles didn't ask. They gave her pleasure, that was enough. Charles watched amiably, his brown eyes amused and loving, as she enthusiastically touched and admired the wonderful bold colors and the exotic floral prints.

"You're insatiable."

"So are you," she answered seductively.

"Only with you." I can't get enough of you.

The conversation began as a tease outside a fabric shop in Lorient, but suddenly became serious and tender. They acknowledged the moment by wrapping their arms around each other and holding tight. The hug lingered, as it always did, and they let go reluctantly after Charles gently kissed her temple and whispered softly, "One more fabric shop."

The day before they left St. Barts, Charles made a trip to the village by himself.

"You'll see," he answered the surprised blue eyes that asked, Why?

When Charles returned three hours later, he found her on the veranda, gazing at the sapphire ocean, lost in thought. Melanie spent the hours missing him and realizing that tomorrow this wonderful perfect dream would be over. *Over,* or just different?

Melanie didn't know. She knew Charles's passion an desire, but she didn't know how he felt about *her. He* never told her. Charles never spoke the words all the other men had always spoken; he never even told her she was beautiful. But Charles held her and kissed her and smiled into her eyes; and Charles made desperate, breathless love to her.

Why was their loving so desperate? Melanie wondered. It was desperate—an urgent need driven by consuming desire—for both of them. As if a deep instinct warned them that it couldn't last. What if tomorrow it was over?

When Charles found her on the veranda, Melanie's fists were clenched and her body was rigid with fear.

"Hi." Charles kissed the back of her neck and felt the tension. "Are you *cold?*"

"No," she whispered, arching her lovely neck against his lips and not turning to face him until the tears vanished. "How was your trip?"

"Successful, I think. You have to tell me." Charles handed her a square white envelope-size box. "The shop doesn't go in for silk-lined velvet, but they had what I wanted."

What Charles wanted, what he left the villa to find, was a long strand of flawless pearls. Charles's discriminating eye knew quality. He would not buy Melanie anything but the best. Charles searched patiently until he found exactly what he wanted. While the delighted jeweller processed the sale of the best strand of pearls in the Caribbean, Charles held them in his hand, admiring the rich luster and imagining them around her lovely neck. He hoped she liked them.

"Charles." Melanie had just vanquished sad, frightened tears. Now new tears—happy, joyous

ones—filled her eyes. Her hands trembled as she tried to fasten the eighteen-carat gold clasp. "Help me."

Charles helped her on with the perfect pearl necklace, and he helped her off with her clothes.

It wasn't over when they returned to Manhattan, but it was different. There were so many hours of each day when they were apart; their busy, successful careers demanded it. They spent the free moments, *all* the free moments, together. They preferred to be alone—they longed for the luxurious privacy of St. Barts—but made the necessary appearances at the required parties, galas, and *events* together.

No one knew when Charles Sinclair and Melanie Chandler fell in love, but everyone knew they *had*. It was so obvious. The New York press, who had followed Charles and his notorious affairs for years, and Charles's friends, who had watched with head-shaking amazement as he ended yet another dazzling liaison, were unanimous in proclaiming this new love to be very special indeed.

"They are *always* holding hands, for God's sake."

"They're in *love.*"

"I never knew what *happy* looked like on Charles."

"The way they look at each other!"

"Melanie seems a little subdued. Where are the famous golden cascades of joy?"

"Who needs cascades of joy when you have radiance? She's more beautiful than ever."

"Do you think he gave her that fabulous pearl necklace? She wears it all the time. So much for diamonds. . . ."

"I'll be back in a few hours." Melanie sealed the promise with a lingering kiss.

"Good," Charles whispered, touching her lips. "Give my regards to Brooke."

Melanie hadn't seen Brooke since their trip to Boston four weeks before. The moments she had with Charles were so precious; Melanie begrudged every minute they spent apart.

But she had to see Brooke.

Not that Brooke had to see *her*. . . . Brooke hadn't called; at least, there were no messages from Brooke on Melanie's newly installed—she spent every night at Charles's penthouse—answering machine. Brooke might refuse to leave a message on a machine, but Brooke *knew* where Melanie was. Everyone in Manhattan knew that Charles and Melanie were together. If Brooke wanted or needed to reach Melanie, she could.

At the end of the fourth week, Melanie called Brooke and suggested Sunday brunch at the Plaza. Melanie and Brooke often met for meals, in the diverting crush of noise and humanity, even though neither ate enough to justify the expense. They nibbled on fruit and drank pots of black coffee and the silences were filled by the bustling activity of the restaurant.

Brooke agreed to meet Melanie for brunch; but, Melanie thought, Brooke sounded reluctant. Maybe it was just Melanie's imagination—her guilt—overreacting. Besides, why should *she* feel guilty? Brooke could have called *her.*

Brooke doesn't care if she sees you or not, an uneasy voice reminded her. The "Save the Chandler Twin" campaign is your project, not Brooke's.

"How are you?" Melanie asked as soon as she and Brooke were seated in the Palm Court at the Plaza.

"Fine," Brooke answered mechanically. "How's Charles?"

Brooke didn't want to ask the question, and she *really* didn't want to hear its answer. But she couldn't help it, and she had to. Charles and Melanie had *happened,* and she had to face it. Brooke tried to desensitize herself by compulsively reading every article about them. She became a habitual watcher of *Viveca's View.* Brooke learned everything the press knew about Manhattan's hottest romance.

Now she was going to hear about it firsthand.

"Charles is fine. He says to say hello." Melanie smiled at her twin. Brooke's depthless blue eyes were dark and serious. Brooke, what's the matter?

"I didn't think you liked Charles."

Melanie drew a breath. Brooke's voice was so stern; it was as if Brooke was informing her silly little sister that one could not go from disliking someone to loving him.

"I didn't really know him."

"And now you do?"

"Yes." *No,* Brooke, I don't know Charles, but I *love* him! We're learning about each other slowly and carefully. He has secrets, I have secrets. . . . Why are you cross-examining me?

Melanie searched her twin's eyes and found the ice-cold answer: Brooke didn't approve. Brooke had *never* approved of what was important to Melanie. But how could Brooke not approve of Charles? Brooke liked and respected Charles, didn't she? Weren't Brooke and Charles—so alike in their brilliant accomplishments—*friends?*

Oh, no, Melanie's heart ached as she understood what the ocean-blue eyes were telling her. It wasn't disapproval of Charles; it was disapproval of *her.*

I've never been good enough for you, have I, Brooke? And now you believe I'm not good enough for Charles, either. . . .

Melanie believed it, too; it was her greatest fear.

"I want to show you something." Charles led her by the hand from his bedroom onto the huge terrace overlooking Manhattan. Dark, rich soil filled the previously empty red-bricked garden wells.

"Dirt." Melanie squinted in the early-morning June sun.

"Topsoil. Ready to be planted. I thought you might like to choose the flowers."

Charles sounded tentative; maybe he had guessed wrong.

"Yes!" Melanie's lips found his and explored for a long, soft moment. Finally she asked, "Do you think roses would grow here?"

"Sure. The drainage is good. We'll probably have to wrap burlap around them in unprotected. . . ."

"You really do know, don't you?"

Charles shrugged, but he did know. He loved the rose gardens at Windermere. As a little boy he had helped the gardeners.

Melanie watched a flicker of sadness darken his eyes. *Tell me what makes you so sad, Charles. I see the deep, painful secrets you try so hard to conceal. Can't you tell me? There is nothing you could tell me that would change the way I feel. . . .*

"There's a nursery in Southampton that specializes in roses," Charles said without answering her question.

"Let's go."

Charles laughed and tightened his arms around her. "OK."

"We need to swing by my place on the way back to get some shorts. Do you have a shovel and trowel—and . . ."

"Whoa. I thought we'd just choose the flowers. I was going to have someone come out next week to plant them."

"Oh."

"You *want* to plant them?" Charles was pleased. He hoped Melanie would like the idea of a flower garden, and she more than liked it.

"*Yes.*"

Six hours later Melanie sat cross-legged on the red-brick terrace surrounded by pots of roses and azaleas. She wore UCLA gym shorts and a pale-yellow blouse knotted under her naked breasts. She was sketching a design of the garden.

"I made you some iced tea," Charles said as he emerged onto the terrace. "How's it coming?"

Melanie told him an hour ago, when he suggested that he begin digging, that it would be at least an hour before she was ready.

"We bought too many Sterling Silvers."

"I seem to remember a pair of earnest blue eyes telling me with the greatest confidence that one could never have too many Sterling Silvers." Charles rested his hand gently on top of her golden head.

"Well, that *is* right. We just didn't buy enough Garden Partys."

"Ah. Let me see what you're doing." Charles felt a little resistance as he took the sketchpad from Melanie's hands.

"Just drawing a picture of how it will look," she explained quickly. "Trying to get the colors to blend."

Charles looked for an amazed moment at the sketch of the garden. It was very good. Curious, he started to flip to the beginning of the sketch-pad.

"Charles, don't."

He stopped. "Why? What is it?"

"It's just sketches of designs for clothes. Silly." Melanie reached for her sketchbook.

"Not silly. But I won't look if you don't want me to."

"Thanks," she said as he handed it back to her. She turned away from him and faced the

271

colorful pots of roses. "I guess we should start digging."

"Melanie." Charles spoke quietly. "The dress you gave Galen. She wondered if you made it. Did you?"

Melanie gave a slight nod.

"I never planned to be a model. I wanted to be a designer." Melanie spoke softly as she told Charles her secret dream. "But when I had photographs taken of me wearing my designs, it was me, not the clothes, that was marketable."

"Just because you *are* doesn't mean your designs *aren't*. The dress for Galen would have been. You must know that. You model clothes with designer labels that aren't nearly as beautiful."

Charles looked in her blue eyes and discovered that Melanie *didn't* know. He urged gently, extending his hand toward her. "Let me take a look."

Melanie sat beside him on the chaise lounge as he slowly, studying each page with great care, looked through her sketchbook. The half-finished sketch on the last page of designs was a dress made of a fabric they had seen on St. Barts.

"Melanie . . ."

"It's just a silly hobby . . . how I relax."

"They're wonderful."

Melanie shrugged.

"I mean it."

"Thank you."

"Are you going to do something with these?"

"No. Maybe next life . . ."

Charles didn't push. For some reason Melanie seemed shy and uncertain about her talent.

"You don't design clothes for yourself, or, at least, there are no sketches of blondes."

"That's true."

"I wonder why."

"I don't know." Melanie tilted her golden head thoughtfully. "I guess it's more fun to design clothes for Brooke and Galen and Fran. I close my eyes and picture them in one of my designs."

"Maybe when you close your eyes and picture yourself what you see—your happiest vision—is a pale-gray sweat suit."

"Maybe." The lovely blue eyes looked a little sad.

"Maybe," Charles whispered gently as he pulled her close to him, "you're a butterfly in search of a cocoon.'

Chapter Nineteen

New York City
June 1986

"And is it your testimony, Mr. Jones, that you were in Atlantic City and not New York on the night of October fifteenth, nineteen eighty-five?" Brooke stood near the jurors. When the witness answered her questions—looking at her because her blue eyes demanded it—he spoke to the jury as well.

"Yes."

"And is it further your testimony, Mr. Jones, that despite the accounts of four other witnesses who saw you in Manhattan—"

"*Objection.*" The defense attorney stood up. "The credibility of the witnesses who *allegedly* saw Mr. Jones—"

"Ms. Chandler?" The judge raised an eyebrow at Brooke.

"If opposing counsel would like a *voire dire* to determine the credibility of the four witnesses." Brooke looked earnestly at the judge.

"Mr. Hansen?" the judge queried.

"No, Your Honor."

"Objection overruled. You may proceed, Ms. Chandler."

Brooke cast a glance of carefully suppressed triumph at Andrew. He answered with a smile that told her, *You've got him now, Brooke.*

"Raise your chin, Melanie," Steve commanded.

"It's *raised.*" Melanie stood up straight, breaking the pose that Steve had been setting and resetting for the past half an hour. Melanie slowly moved her head through a range of motion, relaxing the taut, fatigued neck muscles.

"Christ," Steve hissed.

"I don't know why this is so difficult."

"Do you want me to tell you?"

"Yes."

"And you won't go crying to Adam?"

"I won't."

"You look terrible."

"What?"

"I'm trying to find an angle that won't reflect off the goddamned dark circles under your eyes. They glow *through* your makeup."

"I . . ."

"You've taken your whoring a little too far, Melanie. You're wearing it on your face. As if the whole world doesn't already know you spend all night every night screwing Charles Sinclair."

"You have no right . . ."

"I'm telling you the truth, Melanie. I always tell you the truth. You just don't want to hear it."

Melanie glowered at him, but she didn't move to leave.

"I'll tell you one more thing. It won't last. He'll leave you just like he's left every other woman in this town. You may think you're special, Melanie, but you're not. You're just the only one he's never had before. You could throw away your whole modelling career—you will if you don't get some rest—because of him. Don't do it, Melanie, because it won't last with Charles Sinclair. That's the truth."

"Brooke, you were terrific. What a victory." Andrew raved as he and Brooke walked from the courthouse back to the DA's office.

"Thank you. It feels good."

"It always feels good to win."

"Well, when you *know* the other guy is a criminal." Brooke smiled at Andrew. Andrew played to win. He didn't spend a lot of time dwelling on guilt or innocence. "This win feels good."

"Good enough to have dinner with me, Brooke, to celebrate your first single-handed conviction?"

"Andrew, I can't." *We* can't.

The past four months had been as if the night in March never happened. Andrew didn't mention Allison, nor did he ask Brooke out. Their relationship was as it had been before; the comfortable, professional relationship of respected colleagues.

"Just dinner, Brooke."

"No, thank you."

"Do you have someone?"

"No," Brooke answered truthfully.

"I worry about you."

I worry about you, too, Andrew. I'm sorry your life isn't happy. Brooke met his concerned thoughtful brown eyes and almost relented. Dinner would be nice, but . . .

"I'm *fine,* Andrew."

"So, that's a firm No?" Andrew teased.

"A firm, but flattered No." Brooke laughed softly and shook her head.

"Lieutenant Adrian, please," Brooke said twenty minutes later to the voice that answered the phone in Homicide.

It was a full minute before she heard Nick's voice.

"Nick Adrian."

"The author?"

In the past four months, Brooke had spoken to Nick over the phone several times about homicide cases they were preparing to prosecute, but she hadn't seen him since the night in March. *Reflec-*

tions had been returned to her in the day's official correspondence from the police department the following Monday. There had been a note: *Enjoyed the book. And dinner. And coffee. Nick.*

Yesterday's mail brought *The New Yorker,* with a short story entitled "Manhattan Beat" by Nick Adrian. It was a powerful, gripping, sensitive story. Brooke called to tell him how much she enjoyed it, but suddenly she felt awkward. She didn't know Nick. If he had wanted her to know he could have told her that night, while they were *discussing* short stories.

He chose *not* to tell me, Brooke realized as she waited for him to answer her question. Why am I doing this?

"Yes," Nick answered after a long pause.

"It's a wonderful story, Nick." There. Good-bye.

"Thanks."

Who was going to say good-bye first?

"Why didn't you tell me?"

"Let's see . . . Jason and Charles and Galen and Melanie."

"We spent a lot of time talking about short stories before their names came up. It seems like a conspicuous omission."

"The first time you call me about something other than the strictest of business is after you discover I am published in *The New Yorker.* What does *that* seem like to you, Counselor?"

"You're interrogating me."

"I think it's a pertinent question. To which you know the answer even though you may not admit it."

"What's the answer?" Brooke asked, knowing it, hoping Nick had a different answer.

"The answer is, Nick is suddenly worthwhile. Nick is more than *just* a cop. He's only *slumming* as a cop because that's the sort of thing serious writers do. You know, *living* the material. How am I doing?"

Brooke didn't answer, but her mind reeled. How much of what Nick said was true? Part of it, she realized, hating her own pretension, Part of it.

"You're a goddamned snob, Brooke," Nick whispered angrily just before hanging up the phone.

Nobody said good-bye.

"I made reservations for eight o'clock at Le Cirque. I told Jacques you might splurge and have four asparagus spears."

"A splurge would be three." Melanie smiled.

"So, shall I come by about seven?"

"I can't do Le Cirque tonight, Charles."

"Oh?"

"I need an early night. I'm getting dark circles under my eyes." *That* part of what Steve said was true; but not the rest, even though it was her greatest fear.

"Oh. All right."

"It's OK? I thought I'd try to go to bed about seven-thirty." *So if you come by at seven.*

"It's fine. I'll call you tomorrow."

No, wait, Charles. Don't be angry. I didn't mean we wouldn't be together tonight.

"OK."

"Good night, Melanie."

"Good night, Charles."

Melanie sat by the phone for twenty minutes. Charles had misunderstood. She wanted to see him. She wanted him in bed with her. Couldn't they just hold each other and fall asleep? But what if it was *she* who had misunderstood? What if Charles didn't want to be with her unless they could spend the night making love, having sex, *screwing*.

"No," she whispered. They had fallen asleep in each other's arms every night since St. Barts. Very late, *after* they had made love, yes, of course, *but* . . .

Melanie reached for the phone and dialed his penthouse. She had to talk to him. She needed to know.

The line was busy. He's calling Viveca, Melanie's fatigued mind taunted. Viveca, or any one of a hundred other women. Maybe even Brooke. *No.* He's probably just talking to Jason.

Melanie made herself wait for ten minutes before redialing. When she did there was no answer.

Charles was gone.

"This is Brooke Chandler from the DA's office. Is Lieutenant Adrian there?" Brooke placed the call—to apologize—at nine A.M. The night had been almost sleepless; he was right, and she had to tell him.

"No. He's out on a case. Can someone else help?"

"No. Would you please tell him that I called?"

★　★　★

279

Melanie had never been to Charles's office. They never tried to see each other during their busy workdays. Even now she only had an hour between photo sessions. It was barely enough time, but she had to see him.

Melanie walked along the marble corridors oblivious to the splendor of her surroundings. Some other time—please let there be other times—Charles could give her a tour of the fabulous building.

"My name is Melanie Chandler. I wondered if I could see Charles Sinclair." Melanie's words were unnecessary. The receptionist recognized her instantly and, given another instant, would have guessed what she wanted. *Everyone* knew about Charles and Melanie. "Let me see if he's free."

Two minutes later Charles appeared on the plush carpeted circular staircase at the far end of the reception area. The staircase led to the private executive offices of Charles and Jason and their editors.

"Hi."

"Come to my office."

They didn't speak again until they were inside Charles's magnificent office and the heavy door was closed and locked behind them.

"How are you? Your dark circles look better."

"Yours don't," Melanie whispered, and gently touched the blue-black shadows beneath his dark eyes. Despite her anxiety about their misunderstanding, and what it might mean, Melanie had slept; it was a testimony to how desperately she needed the sleep. But Charles looked as though he had been up all night . . .

"I guess I don't sleep well without you."

"I never wanted you to."

"No?"

"I thought I could go to bed early and you could join me." Melanie shrugged, acknowledging that it was a silly sentimental idea.

"How about if we both go to bed early? Should we try that tonight?"

Melanie answered him with a kiss that would have led to much more if she hadn't miraculously remembered her photo session. She pulled away reluctantly.

"I have to go." As Melanie turned toward the door, her gaze fell on the framed photograph on the wall. Steve must have taken it during the photo session in Central park last winter. Melanie hadn't seen it before now. It was a picture of *her* but not as Melanie Chandler, sophisticated high fashion model. Instead, it was a provocative, seductive portrait of a beguiling temptress. "Oh."

"Steve took that just after you said, 'I won't charge you for this, Charles.'"

"I didn't think you were paying attention."

"Always."

Nick returned Brooke's call at ten o'clock that night.

"You got my unlisted number."

"I thought you were calling about business. I

wasn't able to return the call until now." The message had said *from the DA's office.*

"It wasn't business. I called to apologize."

"Not necessary." Nick sounded tired and defeated. "I was putting my words in your mouth, voicing my own paranoia about the value of what I do for a living."

"Nick, what's wrong?" Brooke decided the flatness in Nick's voice had nothing to do with their conversation yesterday. Something had happened; something *important* and terribly disturbing.

"Bad, bad murder today. Last night, actually." Nick had been at the scene, in her nice secure apartment, all night and most of the day. "It will be on the eleven o'clock news."

"What?"

"A young woman—twenty-seven, beautiful, a very successful broker with a big firm on Wall Street—murdered," Nick answered heavily. The woman had been raped and then knifed to death. Nick didn't tell Brooke that. "Her name is, was, Pamela Rhodes."

"I've heard of her. She did stock market commentary on the morning news shows."

"Yes."

Brooke could feel Nick's horror. He must have seen something unspeakably terrible. It shook him, and it enraged him.

"Do you know who did it?"

"No. Probably someone she knew, or thought she knew. It happened in her apartment. There was no sign of forced entry and she was dressed up." At least she had been, before . . .

282

"You'll find him soon." Brooke wanted to encourage him. She hated the tone—the tonelessness—of his voice.

"I hope so. I hope like hell this isn't the first victim of some crazy."

"Why do you think it might be?"

"Just a hunch. It was so brutal, and not one clue. Not a print to be found. We'll get a blood type from the semen, but other than that . . ." Nick sighed. "It just seems like more than a spurned lover. A little too, uh, professional, *meaning* psychopathic."

"Oh."

"Be careful, will you, Brooke?" Nick asked suddenly, the energy returning for a moment to his voice. Then he had to go. The police pathologist who had just completed the autopsy on Pamela Rhodes walked into his office. "I'll talk to you later. Thanks for calling."

So much BLOOD—too much. It will be less MESSY next time. Next time? Of course! There will be a bloody ETERNITY of next times until SHE understands. She CANNOT treat me this way!!! When she does, someone has to PAY. . . .

He looked at the words he had scribbled into his journal two nights before—only hours after he had brutally murdered Pamela Rhodes—and he smiled at the exciting memory.

283

Chapter Twenty

The July Fourth sun shone brightly on the Liberty Weekend celebration in New York Harbor. The unveiling of the revitalized Statue of Liberty the night before had been spectacular. Today's festivities—the parade of boats and the tall ships—would climax in a phenomenal fireworks display.

"Jason, this is such a thrill!" Brooke exclaimed as she boarded the one-hundred-twenty-foot yacht at the New York Yacht Club. "Thank you for including me."

"I'm glad you could come." Jason smiled graciously.

Brooke hadn't seen Jason for months. He looks a little sad, Brooke thought. His golden, sunny smile had lost some of its shine. Impulsively Brooke gave Jason a brief hug.

"Make yourself at home, Brooke. I'd show you around, but I have to stay here until we cast off."

Brooke wandered among the crowd on the yacht, smiling in recognition at face after famous face. It was after she smiled a familiar hello to the handsome if controversial network news anchorman—and he smiled in return—that Brooke realized with embarrassed horror she was behaving as if she knew them. She did know who they were. She watched them perform on television and film and stage, she listened to their music, and she admired the fabulous clothes they designed. They were recognizable, but she wasn't.

Still, they returned her smiles.

Because I must be *someone*, Brooke realized. I wouldn't be on this yacht on this special day with these special people if I weren't. They just can't place me.

"Brooke!"

"Hello, Adam." A truly familiar face.

"This is kind of exciting, isn't it?"

"A perfect day."

"Let me introduce you to some people," Adam offered.

Brooke and Adam retraced her steps. He introduced her to some of the faces with whom she had already exchanged smiles. Adam introduced her as Brooke Chandler; sometimes he added that she worked in the DA's office. Adam never mentioned that she was Melanie Chandler's *twin* sister.

Brooke hadn't seen or spoken to Melanie since their brunch at the Plaza. She followed Charles and Melanie's golden love affair in the press and wondered when it would end. What if it never did? What if, as the papers and magazines and television proclaimed, their joyous, blissful love was forever?

When Jason called a week ago to invite Brooke to join the Independence Day cruise, she accepted because she needed to see Charles and Melanie together. Brooke needed to find out for herself.

★   ★   ★

Charles loves her, Brooke decided as twilight fell over Manhattan. Brooke had never imagined such softness or such happiness in the dark-brown eyes. Charles loved Melanie; it was obvious. And there was something new—something serene—about Melanie.

"Anything on the Pamela Rhodes murder, Brooke?" the anchorman asked after dinner. Charles, Melanie, Adam, Jason, the anchorman, and Brooke sat on the aft deck, sipping after-dinner drinks in the twilight, waiting for darkness and the spectacular fireworks display to begin. He added pleasantly, "Off the record."

The question surprised Brooke. Then she remembered that Adam had mentioned the DA's office when he introduced them.

"On or off," Brooke replied. "It doesn't matter. I don't know anything."

Except the way Nick Adrian sounded, and his *off-the-record* fear that it was just the beginning.

"You knew her, didn't you, Charles?" Adam asked.

"One of Charles's many—" Jason began, but he saw Melanie's pale-blue eyes widen and stopped mid-sentence.

Charles reacted as if he'd been struck.

Jason, what is wrong? Charles wondered as he recoiled from the bitterness in his brother's voice. There had been an edge to Jason's polite reserve for months. Charles stared at his twin—what is it, Jason?—for a long bewildered moment. Then he answered heavily, "I knew Pamela."

An awkward silence ensued as they all frantically searched their minds for new, safe topics.

"That Jones conviction, Brooke," the anchorman finally murmured. "Really impressive."

"Oh, well . . ." He *does* know who I am, Brooke realized with amazement.

"Andrew Parker had better watch out."

"Oh, no. Andrew's the best. He's taught me everything I know."

"He may have taught you too much."

The last words were lost in the burst of light and color in the balmy July night as a galaxy of dazzling fireworks exploded overhead. Drawn by the magnificent spectacle appearing over the Manhattan skyline, they moved to the shiny brass railing on the leeward side of the yacht.

Only Charles and Melanie lingered behind.

"Melanie?" Charles held her hands in his and spoke softly.

"Why didn't you tell me that you knew Pamela Rhodes?" The light of the sky rockets danced off her pale-blue eyes.

"I knew her before I met you."

"But . . ."

"Darling, it doesn't have anything to do with us."

"Still . . ."

Charles stopped Melanie's lips with his own, and they convinced her, softly and tenderly, not to worry. As they kissed, their passionate faces were illuminated by brilliant rainbows of color in the summer sky. Jason and Brooke witnessed their twins' kiss. . . .

A rush of tingling, excited feelings flooded Brooke, as if Charles were kissing *her*. Brooke extinguished the surprising, wonderful sensations quickly, angry at her own reaction. Face it, Brooke.

Did he kiss Galen like that? Jason wondered with a mixture of sadness and rage. Did Charles seduce Galen as he is seducing Melanie? Of course he did. That was Charles's specialty; he lured his victims into a warm, secure web of love. Then, once trapped, he abandoned them. Jason's knowledge was firsthand. Charles had left him, without warning or explanation or apology, when they were twelve; and he did it again when they were eighteen.

Melanie steadfastly refused to think about her trip to Europe. It wasn't a thrilling adventure any longer. It meant being away from Charles. Each day Melanie's confidence in herself and their love grew stronger; but it was still delicate and fragile and precious. There were secrets they hadn't shared, and their lovemaking still had the desperate urgency of lovers fated to share stolen moments of passion, not a forever-and-always love.

Ten days before she was scheduled to leave, Adam gave her a final copy of her itinerary. There was one weekend, maybe two, that she could fly back to New York to see Charles. Maybe he would join her, maybe he could find a week or two. . . .

Melanie lay awake, safe in his arms, her mind racing, trying to visualize a way to give them a week. She would do photo sessions night and day. She could do that; somehow there wouldn't be dark circles. It seemed, Melanie thought, recalling the schedule that was neatly folded in her purse in Charles's living room, that there was one day with only a two-hour session planned in Rome at Gucci . . .

Melanie gently lifted the arms that held her and slid out of bed. Charles moved, but he didn't waken. When Melanie returned a half hour later—it *was* possible, she would talk to Adam in the morning—Charles was on the opposite side of the bed. Melanie crawled in carefully.

He felt so far away. Maybe he would wake up, find that she was not in his arms, and pull her close, the way they were supposed to be.

Tell me Father, please. I need to understand.
Elliott laughed a mean laugh.
You don't deserve an explanation.
Please.
The sailboat lurched in the heavy sea. Charles's heart ached with the familiar emptiness.
You don't deserve my love, Elliott hissed. Do you want to know why?
Yes, please. And I want you to love me, Charles added quietly.
I'll never love you. No one ever will. You're evil, Charles.
No.
Yes.
Elliott's dark eyes glistened with hatred. There was a sudden deafening crash followed by a frenetic swirl into darkness . . .
After it was over, Elliott lay on the deck. Bright-red blood gushed from his head and his dark eyes no

longer glistened. Instead, his eyes clouded and his lips turned into a mean smile just before he died.

No, Charles pleaded.

"No!" Charles sat upright in bed. His naked chest heaved, and he held his head with his hands.

"Charles?" Melanie touched his damp, cold back.

But Charles didn't seem to hear her or feel her touch. Wordlessly, without looking at her, he left the bed and the bedroom. After a stunned moment Melanie followed.

Charles was on the terrace in the rose garden they loved so much. His hands were clenched tight at his sides. His handsome face was a tormented shadow in the pale moonlight.

"Charles."

He looked at her slowly and without recognition. Melanie gasped when she saw the pain in his dark eyes. She put her arms around him.

"Charles, tell me," she whispered. It was something more than a nightmare; it didn't go away when he awakened. It was what had been there all along, making their love so desperate and so fragile. Tell me, *please.*

Charles pulled away violently. Anger and confusion merged with the pain.

"I need to be alone, Melanie."

"Charles . . ."

He turned away from her "I mean it."

Melanie retreated to the bedroom. She paced in the darkness, taunted by her own fears.

You don't know him, Melanie. And he doesn't want you to know him. He doesn't care enough to share himself with you. You're no different from all the others. This is how it ends with Charles Sinclair.

After an hour Melanie got dressed. She was stopped by his voice as she walked through the living room. Sometime in the past hour he had come in from the rose-scented air.

"Where are you going?"

"I guess I need to be alone, too, Charles."

Melanie looked toward him, but his dark eyes were hidden in shadows.

Stop me, Charles. Don't let this happen.

But Charles didn't stop her, and she left.

"I don't know if you realize this, *dear,* but we're leaving in five days for the most important modelling dates of your career."

"I know that." Five days. It had been five days since she left Charles's penthouse in the middle of the night. In five more days she would leave for Europe.

"So do you plan to look like death warmed over for Yves and Christian and Oscar?"

"I look fine."

"You look like shit," Steve corrected swiftly. Then a mean smile curled on his face. "Oh, God, it *happened* didn't it? He dumped you."

"None of your business."

"This is a new record, Melanie. What was it, less than three months? Even vacuous Viveca kept his attention for longer than that."

Melanie trembled with rage as Steve continued his cruel harangue.

"Are you frigid, Melanie? I've always . . ."

"That's *it,* Steve. I warned you."

Melanie rushed out of the studio and up the flight of stairs to Adam's office.

"Is he in?" Melanie demanded of Adam's secretary. Tears threatened. Stay angry, she told herself.

"Yes. But . . ."

Adam's office door was ajar. Melanie walked in talking.

"I don't have to take it, Adam. If you let him treat me that way anymore I'll leave." Melanie stopped abruptly. Adam wasn't alone.

Charles. What was he doing here?

Business, of course; business as usual. Charles and Adam were seated at a table studying photographs. They both stood up and both moved toward her when she entered.

"Melanie, what's wrong?" Adam demanded, worried.

At that moment Steve burst in, panting, his eyes wild with rage.

Melanie glowered at Steve, then turned back to Adam.

"Him or me, Adam, you choose."

Don't look at Charles, Melanie's mind warned. But she couldn't help it. Her eyes flooded with hot tears. The exhaustion of five sleepless nights and the nervous energy of five days without food converged in a sudden ice-cold shiver. Miraculously, Melanie willed her trembling body to move out of Adam's office and away from *him.*

"Bitch," Steve hissed under his breath. Steve's anger turned to fear as he saw Charles moving toward him.

But Charles rushed past him to follow Melanie.

He found her in an alcove, pressed against a wall, trembling. Charles put his arms around her and held her tight.

"Melanie," Charles whispered softly, his lips lightly brushing her golden hair. "Darling."

Melanie felt his wonderful warmth and strength. Hold me, Charles, don't ever let me go.

He already *has* let you go, a voice reminded her. With great effort Melanie controlled her trembling and pulled free.

"Tell me about Steve. What did he do to you?"

"Nothing." Don't look at me as if you care, Charles. "I'm a little raw, that's all."

"I don't want him going to Europe with you. I'm going to speak to Adam."

"No, Charles, really. It's nothing."

They stood, close, but not touching, for several silent moments. When Melanie spoke, it was about *them*; what happened with Steve was so trivial by comparison.

"I'm sorry, Charles." Melanie forced a smile, but her lips quivered.

"I'm sorry, Melanie. I . . ."

"No." She held up a thin trembling hand. "I shouldn't have pushed you. There's no reason you should tell me."

"You were trying to help." Charles gently moved a strand of tear soaked gold away from her sky-blue eyes. His touch made the tears begin anew.

"Yes, but—" Melanie shook her head helplessly. The tears and emotional exhaustion had won again.

I *would* tell you, darling Melanie, if only I knew. But I don't know, and it has hurt you terribly. I have to let you go. Somehow I will find a way to live my life without you. I have to, but not yet. I can't leave you like this.

Charles cupped her damp cheeks in his hands and smiled.

"You owe me a dinner at Le Cirque. I'll pick you up at seven-thirty."

After Charles left, Melanie returned to Adam's office. Adam stood by the window and Steve sat in dark brooding silence by the door

"I apologize." Melanie addressed her apology to Adam, not Steve.

Adam looked surprised. Melanie wasn't temperamental. It seemed unlikely that the fireworks with Steve had been *her* fault. But the beautiful blue eyes were accepting the blame, or, at least, the responsibility.

Melanie did accept responsibility for what happened. She had let her raw, fragile emotions affect her work; it wasn't professional.

"All right." Adam smiled at her. Then he looked sternly at Steve. Steve had provoked Melanie; there was no other explanation. Adam issued the warning to Steve, "If anything like this happens again, I am going to demand the facts."

Melanie and Charles didn't dine at Le Cirque that night. They spent the evening—and the night and the next day and every minute until

Melanie left for Paris—in Charles's penthouse, loving each other, silently and passionately saying good-bye.

"Siena was founded by Remus. It may even have been his choice for their great city."

"But Romulus preferred Rome, and killed Remus because of it."

"You should go to Siena anyway." Charles smiled and held her closer. "The buildings are made of white-and-black marble, and the view of the countryside from the *campanile* is magnificent. The Paolo, the famous horse race through the town, is held in August."

Charles didn't talk to Melanie about the relationship they both knew was ending. Instead, he told her, as he held her in his arms on their rose-fragrant terrace in Manhattan, about his favorite places in Europe.

He's sharing them with me now, because he won't be with me. Why, Charles? Melanie's heart cried in silent anguish. *I love you so much. And if you don't love me, why are your eyes so sad?*

"You'll love the roses in the Borghese Gardens in Rome. And there's a small hunting lodge with statues by Bellini in the courtyard. It's a little hard to find, I just stumbled onto it as I was wandering—"

"Why don't you show it to me?" Melanie regretted her question the moment she asked it. The sudden pain in his dark eyes matched the depthless ache in her heart. *I'm sorry, Charles, I just don't understand.*

"Jason is going to the America's Cup trials in

Australia. He'll be away from August to November. . . ." Charles couldn't finish the lie. They both knew he *could* get away—they had all planned to spend two months in Kenya filming "Sapphire," hadn't they?—he just wasn't going to.

Charles took Melanie to the airport. They held hands in a distant corner of the Air France first-class lounge until her flight had been called for the final time.

"Au revoir Charles." Until we meet again.

"Good-bye, darling." It's over.

Melanie sat on a park bench in the Tuileries under the hot late-August sun. The Champs-Elysées swarmed with tourists, but the Parisians had vanished, as Charles said they would, escaping to the Riviera for the final month of summer.

Charles. In three and a half weeks, the pain hadn't diminished and the hope hadn't died. It wasn't really good-bye; it was just sadness about the two-month separation. I'll hear from him. There will be a message waiting for me at the Bristol.

But there were no messages at the hotel from Charles.

Melanie looked at the postcards that lay beside her on the bench and thoughtfully fingered the magnificent pearl necklace Charles had given her.

She sighed softly, picked up a postcard, and wrote,

Dear Charles,
    *Greetings from the Jeu de Paume and apolo-
gies to your Monet for once placing it at the
Louvre instead of this magnificent spot!*

Stupid, Melanie thought. She ripped the postcard in half and tried again.

Dearest Charles,
    I love you so much.

No, she couldn't tell him that, even though it
was true. Charles had never told her he loved
her. Of course he hadn't! Because he *didn't.*
    Melanie wasted three more postcards of
Impressionist paintings before writing,

Charles,
    I miss you.
                                    Melanie

Melanie carried the postcard with her for a
week before addressing it, applying the correct
postage—now Italian because they were in
Rome—and mailing it.

Adam watched Melanie's torment with helpless concern. He resisted asking her—it wasn't
his business anyway—because she was trying so
hard not to let it show. Adam noticed the change,
because he had known her before. He knew there
used to be a natural golden joy, a happiness that
glowed from a radiant soul. The gazelle-like

spring had vanished from her stride, and her flawless smile came with effort.

Adam noticed, because he had known the unspoiled, confident, dazzling California surfer girl. But the couturiers of Paris and Rome, who didn't know the old Melanie, marvelled at the new one. They gasped in breath-held admiration at the proud, bewitching, haunted eyes, the austere aristocratic face, and the graceful elegance. They proclaimed her—the Americans were right!—the most beautiful model in the world.

In her suffering, Melanie Chandler had become even more beautiful.

Adam finally decided to speak with her at the beginning of the fifth week. If she didn't want to talk, fine. He just wanted her to know he was available, and he cared.

"Do you have the energy to walk back to the hotel?" Adam asked.

"Sure." Melanie had spent the afternoon being photographed modelling the exquisite, creative jewels of Bulgari. The mental strain of holding pose after pose matched the physical rigors of a fast-paced, high-pressure fashion show; both were exhausting, but after a photo session a brisk walk felt good.

"Are you enjoying Rome?" Adam asked after they had travelled for a block and a half along via Condotti.

"Oh, yes. The roses in the Borghese Gardens—" Melanie began, then stopped. She had only seen Charles's favorite places; she hadn't visited the Colosseum or the Forum or the Pantheon or the catacombs. "Yes."

"Good." Adam waited until they had successfully crossed the chaos of the via Veneto before continuing carefully, "I sort of expected Charles would join you over here."

Melanie smiled a wistful smile.

"It's over, Adam." Melanie needed to speak the words aloud. It made them seem more real, and they were real. Her love affair—her *affair*—with Charles Sinclair was really over.

"I'm sorry."

"You know Charles—he doesn't have long-lasting relationships."

Adam and Melanie walked in silence toward the Eden Hotel. As they approached, Adam said, "I've known Charles for many years, Melanie. What he had with you . . . did you end it?"

"*No.*"

"Then I don't understand."

"Charles just didn't want me anymore," Melanie whispered softly. He never wanted *me.* He only wanted my beautiful body, and once he owned it he quickly became bored.

Adam looked in her lovely sad eyes and thought, How could he not want you? How could anyone not want you?

Adam and Melanie didn't talk about Charles again, but Adam became her friend. Slowly and patiently he tried to resurrect the joy he knew lay buried beneath the unhappiness.

"Adam!"

"What?"

"You're trying to make me laugh!"

Adam had been teasing her as they strolled through the yacht basin in Monte Carlo. He had finally resorted to pretending he was going to push her into the sparkling blue Mediterranean.

"Is that so bad?"

"*Why?*"

"Because I love the way you laugh."

Melanie didn't laugh then. Her blue eyes became soft and thoughtful and she whispered, "Thank you."

Melanie laughed later, and it was a little golden and almost joyous, at the antics of the octopus in Jacques Cousteau's Oceanographic Museum. Adam wanted to acknowledge her laugh with a kiss, but he resisted, settling for gently draping his arm around her as they walked back to the splendid Hermitage Hotel.

"Off with the old and on with the new, eh, Melanie?"

"What?"

Steve gestured for her to lift her chin a little higher before answering. They had driven to Cap d'Antibes for a photo session at the Hotel du Cap. "Charles for Adam."

"You're wrong."

"I'm never wrong," Steve snarled. "Which one is the better lover, Melanie? Or do you ever let anyone actually touch your perfect body? Maybe that's why Charles finished with you so quickly."

"Stop it," Melanie warned.

"You prefer to touch yourself, is that it? Or,

I've got it, you and Fran have always seemed close—"

"That's it," Melanie spoke calmly.

"That's it? You and Fran?"

"No, that's *it*. I warned you."

Melanie took a taxi from Cap d'Antibes back to Monte Carlo. Adam was working in his suite when she arrived.

"That was in *October*? Why didn't you tell me then?"

"I thought I could handle it. I *did* handle it. It was all right—not pleasant, but all right—until about three months ago."

"OK." Adam frowned briefly then smiled. "You're having dinner with me—that is, watching *me* eat—at seven."

"I am?"

"Yes. We have reservations at Gabriella's."

Four hours later, as Adam and Melanie dined at the most romantic restaurant in the principality of Monaco, Steve Barnes drove at breakneck speed toward the airport at Nice. Steve was returning to New York; Adam had just fired him.

"It seems too extreme," Melanie murmured.

"Not extreme enough," Adam corrected swiftly. "There's no excuse for what Steve did."

"Maybe it's me." Melanie frowned.

"You weren't the only one. I made some calls before I met with Steve. He's been doing this kind of thing for years."

"Fran did say he did it to her."

"Why in God's name didn't anyone tell me?"

301

"Afraid, I guess." Melanie tilted her golden head.

"Hey"—Adam reached between the pale-pink candles and touched her flushed cheeks—"never be afraid to tell me anything, OK?"

Melanie's eyes answered with a sparkling, happy flash of blue: "Never?"

"Never."

Melanie laughed softly and cupped his hand in both of hers.

"You're a kind man, Adam Drake."

Charles stood just inside the door. The concierge at the Hermitage told him that mademoiselle and monsieur were dining at Gabriella's. Charles could have waited until she returned, but . . .

He was desperate to see her. He made the trip on impulse, urged by his aching desire and loneliness; he missed her so much! Maybe, if he told her about himself, as much as he *knew*, and she was willing to take the risk, they could try.

Charles was desperate to see Melanie, and in his desperation he had created a fantasy. As he watched her, laughing and happy as she flirted with Adam, the dream dissolved into bitter reality.

You can't guarantee her happiness, a voice deep within reminded him. There is something terribly wrong with you. Let her *go*. You have no right.

Charles turned to leave, but Adam's voice stopped him.

"Charles!"

"Charles, " Melanie breathed. Without looking

at Adam, Melanie left the table and quickly wove through the tables to Charles.

"Hi." I got your postcard. I miss you, too. I love you. "I was in the neighborhood. I just . . . my plane leaves in two hours."

A hush had fallen over the restaurant; interested eyes watched the celebrated couple and ears strained to hear.

"Let's get out of here."

Gabriella's was perched on a steep cliff. Narrow paths wound through terraced gardens. Moments after leaving the restaurant, Charles and Melanie disappeared into the dense green maze.

"Tell me why you came." Melanie spoke quietly when they stopped finally safely out of sight. "You weren't just in the neighborhood."

"No. I came to see you." *To tell you about a wonderful fantasy I had.* Charles sighed. "I came to explain why it—we—will never work."

"Why?" *No, don't tell me, Charles. I don't want to hear it.*

"I'm no good for you, Melanie. Seeing you with Adam—"

"There's nothing between me and Adam! Charles, you can't believe there is."

"No," Charles answered truthfully. "But Adam, or someone like Adam, can give you the happiness you deserve."

"And you can't?"

"I haven't, have I?"

"Yes."

"No. I've hurt you. I didn't mean to, but I did.

It's me, Melanie. I have deep flaws . . ." And you are flawless.

"I can't believe it!" Melanie's eyes flashed with anger "That's *my* line, 'You'll be better off without me.' Can't you do better than that?"

"No, it's the truth." Charles hated the anger and pain in her eyes; he hated himself for causing it.

"Why did you really come, Charles? Just to twist the knife?"

"Melanie."

"So, *twist* it. Tell me the truth. 'You're not good enough for me, Melanie. I'm *bored* with you, Melanie.' " Her eyes filled with hot tears and she had to get away from him.

"No," he whispered as she disappeared into the green maze.

Charles started to follow her, but he stopped. Would it help her? She didn't believe the truth, and she *couldn't* believe what she said about herself. She was *too* good for him; he could spend forever with her and never feel a second of boredom. She knew that, didn't she?

Of course she did. The angry words—full of contempt for his foolishness—made it easier for her to hate him, easier for her to forget him, easier for her to get on with her life.

Charles didn't follow Melanie. There was nothing more to say.

Chapter Twenty-one

"Fireworks in Monte Carlo! Good evening, I'm Viveca Sanders and this is *Viveca's View.*" The camera zoomed in to Viveca's face. "Yesterday, a blow-up between top model Melanie Chandler and celebrated fashion photographer Steve Barnes led to the photographer's precipitous departure from the Cote d'Azur. Only hours after severing her successful business relationship with Mr. Barnes, Ms. Chandler ended the romance that has captivated Manhattan since May."

A photograph of the yacht-cluttered harbor in Monte Carlo appeared on the television screen.

"Last evening," Viveca continued, "Charles Sinclair arrived in Monte Carlo only to discover super-model Melanie Chandler enjoying an intimate dinner with model-mogul Adam Drake. Melanie and Charles vanished for an out-of-view confrontation following which Charles promptly left Monte Carlo."

Viveca's face reappeared on the screen. Her eyes sparkled and her full lips turned into a slight smile.

"Both men returned to New York today. However, neither Charles Sinclair nor Steve Barnes is talking. Meanwhile, on the French Riviera, a new photographer is marvelling at the opportunity to photograph the world's premier model. And perhaps tonight Adam and Melanie's romantic repast will not be interrupted . . ."

"Goddamned bitch," Steve hissed at the television as the camera faded from Viveca's smug face to a commercial.

Across Manhattan, Charles swore at the same face, angrily turned off the television, and stormed out of his penthouse.

Oh, Melanie, Brooke thought. How could you do that to Charles? He cared so much. . . .

The phone rang. It was Andrew, calling to discuss the most effective order of witnesses in the State versus Fortner trial.

"Allison is ill again, Brooke," Andrew said softly after he and Brooke had plotted their legal strategy.

"Andrew, I'm sorry."

"Brooke, if I could just see you. I could use a friend."

Brooke smiled as she thought about her handsome, persuasive friend.

"You're a married man with political aspirations. Even a hint of scandal could ruin your future."

"Let me worry about that. Besides, Brooke, the marriage is no good. As soon as Allison is well enough, I am going to end it."

Brooke knew it was Andrew's frustration talking, not his heart. Andrew would never leave Allison. Maybe Andrew didn't hear the softness in his voice whenever he spoke Allison's name, but Brooke did.

Brooke wondered if Andrew would even be interested in her if he were free. Now she was forbidden fruit and a challenge. The Deputy DA loved challenges and risks, and he loved to win. We're not Edmund Rochester and Jane Eyre, Brooke mused. Ours isn't a passionate, desperate love foiled by a mad wife.

"I have some depositions to read, Andrew, especially now that we've changed the order of witnesses."

"Brooke . . ."

"I can't," Brooke said apologetically. She wasn't rejecting him, she was rejecting the situation. She hoped he knew and understood.

"All right." Andrew laughed softly, easily. "I'll see you in court."

"Yes." Good, he *did* know. Brooke added quietly, "Goodnight, Andrew."

Brooke heard the sirens in the distance. It was almost midnight. Distant sirens and midnight and the too hot humid September weather went together.

But now these sirens were close. Brooke looked out the window and saw NYPD squad cars, two ambulances, and a medic unit arriving at her apartment building. She watched as uniformed men rushed inside.

Brooke quickly changed out of her robe into jeans, a light cotton blouse, and tennis shoes. The hallway outside her apartment was cluttered with other tenants; some rushed to the scene, and others walked slowly, not wanting to go, but unable to resist.

By the time Brooke reached the apartment, two floors below, she had heard one word—whis-

307

pered, gasped, and shrieked—over and over: *Murder.*

The door to the apartment was ajar, but the view inside was completely obstructed by police officers. Brooke knew the woman who lived there. Belinda Cousins was only a few years older than Brooke. She owned and ran a well-known Madison Avenue advertising agency. Belinda and Brooke did their laundry at the same time— eleven o'clock on Friday night. Where were the good men? they laughingly asked each other. They talked about how it was safer to live here, in an inexpensive, low security apartment building, than in a glamorous penthouse on Fifth Avenue. Not that Brooke had a choice, but Belinda did.

Brooke approached one of the officers.

"I'm Brooke Chandler from the district attorney's office." Brooke smiled, remembering her faded jeans and tousled hair, and explained, "I live here. May I go in?"

"If you want to, ma'am, Ms. Chandler." The officer stepped aside.

"Don't let her in!"

"Nick," Brooke whispered. She recognized his voice and saw him, his back, hunched over something.

Instinctively, Brooke walked toward him.

"Get out of here, Brooke," Nick hissed over his shoulder. He didn't turn to face her.

"Nick, I—" Brooke gasped.

Nick's warning came too late. Brooke was already in the middle of the blood-splattered room. And even though Nick tried to protect her from seeing what he saw, using his body to block her view of the mutilated body of her *friend,* Brooke saw enough.

"Oh, my God," Brooke breathed, reflexively covering her face with her hands.

Nick couldn't go to her. He couldn't let her see the face, what had been the face. Nick couldn't even turn around; he could only listen to Brooke's horror behind him.

"Nick!"

"Go back to your apartment, Brooke," Nick whispered hoarsely. "Please."

"I know her, Nick. You can help her, can't you?"

"Jesus Christ, would someone please get her out of here?" Nick yelled angrily over his shoulder.

It was three hours before Nick could leave the murder scene. He had to see it all and think about it all while it was fresh. Nick had to search for clues amidst the carnage. And he had to deal with his own reaction before seeing Brooke.

Nick saw the slit of light under Brooke's door. Of course she wouldn't be able to sleep. Who could? Nick wondered if she was expecting him. . . .

"Brooke," he called softly without knocking.

"Nick?"

"Yes."

Brooke opened the door hesitantly. She was scared. As soon as she saw him, she opened it wide.

"Nick," she whispered. Tears filled her dark-blue eyes.

Nick felt almost as helpless now, two feet away from her, as he felt three hours ago when he couldn't move because he wouldn't let her see the rest of Belinda Cousins' body. Then Nick extended his arms, and Brooke fell against him gratefully. As he held her tight, the helpless feeling vanished. Brooke curled against him, resting her head in the curve of his neck, and cried. Nick stroked her fine chestnut hair, comforting her, wishing he could erase the gruesome image from her brain.

When Brooke finally pulled free, Nick missed her warmth and softness immediately. He needed comforting, too. She had given it to him without even knowing it.

"It was him, wasn't it? The psychopath you were afraid was out there."

"I think so," Nick said. He was sure of it. "What makes you ask?"

Brooke hesitated.

"The way you sounded when Pamela Rhodes was killed. It was as if you had seen something unspeakably horrible. Like this."

"It was the same," Nick said. Come back to my arms, Brooke. Let me hold you.

"I made some coffee."

"It's three in the morning. Aren't you going to work pretty soon? Like in four or five hours?"

"I made enough coffee to last for four or five hours. I made enough for both of us," Brooke answered quietly.

She didn't want to be alone.

Brooke and Nick talked until just past dawn and it was time to get ready to face the day.

After Nick got her to promise that she would have a peephole installed in the door—he expected the apartment manager was already working on it—and a dead bolt lock, they didn't talk about the murder or crime or the law or their jobs. Instead they talked about his writing, about the short story that was published and the new one he had started, and books and plays and movies and songs. And, in little bits, they talked about their lives.

Just before the autumn sun cast a yellow hue over Manhattan, as tears spilled, and she was too tired to care, and she needed to say it out loud to someone, and they were bonded forever by the sight of the dead woman, Brooke told Nick how angry she was at her vain, self-centered, insensitive twin for hurting Charles Sinclair.

You wouldn't care so much about Melanie ending a love affair, Brooke, Nick thought, *if you didn't care so very much about her lover.*

There was less BLOOD this time. I'm getting better—practice makes PERFECT. This one pleaded so frantically!!! I patiently explained to her that it wasn't my FAULT. I had no choice! Another WOMAN had signed her DEATH warrant. I don't think she believed me. At least, this time, there was less BLOOD.

He finished writing and closed the blue leather journal. He carefully washed the bloodstained knife in the sink, dried the shiny blade on a soft cloth, removed the whetstone from his desk drawer, and began to sharpen the lethal weapon for the next time.

There *would* be a next time, he thought with a smile. Unless something happened to stop him—it was up to *her*—he would kill again in precisely one month.

Melanie returned from Europe on October first. She waited until the seventeenth, two weeks before their birthday, to call Brooke. Melanie didn't know if she and Brooke could try again. The progress they had made, the fragile beginnings of friendship, had been shattered in one stroke by Melanie's relationship with Charles. Brooke's disapproval, Brooke's obvious disdain for Melanie's foolishness, made it impossible for them to be together. Except for Liberty Weekend, when they kept a cool, polite distance, Brooke and Melanie hadn't seen each other since the disastrous brunch at the Plaza.

Now Melanie's relationship with Charles had ended, as Brooke knew it would. Brooke was right. Brooke was always right. Melanie didn't know if she and Brooke could begin again, but if Brooke was willing . . .

Why wouldn't Brooke be willing, Melanie wondered as she dialed the phone. After all, Brooke had lost nothing. It was she, Melanie, who had lost everything, including her pride.

"Hello, Brooke. It's . . ."

"Melanie." Brooke asked dutifully, "How was Europe?"

"Fine." Awful. "How is your work?"

"Fine. Busy."

"Are you involved in the Manhattan Ripper investigation?"

312

"The what?"

"The man who killed Pamela Rhodes," Melanie began. Pamela Rhodes was one of Charles's women; like her, a name on Charles Sinclair's long list. "Last night, he murdered Ryan Gentry, the actress. Apparently he killed someone else in September. I'm surprised—"

"Last night? Oh, no," Brooke murmured. She hadn't heard. She had been in the archives of the law library at Columbia all day and hadn't even watched the evening news. "Who is calling him the Manhattan Ripper?"

Brooke knew it wasn't Nick. In fact, it probably infuriated him.

"I don't know. The news media, I guess."

"Oh." Brooke's mind's eye recalled the horrible image of Belinda Cousins. A psychopath was brutally murdering Manhattan's beautiful, successful young women. And he chose as his targets women like Melanie, her *sister*, her *twin*. Brooke felt a sudden rush of emotion. If anything ever happened to Melanie . . .

"I wondered if you'd like to come here for our birthday," Melanie suggested tentatively.

"Yes, Melanie. I'd like to very much."

"Brooke, It's Nick."

"I just heard. I'm sorry."

"I'd like to talk to you about the case. I need to bounce my ideas off someone." Nick's tone was matter-of-fact and businesslike. This *was* their business. The tone softened as he added, "You."

"OK," Brooke agreed uneasily.

313

"Brooke, I'm not going to show you pictures, for God's sake." The softness was suddenly gone. He was so tired—too tired—and his emotions were raw; but he was taking his fury out on her of all people. "Sorry. Maybe this wasn't such a good idea."

"Here's what I was just about to make for dinner—cheese and crackers. There's plenty for both of us."

"Sounds good."

"OK, so?"

"Thirty minutes. Thank you, Brooke."

Nick arrived thirty-five minutes later. He had stopped, it took five minutes, to buy a bottle of champagne.

"I like the peephole and the locks." Nick hadn't been at her apartment, and hadn't seen her, since the last murder.

"You look really tired." The dark circles and cloudy gray eyes told a tale of many sleepless nights.

Brooke knew Nick had been busy. In the past month he had made a few brief calls to her at work. He wanted to see if she was all right. Was she still sleeping with the lights on? Brooke told him, Yes, she was sleeping with the lights on, but she *was* sleeping.

Which was more than she could say for him.

"The unusually hot, humid summer left its share of unsolved murders," Nick explained with a shrug. Brooke's thoughtful dark-blue eyes continued to stare. Nick smiled. "Go ahead, say it, You look terrible, Nick."

Brooke frowned slightly. That wasn't what she

314

had been thinking. She had been thinking, You are so handsome, Nick. It was what everyone said about him; gorgeous, sexy, seductive Nick Adrian, the lieutenant with the bedroom eyes. Brooke had never thought about it before. After all, counting tonight, she had only seen him four times.

"You look hungry, Nick."

They ate cheese and crackers and drank champagne and talked about the case.

"Are they really calling him that?" Nick's annoyance at the Manhattan Ripper label was obvious.

"Yes." Before Nick arrived Brooke had watched the news. Every station used it. Tomorrow "Manhattan Ripper" would be a newspaper headline.

"What *is* there about glorifying criminals? There is no glory in what this man does. He is evil, unbelievably evil." Nick felt his rage surfacing.

"Like when they talk about terrorists *master minding* a hijacking or a bombing," Brooke said quietly.

"That drives me crazy, too." Nick smiled and the rage retreated.

"Ryan Gentry," Brooke spoke the name of the murdered woman quietly. "I read a review about her in last Sunday's *Times*."

Nick nodded. "Broadway's most enchanting actress."

"They've all been so special, haven't they? Young and talented and successful."

"Yes. Just like—"

"My sister."

"Just like *you*. New York's newest and youngest assistant district attorney."

Brooke smiled. "I hadn't even thought about *me*. I'm not like those women."

"Yes you are." Nick's gray eyes were concerned and serious. "You have to be very careful, Brooke."

"I am," she assured him, but it wasn't true. She could wander around Manhattan so totally preoccupied with a case that she was oblivious to her surroundings. She would have to be more careful, even though it had nothing to do with the Manhattan Ripper murders. Brooke added, "These women weren't murdered at random in the streets. They were in their apartments."

"Yes. There was no forced entry and they were all dressed up for the evening."

"So it had to be someone—some man—they all knew."

"If he's there, we can't find him. There doesn't seem to be a personal link between the three."

"OK, then someone they all knew *of* and had no reason to fear. Someone well known, someone you and I . . ." Brooke's voice trailed off.

That was what scared him. The dead women were smart, savvy, and sophisticated; they weren't easily fooled. Yet they had permitted, *welcomed*, this lunatic into their homes. And for all Brooke's success, for as bright and discerning and astute as she was professionally, there was a trusting innocence about her.

"That's one possibility. He could be someone we all would recognize. Who else?"

"Someone with a plausible line."

"Such as?"

"Someone writing a book on career women of the eighties. That's *in* right now."

"OK. So the man is either just famous, and they'd like to meet him, or he approaches them through what matters most to them—their work."

"It seems hopeless, Nick. Where do you start?"

"It's not hopeless, Brooke. It's just going to take time," Nick answered quietly. And it may cost a few more lives, he thought, feeling a rush of ice-cold fear.

Three days later, when Brooke walked into Andrew's office, Nick and Andrew were sitting at the desk staring intently at several eight-by-twelve-inch photographs. Their handsome faces were somber.

"Andrew? Nick?"

"Brooke!"

Andrew and Nick quickly gathered the photographs and covered the stack with a folder.

"What's . . . ?" What were the pictures? Their faces told her it was something she didn't want to see.

"The chief of police and the district attorney have decided the DA's office has to become involved *now* with the Manhattan Ripper investigation."

"Manhattan Ripper? Is that what *we're* calling it . . . him . . . *it?*"

"Afraid so."

"How can the DA's office help with the investigation?" Brooke asked, frowning.

"You can't. At least, not yet, not until we get a lead or a suspect." For now it was Nick's investigation. He could handle it. "This is pure P.R.— I keep Andrew informed and we present a unified front to the press—that sort of thing."

"But Andrew doesn't have to go to the scene of the crime," Brooke said flatly. It was bad enough that Nick had to be there, and Andrew had enough worries of his own.

"No." Andrew smiled reassuringly at her concerned blue eyes. "I don't. Nick will call me right away, so that I know."

"Why did you look at the photographs?" That was what Nick and Andrew had been doing when she walked in, studying pictures of the Manhattan Ripper's victims.

"I thought I should," Andrew answered evenly, but he frowned. "Probably a bad idea."

Brooke nodded in somber agreement.

"I worry about you, Brooke," Andrew spoke to Brooke as if Nick wasn't there. His voice was gentle and concerned. "Being alone . . ."

Brooke shrugged away a shiver of fear.

"I'm *fine,* Andrew."

The intercom on Andrew's desk sounded. "Yes?"

"There's a call for Ms. Chandler from Charles Sinclair," the muffled voice spoke from the desk. "Shall I take a message or . . ."

"I'll take it in my office." Brooke's cheeks flushed pink. "Andrew, I'll be back. Good-bye, Nick."

A half a minute later Brooke depressed the blinking button on the phone in her office.

"Charles?"

"Hello, Brooke. How are you?"

"Fine." How are *you?*

"Good. I wondered if you could have lunch with me one day this week."

"Yes." *Why?* Brooke consulted her appointment book. Wednesday and Thursday she would be in court; she and Andrew would spend the lunch recess planning strategy. Assuming the case ended when they anticipated, she should be free on Friday. "Is Friday all right?"

"Friday's fine."

Charles told Brooke he would meet her at the Court Jester, a restaurant located near the DA's office. He said good-bye without ever telling her why he wanted to see her.

She would find out on Friday. As Brooke pencilled the initials *C.S.* into her appointment book, she realized that Friday was Halloween; her birthday, *their* birthday. On Friday Brooke would have birthday lunch with Charles and birthday dinner with Melanie . . .

"I want to ask you something, Brooke," Charles began after they ordered lunch. "But I don't want you to feel under any pressure."

Please don't ask me to convince Melanie to come back to you, Charles. I see the sadness—the great loss—in your dark eyes. I see how much she hurt you. But . . .

"OK." Brooke's heart pounded. *Please.*

"We really need an attorney full time at Sinclair. I've spoken to John Perkins and he agrees. He can provide us with someone from the firm. That would be fine"—Charles smiled at her—"but it wouldn't be as good as you."

"Me?" Brooke wondered if Charles could hear her. She couldn't hear anything except the roar of blood pounding through her brain. *Me?*

"Of course you. Before we agree to anyone else, Jason and I want to know if you would consider it. I didn't know if you planned to do trials and criminals always or . . ."

Brooke shook her head and breathed, "I don't know."

"You might consider it?"

"Yes. I'd need to think about it."

"Of course. Let me know whenever."

Charles and Brooke spent the rest of lunch talking about her work, and his, and books and theater and even the abrupt wintry end of the long, balmy fall. Charles and Brooke covered many topics, but neither mentioned Melanie.

That evening Brooke gazed in amazement at her twin sister. Melanie looked so tired. Her face was thin and drawn and the bright blue eyes were gray and lifeless.

"Are you ill?" Brooke asked the moment Melanie opened the door.

"No. I'm just a little tired. I've been doing extra work." The demand for Melanie Chandler was virtually limitless. Melanie urged Adam to keep her as busy as possible. She wanted to be too tired to think. She could resurrect beauty and energy and dazzle from her exhausted face if she *tried.* Tonight, for a birthday celebration with Brooke of all people, Melanie had forgotten to try.

"Did you get sick in Europe?" Brooke pressed.

"No. I'm not sick, really." Melanie forced a twinkle into her sparkleless blue eyes.

Melanie led the way into the apricot-and-cream living room in her apartment. A platter of celery and carrot sticks, neatly arranged in orange-and-green rays around a bowl of crab dip, lay on the glass-top table.

"Have you seen Charles, Brooke?" Melanie asked after they sat down.

"Yes." Why do you want to know? Does it give you *pleasure* to know how much pain you can cause? Is that a measure of your own magnificence? Brooke felt her anger surfacing.

"How is he?"

"How do you *think* he is?"

"Fine, I guess." Why was Brooke scowling at her?

"You really amaze me, Melanie. You have to have everything and everyone, and it's still not enough. It's not enough until you throw them away."

"Brooke, what are you talking about?"

"*Charles*. It wasn't enough just to hurt him. You had to humiliate him publicly."

"*What?* Charles left *me.*" Melanie's eyes filled with tears. "I wasn't good enough for him."

"Not good enough? Perfect, golden, beautiful Melanie not good enough?" Brooke stood up. Her dark-blue eyes narrowed at her twin. "What game are you playing now?"

"I'm not playing any game! I've never been good enough for you, Brooke. And from the beginning you made it clear you didn't think I was good enough for Charles."

Brooke paused for a startled moment. What was Melanie talking about? *Nothing* She was simply trying to shift the blame. It wasn't going to work. When Brooke spoke, her voice was ice, "The whole world knows what happened. Why would you *lie?*"

"I'm not lying, Brooke!"

"You *are!*"

Brooke and Melanie stared at each other, glowering and bewildered. In just a few words, years of resentment and bitterness and anger had been revealed. They had finally spoken the painful truths hidden in their hearts. Now they had reached an impasse and neither knew how to find a way beyond it.

"Why couldn't you just stay in California?" Brooke finally broke the tense silence. Without waiting for an answer, she turned and left.

"Brooke," Melanie whispered. "Brooke."

They both cried that night. And they both remembered—and it was probably an omen— they had forgotten to wish each other Happy Birthday.

Chapter Twenty-two

Lake Forest, Illinois
November 11, 1986

"Chicagoland" awakened to snow. It was an early snow and a heavy one, blanketing the entire area with a soft, fleccy layer of pristine whiteness. The snow surprised the weather forecasters and annoyed the commuters. It sent shoppers rushing to the grocery to buy food for pantries and rock salt for walkways and candles in case the electricity went out.

Almost everyone had a reaction to the unexpected heavy snowfall. Most resented it; a too-early harbinger of the hard cold winter that lay ahead. A few ignored it, taking it in stride. And fewer still—the children—enjoyed it.

The children enjoyed it, and Galen enjoyed it. Everything was so beautiful. A cottony-soft fairyland, she thought, gazing out her window across the expanse of untrodden snow toward the lake. The trees, barren for weeks of their leaves, were alive again, dressed in lacy white, decorated for winter.

It was on a day such as this—silent, peaceful, virginal—that she and Jason first made love . . .

Galen sighed. She should work, on this day of all days, on "Sonja." "Sonja" was the story she had to write, the story that told the truth about love. "Sonja" exposed the fantasy of love and the bitter reality of betrayal.

Galen had to write "Sonja," even though it was a painful journey through the memories of Jason.

She had to set the record straight. She had to let her readers know. They trusted her. Their letters were mailed to Sinclair Publishing and forwarded to her post office box in Lake Forest. They believed in the lovely portrait of love Galen painted for them. And now Galen knew the portrait was false. She had an obligation to let her readers know.

But today Galen couldn't make herself carve the painful words from her heart. Today was a day to sit before a crackling fire and watch the snow fall and feel the wonder of the small life that was inside her still.

Still. With each passing day it became more likely that the baby's father was Charles, not Jason.

"I wish you could see this day, little one," Galen whispered softly to her unborn child. "But there will be so many days like this for us to share."

At three in the afternoon, the white-bright sky turned black, bringing with it an early nightfall and a violent winter storm. Snow fell in thick opaque walls, tossed and swirled by the cold, angry wind. Galen watched the awesome drama unfold. Such turbulent beauty! Galen felt serene and content; she was warm and safe and cozy in her gatehouse in the midst of a raging flurry of snowflakes.

The first pain came at three-thirty. Its significance didn't register right away. It was a squeeze, strong and warm, more than a pain. Then the next came, stronger, warmer, bringing with it a little more discomfort. Then the next. Then it was five o'clock and she had had three contractions in thirty minutes.

I have to get to the hospital, Galen realized. I have to call a cab or an ambulance.

But the phone line was dead! Galen depressed the disconnect button again and again. There was no dial tone. The telephone lines were above ground. Perhaps a tree had fallen. They would fix it soon, they *had* to.

The telephone was her only link. Galen didn't own a car—she didn't know how to drive—and walking in this storm would be dangerous if not impossible. The snow was dense and deep. The nearest house, the owners' mansion on the lake, was lost in a whirl of white. The path and trees that could serve as guideposts had vanished in the blinding blizzard.

Galen didn't want to think about what might happen if the phone wasn't restored quickly, but she had to. She needed to make preparations, in case. . . .

Galen gathered blankets and towels and candles and matches. She found scissors and string, carefully cut two pieces of string, and put the string and the scissors in her pocket. As she moved around the gatehouse, gathering items and placing them near the fire, Galen stopped six times because of contractions. And she paused fifty times to lift the receiver of the phone. Hoping, *hoping,* for a dial tone.

The outdoor lights on the barren rose stems cast spiny, twisted shadows on the brick. A frosty wind blew across the terrace, chilling his face and numbing his hands.

Why did you put this off so long? Charles chided himself as he carefully tied the protective layer of burlap over the pruned-for-winter roses. Were you waiting to do it with *her?*

Charles pricked his thumb on a frozen thorn and swore softly. Don't let yourself think about her.

Charles thought instead about her dark-haired twin.

Brooke had called today. She remembered it was his birthday and wished him a happy one. Then she told him she had decided, Yes, she would become the attorney for Sinclair Publishing Company.

"Really, Brooke. That's wonderful."

"I think so, too."

"When?"

"As soon as I can find the courage to tell Andrew, plus about three months."

"He'll be upset?" Of course he would; losing Brooke would be a great loss for the DA's office.

"Yes." Brooke smiled slightly. Andrew wouldn't understand. He loved the courtroom battles and the strategy. Andrew enjoyed the game and relished the triumphant victories. You're so good, Brooke, he would tell her. How can you throw it away? I have to, Andrew, she would reply. *I don't love it. I can't make it feel like a game.*

"I won't tell anyone except Jason until you give me the word."

"Thank you." Brooke frowned slightly. It didn't matter, except Belinda had been her friend, and she and Nick and Andrew were a team of sorts. . . . Brooke added quietly, "I would sort of like to see this Manhattan Ripper business through."

"I didn't realize you were close."

"Wishful thinking."

"To you." Adam raised his champagne glass and smiled. "Belated Happy Birthday."

"Thank you," Melanie whispered. *Her* birthday had been a disaster. Now it was Charles's birthday and she was dining with Adam at Lutèce. She added, forcing enthusiasm, "I think the shoot went well today."

"Very well."

Melanie chewed her lower lip thoughtfully, considering whether to say the next. She had to.

"Adam, I greatly prefer photo sessions and commercials to shows. Do you think—"

"*I think* the truth is that Charles is at the shows," Adam suggested gently.

"Yes." That was why she hated doing shows. She hated his intense dark eyes appraising her as she walked down the runway. *You've seen this body before, Charles, you've owned it,* her mind would scream as she felt his gaze. *I gave it all to you, and you didn't want it. Stop looking at me!*

"Can't you forget about him, honey?" Adam's

blue-gray eyes were concerned and gentle. Adam didn't care if Melanie ever set foot on another runway. He just wanted her to be happy and confident again. The sad sky-blue eyes were proud and determined, as always, but the confidence had vanished. Charles Sinclair had done so much damage. . . .

"I'm trying, Adam." Melanie smiled bravely.

"Try very hard right now. Viveca Sanders is heading our way." Adam stood up when it was clear that Viveca's destination was their table. "Viveca. How nice to see you."

"Adam," Viveca purred. "And Melanie. We've missed you at the parties, Melanie."

"My fault, Viveca," Adam interjected. "Melanie's schedule hasn't permitted it."

"I'll be at the holiday parties." Melanie smiled as if she couldn't wait.

"Oh, good. You really do add such sparkle." Viveca looked as if she was about to leave, but she hesitated. Then, on impulse, she asked, "Melanie, come with me for a moment, will you?"

Melanie sent a plea for help to Adam. His eyes told her it was easier not to resist Viveca; *resisting* Viveca made her suspicious. Without a word, Melanie nodded and followed Viveca into the lavish pink-and-white marble ladies' room.

"I'm not even going to ask you about Adam," Viveca began as she arranged a lock of hair that had fallen out of place.

"Good. There's nothing—"

"I just want you to know that I really admire what you did to Charles. It took guts."

"What?"

"Dumping him."

"But I—"

"I think everyone that's ever been with Charles vowed to end it before he did. But they—*we*—were all addicted. The sex was too good and he was handsome and powerful and irresistible. It's hard not to get hooked on leisurely expert sex, isn't it?" Viveca sighed, took a breath, and continued, "We all overlooked, or forgave, the fact that the bastard never spent the night or held us or gave one small damn. He was quite happy to share his perfect body, but nothing else."

Melanie's mind whirled. *Leisurely expert sex.* It had never been like that with Charles. They were always so desperate for each other, as if it was the first time—and the last time—every time.

The bastard never spent the night. They spent almost every night together, falling asleep in each other's arms and awakening that way, holding each other, reluctant to let go.

He never gave one small damn. No, that was true, he never did.

But Charles was the one who ended it, just as Charles did with all his women. It was the same for her as it had been for the others. Wasn't it?

"Charles has hurt a lot of people." Viveca's voice was solemn, laced with bitterness. "Maybe now he knows how it feels."

"I don't think—"

"Charles comes to the parties, but he comes alone and leaves early."

"Really, Viveca—"

"Is Adam even better? Is that how you could

329

do it?" Viveca held up her hands. "No, I promised, no questions about Adam. You still haven't been on my show, but we can't do anything until this is all ancient history. The viewers would expect questions about Charles and Adam, and I have a feeling you just wouldn't answer."

I would tell the truth, Melanie thought. Even though no one seems to believe it.

At nine o'clock, Galen's gatehouse lost electricity, and, with it, light and heat. Galen lit her scented candles and pulled a layer of blankets over her. The fire had long since died and the heat dissipated quickly.

The labor pains were frequent now, and painful. They pulled her breath from her. But she pulled it back, breathing the way she knew to. She did know. She had seen many babies born, in mud huts of Kenya and on sun-parched fields in central India. She had seen it, and she had helped, once. She and Charles . . .

And now it was *her* baby—and maybe it was theirs, hers and Charles's—and she needed his help. He had helped so much that time. His dark, smiling eyes had given her such confidence. Galen closed her eyes, remembering Charles and the strength he had given her.

This is Charles. He's here to help. Not that we will need much help. Babies deliver themselves, you know. She had spoken those words then, smiling reassurance to the frantic mother-to-be.

Help me now, Charles, *please.*

Galen felt her fingers becoming cold—what if

they were too numb to tie the string?—and fought her own resistance to push. *You have to push, Galen. You know you have to.*

The baby was born at ten. Galen forced herself to push. She felt resistance for a moment, and then none.

And then her baby spoke to her, as if in answer to all the gentle words Galen had whispered to her—to *her*—for all those months. It wasn't a cry or a wail. It was a hello.

Galen gazed at her precious little girl, covered with blood, breathing, moving, silhouetted by candlelight. Galen wanted desperately to cuddle her, but an ancient instinct stopped her. There was one more thing to do first. The most important thing. *You tie the cord in two places and cut in the middle,* she had explained to Charles. *You have to be sure that the string nearest the baby is tied very tight.*

With hands trembling but miraculously nimble, Galen tied the string around the umbilical cord. Then she took the scissors and cut the cord. Galen held her breath. A little blood oozed from her side, the placenta side, but the baby's side was tight and secure.

Then, as her warm tears spilled on the naked head of her baby girl, Galen held her and kissed her. *It was a miracle, Charles . . . a miracle.*

Galen wrapped them both, together, in blankets. Then they talked. Mother to daughter. And daughter, in small coos, to mother. Finally, they fell asleep.

They were awakened at midnight by sudden light, the electricity restored, and the promise of heat. Galen walked to the window, carrying her baby in her arms, and gazed at the aftermath of the storm. It was a fairyland again. Huge, amorphous snowdrifts, like harmless soft monsters, glistened beneath the porch light. The world was still and peaceful and beautiful again.

"What a day this was, my darling," Galen whispered.

Something tugged at the back of her mind about this day. What was it? Oh, yes, today was Jason's birthday. Today was Charles's birthday. And now it was his—*whose?*—daughter's birthday.

Happy Birthday, precious little one.

"Brooke?"

"Hello Charles. Cheers." It was December twenty-third.

"You don't sound very cheery."

"I just told Andrew." She had been *hinting* about it for the past six weeks, but today she told him outright that she was going to leave the DA's office and join Sinclair Publishing.

"He wasn't happy."

"At first, he was furious." The memory of Andrew's reaction still bewildered her. She had expected he would tell her she was throwing away a brilliant career in criminal law, not to mention the political opportunities she was squandering. She expected Andrew might even say she wasn't tough enough after all. Brooke had expected anger, but she hadn't expected him to take it personally.

But he had; it was if she were abandoning him,

too. It must have been a bad time. Perhaps Allison was ill again for the holidays. Andrew's personal reaction was immediate, and it was short-lived. He recovered quickly, teasing her about the expected things, and finally wishing her well.

"At first?" Charles asked.

"Yes. Then it was fine. But—"

"But you're having second thoughts?"

"Not really. I guess—" Brooke stopped. Why had she called Charles? "Tell me I'm doing the right thing."

"From my very selfish standpoint, you're doing a terrific thing. But you have to decide."

"I have decided. I told Andrew I would leave the DA's office sometime in March."

"You'll have the Manhattan Ripper convicted by then?"

"I've decided he's gone. It's been two months. He was just a horrible nightmare."

"I hope so," Charles agreed quietly.

When she saw him, Melanie stepped in front of the Renoir, blocking his view. Jason smiled, turned off the tape player, and removed the headphones.

"Melanie. How nice to see you."

"You, too, Jason. Back from Australia?"

"Yes, for the moment. I'm going back to Fremantle in a few weeks to watch the finals."

"You realize that everyone else in Manhattan is doing last-minute Christmas shopping?"

"Which leaves this fabulous Impressionist exhibit just for us." Jason gestured to the virtually empty gallery.

Melanie nodded. It was why she had come. It was peaceful here, away from the frantic festive holiday crowds.

"I've never known anyone who rented one of those." Melanie's eyes sparkled at the tape player in Jason's hand. "Does it really tell you more than the guidebook?"

"Probably not," Jason replied easily.

They walked together for a while, admiring the fabulous paintings and talking.

"How is Charles?" Melanie asked finally.

"Fine. I was sorry—"

"Me, too." You don't *look* sorry, Jason. You're probably tired of exchanging the end-of-relationship platitudes with Charles's women.

"How's Brooke?"

"Fine." How do I know? I wonder if she hurts the way I do? "Everyone is so consumed with this Manhattan Ripper business."

Jason nodded thoughtfully. At least Galen was away from that fear. She used to wander Greenwich Village as if it were a wild, wonderful, *safe* African savanna. Jason was glad Galen was away from the horrors of Manhattan; he was glad she was away from Charles.

This will be the MANHATTAN RIPPER'S little Christmas present to this wonderful town. THE MANHATTAN RIPPER! What a fabulous name! Viva La Press! I love NEW YORK.

The Manhattan Ripper laughed a low, mean laugh. Then his dark eyes narrowed and he wrote angrily,

More will DIE. It is NECESSARY. Tonight, the

distinguished DOCTOR. Even the ivory tower of academia isn't safe from the MANHATTAN RIPPER. This will be an important LESSON. This will make her understand. It will be the Ripper's formal WARNING before he plunges the knife into the GOLDEN HEART and slashes the lovely GOLDEN NECK.

"Melanie." Viveca clutched Melanie's forearm tightly.

"Viveca?" Viveca's rosy cheeks were ashen.

"I need to speak with you."

Melanie followed Viveca to a far corner of the crowded room. The *Vogue* holiday open house was still in full swing. *Everyone* was here, or had been. Melanie and Adam arrived early and planned to stay late. They had to; *Vogue* was a valued client, and Melanie was the prestigious holiday issue cover. Charles had come, and gone, alone, hours ago. He and Melanie didn't speak, but she felt his dark eyes watching her. He started toward her once, but Melanie quickly turned away.

"Viveca, what's wrong?"

"I just arrived. On the way over I heard a special bulletin on the radio. The Manhattan Ripper . . ." Viveca paused for a breath.

"*What*, Viveca?" Is it *Brooke?* No, please, if anything ever happened to Brooke.

" . . . murdered Jane Tucker"

"Jane Tucker," Melanie repeated softly as relief pulsed through her. Jane Tucker, the name was familiar, why?

"Adam and Jane were once engaged to be

335

married. It didn't work out, but . . . Melanie, you have to get him out of here before everyone finds out about it."

Melanie nodded and left to find Adam.

He went with her, without question, as she had gone with Viveca. Adam saw the sadness and terror in her pale-blue eyes. When they were alone in his car, Melanie told him.

"Oh, my God, *no.*"

"Adam, I'm so sorry."

"When are they going to find the bastard?" Adam demanded, his handsome face twisted with rage and anguish. "When are they going to put an end to this insanity?"

Brooke watched the eleven o'clock news as she got ready for bed.

"The Manhattan Ripper has claimed a fourth victim. Earlier this evening the body of Dr. Jane Tucker, associate professor of neurosurgery at . . ."

Brooke watched the television screen. The cameras panned to the apartment building where the dead woman had lived. Brooke knew that Nick was inside searching the blood-splattered apartment for clues. She knew he was churning with rage. Brooke wanted to talk to him. She would. Nick would call, as he had before.

Brooke hoped Nick knew he could call anytime, even in the middle of the night.

Nick didn't call that night. And he didn't call the next day. It was Christmas Eve, but the city offices were open. Nick could call her at work or at home.

But he didn't call.

At three in the afternoon on Christmas Day Brooke telephoned Nick's precinct headquarters. She asked for him without identifying herself.

"Lieutenant Adrian."

"Hi. It's Brooke."

"Brooke," he breathed. He wanted to talk to her, but he wasn't going to. He would call her *sometime*. Some other time. He would call her sometime when there hadn't been a murder and they didn't have a case to discuss. He would ask if she wanted to go for a walk or to dinner or for a ferryboat ride. Nick had been thinking about calling Brooke on December twenty-third. But then the call came about Dr. Jane Tucker. "Merry Christmas."

"Same to you."

"Uh, why . . .

"I was wondering," Brooke began. I was wondering why you didn't call me. She continued, "How do you hear about the murders? You seem to know the same night."

Very sharp, Brooke. Nick had told Andrew—as DA's office liaison Andrew needed to know everything—but Nick hadn't told her. The press hadn't tumbled to it yet. But the press had only been involved— really involved—since the October murder. Now it was a cause célèbra. "Famous" cases of serial killers were featured in the local papers and on television: Ted Bundy and the Hillside Strangler and the Green River Killer. Would the Manhattan Ripper be the next psychopath to elude the police for months, even years, leaving in his wake terror and death? What was the NYPD doing? Didn't they need a task

337

force instead of just the usual investigation team? Was Lieutenant Nick Adrian really doing enough?

"He calls." Nick's voice was low, the information clearly confidential. It was not even widely known throughout the precinct.

"*He* calls? Have you spoken to him?"

"I did this time," Nick said heavily, remembering the disguised voice and its gruesome purpose. "Now that he knows I'm in charge of the investigation. Before he just left a message."

"What message?"

"Each time he says we should get to the address he gives as soon as possible. Then he hangs up. It's much too quick to trace. This time it sounded as if he was calling from a phone booth."

"As soon as possible," Brooke repeated. "Are they alive when he leaves them?"

"No." There was no question, no possibility, of that. "Has he called at other times?"

"No. He doesn't seem interested in playing psychological cat-and-mouse with the police. Beyond what he is already doing." Nick sighed. "I really don't know why he calls, Brooke, but he calls within half an hour of the murder."

"Maybe he can't stand the thought of them just lying there," Brooke said quietly, shivering. *She* couldn't stand the thought. It was a normal reaction. But was any part of this man, this maniacal murderer, *normal?*

"Is this how you usually spend Christmas? Calling your local PD?" Nick asked suddenly, pulling them both away from the grisly subject of the murders.

"No."

"Are you having dinner with Melanie?"

"No." We tried a birthday dinner together. She repeated softly, "No."

"Do you want to have dinner with me?"

"Yes, I'd like to."

"One ground rule. We don't talk about the murders. We don't talk about murder at all. Or crime. Or law. Or work."

"Then what can we talk about?" Brooke teased. After a moment, she continued seriously, "I know. We can talk about your short stories."

"We can talk about why it makes you so sad that you aren't having Christmas dinner with Melanie," Nick countered carefully. He heard the sadness. He imagined a storm in her dark-blue eyes.

"No," Brooke whispered, "we can't talk about that."

Chapter Twenty-three

New York City
February 1987

"Happy Valentine's Day, Galen."

"Melanie! How nice to hear from you. I was going to call you. The cover of *Fashion* is sensational."

"Thanks." The only problem with the fabulous photograph of Melanie on the February issue of *Fashion* was it meant that she had to attend Sinclair's Valentine's Day party at the Essex House. Adam insisted; he would escort her, of course. "How are you?"

"Fine." *I have Elise and she is joy.* Galen laughed softly, "Except the editors for my next book think my feature story, 'Sonja,' is unpublishable."

"Oh, *that*," Melanie answered gaily. "Isn't the book due to be released next month?"

"That's *Songs of the Savanna*—the stories I wrote about Kenya, minus the *gems*. My next book, the one I'm working on now, is called *Spring Street Stories*. It's about life in the Village."

"What's the problem with 'Sonja'?"

" 'A too bitter portrait of love,' they said."

"Sounds right up my alley," Melanie murmured. She added with genuine enthusiasm, "I'd really like to read it. I may not be an editor, but I certainly am a fan."

"And a friend. Thanks. I'm going to rework it for a while, then maybe I'll send it to you."

"Great. Perhaps I should come there. Lake Forest sounds enchanting."

"It is," Galen agreed. But you can't come here. Galen felt a pang of sadness as she realized she would probably never see Melanie again. Her dear friends could never know about Elise. They would have to remain long-distance voices. Melanie and . . . "How's Brooke?"

"Fine. I guess."

"Looking forward to her new job," Galen suggested carefully.

"New job?"

"At Sinclair Publishing." *Working with Elise's father, whoever he is.*

"Oh." Brooke working with Charles!

"You haven't talked to her, have you?"

"We had an argument."

"I know. Brooke told me almost two months ago."

"What did she say?"

"Nothing. She sounded sad, just like you do. Melanie, can't you two work it out?"

"I don't know," Melanie spoke softly. *I want to. Then why don't you just pick up the phone and call her? Because I can't. Besides, she could call me.*

"What in the world is the assistant DA doing in my office on Saturday afternoon?"

"What are you doing here?"

"Paperwork." Nick gestured at stacks of reports. "And it *is* my office."

"I'm escaping from Jeffrey Martin."

"Ah, but can he escape from *you?*"

"I hope not. I really think it's airtight."

"When do you go to trial?"

"Early this week. Probably Tuesday."

"Well," Nick said after a few beats of silence, "I think it's nice you decided to escape here."

Brooke tilted her head slightly, and her blue eyes became thoughtful. "Actually, I'm here to make a confession."

"Really? Should I recite *Miranda* to you? You have the right to remain silent—"

"No I don't." Brooke sighed quietly. "I should have told you this a long time ago."

"What, Brooke?"

Don't be angry, Nick.

"I'm leaving the DA's office. As soon as the Jeffrey Martin trial is over. I'm—" Brooke stopped. Nick was smiling at her; *smiling,* not gloating or glowering.

"Going to work for Sinclair Publishing," Nick finished her sentence. *Going to work for Charles Sinclair.*

"You knew."

"Andrew told me in December." Nick frowned as he remembered why he had seen Andrew on Christmas Eve; Nick had to give him the details of Dr. Jane Tucker's bloody death.

"Oh." *Oh.* That meant Nick knew when they had dinner together on Christmas Day. "Why didn't you . . ."

"Why didn't I *what?*"

"I don't know. Call me up and say 'I told you so' or point out that I can't save the world by negotiating advertising contracts."

I don't have the right to do that to you, Brooke. And you have the right . . . the right to be with Charles Sinclair if you want to.

"You make choices," Nick answered seriously. He had been thinking about getting out. He was tired of seeing mutilated bodies. He'd been wondering if he could write a novel. He added, "You've probably made a good one."

Brooke smiled. *Thank you, Nick, for making this so easy.*

"How's Melanie?" Nick asked. He hoped the problem Brooke wouldn't talk about at

Christmas was resolved. The sudden storm in her eyes told him it wasn't.

"I don't know."

"You make choices," Nick reminded her quietly.

"Yes." And I don't *choose* this. Then why don't you just pick up the phone and call her? Because I *can't*. Besides, *she* could call *me*. Brooke shrugged, suddenly restless. "I guess I'd better go."

Nick felt her pulling away. He had no right, but . . . "Do you think you'll feel like escaping again in, say, about three hours? For dinner?" To celebrate Valentine's Day?

Brooke hesitated. "Escaping, yes. But no more confessions."

Nick nodded. Enough confessions for one day.

Melanie smiled wryly at the ice-sculpture cupid. His love-drenched arrow aimed ominously at a mountain of caviar.

"Whoever invented Valentine's Day?"

"No cynicism tonight," Adam teased. He touched her cheek lightly with his finger and smiled into her bright blue eyes.

"OK," she agreed easily. Everything was easy with Adam. He made her feel warm and secure and calm. "Do you think it's safe to eat the caviar?"

Adam laughed. "Oh, I see. It might be tainted with love and passion and romance. Would that be so bad?"

Melanie started to speak, then her eyes sparkled at his and she bit her lip. She smiled coyly and said, "I just edited a terribly cynical remark."

Adam and Melanie smiled at each other and a nearby camera flashed, capturing the happy, sparkling moment. The Sinclair Valentine's Day party was the event of the weekend; it was being well photographed for the society pages of tomorrow's *Times*.

It was Charles's party, but, miraculously, Melanie managed to avoid him. She was aware of his presence, dark and handsome and menacing, but she successfully avoided his eyes and artfully kept herself at a safe distance. There was no point in speaking to him; it was almost too painful just seeing him.

Toward the end of the evening, Melanie walked through the elegant French doors onto the terrace. It was cool, but Melanie needed a private moment. The winter moon was full and the dark sky glittered with stars. The roses were wrapped, snug and safe, in burlap.

"Melanie?"

Melanie stiffened at the sound of his voice. It was soft and seductive; the familiar voice of the dark stranger who had taken her to paradise, and back. *Go away.*

Charles moved closer.

"Melanie, I'm glad you came to the party."

Silence.

"You look happy, Melanie. You and Adam look happy."

"I wonder"—the ice in her voice matched the winter cold—"what happened to our roses."

"I covered them with burlap."

Warm tears spilled onto her cold cheeks as she remembered the sunny, happy day they planted the roses, and the pleasure they had sitting in the fragrant, colorful garden. But that was Charles; he took pleasure in beautiful things, like her.

But he didn't care. *He never gave a small damn.*

"I'm surprised." Melanie didn't recognize her own voice. It was empty—a shell without substance—just like she was in his eyes.

"Why?" Charles moved in front of her.

"Because . . ." Her blue eyes met his and she was suddenly consumed with anger. When she spoke again she still didn't recognize the voice, but it was no longer empty. Now it was full, overflowing, with hatred. "I thought you enjoyed watching beautiful things die."

"Melanie."

"You're no better than the Manhattan Ripper, Charles. *Worse,* because your victims survive even though you've torn out their hearts."

Her words caused such pain! His dark eyes became wild with anguish. Melanie had seen the same tormented look the night on the terrace after his nightmare.

I cared then, Charles. I cared so much. But now I'm like you. I don't care.

It wasn't true. As she turned to leave, her heart pleaded, *Stop me, Charles.*

But he didn't move, and she walked away from him, back through the French doors to his fabulous party, and into the curious eyes of Viveca Sanders.

"Melanie?" Viveca looked beyond Melanie to the terrace. She recognized the shadowy silhouette. She was witnessing the aftermath of another off-stage fight between Charles Sinclair and Melanie Chandler. Was he trying, as he had without success in Monte Carlo, to convince her to come back to him? "Melanie?"

Flashbulbs sparkled in Melanie's eyes, and everyone was asking questions. Still bewildered and shaken by the hateful venom of her own words, Melanie stood stiff and mute. Finally Adam was by her side and she whispered, "Get me out of here, Adam. Please."

Adam wrapped a strong arm around her and swiftly guided her through the curious crowd.

"I could kill him for what he did to you," Adam whispered hoarsely when they were finally alone. "For what he's still doing . . ."

"I hate this," Melanie told Adam when he called the following morning. Melanie glowered at the Sunday *Times*. A radiant picture of her with Adam—"The Happy Couple"—smiled back.

"What do you hate?" Did she hate the fact that *they* had been portrayed as a loving couple? Or did she only hate that the accompanying article described Charles as the twice-spurned lover and strongly implied that they had argued about her love affair with Adam?

"All of it. It's all false."

Yes, Adam thought. But I wish it weren't. Adam wished his lovely golden-haired friend *would* become his lover.

"I'm going to call Viveca."

"Viveca! Why?"

"I have to clear the air, Adam."

"You need to tell the world that Charles Sinclair left you?"

"Yes." What if Charles thought *she* was spreading the lies. It doesn't matter what Charles thinks, she reminded herself. Still, it wasn't *true*.

"Melanie, think about it."

"I have."

"Do some more thinking."

"Adam . . ."

"I'll call you from Paris and we'll discuss it. If you still have to do it, let's carefully select the right way. I'm not sure a live, on-camera interview is the answer. OK?"

"OK. You'll call?"

"You know I will. Nothing rash in the meantime, *d'accord?*"

"*D'accord.*" Agreed.

He reached her by telephone in the models' dressing room at Drake two days after the Valentine's Day party.

"This is Melanie."

"Ms. Chandler." He spoke with a slight British accent. "This is Robin Shepard. I write a column . . ."

"Yes, I know." Robin Shepard wrote a celebrity gossip column, "Profiles," for the *Times*.

"I would like to do a piece on you."

"All right." Melanie smiled. Adam must have decided she was right after all. "Profiles" was the perfect forum.

"Where shall we meet? I find interviews in the person's home often the most comfortable."

"That would be fine."

"How would this evening suit you? It's short notice."

"Tonight would be fine." Melanie knew that Robin Shepard was doing a favor for Adam which was really a favor for her. Robin Shepard was too much a gentleman to mention that Adam had arranged it. Melanie almost told him that she knew. "Perfect."

"Ten o'clock? I have a dinner I must attend first."

"Ten o'clock," Melanie agreed and gave him her address.

He arrived promptly at ten and spoke to her through the security intercom.

"Ms. Chandler. It's Robin Shepard."

Melanie pressed the button to release the front-door lock of the building. Somewhere in the back of her mind it registered: his accent was gone. But it was in the back of her mind. In the forefront stood the hope that the interview would go well.

When her doorbell rang two minutes later, Melanie didn't even look through the peephole.

She just opened the door and realized, too late, who she was letting in.

Part III

Chapter Twenty-four

New York City
February 16, 1987

Brooke sat bolt upright. Her heart raced and her breath came in shallow gasps. The dial of the bedside clock glowed ten-thirty. Brooke frowned at the clock. She had only been in bed for fifteen minutes; it was hardly enough time to fall asleep, much less to dream! But something—it *must* have been a nightmare—had forced her violently back into wakefulness.

Only later would Brooke recall that she was already reaching for the phone when it rang. . . .

"Hello," she breathed uneasily as her mind frantically tried to reassure her anxious heart.

It will be Andrew, Brooke told herself. He will be calling to discuss one final detail, one final twist, of the Jeffrey Martin case. logically, the late-night phone call would be from Andrew. But illogically, and fueled with a knowledge that defied logic, Brooke's heart resolutely pumped dread through her body.

"Brooke!" Sheer terror.

"Melanie! What's—"

"He tried to kill me. Brooke, help me!" The terror was strong and pervasive. But the voice wasn't. It was the voice of a body that was badly injured, in shock, maybe dying. . . .

"Melanie," Brooke spoke urgently, "where are you?"

"My apartment," Melanie answered slowly, as if bewildered that something so horrible could have happened in that sanctuary.

"Is he gone?"

"Yes. Brooke it was *him*. The Manhattan . . ."

The Manhattan Ripper. The Ripper didn't leave witnesses, only victims. But Melanie had seen him. And, miraculously, she was alive. *still.*

"Are you hurt?"

"So much blood," Melanie murmured dreamily "So much blood."

Melanie was badly hurt. Her voice faded in and out of reality, drifting away. . . .

"Melanie." Brooke spoke sternly. She had to make Melanie focus on the present—if it was possible, if Melanie hadn't already lost too much blood.

"Yes, Brooke," Melanie answered in a little-girl voice, surprised that her older sister was talking to her so harshly. What had she done wrong?

"Melanie," Brooke continued softly. There had been so much harshness between them, so much for so long. It hadn't always been that way; it couldn't be that way now. Brooke added gently, her voice choked with emotion, "Mellie."

Mellie . . . It was Brooke's special name for Melanie when they were little girls. *Mellie.* The name recalled such happy memories of laughter and love between sisters—twin sisters—still bound by the unique closeness born in their mother's womb, before the realities of life drove a wedge between them. . . .

Brooke shook the memories that flooded her mind. She needed to tell Melanie those lovely memories were with her still, despite the bitter ones. Brooke *would* tell her, but not now. Now she, *they*, had to save Melanie's life.

"Mellie, have you called the police?" Brooke asked, knowing the answer, but hoping.

"I called you!" The voice said clearly, *I called you because you are my sister—my older sister—and I know you will save me.*

"I'm glad you called me, honey. It was the right thing to do. Now listen carefully, Melanie. You have to hang up the phone so I can call the paramedics and the police. As soon as I've done that I will call you right back and we'll talk until they arrive. OK?"

No answer.

"Melanie."

"Uh-huh." The answer came weakly as if from a small child who had answered by nodding her head instead of speaking. Was she getting too weak? Or was she just drifting, too, to the memories of the two happy little girls?

"OK, Mellie. Hang up now. I'll call you right back."

An almost unbearable emptiness swept through Brooke as she heard the phone disconnect. It felt like an end. An ending. The end.

No! Brook shook the thought angrily as she hurriedly dialed the emergency police number.

"This is," Brooke began urgently, then forced control in her voice and assumed her usual professional tone, "This is assistant district attorney Brooke Chandler. I need a medic unit dispatched to . . ."

Brooke provided the necessary information in a matter of moments. Just before the call ended she added authoritatively, "Have the police department contact Lieutenant Nick Adrian. He needs to be there."

"Will do, Ms. Chandler," the dispatcher replied with respect. The police, the emergency unit dispatchers, the paramedics, and the district attorney's office were all coconspirators in the war against crime in New York City. They were on the same team. The dispatcher had no idea that the assistant district attorney's call was more than good teamwork. There was nothing in Brooke Chandler's tone that sounded like emotion. "I'll let Lieutenant Adrian know you think he needs to be there."

Nick needs to be there, Brooke thought as her trembling fingers dialed Melanie's number. He *has* to be. It wasn't because the Manhattan Ripper was Nick's case. Nick needed to be there because he would help Melanie. Melanie . . .

As Brooke listened to Melanie's phone ring, unanswered, her frantic thoughts darted to other people who needed to know.

Five rings.

Her parents. How could she tell them what horror had befallen their golden angel? Would they blame *her* for allowing this to happen to Melanie? New York was Brooke's city. She should have protected Melanie . . .

Brooke would call her parents from the

hospital, as soon as she knew that Melanie was all right.

Ten rings. Pick up the phone, Melanie. Mellie. Please.

Adam needed to know. The society pages of yesterday's—*yesterday's*—Sunday *Times* featured a color photograph of Melanie and Adam taken at *Fashion* magazine's gala Valentine's Day party. Melanie and Adam stood in front of an ice sculpture of Cupid, the perfect backdrop for their fairytale romance. Distinguished, elegant Adam and dazzling golden Melanie, smiling, happy, in *love.*

Adam was the reason Melanie left Charles. It was so obvious. Why did Melanie deny it? Even at the Valentine's Day party, according to the article that accompanied the photograph, there had been a "scene" between Melanie and Charles. . . .

Charles, Brooke's mind whirled. How can I tell Charles about this? How can anyone tell him?

Fifteen rings. Melanie, come *on.*

But Charles needed to know, and Jason needed to know. Charles and Jason, the *other* twins.

Twenty rings. Answer the—

The ringing stopped. So, for a moment, did Brooke's heart. Someone had taken the phone off the hook. Melanie? The Ripper? The paramedics? Nick?

"Melanie?" Brooke whispered.

Silence.

"Mellie, honey," Brooke spoke lovingly to the silence, "I called the paramedics. They'll be there any moment. Hold on, darling. Please. And Nick.

355

He's a police officer. You can trust him, Mellie. He'll take care of you."

Brooke paused, blinking back tears, hoping to hear something, the smallest sound, from her twin. Brooke heard nothing, but she *felt* a presence. Brooke knew Melanie was there, and Melanie would hear her words.

"Mellie. Don't try to talk, just listen. We'll talk when you're better." Tears streamed down Brooke's cheeks. She closed her eyes and saw a little girl with sun-gold hair and bright blue eyes frolicking on a white sand beach. Brooke could almost hear the laughter. "I love you, Mellie, I always have. We need to talk about the things that have come between us. We *will* talk. Remember the summer we spent at the beach when we were five, Mellie? Remember what fun we had?"

Suddenly there was noise—commotion—at the other end. Brooke held her breath. She heard pounding. It lasted only a few seconds. Then Brooke heard a crash as the door gave way.

"Christ."

Brooke felt the paramedic's horror as he saw her twin sister.

Help her. *Please.*

"Is she . . . ?" another voice asked.

"I don't know," the voice, now close to the phone, close to Melanie, answered. "Let me find her carotid."

Please. Please. Please.

Depthless immobilizing fear settled in Brooke's heart as she silently prayed for the other heart; the other heart that once had been so close.

"OK, Joe, let's get to work," the paramedic breathed finally. "She's still alive. . . ."

Brooke strained to hear, but the voices were distant and muffled. The receiver of the phone must have rolled over into the deep pile carpet in Melanie's apartment. Brooke heard bits.

"Can you get a fourteen-gauge needle in her?"

"—so clamped down. Try a femoral or a jugular—"

"—needs to be intubated—"

"—it's a pneumo, not a tension, but she'll need a chest tube—"

Then a familiar voice, worried, asked, "How is she?"

"As stable as we can get her here. We're about to roll."

"What's with the phone?" Nick asked, lifting it with a handkerchief to protect prints—not that there would be any.

"She was holding it when we arrived, *clinging* to it. It took some strength to pull her fingers away." The voice faded as the medics rushed out of the apartment with Melanie.

"Hello." Nick spoke into the receiver.

"Nick. Thank God you got there so quickly."

"We were on our way when your call came."

Of course, Brooke thought, the Ripper always calls to tell them where to find the victim. But Melanie was *alive.*

"Nick?"

"I don't know, Brooke," Nick answered gently. I don't know if she will live. Melanie was badly, horribly injured, but not as badly as the others. The Ripper had left before making the final, instantly lethal cuts Nick knew so well. Something had stopped him, or interrupted him. "Did you call her?"

"No." Tears blurred her eyes. I *wanted* to call her. I was *going* to, *sometime*. "She called me after he left."

"You spoke to her?"

"Yes. She told me that it was *him*," Brooke whispered. She added urgently, "Nick, I have to go now. I have to be at the hospital with her."

Nick could envision Brooke running across Manhattan in the middle of the night. She was trying to sound calm and in control, but he knew better. Nick looked at the blood-splattered room and made a decision.

"I'll be there in five minutes to take you to the hospital."

"But you have to be *there*." You have to be in Melanie's apartment, at the scene of the crime, finding out who did this to her.

"I have to be here. And I have to be at the hospital to talk to Melanie," Nick said firmly. He knew it would be hours before he could talk to Melanie, assuming she lived. It was a very big assumption.

Mostly, Brooke, Nick thought, I have to be with you. He repeated, "I'll be at your apartment in five minutes."

Before leaving Melanie's apartment, Nick ordered the officers to collect prints and photographs and samples, but not to disturb anything. He would return in a few hours.

Brooke opened the door as soon as Nick knocked and was halfway into the hallway when he put his hand on the door to prevent her from pulling it shut. Brooke's hair was tousled, her cheeks were damp, and her dark-blue eyes glistened with fear. She wore jeans and a light cotton blouse buttoned incorrectly.

"Just a minute." Nick guided her gently back into her apartment.

Then, carefully, Nick unbuttoned and rebuttoned her blouse and parted her tousled hair with his hands.

"I don't care how I look, Nick!" But she didn't resist.

"I know." *And you look so beautiful.* "OK. Now, sweater and coat and then we can go."

Brooke pressed against the far door of the squad car, her body rigid with fear. Nick felt her despair and fear as he drove quickly through the treacherous rain-slick streets. He wanted to help her, but he had to concentrate on his driving.

Finally he extended his hand to her. She took it gratefully, wrapping both of her hands, cold and small, around his strong, warm one. When they reached the hospital, when he moved to get out of the car, she moved with him. Unwilling or unable to release his hand she slid across the seat and followed him out on the driver's side.

The emergency room was brightly lighted, noisy and busy. Nick passed through the Authorized Personnel Only signs toward the trauma room. Brooke still held his hand and he felt her hesitation. She was so afraid of what might be behind those electronic steel doors.

What *were* they going to find beyond the impersonal steel doors, Nick wondered. He should have left her in the waiting area. But would she have agreed to stay behind? *Could* she have released his hand? Nick didn't know, because he didn't try, and now it was too late.

"Nick." Frank Thomas, one of the hospital's trauma surgeons, greeted him. Frank and Nick had worked together on a number of cases.

"Frank. How's—?"

"Chandler? She's in the OR now. She's carved up pretty badly, although some of the wounds are superficial and ugly but not life-threatening. She has one chest wound. If we're—if she's— lucky it will be above the liver. And she has several abdominal wounds, probably deep. She's in shock so the best guess is that she's bleeding into her belly. They're exploring her now," Frank explained quickly, looking at Nick. Only toward the end did he shift his gaze to the woman who clung to Nick and whose face radiated such fear. Frank frowned.

"This is Brooke Chandler, Melanie's sister." Nick realized grimly that his impulse to leave Brooke outside had been correct.

Frank shot Nick a glance that said, Christ, Nick, why didn't you warn me? He could—and would—give the same facts to a family member, but he would use different words.

"We are concerned," Frank began again, speaking to Brooke, trying to compensate for *carved up pretty badly* and *bleeding into her belly* and *best guess*. Nick should not have brought her back here, not without checking. What if Melanie was lying, dead, in the room with the plate-glass windows behind him? Frank could tell from

Nick's expression that he knew that. And Frank could tell from the way Brooke held Nick's hand and pressed close to him that this was not a *usual* case. Rules were going to be broken.

Frank continued, speaking to the frightened blue eyes, "We are worried that her spleen or her kidneys may have been injured. They are quite vascular—they bleed easily. Melanie is in the operating room now so they can look for a bleeding site and stop it."

Brooke nodded. She knew not to ask about chances.

"Where can we wait, Frank?" Nick asked. "I want to keep Brooke away from the press."

Nick didn't want the Manhattan Ripper to know, if he didn't already know, that Brooke—Melanie's twin—existed. Nick especially didn't want it known that Melanie had called Brooke after the attack.

Frank led them to a small waiting area near the operating room.

"Will others be coming?" Frank asked.

"Are there people we should call, Brooke?" Nick paraphrased Frank's question.

Brooke nodded, but offered no names. Yes, but how can we? How can we tell them?

"I'll let you know, Frank," Nick said. Then, before Frank left, he added, "Thanks."

Nick held her for a long time, his arms wrapped around her, feeling her silent sobs and the deep, horrible fear that shook her body. Finally Brooke pulled free.

"Adam needs to know." It was so difficult to *think*. All thoughts led to Melanie. "And Charles and Jason. And my parents. We should wait before calling them—they can't get a plane before morning anyway."

"I'm going to ask an officer to reach Adam and the Sinclairs. And I have to call Andrew."

Panic flickered across Brooke's eyes at the thought of Nick leaving. Then, with great effort, Brooke subdued the panic and nodded.

"We reached them all," Nick told her when he returned twenty minutes later. "Adam is in Paris. He'll take the first plane. Jason is coming from Southampton. Charles and Andrew should be here soon."

"Thank you."

Andrew was the first to arrive.

"Brooke," Andrew spoke her name as he entered the tiny waiting room. He put his arms around her gently and whispered, "I am so sorry, darling."

Brooke succumbed gratefully to Andrew's comforting strength and warmth. He held her tight, was still holding her, when Charles arrived moments later.

Nick watched as Charles entered the room. The dark, aristocratic eyes sent a message of deep, unfocused, heart-stopping fear. It was the same look Nick had seen in Brooke's eyes, the look he still saw despite her brave attempts to stay rational.

Nick started to move toward Charles, to help him because Charles Sinclair needed help, but before Nick reached him, Charles spoke. "Brooke?"

"Charles." Brooke pulled free from Andrew and moved to Charles. Her trembling hands briefly touched his handsome, worried face. Oh, Charles.

"How is she?" His voice was hoarse with fear.

"We don't know. She's in surgery." *We.* Brooke realized as she spoke that Charles didn't know Andrew or Nick. "Charles, this is Andrew Parker, and this is Nick Adrian."

Brooke didn't identify Nick and Andrew with their titles. She couldn't say words to Charles like "homicide" or "Manhattan Ripper case."

Charles shook hands with Nick and Andrew. The men nodded solemn greetings, and then there was nothing more to say. All they could do, now, was wait. Brooke retreated to a pale-green vinyl couch. Andrew sat beside her. Charles and Nick pressed against paint-chipped walls on opposite sides of the small, sterile room.

One hour after Charles arrived, a doctor appeared. He wore green surgical scrubs and a turquoise surgical mask. They all stood at attention when the doctor entered the room.

"We have more surgery to do, but we've finished the exploration."

"And you found?" Nick queried.

"Bleeding from the spleen. We've stopped that. Her liver and kidneys are fine."

"And everything else is fine?" Charles asked.

"Well, no. There *are* other knife wounds." The doctor saw the anguish in Charles's eyes. He added reassuringly, "But the abdominal wounds were potentially the most serious, and we have those under control."

"So she is going to live," Charles spoke softly.

"It's too soon to know. I'll keep you posted." The doctor waited a moment before returning to the operating room, but there were no more questions. They had all heard the answer to *the* question. *It's too soon to know.*

"Tell me what happened." Charles turned his dark eyes to Nick. The muscles in his strong jaw rippled. Charles wasn't asking. He was *commanding* with his bigger-than-life power.

"We don't know, Charles." It was Brooke who spoke. "All we know is she was able to call me after he left."

"She called you," Charles breathed.

I wish you hadn't told him that, Brooke, Nick thought. I didn't want anyone, even her friends, even *your* friends to know that Melanie talked to you after she saw the killer.

"Yes." Brooke's eyes filled with fresh tears as she remembered the terror in Melanie's voice.

"What did she say?" Charles demanded.

Why does Charles Sinclair have to know? Nick wondered uneasily. It *could* be a normal reaction for someone who cared very much and was trying to understand, trying to make sense of something that was senseless. But Charles seemed so desperate.

"She told me that it was him, the—" Brooke paused. She wouldn't say it. "She told me she needed help."

"That's all?"

"That's all." Brooke's voice was barely audible.

"I'm going to leave for a while, Brooke," Nick said, purposefully shifting the conversation.

"You're going to her apartment." Brooke's eyes met his.

Nick nodded solemnly. He could leave her now. She wasn't alone. Nick wanted to hold her and promise her that it would be all right. But he couldn't hold her, and he could make no promises.

"Nick, should I?" Andrew was torn. Maybe he should go with Nick—as the DA's office liaison in the investigation— but if he could help Brooke.

"There's no need for you to come, Andrew." Nick shifted his gaze from Brooke to Andrew. Be here for Brooke, Andrew, in case. "Thanks."

"OK," Andrew agreed easily.

As Nick left, he caught a brief but suppressed movement from Charles. He wants to come with me, Nick thought. *Why.* To prove to himself that this nightmare has really happened? To force himself to admit it?

Or is there another reason?

Chapter Twenty-five

Nick returned to the hospital just before dawn. His long and careful search of Melanie's apartment yielded no clues. Nick stopped in the trauma area before rejoining the others.

"Any word, Frank?"

"I heard ten minutes ago that they're about to move her to the Intensive Care unit."

"Great," Nick breathed. She was still alive. "How is she?"

"So far so good. They took part of her spleen and the lower lobe of her right lung. She's very lucky. It could have been much worse."

"What about the skin lacerations?" Nick knew the medical term—*lacerations*—and used it, even though it didn't adequately describe the wounds. What Nick had seen were deep, jagged *gashes* where the assailant's knife had viciously ripped her lovely flesh.

"The plastic surgeons closed them all as soon as they knew she would survive surgery. She'll have scars, but . . ."

She's alive, Nick thought. And for some reason the Manhattan Ripper stopped before inflicting the final, lethal wounds to her face and throat. There was something else the Ripper always did to his victims. Nick asked, "Was she sexually assaulted?"

"I don't know. I saw Sara Rockwell arrive about thirty minutes ago. I assume she's in there now, collecting evidence while Melanie is still under anesthesia."

Moments before Nick entered the waiting room, Brooke and Charles and Andrew and Jason, who had arrived from Southampton, had been told that Melanie was about to be moved to Intensive Care. Nick found Brooke's eyes and saw a glimmer of hope amid the fear and fatigue.

The hope was fragile, no one was offering guarantees, but . . .

"Nick, have you heard?" Brooke smiled a trembling smile.

Nick returned a smile and wanted to hold her.

"Good news."

"Did you find anything?"

"Working on it, Brooke." He had found nothing. But even *that* was confidential police information. He might tell Brooke, but not the others.

Before Brooke could press further a woman entered the room. She wore a dark-blue surgical scrub dress covered by a long white coat. Above the left breast pocket of the white coat, embroidered in emerald-green thread, was the name Dr. Sara Rockwell.

"'Lieutenant Adrian?" Sara scanned the group and settled on Nick. His was the only face—male or female —that Sara didn't instantly recognized. She had seen the others on television and read about them in newspapers and magazines. Andrew Parker, Manhattan's brilliant deputy DA. Brooke Chandler, Andrew's able and impressive assistant, and—Sara had read somewhere—Melanie Chandler's twin sister. And the handsome and powerful Sinclair twins, one of whom was the father of Galen Spencer's baby.

Which one, Sara wondered. Which twin had Galen loved? Or had she loved both? And which twin, or both, had loved her? And was either involved with the beautiful woman she had just examined?

One of them is, Sara concluded as she observed their worried faces. One of them is *very* involved.

"Dr. Rockwell." Nick moved toward her.

"May I . . . shall we . . ." Sara gestured toward the door.

The information was police business, for Nick only.

"Has something happened?" Brooke asked anxiously.

"This is Brooke Chandler, Melanie's sister," Nick explained. "Brooke, Dr. Rockwell just examined Melanie to see if she was assaulted, uh, sexually."

"*Raped,*" Brooke whispered. The others—the other victims—had been raped. Brooke knew that. "She was, wasn't she?"

Sara looked at Nick with a glance that asked, Do you want the answer in front of all of them?

Nick shrugged. Why not? They were all involved, himself included, even though he shouldn't be.

"No," Sara answered definitively. She cast a sympathetic glance at Brooke and then beyond Brooke to the very concerned Sinclair. "No, she wasn't raped."

"No?" Brooke repeated weakly. Relief swept through her. It made a difference. As violated as Melanie already had been, it still made a difference that *that* hadn't happened.

"No."

What made him stop? Nick wondered for the hundredth time that night. Melanie would tell him. . . .

★   ★   ★

No visitors until noon, the doctors said. By then the anesthetic should have worn off and Melanie would be awake.

Brooke and Charles and Andrew and Nick waited in the ICU visitors' lounge. Adam arrived at ten.

"She's going to be all right, Adam." Brooke greeted him with that reassurance. Even though no one reassured Brooke—they couldn't—*that* was what she was going to believe.

"Thank God," Adam breathed.

"She's resting. We can see her at noon." *We.* The doctors had said family only. But Adam was the man Melanie loved, surely he would be allowed. . . .

Adam's tired eyes smiled at Brooke and relief softened the strain on his face. Then he looked beyond Brooke, at Charles, and his face hardened with rage.

"What the hell are you doing here?"

"Adam," Brooke whispered to Adam's back as he moved, fists clenched, toward Charles. "Charles cares about Melanie."

"Cares?"

"Yes." Charles's dark eyes blazed at Adam.

"She really loved you, Charles. Christ only knows why. It almost destroyed her when you left her. You should be lying in there, not her, not Melanie."

"Adam!"

"Mr. Drake, I'm Nick Adrian with the NYPD." Nick casually positioned himself between Charles and Adam. "This really isn't helping."

Adam looked at Nick. "You're a cop? Good. You can get a restraining order. I know Melanie wouldn't want him here."

"I can't do that." Nick's voice was calm and firm.

"Can you, Andrew?" Adam turned to the man who was such a celebrity in his own sphere that his name appeared on important guest lists, such as Adam's exclusive New Year's Eve party.

"Adam." Andrew's calm matched Nick's. "We have to have cause. If Charles wants to be here—"

"He does." Charles held Adam's gaze until Adam looked away. Then Charles turned to Brooke to gratefully acknowledge her support.

But Brooke was distracted, lost in thought. *She really loved you, Charles,* Adam had said. *It almost destroyed her when you left her.* Charles left Melanie? Melanie had tried to tell her that—"I'm not lying, Brooke!"—and Brooke had refused to believe her. But it was true. Brooke saw it in Charles's eyes, and he didn't deny Adam's accusation. Charles had left Melanie.

But there was more in Charles's tormented dark eyes. Charles left Melanie, but he loved her, *still.*

Melanie didn't awaken by noon. She didn't awaken at all that day, or the next. The doctors couldn't explain it. There had been no head injury. They did brain scans and CAT scans and EEGs; all the high technology only confirmed what they already knew. Melanie Chandler should be awake.

But she wasn't.

Brooke and her parents and Adam kept vigil at Melanie's bedside. They talked to her and touched her and held her lifeless hands and pleaded with her to wake up.

Melanie heard Brooke's voice, but she couldn't open her eyes. The lids were so heavy and there was so much pain.

"Mellie," Brooke whispered softly to her pale, unresponsive twin. An ancient promise haunted her.

Brooke, promise me if I die I can be your shadow.

I'm not going to talk to you if you say things like that.

Promise me.

I promise.

No, I don't promise, Mellie. You aren't going to die.

I'm dying, Brooke. Am I already dead? I can't see you. I can't make my eyes open. I can't talk. There is something in my throat. Help me, Brooke.

Brooke gently touched Melanie's forehead above the tape that held the nasotracheal tube through which a ventilator breathed oxygenated air into her twin.

"There's a tube to help you breathe," Brooke answered Melanie's thought. "I'm sure it's uncomfortable. As soon as you wake up they can take it out. You're going to be fine. Oh, Mellie, can you hear me?"

Yes, Brooke, I can hear you! Keep talking to me, Brooke. Don't give up. I can hear you. Please don't leave me. I am so afraid.

"I won't leave you, honey. I never will. Well be friends again—so close—like we used to be. OK?"

Yes! I want to be your friend. I've always wanted to be.

"Today is Wednesday, February eighteenth. You've been asleep for two days. We're all here. Mom and Dad. And Adam. And," Brooke hesitated. She stroked Melanie's blond hair thoughtfully. *She really loved you, Charles. It almost destroyed her when you left her.* Maybe, maybe. . . "And Charles is here."

The long, golden lashes flickered.

Charles is here? Where?

"He's been here the whole time." Brooke watched Melanie's pale eyelids. There was life behind them for the first time in two days! "He hasn't been in because he's not family, but . . ."

Was it her imagination or did Melanie's brow furrow slightly? To hell with the *rules*, Brooke decided impulsively. "I'm going to get him, Mellie. He wants to see you."

Charles had been there almost continually, resolutely keeping his own private vigil in a far corner of the waiting room. Charles was there, even though there was no hope that he would be able to see her, and even though Adam glowered at him and Melanie's parents eyed him skeptically. Only Brooke, when she wasn't in Melanie's room, sat beside Charles.

"Charles?"

Charles stood up. "Is she . . . ?" A spark of hope flickered in the tired brown eyes.

"No. She's not awake, but I want you to talk to her."

Brooke and Charles walked into the ICU. Brooke cast a defiant glance at the nurses. He's my long-lost brother, her blue eyes told them. He only *looks* like Charles Sinclair. No one stopped them.

"This is all right with Lieutenant Adrian," Brooke lied to the guard outside Melanie's room. It *would* be all right. The guard was there in case the Manhattan Ripper tried to finish what he had started. That had nothing to do with Charles.

Brooke led the way into Melanie's room. She and her parents and Adam had adjusted to the sight of the frail, lifeless body of their beloved Melanie, but for Charles it was a heart-stopping shock.

I thought you enjoyed watching beautiful things die. God, why had Melanie said that? Had she somehow known?

Charles took Melanie's pale, cool hand in his and stared at it for a moment. Plastic tubing flowed into a purple vein. It was taped securely, but there were dried bloodstains between her fingers. Did they have to try again and again to find a vein? Had they hurt her?

Charles wanted to take her away.

His lips touched her temple as he whispered, "I love you, Melanie. You have to know that, darling. I believed your life would be happier without me, but I never stopped loving you. Come back to me, Melanie."

She was dreaming and it was a lovely, wonderful dream. His soft, gentle, loving voice spoke words he had never spoken to her before, words she had dreamed he would speak. It was such a wonderful dream. Oh, *Charles.*

Charles felt pressure in his hand and his heart leapt. "Melanie, I love you so much. . . ."

The pale-blue eyes fluttered open and focused slowly on his handsome face. He was so close and so worried. Don't *worry,* Charles.

"Hello, darling," Charles whispered.

Hello, Charles. I thought I was dreaming, but you're here. Did you really say I love you?

"How are you?" Charles smiled through tears of joy.

Melanie began to search her memory for answers. The details didn't come, but there were vague images of something horrible. Her eyes narrowed, trying to make the memory come into focus.

"Hey." Charles gently kissed her cheek. "Don't think about it now. It's over. Just concentrate on getting well. OK?"

Melanie frowned. The foggy memory troubled her. Don't think about *what?* And why couldn't she talk? What was in her mouth?

"Melanie." Charles smiled lovingly at her. "Remember the morning I found you in the rose garden in the park? I wanted to hold you so much. Did I ever tell you that?"

The frown vanished and her face transformed as Charles pulled her away from ugly memories to lovely ones. The lovely memories of Melanie and Charles.

Brooke withdrew quietly from Melanie's room. She didn't belong there, witnessing their private,

374

intimate reunion. Melanie was awake; that was all she needed to know.

Nick was outside Melanie's room, glowering at the guard, when Brooke appeared.

"Its my fault, Nick. I told him it was all right with you."

"*Why?*"

"She needed to hear his voice, Nick. The rest of us, as much as we love her," Brooke's voice faded. Then her eyes narrowed and she asked defiantly, "Why do *you* care if Charles sees her anyway? It may be an ICU rule, but it has nothing to do with the police investigation."

The gray eyes told her nothing.

"Nick?"

"You just shouldn't have done it, Brooke," Nick said evenly. There was something about Charles Sinclair, the intensity of his concern, Adam Drake's vehemence that Charles not be allowed near her. . . .

"Yes I should have," Brooke answered quietly. Her dark-blue eyes glistened. "She's awake because of him. . . ."

Because of how much he loves her.

"She's *awake?*"

Brooke nodded and impatiently brushed away a warm tear.

"Brooke, I'm sorry. I shouldn't have gotten angry. . . ."

The following morning the anesthesiologist removed the nasotracheal tube. Melanie coughed as the tube was withdrawn. Then she gasped for breath. Then she groaned in pain as the deep breath of the gasp caused fire in the right side of her chest where the knife had entered and the surfaces were raw and inflamed. She took a smaller breath and it hurt, but not as much. Then, as the doctors watched, prepared to reintubate her if she was too weak or in too much pain to breathe on her own, Melanie began to breathe.

And talk.

"Oh," she whispered, her voice hoarse from the lingering irritation of the tube. "Oh."

"How are you doing, Melanie?" the anesthesiologist asked. He needed more than one syllable.

"OK," she uttered, then forced a smile. "Better. On balance. Better. I think."

"Is it the chest pain that's bothering you?"

Melanie nodded. It had been there, part of the painful aching of her entire body, before. But now, because of the deep breath she had taken, it was the worst pain.

"Is it better with shallower breaths?"

"Better," she admitted. "But not perfect."

"Let's give her some Demerol," the pulmonary specialist said. They couldn't give her Demerol before extubation because it might have depressed her breathing or her energy. But now they could. She was breathing on her own. "This will block the pain, Melanie, and enable you to take deeper breaths."

"I like these shallow breaths."

"I know. But the lung needs to expand to prevent complications."

"Oh."

An hour after Melanie was extubated, after she had received enough Demerol to diminish the pain without blocking her respiratory drive, Nick was allowed to interview her. Only for a few minutes, the doctors said. She will fatigue easily and she needs her strength.

But Melanie's strength held up well. She made it hold up; she needed to talk about it. Melanie remembered everything in vivid detail. Maybe talking about it would help purge the horror. Until now, she couldn't talk. She had been trapped in a world of choking tubes and puffing ventilators and the sometimes regular, sometimes erratic beeping noises that almost drove her crazy.

"I want Brooke to be here," Melanie told Nick when he asked. "If she wants to be."

Brooke wanted to be. At first, Nick said No, for Brooke's protection.

"Nick, if Melanie knows something, the killer will assume I know it, too. If there *is* something, it's safer for me to know."

Nick had to agree; it was safer. Still, it was ultimately Melanie's decision, and Melanie wanted Brooke to be there.

Brooke held her twin's hand while Nick and Melanie talked.

"Do you have any idea who did it?" Nick asked. If he only had a short time, because of Melanie's energy, he would start with the bottom line.

"I know exactly who did it," Melanie answered simply. "It was Robin Shepard."

"*What?*"

"Robin Shepard," Melanie repeated. "He said he wanted to put something about me in 'Profiles.' I thought Adam had arranged it. . . ."

Melanie's blue eyes clouded briefly as she remembered *why* Adam would have arranged it. She blinked away the horrible memory of the bitter, venomous words she had hurled at Charles. There were enough horrible memories.

"What did he look like?" Nick asked gently.

"I didn't see his face or his hands. He wore a dark stocking over his head, and he wore gloves."

"What about his eyes?"

"They were dark brown. His hair was dark, too. I saw some of it at the edge of the stocking."

"Height?"

"Taller than me with my heels on. Six feet, I guess."

"Weight?"

"I don't know. Slender, but not thin. Strong." Melanie shuddered involuntarily.

"You OK?" Nick was pushing her, and she was doing well; except for the name, it was helpful information.

"Nick, why don't you just go get him? Melanie told you who he is," Brooke urged.

"Brooke." Nick's voice was gentle. Brooke wanted it to be easy for her sister. The attorney part of Brooke knew he needed more than a name, and Brooke didn't know the name Melanie had given him was useless.

"I'm OK, Nick," Melanie said. "Go on."

Nick waited a moment before asking the next question. He knew it would startle her. He asked it softly.

"Melanie, was he someone you knew?"

"I told you who he was—Robin Shepard. I'd never met him before."

"Forget who he said he was, Melanie. Was the man who assaulted you—the strong, slender man who was six feet tall with dark hair and eyes— someone that you knew?"

Nick watched Melanie carefully as she considered his question; it worried her. She hadn't thought about it before, and now that she did, it scared her. Was there something?

Finally she shook her head. No, it wasn't possible. No one she knew would do such a thing to her. No.

"Did you recognize the voice?" Nick pressed. Her head shake hadn't been an emphatic No. There was a trace of doubt.

"No, but it was probably always disguised. Even in my apartment it sounded strange, unnatural."

"And the eyes?" Eyes were so personal. If they were eyes she knew well . . .

"I couldn't see the entire eye. The holes were small. I could just see the color, not the shape."

She had seen enough to make her worry about a man she knew with dark-brown eyes, Nick decided. And not enough to reassure herself it wasn't him.

"Keep thinking about that, Melanie. If it could possibly be someone you know, I need to hear about it," Nick said firmly, sensing that she was worried, a little, and guessing that she wouldn't tell him. That was all right. He could think of a man she knew who fit the description, a man whose name she would never give him.

Melanie nodded.

"Do you want to talk about what happened?" Nick asked gently.

"Yes," Melanie answered, but she sighed. She was suddenly so tired. She wanted to tell it all. She *could* tell it all. She remembered every brutal second of the horror, how it felt and what she was thinking. She had to tell it all, but not now. "Sometime."

"OK. Do you have the energy for two more questions?"

"Nick," Brooke murmured.

"It's OK, Brooke."

"Do you remember what he said in your apartment?"

"Yes. He said, *I have to do this. There is no other way. You understand.*" Melanie frowned. "What could that mean? I *don't* understand."

It could mean that it was someone you know, Nick thought uneasily. Someone with whom there had been love and hate and passion and bitterness. . . .

Nick shrugged and smiled at her.

"All right, final question for now," Nick continued. It was, in some ways, *the* question. "Something must have happened to make him leave. He—"

Nick stopped.

"Didn't kill me," Melanie whispered softly. "I don't know why he didn't."

"Did you say anything?"

"I pleaded with him." Melanie shuddered. "I called for help."

Nick was certain that all the Manhattan Ripper's victims had pleaded and called for help. It hadn't stopped the killer before.

"Called for help. Who did you call?"

"I called for Brooke." Melanie's voice was soft. *I called for the people I love.* She added, even more softly, "And I called for Charles."

Charles, Nick mused.

"Did he stop suddenly?"

Melanie considered Nick's question for a moment. "Yes, I guess he did. He stopped and stared at me. He looked startled and then confused."

"After that he left?"

"Yes." Melanie's energy was visibly fading.

"Brooke?" Melanie asked dreamily, her eyes fluttering.

"Yes?"

"It didn't hurt when he stabbed me. It just felt like pressure, but I *heard* it. It was like . . . remember when we got our ears pierced? Remember how afraid we were that it would hurt?"

"But it didn't." It had been an exciting and scary adventure; they braved it together, half anxious, half giggling. Of course she remembered.

"No. But the sound . . . do you remember what we decided it sounded like?"

"I remember, Mellie," Brooke answered gently. She had been remembering the giggles, but now she remembered the sound of the sharp needle puncturing cartilage. "It was a crunching sound. Like celery."

"Uh-huh," Melanie whispered as her eyes closed. "Like celery."

Chapter Twenty-six

"Would you like to come with me to see Robin Shepard? Or do you have to go to court?" Nick asked as they left the ICU.

"Andrew is single-handedly waging war against Jeffrey Martin."

"Andrew can handle it."

"Andrew has been so helpful," Brooke mused. "He has been such a friend throughout all this."

"Andrew's a nice man," Nick observed carefully.

Brooke nodded thoughtfully. "Yes."

She doesn't see it, Nick thought. Brooke has no idea how much Andrew cares about her. But *that* is Brooke's specialty. . . .

They walked in silence for fifty feet before Brooke said suddenly, "You wouldn't let me come with you to see Robin Shepard unless you knew he had nothing to do with it."

"That's right. But do you want to come anyway?"

"Yes."

They walked through the maze of shiny narrow corridors in the recently renovated building that housed New York City's largest newspaper. Robin Shepard's office was in a remote corner on the fourth floor facing the East River. The door to Robin Shepard's inner office was closed.

"May I help you?" a secretary in the small outer office asked.

"I am Lieutenant Adrian, NYPD. I would like to speak with Robin." Nick showed her his badge.

"One moment please." The secretary retreated behind the inner office door and returned moments later. "Please come in."

Robin Shepard was not the Manhattan Ripper. Robin Shepard was five feet five inches tall with shoulder-length auburn hair, green eyes, and a lovely figure. She was a very attractive woman who smiled warmly at Nick.

"Nick, how nice to see you."

"Hello, Robin. Robin, this is Brooke Chandler."

Robin recognized Brooke and, of course, knew the connection with Melanie; it had been common knowledge since the Liberty Weekend celebration.

"I am so sorry about your sister. How is she?"

"She's OK."

"Good. This is an official visit, isn't it?"

"Yes," Nick replied. He told Robin Melanie's assailant had used her name as his passport into her apartment. Nick also gave Robin Melanie's description of the man.

"Terrific," Robin said grimly.

"He must not know you are a woman," Brooke suggested.

"Not necessarily," Nick said. "He could know very well. He only had to count on the fact that Melanie didn't know. And if she did know, and called him on it, he could have admitted the joke or hung up. It wasn't a big risk."

"I've been reading 'Profiles' for four years and I always assumed you were a man." Brooke smiled at Robin.

"Has anyone ever noticed that it's the *women* who always assume that the other successful career person is a *man?*" Nick asked lightly.

"Touché."

"I wonder if he's used my name each time?" Robin asked, frowning.

"Possibly. All the women would recognize it."

"And welcome me with open arms," Robin observed solemnly.

"It's pretty scary," Nick agreed.

"You can't hide from life because of one crazy," Robin said defiantly. Then she teased, "Besides, do you know how angry *you* would be if some woman you needed to interview told you to come by her office the next day after she checked on your badge number?"

Robin was talking about *them*, how they had met. It had been in her apartment late one night when Nick needed information for a case.

"Police business."

"A great cover."

"Do you have any idea who it *could* be?" Brooke interrupted the repartee. "Someone on your staff?"

"Just because this maniac used my name doesn't mean he is, or ever was, associated with me or the paper." Robin stated the obvious. "The physical description includes more men than it *excludes*, The blue eyes and green eyes and gray eyes may be off the hook, but . . ."

Robin looked at Nick when she said gray eyes.

384

"So we're back at ground zero," Brooke murmured.

"No, not at all," Nick countered confidently. "We have a description plus an MO. I'm going to hold a press conference this afternoon."

"You're going to get a lot of calls. Everyone in the city will know at least one possible suspect."

"That's OK. Someone out there really *does* know him, has seen him, works next to him. And revealing his MO may make women even more cautious."

"I don't know if you've noticed, Nick, but this town is already totally panicked about this psychopath. Describing his MO—and I agree you must—will put an end to meaningful male-female intercourse," Robin paused, smiling, "as we know it."

"I have to tell the press he used your name," Nick continued firmly, ignoring her innuendo. "And why we know it's not you."

"I have never pretended to be a man. In fact I've been pushing the editor for a picture beside my byline for years. This may do it."

"Good." Nick made a move to leave. "Thanks, Robin. If you think of anyone . . ."

"I'll let you know right away. Oh, Nick, I've been thinking about doing a profile on you. Cop and author, something like that. I wanted to do it soon, but now I'm wondering if I should wait until you solve this Manhattan Ripper business, write the book about it, and win the Pulitzer Prize."

"That will be a very long wait," Nick said. Not that he wanted a column written about him *ever*.

"I plan to solve the case right away, but I would never write a book about it."

"Nick, why not? Someone is going to. It might as well be the man who knows more about it than anyone else *and* is a fine writer." Robin smiled.

"All I care about is getting him," Nick said seriously. It wasn't entirely true; all Nick cared about was getting him *before* he hurt someone else—someone like Brooke or Robin. "You be careful, Robin. You're one of *them,* you know."

"Them?"

"Yes. The successful women, his targets."

As Nick and Brooke left Robin's office, Brooke winked conspiratorially at the undercover agent who was assigned to protect her.

"When are you going to give that poor man his freedom?"

"Maybe after the press conference," Nick answered vaguely. Maybe never. He couldn't really justify continued police protection for Brooke any more than for any other young woman in Manhattan.

"But the killer knows that Melanie doesn't know who he is. And, therefore, I don't."

"I'm not taking the protection off Melanie until we get him."

"Melanie's an eyewitness. There really isn't a reason to protect me."

"Except that you are so damned trusting."

"Not anymore," Brooke told him solemnly. "If anyone needs protection it's Robin. She *may* know him. Don't you think it's likely that he worked for her or the paper at some time?"

Nick shrugged. Of course he thought it was

likely. Of course Robin needed protection. That was why he arranged for it when he made the call to schedule the press conference.

"She's pretty fond of you."

"Fond?" Nick asked, surprised, his eyes twinkling.

"Pretty interested in you."

"We're friends."

"I'm surprised you're not married."

"Married? To Robin?"

"To anyone."

Nick didn't answer, but later, as he drove Brooke back to the hospital, he said, "I was married once."

"It didn't work out?"

"No. We met in college. I was a nice, safe English major. After we graduated and were married and I was teaching high school English and thinking about getting a Ph.D., I decided to become a cop. It was a childhood fantasy. I even told her about it before we were married, but I don't think either of us really believed I would do it. Anyway, I did, and it was awful for her."

"Why?"

"Any time I was five minutes late getting home she assumed I'd been killed. And every time the phone rang and I wasn't there she was certain it was bad news. She wasn't being paranoid. Cops do get killed, especially in this town. It was awful for her."

"Was it awful for you?"

"She didn't make it awful. She kept her fear hidden for a long time. But I wanted kids, we both did, and . . ."

"You couldn't."

"She wouldn't," Nick corrected. "Not as long as I was a cop. That's when—how—I learned how much she hated what I was doing. And while I was considering giving it up, she fell in love with someone else. By the time she told me how much she hated the way I was spending my life it was already way too late to save the marriage. So, we divorced and she remarried and has three kids and lives in the suburbs."

"And you're still a cop."

"Still a cop."

"And you would still like to have kids," Brooke added quietly after a few moments.

Nick didn't answer. He didn't have to. They had reached the hospital.

"I'm fine, Adam," Melanie told him two days after the tube in her throat had been removed. "You really need to be in Europe."

"I think I need to be here."

"I have plenty of company, and I sleep most the time anyway."

"Still."

"Go." Melanie smiled through the fire that smoldered, threatening to burst into flames of pain, in her chest and abdomen. She was overdue on her Demerol shot, but she wanted to be awake, and not groggy, for her talk with Adam.

Adam frowned briefly. He would go—she was right—but there was something he had to tell her first.

"Melanie, don't let him hurt you again. I know

388

he's here now." Adam paused. *He* didn't want to hurt her.

"Because of the crisis." Melanie sighed softly. There was a foggy memory of soft, lovely words—Charles's words—*I love you, Melanie.* Was it a memory, or a dream? A *dream,* she told herself firmly. She couldn't allow herself to think it was real. "I know, Adam."

"I don't trust him, Melanie."

"Adam, Charles is your friend!"

Not anymore, Adam thought, remembering their angry exchange and the iciness that lingered. "I don't trust him when it comes to you."

Adam returned to Paris. A day later, at Melanie's insistence, Ellen and Douglas Chandler returned to Pasadena. She was *fine,* Melanie told them lovingly. And Brooke was here, and Charles . . .

Charles spent most of every day at her bedside, reading manuscripts while she slept and talking gently to her, holding her hand, when she awakened. In the evening, when Brooke arrived after a day of battling Jeffrey Martin in the courtroom, Charles left. Charles sensed that Brooke needed private time with Melanie as much as he did. They each had secrets and confessions to share with their precious Melanie.

Brooke and Charles needed to tell Melanie *now,* in the rare moments when her trying-to-heal body allowed her to awaken and the narcotics released their foggy grip. They knew she might not hear, or understand, but they had to tell her.

They would tell her again later, too, when her body was strong and her mind was clear.

"It's a nightmare, Melanie, but it feels so real."

"Charles, you don't have to . . ."

"Yes, darling, I do." Charles sighed softly. He had to tell her about more than the nightmare. He had to tell her about an unloved little boy and the man he had become. He *would* tell her all of it when she was well. For now, he would tell her little, important bits. "The nightmare is about my father. There was always something . . ."

Charles paused. How could he explain something he didn't understand? Charles made it simple. "I was never good enough to earn his love."

I was never good enough for Brooke, either, or for you, Melanie mused dreamily. Her thoughts began to drift to the bittersweet memories of her past, carried by the blurry warmth of Demerol and fatigue, but Charles's loving brown eyes pulled her back. Melanie fought to stay awake, focused on Charles, and the present, and these precious moments with him. "You were saying . . . your father . . . the nightmare . . ."

"In the nightmare, my father and I argue." I plead for his love. Charles frowned, remembering. "There's a violent storm, and a sudden crash, and he dies."

"How awful," Melanie whispered softly just before the narcotics won and she succumbed begrudgingly to necessary sleep.

★ ★ ★

390

"I wanted so much to be you," Brooke told Melanie.

"*Me?*"

"Yes. I was jealous." Brooke smiled thoughtfully and stroked the golden hair. "I guess I still am."

"Jealous," Melanie murmured. "Of me?"

"Yes." Brooke laughed softly. "That surprises you?"

"I wished I could be like you." But I was never jealous.

"*Why?*"

"You did important things. You still do." Melanie's voice faded, then found a final burst of strength. "I am so proud of you, Brooke."

"Oh, Melanie, I am so proud of *you.* I always have been."

One evening, Melanie awakened to find Brooke and Nick and Charles at her bedside.

No, she realized as her just-wakening eyes sharpened their focus, it isn't Charles, but he is vaguely familiar. . . .

"Melanie, this is Andrew Parker."

Of course, the deputy DA! Melanie had seen his picture on television and in the papers.

"Hello, Andrew."

"Hello, Melanie. How are you?"

"Fine, thank you. How's Jeffrey Martin?"

"I think we're closing in." Andrew smiled confidently.

"Good." Melanie returned the smile, then frowned. There was something she meant to tell

Nick. What was it? Oh, yes. "Nick, you told me to let you know if I thought of who he might be."

"Yes?"

Nick and Brooke and Andrew waited in breath-held silence.

"Steve Barnes."

"Who is he?" Andrew asked.

"The photographer Adam fired in Monte Carlo," Brooke answered. "Because of me."

"Have you seen or heard from him since?" Nick asked.

"No. I've heard *of* him. He's working, but it's not the same for him. He's not at the top anymore."

"Sounds like a motive."

"And there's something else. Jane Tucker and Adam were once engaged to be married."

Eight days after Melanie arrived at the hospital—bloody and wounded and dying—she awakened to an almost familiar feeling of strength and energy. The feeling awakened with her, a glimmer of hope, and it didn't fade. Melanie eagerly told the doctors that she wanted to sit in a chair and maybe even walk a little. . . .

"Why are you smiling?" she asked, stopping, breathless in the midst of her requests.

"Because you've turned the corner," the attending physician replied. "You're ready to be well again."

"Yes, I am. *Finally.*"

"Not finally, Melanie. Your whole recovery has been remarkable. Your will to be well is ahead of your body's ability to recover. Your injuries are serious and major. Even though you are in excellent health and very fit, it will take a long time before you are fully recovered."

"So don't get discouraged?" she teased happily. It was such a relief to know that her strength and energy would return. She had worried—a foggy, drugged, fatigued worry—that she would never feel good again. "I won't. So I can sit in a chair?"

"Sure. With *help*. Slow and easy. OK?"

"OK," Melanie agreed readily, but her mind spun with wonderful plans. She would sit, then walk, then take a long hot shower . . . Surely the wounds, carefully hidden by sterile dressings, must be healed by *now*.

That was something else she needed to do. She needed to look under the bandages and see for herself what the doctors and nurses examined with such interest every day. Melanie hadn't seen the wounds. She was lying down when they examined her—she was *always* lying down, but not anymore—and it hurt too much to flex her neck to look, and besides, she had been too tired to care.

But now she cared, again, about everything.

Don't get discouraged, she reminded herself later that night as she lay awake—she could stay awake for hours now—reflecting on her accomplishments of the day. The accomplishments seemed so small when she remembered how much effort and energy they had required.

She sat in a chair three times, each time remaining a little longer, ten minutes, fifteen minutes, *twenty* minutes. Each time she was forced to stop because the weakness would come and her heart would race and her mind would blur and she couldn't think or breathe. The weakness was worse than the pain, but the pain was there, too. The fragile healing fibers of the deep knife wounds pulled and stretched and finally sent hot, searing messages of angry protest.

Why was there so much pain, Melanie wondered. She still hadn't looked at her wounds. Her courage waned because of the pain; so much pain meant they couldn't be healed. She would look at them tomorrow, or the next day.

It was too soon for a real shower, but her doctors approved the nurses' plan to wash their favorite patient's long golden hair in the morning.

Melanie fell asleep, smiling, thinking about her hair being clean and shiny again.

When Charles arrived at eleven the next morning he found Melanie sitting at the edge of her bed, her head bent, her shoulders hunched, her face obscured by a mane of slightly damp golden hair.

"Melanie?" He had knocked, hadn't heard an answer, and now peered in, expecting her to be asleep. At the sound of his voice she looked up. Her pale-blue eyes glistened with tears. "Darling, what's wrong?"

"I can't even brush my own hair." She stared at the brush in her useless hands.

After the nurses washed her hair and towelled it almost dry, they offered to brush it for her. But Melanie said No. She wanted to do it; she wanted to do that one *normal* thing.

But the moment Melanie raised her arm above her head, the pain from the stretched and rebelling wounds became severe. Still she didn't stop. She was getting used to pain. Pain was better than the fogginess of Demerol. But after two strokes her arm became heavy, weak, *useless*. There was nothing she could do. She could fight the pain, but not the weakness. She had to stop.

Without a word Charles took the brush from her hand and very gently began to brush the golden silk.

Melanie trembled at his touch and her mind drifted to memories of last summer. Charles loved to brush her hair, but his strong hands always became too gentle. When Charles found a tangle, she would take the brush and pull impatiently at the snarl of silk. And his hands, suddenly free, would find her face, her neck, her breasts, her thighs; and they would make love, and the gold would be tangled again.

Melanie sighed.

"What a sigh," Charles murmured as he brushed gently, so gently.

"I want to be well, Charles." I want more than that. I want to go back to those lovely memories.

"You will be. You look well now. The doctors are thinking about—what is it they said?— oh, yes, writing you up as a case report of a miraculous recovery."

"But I can't *do* anything. I am so weak." Melanie told him about the weakness, but not the pain. She didn't want to tell Charles about the pain.

"That will pass."

Charles brushed in silence for several moments.

Tell him, Melanie. Even if he already knows it you need to tell him.

"Charles?"

"Hmm?"

"I am so sorry for what I said to you at the Valentine's Day party."

Charles stopped brushing and knelt in front of her. He peered under the curtain of gold until he found her eyes.

"I am so sorry for hurting you. For all the hurt," Charles said heavily, as if weighted down by every pain she had ever suffered, including the horror of the Manhattan Ripper.

"It's OK. I'm OK." *Now, because you're here. But when I get well and you are gone again . . . I can't think about that.*

Charles took her hands in his.

"May I have this dance?" *May I have this life, this love?*

"Yes."

Charles stood up and pulled her gently to him. He folded her arms against his chest, because he sensed that she couldn't lift them to his neck. Then he wrapped his arms around her and held her tight, providing support, as they swayed gently together.

"Am I hurting you?" His lips brushed her clean gold hair.

"No," she whispered into his chest. It all hurt, her whole body hurt. But beyond the pain was something so wonderful. Beyond the pain was Charles. His hands, his arms, his lips, his body, his warmth, his strength. *Charles.* Nothing else mattered.

If only this moment could last forever.

But it couldn't. The weakness came suddenly and without warning, drenching her in overwhelming fatigue that, unlike the pain, she couldn't fight or control. She could conquer the pain, but not the weakness. It won every time.

Charles sensed it immediately; her body shuddered and became limp. Quickly, carrying her easily, Charles laid her on the bed.

"Are you OK?" he asked anxiously. "Should I get the doctor?"

"No, Charles," Melanie reassured the concerned brown eyes. "This happens all the time."

"I shouldn't have —"

"Yes, you should have." Melanie forced her eyes to stay open a little longer. It was a small conquest over the fatigue that was demanding she go to sleep *now.* She looked at him and whispered, "Thank you."

Melanie didn't know if it was just a lovely wish or the beginning of a happy dream or if it was real. It *felt* real. It felt like the touch of his lips, so soft, so tender, pressing lightly against hers as she fell asleep.

Melanie awakened two hours later. Charles was gone. But the memory filled her with warmth and joy and hope. *Maybe.* She would be out of the hospital soon. Maybe they could begin again. . . .

Melanie got out of bed and walked to the sink, above which hung a small mirror. Melanie needed to see how soon it would be. *Surely* the wounds were almost healed. . . .

Melanie pulled the paper tape that held the edge of a large bandage over her left breast. The bandage fell free, exposing a thick pink-purple scar that puckered her skin and redefined the shape of a breast that *used* to be perfect and round and firm and proud. Now it was misshapen, stretched and twisted into a new, ugly shape by the gruesome scar.

Melanie gazed in horror.

No. *No.*

Melanie felt her dreams die. She and Charles could never begin again.

It was over.

Chapter Twenty-seven

When Brooke arrived at six o'clock that evening she found Melanie staring trancelike at her hands.

"Melanie?"

"Oh, Brooke. Hi." Melanie's voice was flat.

"You look great."

Brooke noticed the shiny golden hair at once. As she moved closer she saw the tears.

"Mellie?" Brooke asked gently. "What's wrong?"

The softness of Brooke's voice made the tears spill faster. Melanie shook her head, unable to speak. Brooke sat on the bed beside her, touched her hands to Melanie's shoulders, and waited.

Finally Melanie spoke.

"Brooke, I saw what I look like today," she whispered bitterly. "I looked under the bandages. You have no idea. . . ."

"I do know, Melanie. I was here one day when they changed the dressings. You were half asleep."

"So you know how ugly."

"They are just beginning to heal. The doctors say they will become fine white lines."

"Fine white lines all over my breasts and abdomen," Melanie murmured. Then her eyes flashed, "And you know they won't be fine, Brooke. You've seen them. They'll be thick and ugly *always.*"

"So you won't model swimsuits anymore," Brooke suggested carefully.

Melanie looked at her twin with surprise. She hadn't even thought about her modelling career. It was over, too. She could still model clothes that covered her torso, but she *wouldn't.* She wasn't beautiful anymore. She no longer had a beautiful body to wear under the beautiful clothes.

"No, I won't model," her voice faded. *And I won't be with the man I love.*

"You'll have a few scars, Melanie." More than a few, Brooke knew. And they *would* be horrible and disfiguring. She added truthfully, "But you can model if you want. And . . ."

Brooke couldn't say it. She couldn't say with certainty that it wouldn't matter to Charles. Brooke *believed* it wouldn't, because she had always believed in Charles. But what if she was wrong? What if the blood in his aristocratic veins really was ice-cold after all? Charles had hurt Melanie before.

Brooke knew Charles loved Melanie; she only hoped he loved her twin *enough*. . . .

Melanie awoke the following morning with the certain knowledge that she had to get out of the hospital as soon as possible. She had to begin her new life. The doctors agreed that with a visiting nurse and careful follow-up, she could, in keeping with her miraculous recovery, leave in two days.

Usually Charles arrived at the hospital by midmorning, but not today. By the middle of the afternoon she still hadn't seen him. Maybe he knew; maybe he had felt the scars, the ugliness, beneath the sterile dressings as he held her against him. Like the princess and the pea, Melanie mused. The prince and scars.

It was just as well, she decided. It would be easiest if Charles made the decision to stay away.

Jason arrived at three o'clock.

"Jason, how nice of you to visit." Melanie hadn't seen Jason since the day in the art museum before Christmas.

"You look good, Melanie." Jason smiled. "Charles asked me to tell you he'll be over this evening. There was a problem with the copy for *Images*. . . ."

"I know he's very busy, Jason. Tell him there's no need to visit every day. I'm getting much better. In fact, I'll be leaving soon."

"Leaving soon?" Nick echoed her last two words as he entered the room. "Hello, Jason. Leaving soon, Melanie?"

"Oh-oh," Melanie explained pleasantly to

Jason. "Here comes trouble. Nick has a fantasy about stashing me away in a safe house until You Know Who is caught."

"Not a fantasy, my dear eyewitness," Nick replied with matching pleasantness.

"See? He's not about to let me wander the streets of Manhattan. Safe house is a euphemism for jail."

"Have you already found a place?" Jason asked.

"No," Nick answered. "This is the first I've heard about leaving soon."

"I have an estate in Southampton. The house has a state-of-the-art alarm system. Guards placed at a few strategic locations would make it virtually impenetrable. I assume Melanie's safety is the major concern."

"Yes."

"I think she'd be safe there. And it's beautiful and peaceful. You're welcome to it." Jason made the offer first to the steel-gray eyes and then to the pale-blue ones.

"Jason, that is so generous," Melanie breathed.

"It's very generous, Jason," Nick agreed.

"Does that mean . . . Nick?" Melanie asked eagerly.

"I need to go look at it, arrange for guards, make sure it's safe."

"I know it will be," Melanie said confidently. "Jason, I can't believe this. It's so nice of you."

"It's really nothing." Jason was happy to help.

"Jason, I just thought of something." Melanie's blue eyes sparkled. "There's probably a beach, isn't there? Somewhere nearby. Maybe

I could go for drives in a squad car to see the beach?"

"The house is on the beach, Melanie. Lots and lots of beach."

Nick agreed to Southampton because it would be nice for Melanie. She had been through so much already. This way she could be near Brooke, and Charles.

Charles. Nick would feel better if he could find Charles even something *close* to an alibi. Nick had been trying to do it without actually asking him, but he was coming up empty. No one seemed to know where Charles Sinclair was on the nights of the Manhattan Ripper's brutal attacks.

Yesterday Nick had received the report from the Southampton police on the death of Elliott Sinclair. The death was ruled an accident. Note was made of the fact that Charles Sinclair, the estranged son who was working with the Peace Corps in Africa, had mysteriously appeared moments after news of Elliott's death. It was regarded as an interesting, but not troublesome, coincidence. The report did not include interviews with anyone at the Peconic Bay Yacht Club who might have been able to tell them if Elliott Sinclair was alone when he sailed into the storm. . . .

After Nick received the report, he made some calls. He spoke with the Southampton police officers who interviewed Charles at the time. They told him that Charles was distraught, *naturally.* Charles's explanation for his mysterious reappearance, they recalled, was that he "just had a feeling" Jason needed him. Nick next spoke with John Perkins who was unable to shed light on the estrangement of Charles and Elliott Sinclair. Nick planned to speak with the harbormaster at Peconic Bay Yacht Club—the man who might know if Elliott sailed to his death alone—upon his return from vacation next week.

Nick would feel better when he had at least one airtight alibi for Charles Sinclair for a night that the Ripper attacked. He also wanted convincing evidence that there really was no mystery about Elliott's death. Best of all would be if one of the hundreds of daily "tips" called in regarding the identity of the Manhattan Ripper paid off.

Until then Charles Sinclair was a suspect, but Nick couldn't prevent him from seeing Melanie.

"You'll be staying at Windermere?" Charles asked when she told him four hours later.

"Yes." *Why does that bother you, Charles?*

"You could stay at the penthouse. It would be much easier to guard than Windermere. I'm going to talk to Nick—"

"No," Melanie said swiftly. *I can't stay with you, darling. I can't be with you. I can't ever let you see the way I look.*

His dark eyes—loving, questioning, bewildered—met hers.

"Being at the beach . . . in the country . . ." Melanie fumbled. *None of that would have mattered if she hadn't seen the scars. All she would have cared about was being with Charles.*

Charles started to speak, but at that moment Brooke and Nick arrived. The four of them talked about Melanie, how well she looked; and about Windermere, how wonderful that would be; and about the Jeffrey Martin trial, how well it was going.

After thirty minutes, Nick stood up to leave.

"I'd better go," Nick said. He added, as if it were an afterthought, "Charles, I wonder if you would let me know where you were on the nights—"

"*What?*" Charles stood up and faced Nick. His dark eyes flashed with anger.

"I need to know," Nick said evenly.

"Nick, you can't possibly—" Brooke began.

"Think I'm a suspect?" Charles finished Brooke's sentence. His voice was low. "That's exactly what Nick thinks."

"No," Melanie whispered.

"It's routine. Charles matches the description," Nick explained, carefully watching Charles's reaction.

"It's not routine," Charles hissed. "You aren't collecting alibis from every man fitting the description who knew Melanie or the others."

"I would appreciate your cooperation in this, Charles." Nick's gray eyes sent a challenge.

"You have no right, Nick. And it's more than insulting to even suggest—"

"Do you know the dates?"

"No I don't."

"June nineteenth, September seventeenth, October seventeenth, December twenty-third, and February sixteenth."

February sixteenth. That night Melanie had been the victim.

Charles forced the anger for Nick from his eyes and looked, gently questioning, at Melanie.

Do you believe I could have done that to you, Melanie? Is that why you don't want to stay at the penthouse?

"Charles," Melanie whispered.

"Don't you know," Charles began. His voice was hoarse, a tenuous balance between tenderness and rage.

Yes, I know, Charles, I know.

Charles turned back to Nick. When he spoke his voice was ice. "You had no right to ask me in front of them."

Charles held Nick's eyes for several angry moments. Then he left.

Brooke and Melanie stared at Nick in stunned silence.

"This is a murder investigation," Nick said finally, firmly, first to the sky-blue eyes and then to the ocean-blue ones. He repeated before he, too, left, "Murder."

"I'll be back, Melanie." Brooke followed Nick out of the room.

"Nick."

Nick turned and waited.

"How dare you?"

"How *dare* I?"

"How dare you imply that Charles—"

Nick took Brooke by the arm and guided her out of the bright lights of the hospital corridor into a dimly lit supply room.

"Brooke. I know what I'm doing."

"Then tell me. Make me understand why you would do that."

"I've told Andrew. You know he's the contact in the DA's office."

"Tell *me.*"

"You're too personally involved." Nick found her dark-blue eyes in the shadows. *Just like I'm too personally involved, only you don't know it.*

"Melanie's my sister, but—"

"And you're in love with Charles." Nick spoke softly.

Brooke's eyes became thoughtful and serious. Maybe once I was, or *thought* I was, she mused. But not now.

Finally she smiled a soft wistful smile and said, "I'm not in love with him, Nick. I care about him. I care about him and Melanie. I admit that. But I'm a professional, too, Nick. You can trust me with whatever you have."

Nick decided to trust her. He wanted to trust her, and he wanted to believe her.

"Charles fits the physical description. His blood-type is O, and he is right-handed."

"Right-handed?"

"Andrew really hasn't told you anything, has he?"

"I guess not."

"We know the Ripper is right-handed. At least he—"

"Uses a knife with his right hand," Brooke completed the sentence. I'm not that fragile, Nick, she thought bravely as an ice-cold shiver pulsed through her.

"Yes. And I can't find an alibi for Charles for any of the five nights."

"He must have been at a party or a theater opening or . . ."

"I've really checked, Brooke. He was at a party on December twenty-third, but he left early, and alone. That's why I had to ask him."

"In front of—"

"If he has nothing to hide, it's just an insult from a lowly cop. But . . ."

"He was very angry," Brooke whispered. "But that doesn't mean guilt. Charles is very proud."

"An expensive luxury."

"What about Steve?" Brooke asked suddenly. "Have you followed up on him? He has reason to want to harm Melanie and Adam. . . ."

"Of course I have followed up. Steve isn't the Manhattan Ripper." Nick paused. *Hear this, Brooke.* "Steve Barnes is left-handed. His blood type is B. He was in Tokyo on the night of the attack in October."

"He knew two of the victims. . . ." Brooke protested weakly.

"So did Charles, *at least* two." *Charles was* involved *with two; and he knew, or certainly had met, Jane Tucker when she and Adam were together.* Nick watched Brooke's face in the shadows.

Brooke frowned and shook her head slightly. *It's not possible.*

"You knew that, didn't you?" Nick asked. "You knew that Charles and Pamela Rhodes were lovers."

"Yes, but . . ." *There had to be more. There*

was still something Nick hadn't told her. "What else, Nick?"

Nick sighed. Brooke said she wasn't in love with Charles, but she was blinded to the facts of the case. Her logical, incisive mind was cluttered and confused by emotion. Maybe if he told her everything. . . . She needed to be aware. She needed to be careful.

"Thirteen years ago Charles's father died in a yachting accident. He was killed by a severe blow to the head. It happened during a storm. The police report says he was hit by the boom of the sailboat."

"So?" Brooke heard the defiance in her voice. Nick was about to tell her something that might make Charles Sinclair's blood type and physical description and right-handedness and lack of alibis suddenly more than circumstantial, and she didn't want to hear it.

"Less than an hour after Elliott's body was found, Charles arrived at the family estate. His clothes were torn and dirty and soaking wet."

"So?"

"Charles had been away—in Africa—for three years. Until that moment no one knew he had returned."

"Coincidence. He missed his father and twin—"

"Elliott disowned Charles four years before."

"Why?" Brooke knew it was true. It explained why Jason, not Charles, signed all the contracts for Sinclair Publishing. She repeated softly, "Why?"

"No one seems to know."

"Charles must have had a reason for why he returned *then* from Africa."

"He told the Southampton police he 'had a feeling' Jason needed him." Nick paused. Then he added skeptically, "Charles began his journey home from Kenya a week before Elliott's death and arrived in New York the day before Elliott died."

Brooke retreated deeper into the shadows of the supply room.

"Brooke?"

"When Melanie and I were fourteen I signed up for an overnight camping trip in Yosemite Park with my science class." Brooke's voice was distant with the memory. "It wasn't the sort of thing I usually did. Melanie was the outdoors one, the athlete. But, sometimes, I pretended I was Melanie."

Sometimes I wanted so much to be Melanie. Brooke sighed.

"Anyway, I guess I was pretending I was her, because I left the group and climbed a steep rocky hill. I scampered up it like a mountain goat, just like Melanie would have. When I got to the top, where it was flat and safe, I was clumsy Brooke again and I tripped on a tree root and badly sprained my ankle. I couldn't walk. I had wandered too far for anyone to hear my calls for help.

"When they discovered I was missing they began a search. My parents and Melanie drove up from Pasadena. Moments after Melanie arrived she started urging the rangers to climb the steep, rocky hill. Naturally the search was

409

centered in the opposite direction toward the flat, dense forest. No one would expect *me* to climb the hill. They would have ignored anyone else, but even then Melanie was beautiful and charming and persuasive.

"Apparently she finally threatened to search by herself. That convinced a ranger to go with her. When they found me it was pitch-black. I didn't even hear them coming." Brooke's voice choked with emotion as she remembered how she and Melanie had downplayed it at the time. It was just a lucky coincidence! She was no part of Melanie and Melanie was no part of her. There was nothing special about *them;* it wasn't because they were *twins* and there was a bond. "Melanie knew where I was. She knew I needed her. Something told her. . . ."

Nick moved into the darkness until he was very close to her.

"Brooke, Charles left Africa seven days before a completely unexpected storm hit Long Island. There was no way. . . ."

Brooke spun and faced him. Her blue eyes flashed. "I don't *care* if it makes sense, Nick. It can *happen!*"

The moment Brooke returned to Melanie's hospital room, Melanie asked, "What did Nick say, Brooke? He doesn't really think that Charles—"

"He has to pursue every possibility no matter how remote," Brooke answered vaguely. Then, purposefully shifting the conversation, she said, "Galen called today. She just found out. She wants to talk with you, but she doesn't want to disturb you."

Melanie smiled. Shy, thoughtful Galen.

"I'll give her a call in the morning."

Brooke and Melanie talked about Galen for a while. Before Brooke left, she asked, offhandedly, "Do you know anything about Charles and Jason's father?"

Why, Brooke? Does it have something to do with why Nick suspects Charles?

"Not really." *Just that Charles has a nightmare about an argument with him, during which his father dies, and the nightmare is so real that it awakens him, gasping and frightened and tormented. . . .*

"How is 'Sonja'?" Melanie asked Galen after she had assured and reassured Galen that she was fine.

"Still unpublishable. I can't change it." *I can't even try.*

"Send it to me," Melanie urged eagerly.

"Oh, no . . ."

"*Yes.* I need some good reading. . . ."

"This isn't good." Galen hesitated. "But I'll send you 'Sonja' and the rest of *Spring Street Stories* and the bound galleys for *Songs of the Savanna.* Hopefully, the others will offset 'Sonja.' "

"What a wonderful care package!"

"Shall I send it to the hospital?"

"No." Melanie would be leaving for Windermere in the morning. Nick told her to tell no one when or where she was going. "Could you send it to Brooke?"

After Melanie finished talking to Galen she studied the 1986 calendar the nurses had found for her. Perhaps *she* could provide an alibi for Charles. Last June they had been together almost every night. *Almost.*

June nineteenth. Melanie's heart raced and her stomach ached as the realization settled. June nineteenth was the night she had gone to bed early and alone. She had called Charles back and reached a line that was at first busy and then unanswered. Melanie had no idea how Charles spent the night of June nineteenth. Except that, perhaps, he was angry with *her* . . .

September seventeenth. On September sixteenth, Charles arrived in Monte Carlo to say good-bye, again, forever. By the night of the seventeenth, Charles was back in New York. Melanie remembered her angry question—"Why did you really come, Charles? Just to twist the knife?"—and shuddered.

October seventeenth. Melanie had no idea where Charles was that night. He wasn't a part of her life then, anymore, even though he was still a part of her heart. Melanie knew she missed him that night, as she missed him every night.

December twenty-third. Melanie's heart leapt. She had seen Charles at the *Vogue* holiday open house. She had seen him from a distance. He was alone. He had started toward her—perhaps to speak with her—but she had turned away. Melanie remembered seeing Charles leave, several hours before Viveca told her that Jane Tucker had been murdered.

February sixteenth. Melanie could not give

Charles an alibi for that night, except he was *not* with her. The wild, dark eyes and strong, lean body and brutal, savage hands belonged to someone else. They belonged to a stranger who stopped his merciless assault when she called Charles's name. . . .

Melanie tossed the calendar aside. She had come up empty, worse than empty. Exhausted, Melanie sought refuge in sleep. But her dreams were confusing, horrible scenes of Charles and Nick and Brooke. Nick's wounded head spurted bright red blood as Charles laughed. Or was it *she* who was laughing? And why did Brooke have that knife?

When Melanie awoke, gasping, it was dark outside. She had spent her last day in the hospital thinking about him and dreaming about him. But she didn't see him that day. Charles didn't visit. And he didn't call.

Chapter Twenty-eight

Melanie left the hospital by ambulance at six-thirty the following morning. The ambulance provided an excellent cover, and, despite her strong will, there was no good evidence that Melanie could sit up in a car all the way to South-ampton.

Since no one expected Melanie to be well enough to leave the hospital for at least another week, it would be days before the discovery was made by the press. Then, and only then, would Nick issue a statement that she had been moved to a safe house in another part of the state.

The guards, off-duty police officers, were already in position by the time Melanie arrived. Nick had spent the previous afternoon at Windermere with Jason making all the arrangements. Before leaving, Nick gave Jason three automatic telephone dialing machines and asked Jason to program the machines with numbers Nick gave him to the Southampton police, Nick's office, and Nick's apartment. Jason nodded. He would see to it that it was done, even though, because he couldn't read the instructions, he couldn't do it himself. Maybe one of the guards wouldn't mind.

"Jason," Melanie breathed after the ambulance left and she was settled in the spacious charming first-floor bedroom that had once housed the live-in cook. Cheerful flowery paper adorned the walls, and yellow-and-white lace curtains framed the window. Melanie gazed out the window toward the emerald lawn and beyond to the white sand beach and gray-green sea. "This is wonderful."

"I thought it would be best for you to be on the first floor. The kitchen is nearby, and it's a short walk to the great room and library."

"But you chose this room because of the view, didn't you?"

"You did mention something about beach." Jason smiled. "Although most of the rooms have views. You'll see. When you're rested we can take a tour."

"I'm rested."

"I meant in a few days."

"Let's see how far we can get today," Melanie urged, standing, encouraged by the legs that supported her and seemed willing to move.

"OK," Jason agreed and offered his arm.

Melanie curled her hand around his forearm and they walked slowly into the huge entry hall. Melanie paused a moment, marvelling at the white marble floor, the huge crystal chandelier, the rich, colorful Oriental rugs, the shiny brass planters filled with luxuriant jade plants, and the lovely, bright paintings that hung on the natural wood walls. She frowned slightly as her eye fell on something that was distinctly out of place.

"What are those?" she asked, gesturing to a stack of boxes.

"Automatic telephone dialing machines. Nick wants one at your bedside, one in the entry hall, and one in my bedroom, all programmed to reach him and the local police."

"Did you explain to him that the high tech look really clashes with the overall tranquillity of the place?"

"No," Jason answered, frowning slightly.

"Jason?"

"Would you be willing to program them?"

"Sure. That's just the kind of project I need."

Melanie didn't ask why. Maybe Charles had already told her, but Jason doubted it.

"Melanie, do you know why I asked you to program the machines?"

"No. Probably because it will be one less game of backgammon you have to play with me to keep me amused," she guessed lightly. Then, watching his face, seeing uncharacteristic doubt in his confident handsomeness, she added quietly, "No. Why?"

"Because I can't read. That's something you probably should know." For your safety.

Can't read? What did that mean?

"You mean you don't read well." Melanie's mind searched for facts. She had never seen Jason read anything. But why would she? Then she remembered the day in the art museum when she teased him about listening to the recorded tour. *Teased* him.

"I don't read at all. I only write my name."

"It must be so frustrating," Melanie spoke softly, almost to herself.

"It's a little frustrating," Jason admitted.

"Understatement of the year?"

"Understatement of the first twenty-two years of my life." *Until I discovered my painting.* "Now I almost forget about it until something comes up like programming automatic dialing machines."

"Consider them programmed, *after* my tour."

Melanie smiled and nodded appreciatively as Jason led her through the elegant mansion. Each room was a masterpiece of style and art and exquisite taste. Throughout, on wall after wall, hung magnificent paintings.

Finally, because she had been silently admiring them, Melanie moved to one of the paintings for a closer inspection. The scene was dramatic, a violent storm painted in shades of gray. Melanie felt the force of the tormented angry sea battling the raging turbulent sky. Melanie gazed at the painting for many moments before her eyes drifted to the signature.

"You did this?"

"Yes."

"No wonder it's only a *little* frustrating being unable to read. What talent, Jason!"

"Thank you."

"You're welcome! Who is Meredith?" The painting next to Jason's, a lovely, colorful, full-bloom garden of roses, was signed *Meredith Sinclair.*

"My mother. Our style is similar. Her paintings are a little more pastel, a little softer than mine," Jason answered thoughtfully. There was a reason for the difference in style. Meredith's eye didn't see violence and death and tragedy in a summer storm the way his did. . . .

"Your mother. Is this—Did you and Charles grow up at Windermere?" Melanie turned to face him. As she turned, the weakness hit her, sudden, unexpected, and overwhelming, as always. *"Oh."*

Jason guided her swiftly to the sofa and helped her lie down.

"Talk about a little frustrating," Melanie said after the fogginess in her brain cleared slightly. "It comes without warning."

"I think it's because you push to the absolute limit," Jason observed mildly. "Do you want to settle in here for a while? I can get a comforter for you."

Charles telephoned Windermere just as the winter sun was setting.

"She's fine." Jason smiled at Melanie. "She keeps looking wistfully at the beach and talking about jogging. How's . . ."

Melanie watched as Jason discussed the business of Sinclair Publishing Company with his twin. After fifteen minutes Jason said, "She's right here."

Jason handed the receiver to Melanie and quietly withdrew from the great room.

"Hello, Charles."

"Are you all right?"

"Yes." Are *you?* "It's so lovely here."

"Uh-huh. I just spoke with Brooke. She has an express mall package for you from Lake Forest."

"From Galen."

"Brooke says she and Andrew have to spend tomorrow working on the trial so she won't be able to visit until Sunday."

"Brooke should rest. I'm *fine.*"

"I thought I could bring the package out tomorrow."

"Oh." Yes, *do,* so I can tell you that I believe in you and trust you and love you.

No. The image of her horrible wounds became vivid. Don't come. There is no point.

"Is that a Yes?" Charles's voice was quiet and tentative. And hopeful. Trust me, Melanie.

"Yes," she whispered.

The police-appointed visiting nurse arrived at Windermere at nine Saturday morning. After removing the sterile dressings and carefully inspecting the wounds, she announced, "You don't really need all these dressings anymore."

"I don't?" Melanie asked, surprised. Wouldn't it be best to keep the scars covered *forever?* Wouldn't it be best to hide the ugliness *always?*

"No. Except for the abdominal surgical incision, which should be covered until I remove the sutures on Monday, you don't need the dressings. The wounds are healing beautifully. There's no evidence of infection."

Melanie had stopped listening. The words *healing beautifully* were swirling in her brain. What could the nurse possibly be *thinking?* Of course, maybe from a professional standpoint, there was something wonderful about the way the mutilated tissue had formed a clean, tight mesh. Perhaps it did make a statement about the remarkable recuperative properties of the human body, but from a personal standpoint . . .

"So what do you say? Shall I just re-dress the abdomen?"

Melanie nodded absently. Then she asked, searching for a glimmer of hope, "Does this mean I can take a shower?"

"Are you strong enough?"

"Yes," Melanie answered confidently. If she could take a nice long shower and wash her hair before Charles's visit . . .

Wait a minute, a voice told her. Do you want him to brush your hair again? Do you want him to dance with you? Have you forgotten?

No, she told the nagging voice of reality. I haven't forgotten. The shower is for *me.*

"All right, but keep the abdominal wound as dry as possible. Shower with the dressing on and re-dress it afterward. I'll leave extra dressings in case it gets wet." The nurse smiled. The abdominal wound was virtually healed. A little water wouldn't hurt, and the benefit of letting Melanie take a shower was worth it. "Shall I stay while you take your shower?"

"No, thank you. I'll be fine. I'll see you Monday."

Melanie *was* fine, until the end. Then it came, as it always did, without warning. She felt herself falling. She fell against the tile wall of the shower stall and slid, her fall broken slightly by her outstretched arms, to the tile floor. Her whole body trembled with pain; every previously injured and still raw nerve fiber screamed out against the sudden violent motion. It was all old pain—a vivid reminder that she was not yet healed. There was no new injury.

It was minutes—five, ten, she didn't know—before she could find the strength to reach above her head and turn off the water. The movement triggered a new round of pain. Sharp shooting tremors ricocheted from one side of her body to the other. Melanie suppressed a scream. The weakness hadn't subsided and the pain was almost beyond her control. She needed help.

No, she told herself firmly. This is just weakness, which will pass, and pain, which you can control. You can help yourself. You *have* to.

Twenty minutes later, still curled on the tile floor of the shower stall, Melanie began to shiver from the cold. She crawled out of the shower onto the plush, carpeted bathroom floor. Her strength surprised her. *This is just weakness. It will pass.* It was passing, gone until the next unexpected moment. The pain was less, or she had more strength to control it.

Melanie pulled herself up from her knees by clinging to the marble vanity. She gasped as she saw the reflection of her naked body in the mirror above the vanity. Melanie had made no effort to see all her wounds—the glimpse, in the hospital, of the purple scar on her breast had been enough—but she tormented herself with how ugly and disfiguring they might be. Now she removed the one remaining dressing, completely saturated with water anyway, and saw the full measure of the destruction. It was even *worse* than she had imagined. She had to force herself to face it.

This is me, Melanie thought. This is how I look. This is how I will always look.

Tears spilled from her pale-blue eyes as she gazed in horror and disbelief at the purple-and-pink tracks that lined her once lovely breasts and now bony rib cage and the abdomen that used to be so flat and the hips that used to curve into a smooth roundness. The scars were *more* than ugly, uneven, discolored markings, more than superficial graffiti, more than skin deep. The scars took away her shape. They destroyed the soft, lovely contours and permanently dimpled and distorted the firm smoothness.

Carved, she thought, shuddering. I've been carved. He took my beautiful body and carved a new, grotesque one.

Melanie was filled then, for the first time, with an unspeakable hatred for the man who had done this to her. Until now she had thought little about *him.* He was not part of her life. He had only been part of her life for those few terrible minutes. But now Melanie realized that he—and that night—would be with her always. She hated him for what he had done to her. Every time she looked at herself she would be reminded of that hatred.

I just won't look, she decided firmly, reaching for a clean silk nightgown and robe.

Why should she look? It wasn't her body anymore. It didn't belong to her. She could keep it covered—and keep her distance from anyone who might want to know what lay beneath—and no one would ever know. Her face was still hers. Her lovely face and . . .

Neck. Melanie drew in a breath as she saw that one scar tracked above her clavicle toward the angle of her jaw. It had been covered until today by the pristine white dressings. But now its purple-pink tentacles were exposed, reaching defiantly above the collar of her robe.

After I dry my hair and brush it I can pull it forward, she thought. It will cover the scar. And I can buy blouses that will cover it enough.

But for today the hair will do. Charles will never notice. She didn't want Charles to know about the ugliness. She didn't want him to know what she had become.

A familiar aching consumed Charles as he approached the brick pillars that marked the entrance to Windermere. He hadn't been here since Elliott's funeral, three days after Elliott's death. Even after Elliott was gone, even when he might have lived here with his brother, Windermere was not his home.

Charles was stopped by police guards at the entrance of the estate. They checked his identification, confirmed his name and photograph on their list, called the house to notify Jason, and let Charles pass. As Charles drove along the red-brick drive, he noticed that the white ash and sugar maples were taller and the emerald forest seemed more dense.

Jason met Charles on the porch, a gracious host greeting his guest. It had always been that way.

Melanie appeared in the entry hall just as Charles and Jason walked inside.

"Should you be up?" Charles asked, concerned. He moved toward her. The package from Galen was tucked under his arm.

"You can't keep her down," Jason explained.

"Until she falls down," Melanie added.

She glanced at Charles and saw desire—familiar, desperate desire for *her*—in his eyes. *No, Charles. You wouldn't want me if you knew. We had our chance.*

"My goal for today is to make it to the day room," Melanie announced gaily, avoiding Charles's eyes.

Charles smiled, and Jason frowned for a moment. It wasn't a big frown or a persistent one. It was just a brief, passing worry, something about the day room.

Melanie accepted the offer of a strong arm from each twin. They strolled from the foyer through the great room and beyond to a long hallway lined with paintings.

The mansion was brighter, more cheerful and colorful, than Charles remembered. It was the paintings, Charles decided. There had never been this many before. But they were Meredith's; he recognized the style. Charles wondered where they had been all the years he lived at Windermere.

Melanie felt Jason's pace slow slightly, a final moment of hesitation, as they approached the day room. . . .

The day room was light and cheery, a bouquet of soft pastel pillows, white wicker chairs, and delicate porcelain lamps. Bay windows provided panoramic views of the sea and the gardens and the woods. A single painting—a breathtaking portrait of Galen—hung in the room.

Charles froze when he saw the painting. After a stunned moment he turned to Jason with a look of utter incomprehension. Jason didn't meet his gaze; his eyes were focused on the portrait.

Melanie marvelled at the magnificent painting. Galen's lovely emerald eyes sparkled courageously, sending messages that were at once naive and seductive. Jason had perfectly portrayed the magic of a girl becoming a woman, capturing the precise moment when innocent hopes and dreams become confident knowledge, and there is no longer any fear.

It was a portrait, Melanie realized, that could only have been painted by a man who knew Galen well and loved her deeply.

"It's lovely, Jason," Melanie whispered.

"Jason?" Charles's eyes fell to the signature on the painting. *"You* painted this?"

Melanie stared from one twin to the other. Charles didn't know that Jason could paint? How was that possible? How long had it been since Charles had been here?

"Yes," Jason answered flatly, defiantly.

"When?" Charles pressed.

"I finished it about a month ago."

"Have you seen her?"

"No. I did it from memory."

There was a long, tense silence. Charles and Jason were lost—caught—somewhere in a tangle of the past and its secrets.

"Why didn't you tell me?" Charles asked finally. *Why didn't you tell me about your painting? Why didn't you tell me about Galen?*

Jason answered his twin with an icy stare. His pale-blue eyes sent their own set of questions to the dark ones. Why haven't you ever told me why Father disowned you? Why did you mysteriously return on the day he died? Why didn't you tell me about you and Galen? *Galen.* I loved her, and she loved you, and you hurt her so much she left both of us.

Melanie watched, horrified by the sudden anger in their eyes. Charles and Jason were always so polite with each other, so civil, so unemotional. There was emotion now— deep and angry and disturbing.

The ringing telephone shattered the tense silence. Jason retreated to a distant room.

"You'd better sit down." Charles guided

Melanie to a white wicker couch with green and mauve cushions.

"So had you."

Charles smiled briefly. "Too many surprises."

"It must have been Jason," Melanie whispered.

"Yes," Charles breathed. Why hadn't Galen told him? Why hadn't *Jason* told him?

"I wonder," Melanie mused as she remembered the title of Galen's short story. "Charles, would you open the package for me?"

Charles tried for a moment, but was unable to easily tear the sealing tape with his fingers. He withdrew a small jackknife from his pocket. At the sight of it Melanie shivered involuntarily.

"Oh, Melanie," Charles whispered softly as he realized what had happened. He quickly returned the knife to his pocket and put his arms around her. "I'm sorry."

"It's OK." She pulled free and tossed the mane of golden hair courageously. "I have to—"

Melanie stopped because Charles wasn't listening. He was staring at her ivory neck and the purple-pink scar revealed by the toss of her head. Instinctively, Melanie reached for her neck, covering the ugliness with her lovely, tapered hand.

Charles looked at her for a minute, then took her hand away. He bent toward her and gently traced a path along the scar with his lips. At his touch, his *kiss,* she trembled. Oh, Charles.

No. I'm not the woman you remember. Your body won't want mine as desperately as it used to. This ugliness is only the tip of the iceberg.

Alone the scar on her neck could be tolerable,

a pastel-pink badge of courage, a grim novelty of sorts. But it was only the tiny tail, a small tentacle, of a large ugly monster.

"Charles, don't."

"Melanie."

"Please," she began. She found some control—the image of herself in the mirror could stop the pounding of her heart and the trembling and the desire—and said firmly, "Please open the package, with your knife."

"I can—"

"No."

This time the cold chill inside her when she saw the knife again—it was a trivial knife compared to what *he* had used—didn't erupt into a shiver. She wouldn't let it. She found control, amazing control. Charles opened the package quickly. His hands were efficient and expert with the knife. He closed the knife and returned it to his pocket before handing her the manuscript.

Melanie read the title page: "Sonja."

"Galen said her story—it's a story about a love that didn't last—is unpublishable." Melanie handed the manuscript to Charles. "Tell me if it's about Jason."

Charles stared at the title. Of course it was about Jason. It was written by someone who knew all about him. Someone Jason trusted enough to tell his greatest secret.

"What do you think?" Charles asked carefully.

"I think it's the way someone with dyslexia might see the word Jason," Melanie answered. Jason. Sonja. The same letters, but in a different order. Melanie watched Charles's reaction to the news that she knew about Jason's dyslexia. It *hurt* him. "He had to tell me, Charles. Nick left some automatic dialing machines. Obviously Jason couldn't program them. He had to tell me."

"Too many surprises," Charles repeated heavily.

"Too many secrets," she added softly.

Charles and Melanie fell silent, each reflecting on their own surprises and secrets, each wishing there were none and that there wouldn't have to be more, each knowing that there always would be.

He can never know about my scars, she thought.

I have to tell her everything I know about myself, and what I don't know, so that we can go on. . . .

Jason's return to the day room interrupted the silence. Jason's handsome face was calm, free of emotion. Jason's anger toward his twin was apparently vanquished, or, at least, hidden beneath a polite veneer.

"That was Nick," Jason said. "He's at the police station in Southampton. He'll be by in about twenty minutes."

"The police station in Southampton," Charles breathed. What the hell was Nick doing there? *"Why?"*

Jason shrugged. "Probably making sure the weekend shift knows that Melanie is here."

"What other reason could there be?" Melanie asked quietly. Her pale-blue eyes searched Charles's for the answer. But she couldn't find answers in the darkness. She only saw secrets and torment and pain. Charles, what is it?

"None," Charles replied flatly. "Melanie, you don't believe . . ."

"No, Charles, I don't." Their eyes met for a moment. The intensity of his seductive dark eyes became too great—he wanted her and she knew it could never be— and her eyelids fell, casting doubt.

Charles watched her for a moment in stunned silence. Then he stood up.

"I'd better go."

Charles touched Melanie's cheek lightly with his hand before he left. He tried to look at Jason, but it was only a sidelong glance accompanied by a barely civil smile.

"He doesn't want to see Nick," Melanie explained after Charles left. "Damn Nick."

"Why?" Jason asked.

"Because Nick is treating him like a suspect, Jason. How—"

The look in Jason's eyes stopped her.

Oh, my God, her mind screamed. Jason believes his twin *could* be the Manhattan Ripper.

Chapter Twenty-nine

Melanie read and reread Galen's short story. Not that "Sonja" was good. Another reader would put it down. In its present form "Sonja" probably was unpublishable. But Melanie read it because it was the story of two people she cared about. It was the story of Galen and Jason.

After she finished reading the manuscript Melanie lay awake, troubled by what she had read; it didn't make sense. Galen had written of love and betrayal and disillusionment. She had written about a man who deceived her, a man who had never truly loved her. Melanie had seen the just-completed portrait; it was painted by a man who was deeply in love, *still*. Melanie remembered the look in Jason's pale-blue eyes. He seemed more betrayed than betrayer.

A piece was missing.

The next morning, after a few hours of fitful sleep, Melanie found Jason at his easel in the great room.

"Good morning." Jason paused to smile at her.

"Good morning." Melanie smiled in return. Then, before she could change her mind, she asked abruptly, "What happened between you and Galen?"

"What?" Jason looked up in surprise. "What do you mean?"

"Why did you fall out of love?" Melanie asked boldly, making assumptions, but convinced they were correct. As she watched his pale-blue eyes Melanie knew she was right. Jason *had* loved Galen. He still did.

"I didn't," Jason answered quietly. "She did."

Melanie thought for a moment. Could Galen have written the story in reverse? The letters in his name were jumbled to make the heroine's name. Was she really telling the story from *his* perspective? No, Melanie decided. Galen's words were too personal, the hurt too visceral, the pain too intimate. Galen believed that Jason had betrayed her.

And Jason believed the same of Galen.

"Are you sure?"

"Yes. She was in love with someone else the entire time."

"How do you know?"

"Because I know who he was." Jason sighed and added flatly, "Galen was in love with Charles. And when that didn't work out, *because* it didn't work out, she left."

"No."

"*No?*"

"Galen and Charles were never in love."

"Melanie, you can't know that. You weren't even—"

"I *do* know, Jason. Charles told me Galen was devastated by a love that didn't last. He thinks that's why she cancelled the film contract for 'Sapphire' and left New York."

"The love that didn't last was with Charles."

"It's not true, Jason."

Melanie watched Jason's eyes narrow, searching the painful memories, trying to find a different explanation. He wanted to believe her.

"Galen thinks you betrayed her, Jason."

"How . . ." he began weakly. There were too many questions. How do you know? How could Galen believe *that?* And there was the exhilarating hope that what Melanie was saying might be true.

"I just read a short story she wrote. It's called 'Sonja,' " Melanie said meaningfully.

Jason shrugged. It meant nothing to him. Of

course it doesn't, Melanie realized, Jason wouldn't know that Sonja was an anagram of Jason.

She told him.

"The story is about me and Galen?"

"Yes. Your identities are concealed of course," Melanie said. Galen's anger apparently did not extend to revealing one of publishing's best-kept secrets—that Jason Sinclair couldn't read. "It's about a talented musician, Sonja, who falls in love with a poet who is deaf. So . . ."

"So he can't ever know her talent because he can't hear," Jason finished softly, remembering how much he wanted to be able to read Galen's words, the words that sprang from her soul, words she could write but was afraid to speak. They spoke to each other with their eyes and their hearts; they found their own language of love. "But they learn to communicate."

"The beginning of the story, as they fall in love, is magical. . . ."

"What happens?" Jason asked urgently. He needed to know. If only he could read the words himself. He was dependent again—dependent on Melanie—but she wanted him to know. Melanie seemed to care.

"He betrays her."

"How?"

"She discovers he is in love with another woman. He always has been. The mood shifts from wonder and magic to pain and rage and disillusionment and bitterness."

"How does she learn about the other woman?"

"She is scheduled to give a concert at

Carnegie." Melanie knew the details of the betrayal wouldn't be exactly what had happened between Jason and Galen, but there might be bits of fact that would help Jason understand. "They come to New York for the week. She returns to the hotel early one night—the conductor has become ill and the rehearsal is cancelled—and sees him leaving their room with the other woman, a woman from his past. They are embracing, smiling, gazing at each other, obviously in love."

"And she never tells him she saw them," Jason whispered.

"No. She doesn't want to hear his lies."

Jason held his head in his paint-spattered hands. Finally he looked up and stared out the bay window toward the gray green sea. But Jason wasn't staring at the sea; he was staring at a distant memory.

"I asked her if she came over that night." Jason spoke softly to the memory. And Galen didn't answer, he remembered suddenly. She had *avoided* answering.

Melanie watched the emotion and pain in Jason's unfocused eyes.

"So it was true," Melanie breathed finally. Jason *had* betrayed Galen.

"No."

"But she might have seen something that looked obvious?"

"Yes." Jason's voice was bitter. If Galen had seen him with Fran why didn't she tell him about it? Because, like Sonja, Galen didn't want to hear lies, Jason realized. Galen knew what she had

433

seen and could find no explanation in her heart, or in her experience, that could make it less than it appeared. "Fran came over one night."

"But you weren't in love with Fran." Melanie knew that.

"No. I was in love only, always, with Galen."

They sat in silence for a moment. Jason, lost in his memories, and Melanie, thinking about "Sonja" and about Galen and Jason . . .

"Go to her, Jason," Melanie urged suddenly, startling him. "Tell her what happened."

"What makes you think she'll listen? You just told me the story ended with rage and disillusionment and bitterness."

"Yes, but it doesn't ring true. No matter how hard Galen tries to tell the reader that love is a myth, that there never was love between them, that she hates him, *you*, it's unconvincing. She doesn't really believe it herself. Galen has never stopped loving you, either."

"Do you know where she is?"

Melanie answered by telling him the telephone number and address for the gatehouse on Mayflower Lane. Jason memorized them instantly.

"When are you going to go?" Melanie asked eagerly.

"After this business is all over." Jason used "this business" as the euphemism for the Manhattan Ripper.

"No, Jason, go now. Don't stay here because of me! I'm fine, and you are a dear man to keep me company and let me stay in this lovely place, but you don't need to be here. You know I'm safe. Even though we don't see them we are surrounded by guards. I'll tell Nick that you'll be away and if he wants to have one of the guards stay inside the house that's fine."

"You're serious, aren't you?"

"I'm an incurable romantic just like everyone else. If you and Galen could work this out . . ." Melanie's eyes sparkled. "Bring her back with you, Jason."

Jason's eyes sparkled in return. If only it were possible.

"I'll go in the morning," Jason breathed. He couldn't lose any more than he had already lost.

Jason rehearsed it, what he would say to Galen, a thousand times. He rehearsed it last night in his bed, *their* bed; and on the plane from La Guardia to O'Hare; and in the limousine as it sped north along the tollway, exiting after thirty minutes at Lake Forest; and, one last time—he sensed they were near—as they passed green-and-white signs he couldn't read labelled Deerpath and Onwentsia and Sheridan and, finally, Mayflower Lane.

The rehearsals were all for naught. Then Jason saw her beloved, bewildered emerald eyes, he couldn't speak.

"Jason."

He extended his arms toward her, but she backed away.

"Galen." Jason's arms fell, heavily, to his side.

"Why are you here?" she asked helplessly. Don't look at me like that, Jason, not like that. I used to believe that look was love.

"Because I love you."

"*No.*" Galen said swiftly.

"Melanie told me you wrote a story about us."

"Yes." Galen lifted her chin defiantly. "About how you betrayed . . ."

"I never betrayed you, Galen."

"You *did.*" The eyes flashed with emerald anger.

"No."

"Jason, I *saw* you in bed with her." The pain of the memory washed through her, leaving in its wake the familiar, horrible ache.

Jason grimaced. Galen had seen them in bed together! No wonder . . .

"Galen, may I come in?"

"*No.*" Galen frowned and her eyes filled with fear.

Galen, don't be afraid of me, Jason's heart cried. She was so far away.

"Please let me tell you what happened."

Galen shrugged, but she didn't close the door.
Please listen to me, Galen.

"Fran came over that night, uninvited. She was upset. I had explained to her that it was over, but she didn't accept it. We talked and drank bourbon, she much more than I, until very late. Then she asked if she could stay." Jason sighed. He should have said No; if only he had said No.

"She said she needed to know that I could be in the same bed with her without wanting to make love to her," he continued heavily. "Somehow that would help her believe, finally, that it was over. She was exhausted, upset, a little drunk. I said Yes. We slept. If you saw us you would know we were both wearing pajamas. Nothing happened, Galen, *nothing.*"

He watched the lovely eyes struggling, trying to understand, wanting to.

"Why didn't you tell me?" Galen asked finally.

"I was going to. Even though nothing happened, and even though I wasn't sure you would understand, I was going to tell you." Jason shook his head. "In the light of day it felt so wrong. Even though—"

"But you didn't tell me."

"I never had a *chance.* You told me you were going away with Charles. You told me our relationship was over."

"But you must have known it was because I had seen you with Fran!"

"I *asked* you," Jason reminded her gently. "And there was always something special between you and Charles."

"You thought I was in love with Charles?"

"What other reason could there have been?"

"You never even tried to explain. It seemed like more proof that you had never cared about me or us."

"You were never in love with Charles?"

"No, Jason." Tears spilled from her eyes and her lips trembled. "I was never in love with anyone but you."

Jason extended his arms again and this time she came to him.

"Galen," he whispered hoarsely. "My darling Galen. I love you so much."

"Jason, I love—"

Galen stopped abruptly and stiffened slightly.

It was a sound that only Galen heard, or maybe she only sensed it. It was their way of talking, mother and daughter. Elise rarely cried. When she awoke, when she wanted her mother, she made soft, cooing sounds.

"Galen?" Jason asked.

Galen stared at him for a long moment. *Oh, Jason, there is so much more . . .*

Jason smiled at her, reassuring her, caressing her with loving eyes. *Galen, tell me . . .*

Galen sighed softly. Then she took his hand and led him into the gatehouse, across the living room, up the carpeted stairs to her bedroom. At the bedroom door she released Jason's hand and entered ahead of him, smiling at the huge blue eyes that sparkled when they saw her.

The cooing increased—happy, excited talking.

Galen lifted Elise gently from her crib and kissed her soft sleep-flushed cheek. Elise's tiny dimpled hands touched her mother's face in delighted welcome.

"Are you hungry? Yes? Of course you are." Galen sat on the bed and unbuttoned her blouse. Only after Elise was tugging contentedly at her breast did Galen raise her glistening eyes to Jason's.

"Galen, is she," Jason's own emotion, and something in Galen's new tears, made him stop.

She shook her head slightly. "I don't know, Jason. She could be yours. I want her to be yours. She was born on your birthday." Galen's smile quivered.

"Then she is mine. She has my eyes." Jason

moved closer and ever so gently touched Elise's rosy cheek with his finger.

It was true. Elise had beautiful pale-blue eyes, Jason's eyes. And she had dark curly hair. Neither her hair nor her eyes were inherited from Galen.

Galen sighed. She had to tell him the truth—all of it. It had been a terrible mistake not to tell Jason she had seen him with Fran. Because she hadn't told him *that* truth there had been so much pain. . . .

And now, when there was a chance that they might be able to find the love again—the love that had been, simply, misplaced—the truth could destroy it all. How could she tell him? How could she *not?*

"Galen," Jason urged gently, watching her struggle. "Tell me."

"She has your eyes, my darling, and she has Charles's hair."

She felt the shock of her words hit his body like a punch. After a few moments he lifted her chin, so gently, and made her look into his watery eyes.

"You said . . ."

"I didn't love him. I slept with him once, because I needed to know how it felt to make love with someone you didn't love. I needed to understand how you could have made love with me all those times and been in love with Fran."

"But that didn't happen."

"I know that now."

"But you did make love with Charles. What did you learn?"

"I learned it was possible, but that I still loved

439

you. And, I learned again—I had always known it—that Charles is sensitive and kind." Galen frowned. "That's something I don't think you know."

Jason avoided her eyes. It was true; Jason *didn't* know that. And Galen didn't know about Nick Adrian's suspicion about Charles, or about what happened between Charles and Elliott.

"Does Charles know?"

"About Elise? No. No one does."

"Elise," Jason spoke softly. "That's beautiful."

"It's my mother's name. Her middle name is Meredith, for your mother. Elise Meredith. She is such a joy." Galen idly weaved her fingers through the dark-brown curls as Elise nursed.

Jason stroked the dark curls thoughtfully for a moment. Then he walked across the room and stared out the window toward Lake Michigan.

Galen watched helplessly.

What if he decided that *her* betrayal was too great? What if he decided, now that he had learned the truth, that it really was over? What if he couldn't live with the fact that she had made love with Charles? What if he could never forgive her for that? And what about Elise? What if he could never love her as long as the uncertainty persisted about whose baby she really was?

"There's something I need to know." Finally Jason spoke, and, when he did, he turned to face her.

"Yes?" *Please don't say good-bye Jason. Please give me another chance. . . .*

"I need to know how you feel about me—us—now."

440

"I love you, Jason," she whispered.

Jason nodded seriously.

"How do you feel, Jason?" She held her breath. *Please.*

"I love you more than anything in the world, Galen. I will love Elise, no matter what. Is there any way . . . ?"

"Oh, Jason, I have caused you so much pain." Galen gazed at the pale-blue eyes that desperately wanted to know that the precious little girl was really his.

"So much joy," Jason corrected quickly, lovingly. His question was still unanswered.

"You and Charles have the same blood type." Galen answered the question he had begun: Is there any way to know whose daughter she is? "There are more sophisticated genetic tests. I never looked into them because they would require samples of your blood and Charles's."

"We'll need to do that."

Galen started to answer but was stopped by Elise, who wriggled away from Galen's breast, now fully awake and no longer hungry. Elise gurgled happily and strained to focus in the direction of the strange, deep voice that was speaking to her mother. Her pale-blue eyes met Jason's and her face erupted into a gleeful smile.

Jason moved to her, arms extended, and looked questioningly at Galen.

"Of course you can hold her, Jason." Galen carefully transferred the eager bundle from her arms to his.

Elise knew very few people aside from her mother. The doctor, of course, for routine checkups, and the faces at the post office and grocery who smiled at her but didn't touch.

Few people, aside from Galen, had ever held her.

But Elise went to Jason without a flicker of uncertainty. She boldly studied his big blue eyes and patted his chin with her soft hands and tugged at his collar and cooed. Jason held her tightly. Too tightly, Galen thought, but Elise didn't seem to mind the constraint. She didn't struggle to be away from him. She only pressed closer, intrigued by his mouth and his smile and his eyes and his warmth.

Galen saw the happiness in Jason's eyes, as he naturally and unselfconsciously cuddled Elise. She has to be his, Galen thought. She has to be.

After a while Galen and Jason took Elise downstairs. They spread a soft pastel blanket on the living-room floor and Elise played between them, her blue eyes flashing with delight, her soft laugh almost constant. Galen and Jason watched the baby—*their* baby—but once their hands fell on the same toy together and the touch lingered and their fingers entwined.

Elise fought the sleepiness that overcame her for as long as she could. They watched her gallant struggle to keep her eyelids open and smiled gently and lovingly.

"Don't be afraid, little one," Jason whispered, cradling Elise as she finally succumbed to the happy exhaustion. "We'll be here when you awaken. And we'll play again. Over and over."

Jason kissed the sleepy face and looked at Galen. "Shall I take her upstairs?"

"She can sleep down here." Galen arranged a soft protected bed out of the cushions on the sofa.

Jason slowly lowered the sleeping baby into the bed Galen had made. Elise stretched when he removed his hands, then curled, contented, safe into the familiar feel of her blanket and the sofa.

Galen and Jason watched the sleeping baby for a few moments. Then Jason turned to her and smiled.

"Galen." He touched his hands to her face and gently laced his strong fingers into her silky hair. She trembled at his touch. Or was it only his own trembling that he felt "How are you?"

"Oh, Jason," she whispered. "I am so afraid."

"Of what?" he asked carefully, pulling her close, hiding his own fear, showing her that *she* had nothing to fear.

"Of waking up from this dream," she murmured as her lips met his.

Chapter Thirty

"Charles?"

"Melanie."

They hadn't spoken for four days; not since Melanie couldn't hold his gaze when he asked if she believed he could be the Manhattan Ripper. Now she was calling him, and he sounded so sad.

"Hi." That *wasn't* why I couldn't stand to look in your eyes, Charles.

"Hi." His voice was gentle, gentle and sad and far away.

"Do you know the follow-up on 'Sonja'? Have you spoken with Jason?"

"No." Jason hadn't been in the office all week. Charles assumed he was staying in Windermere with Melanie. There had been no pressing business, no reason to call Jason.

"Oh." Melanie frowned. Charles needed to know. "Jason believed that Galen left him for you."

"For *me?*"

"She didn't, did she?" Melanie asked quietly.

"No. I told you last summer . . ." Charles's tone softened as he said *last summer.* "Galen believed he never loved her."

"But he did." Melanie paused. She didn't want to talk to Charles about love. "Anyway, the reason Galen left New York, the reason she couldn't be filming in Kenya in November, was because she was carrying Jason's baby."

"*What?*"

"She was pregnant. She had their baby—Elise, isn't that a lovely name?—in November. On his, your, birthday."

Charles's mind whirled. November. He and Galen had made love in February. Jason's baby or his?

"How do you know all this?"

"Jason went to Lake Forest. They're coming home tonight. They plan to be married next week."

A long silence followed. Melanie had finished her reason—her *excuse*—for calling. She called under the pretext of giving Charles some good, happy news, but she really called because she wanted to hear his voice. And she wanted him to know that she believed in him.

"How are you, Melanie?" Charles asked finally.

"I want this all to be over."

"So do I, darling." *So do I.*

"Are you confident you'll get a guilty verdict, Ms. Chandler?"

A crush of reporters swarmed around Andrew and Brooke as they emerged from the courthouse. The closing arguments were over and the jury had retired to deliberate on Jeffrey Martin's guilt or innocence.

"I'm confident that we *should*," Brooke spoke to a television camera. Then she tossed her head toward Andrew and smiled.

Brooke felt wonderful. The trial had been faultless. She and Andrew had worked so well together. It was a perfect ending; as soon as the jury returned its verdict her job as assistant district attorney would be over. By this time next week she would be sitting in her office at Sinclair Publishing reviewing advertising contracts.

"Are you really leaving the DA's office?" another reporter asked.

"Not if I can help it," Andrew answered amiably, smiling his gorgeous, confident smile.

"Yes." Brooke's blue eyes sparkled at Andrew. "Yes, I am."

★   ★   ★

Charles arrived at Windermere an hour after twilight. He hadn't planned to return to Windermere at all. As much as he wanted to see Melanie, he had to stay away for now. Charles wouldn't push her, and he couldn't stand the doubt in her eyes.

Charles hadn't planned to return to Windermere, but he needed to see Galen. He needed to see Galen's *baby*.

The house was surprisingly dark. Charles walked toward the kitchen, guided by a yellow beam of light.

Charles paused a moment, his heart pounding, when he saw the red-gold head bent lovingly over the dark brown one cradled in her arms. Charles walked across the kitchen. Galen didn't hear him above the whistling of the teapot and the cooing of her baby. Charles touched her gently on the shoulder and said quietly, "Welcome home."

"Charles!" Galen smiled, happy to see her dear friend. After a moment she could no longer hold his intense gaze; the serious dark eyes were asking questions that demanded answers.

"Your tea is ready," Charles observed. Instead of moving to the stove to remove the hissing teapot, he extended his arms to Elise.

Galen watched her precious baby girl go to Charles as easily, as eagerly, as she had gone to Jason. Elise laughed and nuzzled her dark head against his, her curls intermingling, an exact match, with his. Elise wrapped her tiny hands in Charles's hair as he whispered to her.

Elise didn't go to strangers. Even with Melanie, Elise kept a careful eye on Galen and Jason. But

Elise went, without worry, to Jason, and now to Charles. A deep, confident instinct told Elise that she had nothing to fear; she was where she *belonged.*

Galen had convinced herself—because they wanted it so desperately and because of how Elise responded to Jason—that Jason was Elise's father. The sophisticated genetic tests were hardly necessary, or *were* they? Galen wondered helplessly as she watched her daughter with Charles, and Charles with Elise.

Galen's hands trembled as she poured the hot water over a tea bag.

"Would you like something, Charles? Tea? Coffee?"

"No, thank you, and yes. I would like to know," Charles spoke with great control, "if she is mine."

"I don't know, Charles." Galen forced herself to find his eyes. "I don't know."

"I need to know."

"We all need to. There are some tests. They may not be conclusive since you and Jason are twins, so genetically alike, but . . ." Galen stopped and gazed, startled, beyond Charles toward the kitchen door. Galen whispered, "Melanie."

Charles spun, catching Melanie's eyes before she could change the look. Melanie knew; she had heard it all.

"Hello, I'm sorry, I'm interrupting," Melanie mumbled, backing away.

"No," Charles and Galen said in unison. For

447

different reasons they wanted the conversation to be over.

"No," Galen repeated. "In fact I was just about to leave. It's time to give Elise her bath and get her ready for bed."

Galen took Elise from Charles and left quickly, her tea still brewing on the kitchen counter.

"Hi." Charles smiled gently at Melanie. "How are you?"

"I'm better. Stronger." *Why did you lie to me about you and Galen? How many other lies have you told me?*

"We were never in love," Charles said quietly as he moved close to her.

"What?" Melanie breathed weakly. They *had* been in love; in her fantasies and her dreams and her lovely memories of last summer. She had even dared to hope. . . . But then she looked at herself in the mirror and she knew it was over. Why did he have to tell her it had never existed at all?

"Galen and I were never in love."

"Oh." It didn't matter.

"We made love once. We weren't in love. There were other reasons."

Melanie understood other reasons. Other reasons were all she knew before she fell in love with Charles.

"I understand. And I understand that you need to know if you are Elise's father."

"I've never been—" Charles stopped before he said the rest, *in love with anyone but you.* He stopped because he promised himself he wouldn't push her.

"You need to know," Melanie repeated quietly.

"I need a drink. Will you join me?"

"You, not the drink."

"Something else? Hot chocolate?"

"No, I'm fine."

"Shall we go to the library?"

"Sure."

Melanie sat curled in a huge leather chair in the wood-panelled library and watched Charles pour himself a large glass of undiluted bourbon.

"How about a roaring fire?" Charles asked before he sat down. The kindling was already laid. Charles added two logs and lighted the paper beneath the grill. The dry wood caught instantly; red-orange flames danced, sending light and warmth and cheerful crackling into the room.

Charles settled in a leather chair facing Melanie. Charles started to say something to her, but the library door opened and his attention was drawn away. Charles stood up.

"Hello, Jason," Charles said flatly.

"Hello, Charles. I wanted to be the one to tell you about Elise."

Jason doesn't know I'm here, Melanie realized suddenly.

Jason was behind her, and she was completely obscured by the enormous leather chair, her legs curled beneath her, her head a full foot beneath the top. Melanie looked at Charles, but his dark eyes were focused on his twin.

"Why? It's none of your business. It's between me and Galen." The bitterness was deep.

"It's between all of us. It has to do with that precious little girl's life."

"Yes. And her fortune," Charles whispered. "It's too bad it's between us—the three of us—because we're not a very responsible group."

"Meaning?"

"I'm disgusted with you and Galen and myself. Disgusted and disappointed. None of us behaved even like trusted friends, much less like brothers or—"

"Trust?" Jason interjected angrily. "That's a funny word to come from your lips. You certainly don't know what it means. Next you'll be talking about brotherly love and honesty. Go ahead, it will make the sham complete."

"What the hell are you talking about? My God, Jason, when have I ever betrayed your trust? *Ever?* When have I ever been dishonest with you?" Charles demanded, incredulous.

"When? I'll tell you. When it was most important for us to be brothers, to love each other and care about each other and trust each other. That's when. You set the ground rules of mistrust and dishonesty, not me."

"I don't know what you're talking about, Jason," Charles whispered. "When? Tell me."

"When Father died. You wouldn't tell me why he disowned you."

"I told you I don't know why."

"That's the lie."

"It's not a lie."

"I don't believe you. But you believe this, Charles, if Elise is yours, I will fight for her." Jason's voice turned ice-cold and threatening. "I will do whatever I can to get her away from you. I may not have to do anything. Nick seems a little worried about your mysterious reappearance the day Father died. . . ."

"You can't believe," Charles breathed. His eyes met his twin's and he saw hatred. "Oh, my God, you do."

"Yes, Charles, I do."

Jason stared at Charles, his pale-blue eyes unrelenting. Finally, without speaking, he turned and left.

Charles fell heavily into the chair and held his head in his hands. Melanie watched the torment stiffen his body then send shudders of rage and hopelessness through it. How could she help him? She would offer him her love, but she *couldn't*. Besides, Charles had forgotten she was there. It would be best if she just left, quietly, before he remembered.

Melanie stood up to leave, but the voice that told her legs to move toward the door wasn't as loud as the commands of her heart. She walked over to him and gently touched his shoulder. Charles looked up, startled, his face white, his eyes wild. He forced control into his eyes, found a look of concern just for her, and took her hands in his.

"I am so sorry you witnessed that."

"It doesn't matter," Melanie told him truthfully. *I believe in you, Charles.*

It was a terrible MISTAKE not to murder her. I let SENTIMENTALITY obscure my MISSION. It won't happen again! This time there will be enough

451

BLOOD for two murders. This time there will be TWIN BLOOD!!!

The Manhattan Ripper frowned briefly. He wondered if he had ever murdered a twin before. . . .

"You're the second person to ask me that this morning," the harbormaster at Peconic Bay replied.

"Really? Who was the other?" Nick asked. Charles?

"Jason Sinclair was here bright and early."

"What did you tell him?"

"The same thing I'm going to tell you—the truth. Elliott Sinclair sailed into that killer storm alone."

"You're sure?"

"Yes," the harbormaster answered a little impatiently. Jason Sinclair had pushed him, too. "I saw him arrive. I helped him load the boat. We talked about the storm clouds in the distance. I cast him off and watched him sail away."

With the last words, his voice softened, as if he should have known to prevent Elliott from making that fateful sail.

"What's this all about?"

"We just wondered if someone had been with him."

"Well, no one was. Besides, anyone with him would have been killed, too. There was almost nothing left of the boat."

Nick knew that. He had seen the pictures. Nick had seen pictures of the boat, and pictures of Elliott Sinclair.

"So Jason was here," Nick mused.

"He's a fine sailor, like his father was. Of course he mostly sails out of New York Yacht Club these days . . ."

"How about the other son, Charles?"

"Not a yachtsman."

"He didn't spend much time here?"

"None."

"Would you recognize him?"

"Of course. He looks exactly like Elliott."

As he drove from Southampton to Manhattan, Nick decided that the Southampton police were right; Elliott Sinclair died alone in a violent storm. Charles's reappearance was simply coincidence; and even if it was something more, some mystical precognition, it was still far from a crime.

And maybe the wild torment in Charles's dark eyes the night Melanie was attacked, and his rage when Nick suggested that *he* might have done it, were not signs of guilt, either. Maybe they were only the emotions of a passionate man who was deeply and desperately in love.

I need to talk to him, Nick thought.

On impulse, Nick decided to go to Charles's office. Nick was able to see Charles within ten minutes of his arrival.

"I haven't received your alibis," Nick said.

"That's because I don't have any."

"No?"

"Except for December twenty-third, when I was at the *Vogue* party for a short, time I was alone each night for the entire evening."

"Isn't that a little unusual for you?"

"No."

"What did you do those nights by yourself?"

"I don't know. Took a long walk, read, drank. I don't know."

"That's not very specific."

"I don't need to be." Charles glared at Nick. "Is that all?"

"Guess so."

"Are you done investigating my father's death?"

"Yes."

"And?"

"His death was accidental. He died alone in a storm."

"I wish you would tell my brother that," Charles murmured under his breath.

"Jason knows."

"Oh?" It hardly mattered. Jason had believed it was possible that Charles had murdered Elliott; *that* was what mattered.

"Yes." Nick looked for a moment at Charles before leaving. I hope like hell you aren't the Ripper. I hope it for you and Jason and Melanie. And Brooke . . .

I hope it, Nick thought as he walked down the circular staircase from the executive suites, but I don't know it . . .

"I really believed Charles might have been on the boat," Jason told Galen.

"And that he killed your father?"

"I don't know." Jason had never allowed the

454

worry to mature. His mind had placed Elliott and Charles together on the yacht a thousand times, but after that . . . "Maybe an accident."

"But Charles *wasn't* with him. You believe that now, don't you?"

"Yes."

"I don't understand, Jason. What would even make you think it? Why would Charles . . ."

Without answering, Jason led Galen past the room where Elise lay sleeping to Elliott's study. He removed a small brass key from the top drawer of Elliott's carved-oak desk.

"My father's personal papers are locked in these drawers. I know there are letters and I think there is a journal." Jason had looked through the desk, once, a year after Elliott's death, hoping he could find an answer. But if an answer was there, it lay in words he couldn't read. Jason had relocked the desk, wondering if its secrets would ever be revealed. Now, twelve years later, he was handing the key to Galen. "Will you read through them, Galen?"

"Oh, Jason." No.

"I need to know about Charles. We both need to, because of Elise."

Galen nodded slowly. If there was something about Charles, something that made gentle, loving Jason believe his twin capable of murder, they needed to know it.

Elise cooed softly in the distance.

"I'll go," Jason whispered.

Galen nodded again. It would be easiest to go through the papers without Jason watching. It would be difficult enough to do alone. It was such an invasion of privacy, and what if she learned something *terrible?*

Galen sighed softly and gingerly unlocked the top right-hand drawer of the carved-oak desk.

"Jury's coming back, Brooke."

"Really? So soon?"

"It has to be good news." Andrew smiled confidently.

"I hope so." Brooke grabbed her briefcase and coat and glanced at her watch: one-fifteen. If the case was really over, if she and Andrew had won the conviction, this would be her last afternoon in the DA's office. It wouldn't take long to empty her desk; she could do it before she left work tonight. Brooke smiled at Andrew. "Okay, let's go."

Chapter Thirty-one

"Nick, there's a woman here to see you. She says it's about the Ripper."

Nick looked up from his cluttered desk and cocked his head at the detective. There was a steady stream of people coming to the precinct with information about the Ripper. So far none had paid off. Usually Nick didn't even get involved. The fact that the detective was bringing the woman to him might mean something.

"You think she's got something?"

"I don't know. She won't talk to anyone but you."

Nick grimaced; it was one of the many drawbacks of the publicity that the Manhattan Ripper was *his* case. "Where is she?"

"Sitting just beyond Larry's desk."

Nick stood up and looked through the bulletproof plate-glass window surrounding his office. All he could see was her softly curled chestnut hair and her head tilted the way she tilted it when she was thinking.

Nick smiled. It was Brooke, paying a surprise visit. Maybe she wanted to tell him about the Jeffrey Martin verdict. Nick had just heard; he could pretend he didn't know.

"I'll see her."

Nick's smile faded as he approached. A swirl of dark smoke hovered above her chestnut hair and her clothes were plain and drab. She wasn't Brooke.

Nick stopped a few feet away from her.

"Hello. I'm Lieutenant Adrian."

She turned her head slowly. Nick drew a breath when the dark-blue eyes met his. She had Brooke's eyes, Brooke's *face*. Nick thought, She is an older, haggard version of Brooke. Once this woman had been beautiful; once she had looked very much like Brooke. Who *was* she?

She stood up, transferred her cigarette into her left hand, and extended her thin right hand to Nick. He noticed a fine tremor.

"Lieutenant Adrian." Her voice was rich and deep. "I know who he is. I will need your protection."

Nick nodded and gestured toward his bullet-proof, soundproof office. He waited as she gathered her purse and a dark-blue leather folder. The purse was frail and battered—like she was—but the leather folder was new, expensive, and elegant. Nick didn't know who she was, but instinct told him that she held the clue to the identity of the Manhattan Ripper.

It scared him to death that she looked so much like Brooke. . . .

She didn't speak again until they were inside his office and he had closed the blinds. Then she told him her name.

"You're his . . . ?" Nick asked as his mind whirled. Oh, my God. . . .

"I'm his wife. I'm not as old as I look." She smiled wistfully. It was a beautiful smile, Brooke's smile.

"Why do you think it's him?"

"I don't think it, I know it." She paused and reached into her purse.

Another cigarette? Nick wondered impatiently. Talk to me. If it's true, I need to do something *now*.

But she didn't withdraw a cigarette; she withdrew a whetstone.

"I didn't find a knife, and I didn't find blood-stained clothes, but I found this."

Nick took the whetstone. Even if there were traces of blood, it proved nothing. He needed much more. Nick didn't even know if this strange woman with the bewitching face was who she said she was; it seemed unlikely.

As if reading Nick's mind, she handed him

a photograph. It was a wedding picture—their wedding picture—and she was young and lovely and her ocean-blue eyes sparkled with joy and she *was* Brooke.

"What else," Nick breathed. He needed more, legally. He fought the strong urge to reach for the phone and have him arrested; *just cause* be damned!

"His journal." She handed him the blue leather folder. "It was locked in the desk in his study—so was the whetstone—but I broke the lock. It's all legal, all admissible. It's my house, too. I was an attorney once. . . ."

Nick was vaguely aware of her words. He had opened to the first page of the journal and was reading the entry:

So much BLOOD— too much. It will be less MESSY next time. Next time? Of course!

In the back of his mind he thought, This is a lot of evidence, but no *proof.* What if this woman, who Nick wanted to believe because she looked like Brooke, was crazy? The woman looked a little crazy. What if she was trying to *frame* her husband?

Nick needed a handwriting analysis of the journal, and he needed a search warrant. It would all take time, and, if she was telling the truth—if *he* was crazy and *she* was sane—there was no time to waste.

"Why did you break into his desk?" *What made you suspect your husband of a crime so heinous?*

"I saw Brooke Chandler on television this morning. She was interviewed as she left court yesterday. I used to look like her. I used to be smart and bright and beautiful like her. And he wanted me desperately." She sighed and the blue eyes clouded. When she spoke again her voice was low and haunting. "He wanted me so much he murdered my roommate."

"*What?*"

"I didn't know it until I read his journal today. I guess, over the years, I have wondered. We met at Princeton. He was obsessed with me. He hid the obsession well beneath his easy charm and confidence. I was flattered, but I was happy with my life and my plans for a career in law. I liked him, but I didn't need him."

She paused. Her dark-blue eyes narrowed as the horrible distant memory came into vivid focus. "So, he made me need him."

"How?"

"My roommate was murdered. She was raped and stabbed to death. It happened in our room. I was the one who found her . . ." Her voice faltered. She took a deep breath. "Anyway, after that, I was devastated, and he was strong and supportive. He convinced me—and I believed it—that I needed him."

"And now?"

"Now I have nothing left. Little by little he has taken everything away. I was a good attorney, but it was too threatening to him. He convinced me— he can be very persuasive—that a good wife doesn't work. I used to be very close to my family, but he drove a wedge between us. He stripped me of everything until he had complete control. *Almost* complete." She smiled wryly. "Every so often, to escape, I spend a month or two in a

sanitarium. It makes him angry; he feels abandoned."

"But you're not crazy." *He* is.

"Isn't it crazy not to have left him? Isn't it crazy
to have allowed this to happen?"

"Why didn't you leave him?"

"Fear, I guess. I am nothing—I have no identity anymore—without him."

"But . . ." That's nonsense.

"I know I still exist somewhere, buried deep,
but it is so hard to dig out." The exhaustion in her
voice betrayed years of emotional chaos. "And he
is still obsessed. He still tells me of his desperate,
endless love. In his warped mind, I am still young
and strong and beautiful, like . . ."

Brooke. Nick had heard enough; he believed
her. He needed to do a lot of things all at once,
but the only one that mattered was making certain
Brooke was safe.

She *is* safe, he tried to convince himself. Brooke
is the one woman in the world he won't harm.

Except, an uneasy voice warned, Brooke isn't
behaving as he wants her to. Brooke remained
strong and independent, even when his victim
was her *twin*.

And Brooke is making changes that might
anger and provoke him very much. . . .

The mansion at Windermere was silent and
somber, as if grief-stricken by the argument
between Jason and Charles. Melanie spent most
of the day in her bright-yellow first-floor bedroom. Jason and Galen and Elise kept to

themselves in their distant, private wing of the mansion.

Jason played with Elise in front of the fire in the bedroom. As he played with the precious little girl who might be his daughter, Jason's mind drifted to Galen and the solemn task he had given her. What was she learning? Were there answers? After two hours, Jason gathered Elise and returned to Elliott's study.

Galen was sitting on the floor. The contents of the desk—letters in shoeboxes and a leatherbound journal—surrounded her; they were pieces of a puzzle whose answer horrified her.

"Galen?"

She looked up from the journal. Jason could tell that she had been crying.

I am so sorry I made you do this, Jason thought his own helplessness haunting him.

"It doesn't seem possible," Galen whispered. How did Charles survive? *Did* he survive? And who could blame Charles for anything he might do?

"What, darling?"

"Your father held Charles responsible for your mother's death. He never forgave Charles, and he never even tried to love him."

"But my mother died when we were born."

"Yes. But you were born first. And"—Elliott had described the scene with Meredith in her hospital room after the birth of their beloved Jason—"your mother seemed fine. No one knew she was carrying twins. She started to hemorrhage. They discovered the second baby—

462

Charles—while they were unsuccessfully trying to save her life."

"I never knew that." Jason frowned. He added firmly, "It doesn't make sense anyway. She died because she was carrying twins. It had nothing to do with *which* twin."

"To your father it did. He never wanted Charles to live. Charles spent the first two months of his life in the hospital. Did you know that?"

Jason shook his head. He sat down on the floor beside Galen and whispered softly, "Tell me everything."

Elliott's journal was a detailed, eloquent, beautifully written chronicle of the birth and lives of his twin sons. The pages were filled with emotion and passion; his great love for Jason, and his hatred for Charles. Elliott was a brilliant, insightful, critical man. He recognized that his hatred of his youngest son was irrational. Elliott despised himself for hating Charles. Elliott knew what harm he inflicted on the little boy with the bewildered brown eyes. Elliott knew, but he couldn't help it, and he couldn't stop.

"Did you and Charles have your own language?" Galen asked. She bypassed the twins' infancy and early childhood. Jason wouldn't remember it, and she couldn't tell Jason about the long, dark, lonely nights Charles spent in his crib while Jason played with his loving father. It filled Galen with such rage. How could anyone do that to a helpless, innocent child?

"Yes, we did, until Charles decided he didn't want to speak it anymore."

"Elliott made him."

"No."

"Elliott threatened to send Charles away unless you started to speak English." Galen blinked back tears. This was so difficult. Jason needed to know the cruel dark side of the father he loved so dearly; it was the only way that he and Charles could go on. Galen hated to shatter the memory of Elliott's love for Jason—that was real, too—but Jason had to understand how much damage Elliott had done to his twin. Galen continued, emotionally, "Jason, Charles was only four and a half! Elliott threatened to send him away."

"No. He never would have."

"Yes, Jason, he *would*. Elliott sent Charles away when he was twelve, didn't he?"

"Charles wanted to go. He was bored being with me. Charles was so bright; it slowed him down to be here, learning at my pace. . . ."

"No. Charles pleaded with Elliott not to send him away."

"When Charles came home at vacations, he seemed restless and distant. We weren't as close."

"Maybe that's because you never answered any of his letters." Galen spoke softly.

"His letters?"

"Charles wrote to you every week for the first few years. Later, the letters weren't as frequent. They are all here, in order by postmark, unopened." Galen gestured to the shoeboxes that lay on the carpet.

"No." Tears filled Jason's eyes and his voice broke. His hand trembled as he reached for the nearest shoebox. He removed a letter and stared at it with unseeing eyes. "What does it say?"

"The envelope reads, 'Master Jason Sinclair, Esquire.' " Galen smiled thoughtfully at the large, boyish handwriting and the little-boy humor. Charles and Jason had been good friends, once. They could have been such good friends if Elliott . . . "It was mailed in care of Elliott."

"Will you open it and read it to me?"

Galen opened the envelope. It had been sealed for over twenty-three years. It was the first letter Charles had written. He wrote it the day after he arrived at Morehead. Charles wrote enthusiastically about his new school. He told his twin about the ancient haunted buildings and about the headmaster, "straight out of *Oliver Twist.* " Galen read the letter with enthusiasm, as it had been written; but they both felt Charles's loneliness. Charles was trying to sound happy for his twin, to share this *adventure* with him, but he missed Jason so much!

"I can't . . ." Jason held up his hand. *I can't hear anymore.*

Galen and Jason sat in silence. Elise cooed softly on a blanket on the floor between them. She had been quiet, as if she understood that she was learning something very important and very sad about her father. Whoever he was.

Jason leaned over and kissed her velvety-soft cheek and idly stroked her dark-brown curls.

"And he disowned him because?" Jason began finally. "Because Charles was eighteen and no longer needed a legal guardian."

"Did he ever tell Charles why?" *I told you I don't know why. It's not a lie.* Jason held his breath.

"No." Elliott had meticulously described Charles's reaction to the news; bewildered, uncomprehending, deeply hurt. After all the years of rejection, until that moment, there had still been hole and love in his son's sensitive brown eyes. "Charles never knew."

"How he must have hated Father."

"Oh, no, Jason. Charles loved him. There are letters here from Charles to Elliott. They were unopened, too, but I read some. Charles desperately wanted Elliott's love. Everything Charles did was to please Elliott."

"How could he love him?"

Galen shrugged. "Charles didn't know what Elliott was doing, or why. And he saw how much Elliott loved you, how loving Elliott could be."

"I should have told Charles about the papers in the desk years ago. But I didn't trust him. I was sure that Charles had done something. . . ."

"How could you know? How could you even begin to guess?"

"I have to tell him now. He needs to know."

Their eyes fell on Elise. If she were Charles's daughter. . . There was nothing wrong with Charles; there was no reason for her to be kept from Charles.

"What are you doing?"

"Packing." Brooke had been gradually moving out of her tiny office. Today, her last day, only a small boxload of items remained.

"I can't believe you're leaving. After today . . . wasn't it exhilarating to win?"

Brooke smiled. "It was a perfect swan song."

"Stay."

"Andrew, we've discussed this. This isn't for me, even though I've loved working with you. I want to go to Sinclair. It's my choice."

"You are throwing away a brilliant career."

"I'm doing what I want to do."

"How can you *choose* to work for a man who is the prime suspect in the Manhattan Ripper case?"

"Prime suspect?" Was there something— *evidence*—that Nick and Andrew hadn't shared with her? Was there something more than loosely connected circumstance? "There isn't anything."

"I talked with Nick this morning. Charles doesn't have one goddamned alibi. Don't you think that's a little suspicious for Manhattan's most high-profile bachelor?"

"Charles doesn't *need* alibis."

"Brooke, it scares me so much that you trust him."

"I do trust him, Andrew."

"Charles already attacked Melanie. How much closer does he have to get?"

"He *didn't.*"

"You're blind, Brooke, why can't you see?"

"Stop it, Andrew."

Brooke's eyes flashed with anger. *Leave me alone. I'm going, and I'm going to work for Charles.*

"Brooke, I care about you." Andrew's voice was gentle.

"Well, *don't.* I don't need your concern. Just

leave me alone, *please.*" Brooke stared down at her hands; they were trembling.

"I don't want it to end this way," Andrew whispered softly.

"But this is the way it is going to end, Andrew." Brooke's eyes met his defiantly. "It's over."

Andrew held her gaze for several moments. His brown eyes met the ocean-blue ice with soft concern, but the ice didn't melt. Finally, reluctantly, Andrew left her tiny, almost empty office.

As soon as Andrew left, the trembling that Brooke had controlled with great effort erupted into a cold shiver. On impulse, she reached for the phone and dialed the number for Sinclair Publishing Company.

She had to speak with Charles. Why? For reassurance? Charles, tell me that you're not a psychopathic murderer. Charles, look again at your calendar, find an alibi. Surely there must be a beautiful woman—an *alive* beautiful woman— who spent one of those nights in your arms. . . .

"Charles Sinclair, please. This is Brooke Chandler calling."

"One moment please."

Hang up, Brooke, a voice told her.

"Brooke."

"Charles." He didn't sound like a psychopathic killer.

"Hi."

"Hi. I called to tell you that Jeffrey Martin is over—we won—and I'll be able to start work on Monday."

"Terrific. But you don't sound terrific."

"I just had an argument with Andrew."

"About?"

"My brilliant career." *About you.*

"Are you having second thoughts?" Charles didn't want to force her; Brooke had to be certain.

"No," Brooke answered firmly. *I know you're not the Ripper.* "Of course not."

"Because if you are—"

"I'm *not.* It was silly of me to call. I'll talk to you later." Brooke hung up quickly. Afterward she thought of safe topics she could have discussed with him. *Are you going to Windermere this weekend, Charles? Have you seen Galen and her baby? Are you going to see Melanie, the woman you love, the woman Nick and Andrew think you brutally attacked?*

Brooke sighed. There weren't safe topics. When was this going to *end?*

Melanie finally emerged from her room in the late afternoon. Dark-gray storm clouds were gathering outside, and the mansion was still strangely silent. Melanie walked into the great room and felt a sudden cold breeze. The french door leading into the rose garden was open.

As Melanie moved to close it, she saw Jason. He stood in the garden, coatless in the bitter cold air, staring at the sea.

"Jason, hello." Melanie joined him. "You left the door ajar."

"I wanted to hear the phone." Jason spoke into the wind. "I'm waiting for a call from Charles."

Charles usually returned Jason's calls promptly, but not today, not after last night. If Jason didn't hear from Charles soon he would drive into town. Jason had to find Charles and tell him everything.

"Oh."

"Have you spoken with him today?"

"No." Melanie hesitated. She had to clear the air. "I was in the library last night, Jason, when you and Charles argued."

"I know some things I didn't know last night. I need to tell him, apologize to him—"

Jason stopped abruptly because Melanie suddenly shivered.

"You're cold, let's go in."

"No." Melanie frowned. "Jason, I . . ."

"What, Melanie?"

"I feel as if Brooke is in great danger." Melanie's voice was distant and eerie. "I need to reach her and warn her."

As Melanie spoke, a clap of thunder sounded off shore. She shivered again. Jason stared at the dark, turbulent sky and the storm that was rapidly approaching. Jason remembered a storm like this, coming out of the blue, bringing with it death and destruction.

"Let's go call Brooke and Charles," Jason said firmly. Jason was suddenly all the more determined to speak with *his* twin, because, as if Melanie's premonition were contagious, Jason sensed danger for Charles.

The lamplight flickered as they made their calls.

Melanie called Brooke at work and was told Brooke had left. Melanie dialed the number to Brooke's apartment and there was no answer.

"I guess she's on her way home," Melanie murmured as she handed the receiver to Jason.

"Didn't you give him my messages?" Jason demanded with uncharacteristic annoyance moments later as Charles's secretary told him that Charles had gone for the day.

"Yes, I gave him all of them."

Jason depressed the disconnect button and started to dial the number to Charles's penthouse. Halfway through, the line went dead.

Chapter Thirty-two

"Brooke left about five minutes ago, Lieutenant Adrian."

"Was she alone?"

"Yes."

"Where did she go?"

"Home, I guess. She was carrying a small box. It was her last day here." The clerk paused. "Is there someone else who could help you?"

"No." Brooke's last day. "Yes. Let me speak with Andrew Parker."

"Oh, dear. He's gone, too."

"All right. Thank you."

Nick dialed the number to Brooke's apartment. There was no answer.

If the officer he had just assigned to follow her and protect her had gotten to the DA's office in time . . . Nick looked at his watch. In five minutes he would try her apartment again, and if she wasn't there he would find her.

Brooke walked briskly. The wind was cold, and large raindrops had started to fall. Gray-black clouds hovered in the distance over Long Island. The wind was invigorating and the raindrops felt cleansing. Brooke decided to stop at her apartment, leave the box, change, and go for a long walk.

Brooke pulled on her jeans and found a wool plaid scarf in the back of her closet. She opened her apartment door just as the doorbell sounded.

"Oh!" she exclaimed. "Hi. I'm glad you came over. It was stupid."

"Can we talk?"

"Sure. Come in." Brooke turned and led the way into her small living room.

"I need to have you with me." His voice was a whisper.

"What?" She spun, smiling, but the smile faded quickly when she saw his wild dark eyes. Brooke repeated, her voice barely audible, "What?"

"You just don't understand."

"No." *Yes.* Brooke's heart raced. Could she get to the door? Could she dash past him?

"Maybe if Melanie hadn't lived." His voice was so strange. "Maybe then it would have been enough."

"But she lived, and I'm so glad." Brooke didn't know how to talk to him. He was no one she knew, no one she *cared* about. When he wasn't like this—when he wasn't insane—she could

472

cajole him. "It's so wonderful that Melanie didn't die."

"She called your name. That was the only thing that saved her."

"Good," Brooke whispered. She started to edge toward the door, but he blocked her path.

"But nothing can save you."

The shiny, menacing hunting knife looked incongruous in the hands of a man wearing a perfectly tailored three-piece gray suit. But the lethal weapon was *real*, and was going to kill her.

"Why?"

From the hallway, as he approached Brooke's apartment, he heard their voices. The door was ajar. He tapped lightly, waited only a moment, then pushed the door open wide.

"You really don't know?" He gave a short, ugly laugh. "I was so patient with you, Brooke, *too* patient. We could have been so good together. I would have taken such good care of you. He doesn't even love you. He loves your sister!"

"Why don't we try?" Brooke was pleading for her life.

"It's too late. You betrayed me."

He raised the knife above his right shoulder.

"Please," Brooke whispered. "Please don't."

As the razor-sharp blade plunged at its target, Charles grabbed him from behind, startling him, and averting the lethal blow.

"Charles."

"Run, Brooke."

Charles should have had the advantage; he attacked Andrew from behind. Charles was strong, but Andrew's madness gave him extraordinary strength. Andrew twisted out of Charles's grip and spun to face him. He stared at the man who in his deranged mind had become his greatest enemy. Charles had stolen Brooke from him!

"You," Andrew hissed.

Andrew slashed with the knife, and Charles spun away. Andrew slashed again and again, relentless in his madness. His lips turned into a half-smile and his brown eyes were wild and blazing. Charles repeatedly dodged the blade, but he was fatiguing. The sight of blood—his blood—on the knife blade told him Andrew was winning.

"Nick." Charles heard Brooke's voice from the hallway. "In there, please hurry!"

Nick ran past Brooke into her apartment with his gun drawn. Brooke followed.

"Drop it, Andrew." Nick pointed his gun at Andrew's heart.

Andrew smiled a half-smile and stood up straight.

"This is quite a party, isn't it?" Andrew glanced from Charles to Nick to Brooke. "All the boyfriends, or should I say *lovers?* Of course, that doesn't apply to me. But you, Charles. And you, Nick."

Andrew's voice had an eerie singsong quality; he was mesmerizing them with his madness.

"It's over, Andrew. Drop the knife."

"You won't shoot me, Nick. You *can't.* We both know the rules."

"I will shoot you, Andrew. Look at Charles, he's bleeding. I had to shoot you to stop you from killing him. *Look* at him," Nick commanded. Nick didn't think it would work. Andrew knew that he hadn't gravely injured Charles, but if Nick could make him look—drop his guard—for even a fraction of a second . . .

Andrew didn't turn his face or body, but he let his eyes dart briefly toward Charles. It was enough. Nick dropped his gun and grabbed Andrew's right arm at the wrist. Nick's hands held tight, cutting off circulation, and his strong fingers worked to pry the knife away.

The knife fell to the floor. Nick released his grip on Andrew's wrist and tried to find a new hold that would subdue him. But Andrew spun free, laughing, and backed away from Nick.

Andrew backed away, stepping into the small box that Brooke had brought home from the office. He lost his balance and fell backward. As he twisted to break the fall, Andrew's right temple struck the metal radiator.

The blow—the full weight of his strong body against the metal—was instantly lethal. Andrew's lifeless body slumped down the wall and onto the floor. His head, propped against the wall, faced them. Bright red blood pulsed from his temple into his dark-brown hair and spilled onto his cheeks like crimson tears. The bleeding stopped quickly; there was no heartbeat to sustain it.

Andrew's dark-brown eyes, now clouded and bewildered, stared at them.

Nick solemnly retrieved his gun and made a call to the precinct to arrange for the homicide squad and the coroner. Brooke followed Nick away from Andrew. Brooke expected Charles to follow, too, but when she turned around she found that Charles hadn't moved.

He still stood in front of Andrew, his eyes staring into the dead dark eyes, unable to move. Charles didn't see Andrew, the psychopathic murderer. Charles saw Elliott—the Elliott of his nightmares—with his taunting dead eyes and his head crushed from the strength of the storm.

"Charles?" Brooke moved beside Charles and touched him lightly on the forearm. It was wet where she touched, wet with Charles's blood! "Charles, are you hurt?"

Charles didn't seem to hear her. He was mesmerized, transfixed, lost in a private horror. Brooke looked to Nick for help. He was still on the phone.

". . . No, I'll tell Mrs. Parker myself." Allison was safe, under police protection, in a room at the Excelsior; now she was safe and *free.* Nick hung up the phone and crossed the room to Charles and Brooke. He spoke firmly, "Charles, what is it?"

Charles squeezed his eyes shut and pressed his strong, trembling fingers against his forehead.

"What, Charles?" Nick pressed. Charles was in some form of shock, but why?

"My father." Charles's voice was heavy. "The way he died. It must have been like that. He must have looked like that."

No, he didn't look like that, Nick thought. Nick had seen Elliott Sinclair's head injury, and Charles *hadn't*. It was more proof—unnecessary now—that Charles was innocent. Charles was innocent of all crimes.

"Let's drive into town," Melanie suggested after forty-five minutes had elapsed and the phone line was still dead.

"There are probably trees across the road. That's why the phone is out. There might be power lines down, too," Jason explained calmly. Jason didn't feel clam. A sense of dread pulsed through him for his twin, and he kept remembering a storm like this thirteen years ago.

"The power lines aren't down," Melanie protested weakly. The lights had flickered but, so far, the electricity had held.

"Why don't I turn on the television for local news? Maybe we can find out about the roads," Galen suggested. Not that Melanie could leave Windermere anyway: It was her *safe* house.

As the television picture came into focus, Melanie whispered, "That's Brooke's apartment building."

It was a special bulletin. The camera crew was positioned outside, in the waning twilight and pouring rain. The building's entrance was cluttered with police cars, medic units, the coroner's van, and numerous police officers.

"The information is unconfirmed—we are waiting for the appearance of Lieutenant Nick Adrian or Deputy District Attorney Andrew Parker, the two authorized spokesmen of the Manhattan Ripper investigation—but we understand that the Manhattan Ripper is dead. We know that this is the apartment building of Brooke Chandler, assistant DA and twin sister of the only surviving Manhattan Ripper victim, super-model Melanie Chandler. Unconfirmed sources report that Brooke Chandler, Nick Adrian, and Andrew Parker—as well as magazine mogul and sometimes companion of Melanie Chandler, Charles Sinclair—all entered the building in the past hour and a half. It is possible that a trap was set by the PD working with the DA's office. It appears, if so, that the trap was successful. That's all we have now, Burt, but we'll stay here until we have all the answers. Back to you in the studio. . ."

"They are all right," Jason whispered unconvincingly.

"You know they're *not,* Jason," Melanie countered. "We have to go to them."

"We have to wait here. There is nothing we can do. We have to wait." Jason's heart fluttered with fear. He had waited here once before, helpless in a violent storm, until the sirens brought news of death.

By the time the first news crew arrived outside Brooke's apartment building on West Fifty-seventh Street, Nick and Charles and Brooke were already in Nick's office at the precinct.

"The phone lines are down to all of east Long Island. I'll have dispatch radio the guards at the estate and tell them that you are safe."

"Thank you." Brooke smiled at Nick then touched Charles's bloodied sleeve. "Maybe a doctor . . ."

478

"It's a flesh wound, Brooke. It's nothing." It's nothing compared to what he must have done to Melanie, or what he was planning to do to you.

"Why did you come to my apartment, Charles?"

"I didn't like the way you sounded when you called. I didn't think I'd heard the whole story."

"You hadn't." Brooke closed her eyes briefly. "Andrew had just made a point of reminding me that *you* were a suspect."

Charles sighed and looked from Brooke to Nick.

"I'm sorry, Charles. I never *wanted* it to be you." Nick shook his head slowly. "God, I was so wrong. I never even considered him."

"Why should you have considered him, Nick?" Brooke asked swiftly. She had never considered Andrew, either, but she had spent many tormented hours convincing herself that it couldn't possibly be Charles. "He didn't even know Melanie. . . ."

Brooke frowned. She suddenly recalled the crazy words Andrew had spoken before he lunged at her with the knife. Andrew didn't know Melanie, but he knew *her*. Andrew wanted *her*. Was it her fault?

"Why did you come over, Nick?"

Nick told them about Allison Parker. There was no way Nick could tell the story without mentioning Brooke's resemblance to Allison.

"Andrew loved Allison," Brooke said softly. "But sometimes he felt betrayed and abandoned by her."

"All Andrew's emotions about Allison were

disturbed. She was his obsession. Andrew murdered her roommate at Princeton to scare Allison into needing him.''

''And he was doing that with me? Oh, *no.* ''

''Brooke, this is not your fault. You happened to look like Allison, that's all.''

''He wanted me!''

''I think he wanted Allison—young, strong, beautiful Allison—back again. You said he felt she was abandoning him.'' Nick spoke the next very quietly, ''Brooke, Andrew tried to *murder* you.''

''*Still* . . . What he did to those women, and Melanie!'' Brooke's horrified blue eyes looked at Charles.

''It's not your fault.'' The brown eyes tried to reassure her.

''He was crazy, Brooke.''

Nick's phone rang. ''Ten minutes. All right. Sure. Thanks.'' He hung up the phone. ''Press conference in ten minutes.''

''You don't need us for that, do you?'' Charles asked. ''I want to get changed and drive to Windermere. I can bring Melanie home now, can't I?''

Home, Brooke mused.

''Yes. Of course.''

''Brooke, do you want to come?''

''Oh, I . . .'' Brooke faltered.

''I could use your help tonight, Brooke,'' Nick interjected swiftly.

Brooke nodded. Somehow it was right for her to be here, with Nick, as they wrapped up the Manhattan Ripper case. She had imagined a night like this, when it was over, when she and Nick and Andrew—

Andrew. Brooke's blue eyes grew dark and thoughtful.

"Brooke," Nick continued firmly. *Don't think about it now, Brooke. It's too fresh. Focus those beautiful eyes and that bright mind on the mechanics. There's a lot of work left to be done, even though he's dead.* "I need to check on a few things before the press conference. I'll meet you downstairs in ten minutes. OK?"

His words, *check on a few things,* jarred her legal mind.

"Was his blood type O?" she asked quietly. Brooke knew Andrew was right-handed with dark eyes and dark hair, and she knew that he intended to kill *her.* But was Andrew Parker the Manhattan Ripper? They had to be certain before they told Manhattan to breathe a sigh of relief.

"Yes." Good, she was with him. "I'm going to check with the handwriting expert now. If he hasn't finished comparing the journal entries with the samples of Andrew's handwriting I got from the DA's office, we'll wait."

"We need to go over all the evidence."

Nick smiled. He already had. More evidence was being collected at Andrew's apartment. In a remote corner of a closet the officers had already found something Allison Parker had missed—a blood-splattered black stocking with eyeholes.

"We will." Nick turned to Charles. Nick had two messages for Charles; both were important, and both were emotional. "Thank you,

Charles, for saving Brooke's life. And I'm so sorry about—"

"You were doing your job. I fit the description. Melanie and I had our share of well-publicized problems."

"That's gracious of you."

"I'm just glad it's over. I was afraid . . ." Charles faltered.

"We couldn't have pressed charges."

"You already had," Charles replied flatly as his dark eyes found Brooke. *You already had with the people who counted.*

"I'm sorry," Nick repeated hoarsely before he left his office. Nick knew that even his *suspicion* of Charles had done damage to Charles with the people he loved—Melanie and Jason and Brooke.

After Nick left, Brooke moved closer to Charles. "Charles, I never . . ."

"But it worried you." It worried you, and it worried Melanie. And *Jason;* Jason *believed* it was possible.

"I just wanted it to be over, too." Brooke sighed softly. She needed to tell him; if they were going to work together, and if he and she and Melanie . . . "Charles, what Andrew said about you and me . . ."

"Andrew was crazy, Brooke. Nothing he said—" Charles caught the look in her eyes and stopped abruptly. He smiled gently and touched her flushed cheek with his finger. "Not so crazy?"

"I remember a wide-eyed law clerk who was pretty enchanted," Brooke admitted shyly.

"Brooke." Charles lifted her chin slightly and gazed into her eyes. "I'm very flattered."

The brown eyes told her it was the truth; Charles meant it.

"I'm flattered that you're flattered." Brooke laughed softly, and her heart didn't ache. Charles could be her dear, beloved friend. Brooke continued easily, so easily, "Next life. This life is with Melanie."

"Yes," Charles whispered quietly.

Brooke smiled. "Give her my love."

Chapter Thirty-three

Charles drove along the rain-slick roads toward Southampton. The driving was treacherous. Branches cluttered the roadway and the wind swirled and the rain pelted. It would have been smarter to wait until morning. . . .

But Charles could not wait to be with Melanie. If only he could avoid seeing Jason. Maybe Melanie would be alone in her cheery yellow bedroom, or in the library, and they could leave unnoticed.

"Andrew visited me in the hospital," Melanie breathed in amazement after they watched the latest special bulletin.

The electricity had held, despite the storm, but the phone line was still dead. Melanie wanted to speak with Brooke, but she was reassured to see her—safe and calm—at the press conference. Melanie looked for Charles, hailed by Nick as the hero of the piece. Brooke gave Charles *and*

Nick equal credit for saving her life. Melanie looked for Charles, but she didn't see him.

"He *visited* you?" Galen asked.

"Yes. It was probably a test to see if I could recognize him. But I looked into his eyes and told him how much I believed it was Steve Barnes." Melanie shivered.

"Thank God it's over," Jason said. He wished it was all over. He wished he already had spoken to Charles and somehow everything would be all right. Restless, even after the special bulletins told them Brooke and Charles were safe, Jason reached repeatedly for the still-dead phone.

When they heard the front door open, they all stood up. They listened in silence as he tapped softly on the door to the yellow bedroom and called her name.

"Charles." Melanie crossed the great room toward the foyer. Jason and Galen followed.

Charles appeared, his dark hair darker from the pelting rain, and his face cold from the bitter wind. Charles didn't look at Jason or Galen. "Melanie, it's over, let's—"

"Charles, I've been trying to reach you," Jason interjected. "Didn't you get my messages?"

The soft, loving look for Melanie vanished as Charles turned toward Jason.

"I don't think we have anything—" he stopped abruptly when he saw the look of worry in Jason's eyes; Jason's eyes and Galen's eyes. Charles breathed, "Oh, my God, is it Elise? Has something happened?"

"No," Galen answered swiftly. That precious child is well, sleeping peacefully in a home where another child suffered horribly. Oh, *Charles.* Galen blinked back tears.

"What is it?" Charles pressed. He looked to Melanie for the answer, but she didn't know. Galen and Jason hadn't told her.

"Charles," Jason spoke softly. "This afternoon I asked Galen to go through Father's desk. I knew there were letters and a journal."

"Yes?" Why hadn't he ever known that?

"We know why he disowned you."

"Tell me." Charles's voice was barely audible.

"Maybe I should leave," Melanie suggested quietly. She had already been an unwitting witness to the argument between Charles and Jason.

"No." Charles looked at her with surprise. There can't be secrets between us, Melanie, not anymore. Charles knew he was taking a risk; Melanie might learn something that would turn her against him. But it—whatever it was—had already separated them once. Charles sighed. "You need to hear this." Whatever it is.

They walked into the great room. The fire crackled cheerfully. Elliott's journal lay on the marble end table. Jason moved toward it, glowering at the words he couldn't read written by the man he once had loved. *Once.*

"Father blamed you for our mother's death." The pain of his words and their meaning flickered in Jason's pale-blue eyes.

"What?" Charles didn't understand.

"She died while you were being born," Jason said heavily. "And he blamed you for it."

"No." Charles shook his head.

485

"Yes."

Galen saw the look of bewilderment and hurt and sadness in the beautiful brown eyes. Galen recognized the look. Elliott had described it so well; when he left Charles alone in his crib, when he spanked him viciously, when he openly loved Jason and neglected Charles, and finally, the last time, when Elliott disowned him.

"Your father was a mean and irrational man," Galen said emotionally. She hated the man she had never known.

"No." It was Charles who spoke, defending the man whose love he had wanted so desperately and who had treated him so cruelly. "No."

"I didn't know until today that you had ever written letters to me, Charles," Jason told him apologetically. Believe it, Charles. Our father was a man who deserved hatred, not love.

"So many letters," Charles breathed. He closed his eyes for a moment and felt the pain of a young boy—his pain—whose loving letters had never been acknowledged. But still he wrote, sharing the secrets of his heart and soul with his twin. "He never . . ."

"No."

The impact of what Charles had just learned suddenly hit him. Emotions swirled within him. He needed to be alone with this; he had to try to make sense of it. Charles clenched his fists and felt a warm wetness on his forearm where the knife wound had reopened and started to bleed.

"I . . ." Charles couldn't speak. He had to get away. Charles saw concern, and love, in the three sets of eyes; hurt they couldn't help him, not now.

Charles shook his head slightly, then crossed the great room to the French doors that led to the rose garden and the sea beyond.

After a moment Galen took the leather journal from the marble end table and rushed after Charles into the storm.

"Charles, wait."

Galen didn't know if he heard her voice above the wind. He moved swiftly into the storm and the darkness.

"Please."

Charles stopped, hut he didn't turn around. "Galen, I need to be alone."

"Yes, I know." She stood close behind him. "But you need to read this. You need to read his words."

Charles turned and stared at her with wild brown eyes wet with rain or tears or both. *"Why?"*

"It will help." Galen forced Elliott's journal into his hands. Galen didn't know Elliott, but she hated him. Charles had known him and loved him. Charles had called to him desperately as he lay alone and delirious and maybe dying in Africa. Charles needed to know how Elliott really felt, how torn he had been, how much it had hurt him to treat Charles the way he did. Charles needed to know how much Elliott really had loved him and how much Elliott hated himself for being unable to show Charles that love. "Please read it, Charles."

Numbly Charles took the leather journal and slipped it under his windbreaker. Then he turned and disappeared in the darkness toward the angry sea.

What if he doesn't stop at water's edge, Galen wondered. What if he walks into the sea to die as Elliott had died in a storm-tossed watery grave?

Galen sighed. Charles was his own man; but somewhere in the emotions that tossed and turned within him was a deep love for Melanie. Galen had seen it in his eyes. Charles would remember Melanie and it would save him.

"Where is he?" Melanie asked anxiously when Galen reappeared at the French doors.

"He went for a walk toward the sea."

"He'll probably go to the beach house. There's light there and protection from the rain." Jason moved to the bay window as he spoke. He thought he saw a dark figure on the lawn; but it was a night of dark shadows. Jason couldn't be sure. A few moments later he saw his twin's figure on the lighted porch of the beach house. Charles stood, motionless, and faced the endless darkness of the night and the sea. Then he sat, bent over, and started to read. "He's there now."

Sometimes I want to love him so much, but I can't. I look at him and I remember Meredith and it makes me hate him all over again.

Charles read Elliott's words and knew why Galen had given him the journal. Buried deep beneath the hatred, between the careful, horrible chronicles of abuse, were glimmers of love.

I read one of his stories today, the headmaster sent it to the office. God, Charles is talented! He is so bright and creative and sensitive. I should tell him how proud I am.

Why didn't you tell me, Father? Just *once . . .*

Oh, those bewildered brown eyes when I told him to leave. He doesn't understand, but his life will be happier away from me forever. Charles will begin his own magazine, and it will be far better than Images *ever was.*

I wish him happiness, now. I hope someday Charles will find someone to love.

After Charles read every word—the hatred and the love—he held his head in his hands and cried.

"Go to him, Jason," Galen urged gently.

They were in their bedroom. She was nursing Elise, and Jason stared out the window at the beach house. After Charles left the great room, they had disbanded in silence; Melanie went to her bedroom, and Galen and Jason went to theirs.

"I have to wait until he comes back to the house. Charles needs this time alone."

Jason watched as Charles finished reading and held his head in his hands. Eventually, Charles got up and walked off the protected porch. But he was still there, facing the angry sea.

Jason's view was of the beach house and the sea beyond. The lawn and gardens directly below were obscured by the structure of the mansion. Jason didn't see Melanie as she walked—her golden hair whipped by the wind, her slender body wavering like a young tree—along the white stone path toward the beach house. *Had* he been watching, had anyone been watching, he would have noticed her slow, determined path and admired her courage.

And he would have seen her fall.

It came like all the other times—but it hadn't happened in almost a week, it wasn't supposed to happen anymore!—the sudden unexpected weakness that commanded her to lie down, *quickly*. She couldn't lie down in the middle of the path in the heavy rain and the bitter-cold wind. She couldn't and *wouldn't*. This time she wasn't going to let the weakness stop her; she was going to be with Charles. Melanie could see him in the distance, his back to her, looking at the sea.

This time she would conquer the weakness, she decided defiantly.

But her body betrayed her. She had pushed too hard. Her arms wouldn't even reach out to break her fall. She screamed with pain as she fell on the stone path. Her fall was heavy, unbroken, and hurled by the angry wind. Her scream was a reflex; it was a scream from a pain that was the *sum* of all pain that had come before.

Breathe, her mind told her. But the pain stopped her from breathing. In a moment it would stop her heart. The pain was within her, surrounding her heart and her lungs and her brain; and the pain was on the surface, relentlessly battered by the wind and rain. All of her, every cell of her, was a raw, gaping wound. Every nerve root, *almost* mended, was torn again and angry and screaming at the insult.

Melanie forced a breath, and another. She was breathing. Melanie knew because each breath made her chest sear with white-hot pain. She couldn't move. She couldn't even raise her head off the ground. She felt sharp pieces of stone digging into her cheeks, but her head was too heavy to lift. Her whole body began to shake, chilled from her drenched clothes and the bitter cold, and the trembling made it all hurt even more.

How could it hurt even more? But it did.

Then he was there, bending over her.

"Melanie," he whispered.

Charles cradled her in his arms and caused a new round of pain as he pulled her against him. He had heard the scream, a heart-stopping human wail, above the noises of the storm. At first he hadn't seen her in the darkness; the direction of the scream, tossed by the swirling wind, had been vague. Finally he saw the shimmer of gold and he ran to her.

"Charles." Her lips formed the word, but there was no sound. When she opened her eyes, Charles saw the disbelieving glaze of pain and a faint flicker of happiness for him.

Charles lifted her shaking body in his arms, suddenly aware that he had caused her more pain. He hesitated. Putting her down would hurt her more, again. He already had her in his arms. He would carry her to the house, to warmth and safety. Charles walked on the grass beside the path; maybe it would be less jarring.

As he neared the veranda Charles saw another figure. Jason had seen Charles's sudden dash from the beach house and went to the great room to meet him. Jason assumed that Charles was dashing against the storm, dashing for the cover of the house. But Charles was carrying Melanie. . . .

"Charles, is she all right?"

"Jason, thank God. I didn't know how I would open the doors without—" Charles stopped. Without putting her down and hurting her more. "We'll need lots of warm towels, and scissors to cut her out of her clothes."

Jason led the way, holding doors, helping Charles take Melanie to her bedroom. Charles set her gently on top of the bed. Jason brought a stack of plush dry towels and a pair of scissors.

"How is she?" Jason asked.

Melanie opened her eyes and nodded slightly.

"I think that means she's OK," Charles answered gently, looking in the sky-blue eyes for confirmation. Melanie smiled a shaky smile. "I'm going to get her dry and into bed."

"Do you need help?"

"No. I think we can manage."

"I'll be in the kitchen if you need me."

"Thank you," Charles said. "Thank you, Jason."

Charles talked to her, like a father talking to a child who would understand but was too young to answer. He didn't want her to try to talk, but he wanted her to know what he was doing.

"I'm going to dry your hair a little then wrap it in a towel," Charles explained as he did just that. When he finished he said, "I think it will hurt the least if I cut your clothes off."

Melanie's eyes opened and Charles saw fear.

He remembered her fear when he used his knife to open the manuscript from Galen.

"Oh, Melanie darling. He's dead. He can't hurt you. And I would never hurt you. Don't you know that?"

Melanie didn't answer and closed her eyes.

Carefully, pulling the wet cloth away from her skin, protecting her from the touch of cold steel with his warm fingers, Charles cut away the cashmere sweater and the cotton shirt beneath it. As the wet clothes fell away, until all she wore above her waist was the rain-soaked bra, Melanie began to tremble.

She was afraid to open her eyes. She couldn't bear to see the expression on his face—his horror and revulsion at her scarred grotesque torso. She felt his hands, warm and gentle, as they removed her bra and dried her with a soft fluffy towel.

"Hey," he said softly. "What do you want to put on?"

"There's a nightgown in the top dresser drawer." Melanie was surprised by the strength in her voice. The pain was subsiding. The startling, breathtaking hot stabs of pain had muted into a constant dull throb and her strength was returning. But it was all too late; Charles had seen her scars. "I'm better now. If you can just hand me the nightgown, I can do the rest."

She heard him open the dresser drawer.

"Is the light too bright?" Charles asked when he returned. It wasn't bright at all. The room was softly illuminated by the light from the bathroom. It was just a gentle glow. Still, her eyes were closed.

"No." Melanie forced them open. It was all right as long as she didn't look at him.

"Can you sit up? Just for a moment. I'll help you. Then I can slip this over your head."

Charles put his arms around her to help her and met resistance. She pushed herself against the bed; her body stiffened with pain.

"Melanie?"

"I'm all right, Charles, really. I'm warm now. The pain is less. I can get dressed and undressed on my own. Thank you." She took the nightgown and covered her breasts.

"I want to stay here—with you—tonight. I can sleep in the chair." I want to be with you, Melanie. What I have just learned—as difficult as it was—has set me free. I can love you. There is no reason—

"*No.*" Melanie looked at him then. She saw his surprise and concern; she read it as pity "No, Charles. Please, just go away"

"Melanie."

"Please."

Charles watched her for a moment, but her eyes wouldn't meet his again. Finally he kissed her on the cheek and left the room.

After Charles left, Melanie touched the spot where he had kissed her. Then she warmed her still-cold face with her own hot tears.

Good-bye, darling Charles. Good-bye, not *au revoir*.

Charles went to the kitchen. He needed a cup of coffee before beginning his drive back to Manhattan. He was exhausted, but he couldn't stay at Windermere unless he was with Melanie. He would return in the morning to get her

Melanie would come with him, wouldn't she? The doubts were behind them now, weren't they? His doubt about himself, about what was wrong with him, no longer existed. And if she had ever doubted him, ever believed that he could have been the Manhattan Ripper . . .

It was over. And she had braved the angry storm to be with him. And even though just now she had asked him to leave . . . Charles frowned slightly.

Charles's frown deepened when he entered the kitchen. He had forgotten that Jason would be there. Jason sat at the kitchen table drinking coffee.

"How is she?" Jason asked.

"Tired. Hurt. Discouraged," Charles answered. He was describing himself, too.

Jason nodded and poured a cup of coffee for Charles. They sat at opposite ends of the table.

"I didn't even know Melanie had gone out," Jason said after several silent minutes "I was watching you. When you left the beach house I went to meet you."

Charles stared vacantly at Jason. I can't talk about it now, Jason.

"There is something I am going to do as soon as possible."

"Oh?" Charles asked without curiosity.

"I'm going to give you half of everything. Sinclair Publishing, Windermere, everything."

"What?"

"It's your rightful half. If I'd known the reason that Father disowned you . . ."

"He made you promise never to let me have it," Charles reminded him.

"A promise to a man like that!" Jason's voice was bitter.

"Oh, Jason," Charles sighed. "Don't hate him."

"How can you say that?"

"He loved you, Jason, very much." Charles smiled slightly. "And he loved me, too."

Jason frowned.

"He did, deep down, but he never really recovered from our mother's death."

"How can you be so forgiving?"

Charles shrugged. "Maybe it is just such a relief to know, finally, there is nothing wrong with *me.*"

They sat in silence for a moment.

"Charles, about last night, about accusing you of Father's death, I . . ."

"Nick said you spoke with the harbormaster. You know I wasn't there." Charles's voice was edgy.

"I know you weren't there anyway." Jason's eyes met his twin's. "Tonight, before you went to Brooke's apartment, I sensed that you were in great danger. I tried to reach you, to warn you. . . ."

Charles nodded. Jason was trying, and he *would* try. If they could free themselves of the secrets, maybe they could be close again. *If* . . . there was one more secret, and it was the most important, the most precious. . . .

"I need to know if she's mine, Jason," Charles whispered finally.

"I know."

"I don't even know what I will do if she is. I know she belongs with Galen and I know Galen belongs with you. But if she's my daughter, if she's part of me . . ."

Jason looked at his brother—the twin who had been deprived of so much that should have been his—and Jason understood, then, how much it meant to Charles. It wasn't that Charles wanted Elise to be his daughter—they all knew it would be best if she were Jason's—but, if she were, Charles wanted to know. Charles wanted to love her the way a father should love his child.

"You know what I've been thinking about all night?" Jason asked as he made a vow to himself that if Elise were Charles's daughter they would work it out. He and Charles and Galen would make it work. They had enough love, more than enough, for the little girl and for each other.

"What?"

"All those hours you used to read to me when we were little boys. Those were such happy times." Jason's voice broke.

Charles smiled, his dark eyes suddenly moist. "Those were happy times for me, too."

Melanie lay in her bed, her entire body throbbing, unable to sleep. Finally she forced herself out of bed to the window overlooking the drive. Charles's car was still there. It was one-thirty in the morning. Charles was probably planning to spend the night.

I can't see him. It was a knowledge that surpassed all the pain. She could not see Charles Sinclair again, *ever*. Charles had seen her wounds; he knew what she had become. She couldn't face him; she didn't want to see his pity or his contempt.

Melanie squinted as she looked into the driveway and realized that the brightness was the full moon. The storm had passed. The night was crisp and clear and still and bright. Maybe . . .

Melanie moved slowly, her pace limited by pain, toward the bedside table and the telephone. She held her breath as she lifted the receiver.

There was a dial tone! Someone could come to take her away. She could be gone before morning. Melanie pressed the button that automatically dialed Brooke's apartment. There was no answer.

Of course Brooke wouldn't be there. Her apartment was the scene of a crime. There would be blood. . . . Melanie wondered about her own luxury apartment. Had someone—Adam, Brooke, the landlord, the police, *who* handled that sort of thing?—removed *her* bloodstains from the furniture and replaced the expensive wool carpet and washed the walls?

Melanie pressed the button that automatically dialed the direct line to Nick's office.

"Adrian," he answered. Melanie heard the fatigue in his voice.

"Nick? It's Melanie."

"Hi. You made it into town?"

"What? No, I'm at Windermere. It's all right for me to leave, isn't it?"

498

"Sure." Nick frowned. "Didn't Charles drive out this evening?"

"Yes. He's spending the night. I sort of hoped I could leave now." Melanie's voice faltered. She didn't want to explain why. She just wanted to leave.

"Well, we do run a round-trip service for our safehouse guests," Nick said easily, but he was worried about her. What was going on? "I've already turned the guards loose, but I'll find someone. When will you be ready?"

Nick guessed her answer before he heard her relieved grateful voice whisper, "I'm ready now, Nick."

"Realistically, it will be thirty minutes. Would you like to talk to Brooke?"

"*Yes. Is she there?*"

Nick didn't answer, but he handed the phone to Brooke.

"Melanie?"

"Brooke, are you all right?"

"Yes." Melanie's question recalled the horror of Andrew's attack. For the past six hours Brooke had forced objectivity, helping Nick with the legal details. Now she shuddered, remembering her own fear and thinking how very much worse it had been for her twin. "Are you?"

"Sure," Melanie answered swiftly and unconvincingly. "Brooke, do you know if my apartment is . . ."

"Yes. It's fine."

"Good. Why don't you plan to stay there until yours is fixed?" Melanie didn't ask, Why don't you plan to stay there, *too?* She knew she would only be in her apartment long enough to pack.

"Thank you."

"Nick is sending someone to get me now."

"I'll be here, at the precinct, when you arrive and then we can go to your apartment." Brooke frowned. "Melanie?"

"Yes?"

"It was because of me." Brooke knew that Charles wouldn't have told her. It was something the press didn't need to know, but Melanie did. Brooke had to tell her.

"What was?"

"Andrew was trying to frighten *me.*"

"Tonight?"

"No. From the beginning. That was why he killed. That was why he attacked you."

Melanie's hand tightened around the receiver and she tugged at her lower lip with her teeth. It was because of Brooke? There was a *reason* in Andrew's warped violent mind? No, it wasn't possible. . . .

"He stopped when I called your name," Melanie whispered finally. It was possible. It was true.

"Oh, Melanie, I am so *sorry.*"

"Brooke," Melanie said softly. She *felt* the pain of her twin's guilt. "It's not your fault. I would never blame you. . . ."

Melanie said it again when she embraced Brooke in Nick's office three hours later; and she repeated it an hour later when they arrived at her apartment. Each time Melanie said it with finality, as if it was absurd for Brooke to even *imagine* that she would blame her. Brooke would believe it for a while; until she looked at Melanie, stiff and pale from pain, and saw the deep sadness in her sky-blue eyes. Then Brooke's eyes would fill with sorrow again; and Melanie would notice and remind her anew that it wasn't her fault.

Melanie entered her apartment hesitantly. She was glad Brooke was with her.

"It looks, uh, *normal,* doesn't it?" Melanie asked with relief. Not that anything was normal anymore. She had to find a new setting for normal. "You're welcome to stay here, even after your apartment is all right. I'll be away for at least two months."

"Away?"

"Yes." Melanie looked at Brooke and told her the truth. "I'm changed. I need to find out who I am *now,* what I want, where I'm going."

"I know you do. I hoped I could help."

"You have. You can. I need you to be my friend."

"I am. You know I am."

"Yes." Melanie smiled at her twin. "Brooke, first I have to go away for a while."

Brooke nodded. "Where are you going?"

Melanie shook her head slightly. "I can't tell you, but I'll be safe. I'll call you, and Mom and Dad. I don't want you to worry."

"You found me once, when I was lost on top of a remote mountain."

"You don't need to try to find me, Brooke. I won't be lost."

"OK. When do you leave?"

"The plane departs at nine." It was true. The plane Melanie planned to take, tomorrow or the next day or whenever she was strong enough and had made all the travel arrangements, departed daily at nine. She wouldn't be on the plane today. It would take all her strength to pack and take a taxi to an airport motel where, hopefully, no one would recognize her under her hooded jacket. She would rest and recover there until she was fit to travel. "I'd better start packing."

Brooke watched Melanie pack turtleneck shirts and jeans and scarves and tennis shoes. Brooke watched her sift through her drawers of carefully folded colorful clothes and select the few that were drab and old and colorless. Brooke shuddered inside as Melanie slid her graceful hands under the layers of designer swimsuits she would never wear again and retrieved a neatly folded pair of gray sweat pants and a matching sweat shirt.

Once Melanie had finished packing the clothes in the small suitcase, she added two sketchpads, a container of colored pencils, a pincushion silvery with pin heads, a large pair of scissors and a box of needles and thread.

"Remember how much I enjoyed sewing and drawing clothes designs in high school?" Melanie asked offhandedly by way of answer to Brooke's obvious curiosity.

"Not really." We weren't friends, then.

"It's a hobby." Melanie hoped it could be something more. She had always hoped it. Now she would find out. Now it was all she had left.

Melanie insisted that Brooke not accompany

her to the airport, and Brooke acquiesced. Melanie didn't want her to have any idea where she was going.

Melanie doesn't want me to know where she is going because she doesn't want Charles to find out, Brooke decided. *Why?* Charles had gone to Windermere to bring her "home." What had happened?

"What about Charles?" Brooke asked finally as she walked Melanie to the waiting taxi cab.

Melanie's blue eyes glistened as she met Brooke's.

"Take care of him, Brooke," Melanie said quietly. *Love him.*

Chapter Thirty-four

"She's gone, Brooke?" Charles asked, incredulous, when he called Melanie's apartment three hours after Melanie took the taxi to the airport.

Charles had awakened early—he had barely slept—and taken a long walk on the storm-tossed beach and finally, at ten, tapped gently on her bedroom door. Melanie left a note, thanking Jason for his kindness in offering her refuge at Windermere and saying good-bye to Galen and Elise; but that was all. There was no note, no message, for Charles.

"Yes."

"Why?" It was a soft whisper of despair.

"I don't know, Charles." *Don't you know?*

Brooke assumed that something had happened with Charles. Melanie's urgent departure, and the deep pain in her eyes, could only have been because of Charles.

"Where did she go?"

"I don't know."

"How was she when you saw her?"

"She looked tired." *And so sad. Melanie looked the way you sound, Charles. What happened?* Brooke added hopefully, "Maybe getting away will be good for her."

The Manhattan Ripper was dead; and Melanie Chandler vanished; and Brooke Chandler joined Sinclair Publishing Company; and Jason Sinclair and Galen Elizabeth Spencer were married; and Lieutenant Nick Adrian refused numerous offers to write a book about the psychopath, as did Allison Parker, who, it was rumored, was going to resume her career in law; and Charles Sinclair was no longer at the parties; and then there was nothing more to say.

The press left them alone to get on with their lives.

Three weeks after Galen spent a somber afternoon reading the journal of Elliott Sinclair, she and Elise and Jason and Charles went together to the office of the geneticist who would tell them which twin was Elise's father. Elise squirmed in her mother's arms as they sat in tense silence in the doctor's waiting room.

"Elise," Galen whispered to the wriggling child. Galen thought about it for a brief moment, then she handed her lively, happy daughter to

Charles. Galen smiled softly at the surprised brown eyes. "Entertain her, will you, Charles?"

Charles didn't need to entertain Elise. Just being in his strong arms, patting his cheeks, and hearing his deep gentle voice was entertainment enough. Elise cooed contentedly and was no longer restless.

After Galen gave Elise to Charles, she reached for Jason's hand. Her fingers touched his gold wedding band, new and shiny and matching hers.

This is going to be all right, Galen reminded her fluttering heart. No matter what, we will make it all right.

Jason still held Galen's hand, and Charles still held Elise, when they sat in the doctor's office and heard the results.

"You are genetically very close." The doctor looked from one twin to the other. Physically, they were so different, but genetically . . . "However, there are two markers that are quite distinct. Elise has them, and Galen doesn't, and Jason does."

Galen and Jason greeted the wonderful news with silent tears of joy and an even tighter squeeze of the hands that already held so tight. Galen looked through her blur of tears toward Charles, but she couldn't see his reaction. His face was hidden, nuzzled in Elise's dark-brown curls. When he looked up finally, his eyes were dry.

Charles carried Elise—neither Galen nor Jason made a move to take her from him—until they reached the hospital lobby.

"I think I'll walk back." Charles broke the silence that had been with them since leaving the doctor's office. Charles gave Elise to Jason, met his twin's eyes, and smiled a shaky smile.

Jason returned the smile, and the thoughtful pale-blue eyes sent a message.

Tomorrow, or the day after, or the day after that, Charles, when this is behind us, we need to begin again.

We will, Jason, Charles pledged, perfectly understanding Jason's thought. *I just need a little more time.*

Three hours later, when Brooke walked into Charles's office to discuss a contract, she found him staring at the provocative, seductive photograph of Melanie as Sapphire. In the three weeks since Melanie left, Charles hadn't mentioned her. But Brooke knew he thought about her, missed her, every minute. Brooke saw the depthless, silent sadness.

Take care of him, Brooke, Melanie had said.

How can I? Brooke wondered. *He is so private.*

Now, in this rare, unguarded moment, as Charles gazed at the picture of the woman he loved, Brooke saw his immeasurable sorrow. Charles didn't know she was there; she was intruding. Brooke turned to leave, but her movement drew his attention.

"Brooke."

"Charles, I'm sorry." *I'm sorry to have disturbed you, I'm sorry about Melanie. How can I help you?*

"Have you spoken to her, Brooke?"

"Yes." Brooke smiled wistfully at his hopeful brown eyes. *She doesn't talk about you, Charles,*

506

but I feel her pain. "I don't know where she is. If I knew, Charles, I would tell you."

Charles nodded gratefully. Brooke would help if she could.

"How is she?"

"I think she's better," Brooke answered truthfully. Sometimes Brooke heard a slight lilt in the long-distance voice.

"Does she still plan to be away for two months?"

"Yes." Brooke didn't tell Charles the rest; it was only a guess. *I don't think Melanie is ever coming back, not here, not to New York, not to you.*

"Is Lieutenant Adrian in?" Brooke asked the receptionist at the precinct. Brooke could see Nick's office, but the blinds were closed.

"Oh, Ms. Chandler, how nice to see you! Yes, he's in."

"Is he alone?"

"Yes. Go on in."

Brooke hadn't seen Nick or spoken to him for over five weeks, not since they spent the night wrapping up the Manhattan Ripper case and she left at dawn with Melanie.

"Nick?" Brooke tapped softly on the door that was ajar.

"Brooke." Nick opened the door and smiled. "How are you?"

"Fine. And you?"

"Consumed with paperwork, as usual. Come in."

Nick shut the door, and they were alone in his

blind-darkened office, and Brooke suddenly felt anxious and shy. She had come for a *reason*—another confession to Nick Adrian—but she might not find the courage to tell him. There was the reason, that might leave, unspoken, with her; and there was the *excuse*. . . .

"I thought of a name for your book—*In Flagrante Delicto.*"

"My book?"

"About, uh, the case."

"I'm not going to write a book about it."

"I read that in Robin's column, but—"

"I'm not going to."

"Why not?"

"Because," Nick spoke solemnly to the ocean blue eyes, "of the innocent victims."

There were the innocent victims who had died. And there were the innocent victims who had survived: Melanie and Charles and Allison and Adam and *her*. Nick refused the lucrative book offers because of all of them; but, mostly, he refused because of Brooke.

"Nick . . ." Thank you.

"Besides I'm writing a novel."

"About?"

"About life." *About love. About you.* Nick shrugged. "So, how's your new job?"

"It's good. It was the right decision." Brooke frowned slightly.

But something isn't the way she hoped it would be, Nick mused. Some*one* isn't what she had hoped. Was Brooke here to tell him, her good friend Nick, about the love that wasn't happening with Charles? If so, Nick thought impatiently, let's get it over with.

"How is Charles?"

"Charles?" Brooke sighed softly. "Charles is so sad. I don't think Melanie is coming back to him."

"And that's bad?"

Brooke looked at Nick with surprise. "Yes. For both of them."

"But that isn't why you frowned when I asked you about your job?"

Brooke shook her head slowly and her cheeks flushed pink.

"What then?" Nick asked gently. Maybe . . .

"No homicides."

"Which means?" The seductive, inquisitive gray eyes wanted to know the real reason she was here; they demanded it. "Brooke?"

"Which means," Brooke whispered, "I don't see you."

"Brooke." Nick touched her face and felt her tremble. Then he kissed her. "Brooke."

"Nick."

They spoke between long, deep, tender kisses. "I have wanted you."

"Yes?"

"So much."

"Yes." *So much.*

Charles noticed Adam Drake's name on his appointment calendar and frowned. Tomorrow you go away—*run away*—to St. Barts, Charles told himself. Get it all behind you before you leave.

"I'm here to apologize, and it's long overdue."

Charles had never seen doubt in Adam's blue-gray eyes, but he saw it now.

"There's no need to apologize, Adam. It was an emotional time for all of us."

"I was wrong," Adam insisted.

"No, you were right. I hurt her terribly." So much that even though I am finally free of the secrets that made me unable to trust myself with her love, she can't trust me enough to try again. "I hurt her too much."

Charles sighed.

"Besides, Adam, you were involved—"

"No, we weren't. I think I was the only man Melanie even *saw* after you, Charles, but we weren't lovers."

Melanie had been faithful to him? For a moment Charles's heart pounded with hope. He had been faithful to her and the wonderful memory of their love. Had she been faithful to that memory too?

No, Charles decided sadly. Melanie's aversion to new relationships wasn't fidelity; she was merely afraid of getting hurt again.

"That explains why you returned to Paris."

"Yes. Didn't Melanie tell you that there was nothing between us?" Why not? Adam wondered. Revealing that truth had been so important to Melanie. It was all she cared about the day before she was attacked by the Manhattan Ripper.

"In Monte Carlo, but not since." Charles

frowned. Melanie and Adam may not have been lovers, but they were friends. Maybe . . . "Have you talked to her, Adam? Do you know where she is?"

"She called last week." Adam heard the quiet desperation in Charles's voice; it matched the emptiness in hers. If Adam knew where Melanie was, he would tell Charles. *I don't trust him when it comes to you,* Adam had told her once. It wasn't true any longer. Adam sighed. "I'm sorry, Charles, I don't know where she is."

"Why did she call?"

"To tell me she was never going to model again. She doesn't think she is beautiful anymore."

Doesn't she know that her magnificent looks are just a tiny part of her true beauty? Charles closed his eyes briefly, his mind tormented by the question. *Oh, darling Melanie, where are you?*

Charles finished packing and gazed at the sapphire-blue Caribbean. His week on St. Barts was over.

Charles had come to the lovely tropical paradise—where the rich and famous go to mourn losses, and rediscover themselves, and fall in love—to say good-bye to the memory. Charles hadn't been able to rent *their* villa on such short notice; it was already taken. Maybe it was just as well; it had been painful enough here, a mile away.

"Monsieur is leaving today?" the housekeeper

asked as she emerged from the just-swept living room onto the terrace.

"*Oui.*"

"*Dommage.* Your friend is staying for two more weeks."

Charles spun around. "My friend?"

The housekeeper look confused. She had taken care of the villa when Charles and Melanie were there a year ago. She had assumed . . .

"My friend?" Charles repeated.

"With the long golden hair."

"Where is she?" Charles could barely speak.

"At the villa where you usually stay. Perhaps I shouldn't have told you. . . ." The housekeeper frowned.

"Oh, yes, you should have. Thank you."

Hopeful, wonderful thoughts swirled in his mind as Charles drove the mini-Moke toward the villa. Melanie had chosen to come here, to the place where they had fallen in love. . . .

Charles knocked softly on the villa door. He didn't want to frighten her. There was no answer. Melanie still didn't answer as the energy of his knocking increased. She must be on the terrace or in the cove.

On impulse, Charles turned the doorknob. It was open! Doors were left unlocked on St. Barts. There was nothing to fear. But there had been such horrible, unwelcome intrusions in her life. Charles was glad, despite everything, Melanie felt safe here.

Charles called her name as he walked through the familiar villa. Everything was familiar but the living room. It had been transformed into a designer's workshop. Melanie was designing clothes from the wonderful, vivid tropical fabrics of St. Barts. Some of the fabrics lay neatly folded; others had already been sewn into breathtakingly beautiful creations. Sketches of designs lay on the table beside orderly rows of colorful thread.

Charles blinked away a rush of emotion, then walked beyond the living room onto the terrace. Melanie wasn't there; she had to be at the beach in the private cove. Charles's hands trembled as he opened the forest-green wrought-iron gate.

Melanie sat on the white sand at water's edge. She could be naked here—she had been naked, always, with him—but now she wore a modest white cotton cover-up. She didn't hear his footfalls on the soft sand, but something made her turn toward him as he approached.

"Charles."

"Hi." He knelt on the sand beside her.

"How . . .

"I didn't know. I never even thought to look for you here."

"Look for me?" *Why would you look for me?*

"Yes, of course." Charles frowned briefly, then asked softly, lovingly, "How are you?"

"I'm fine." Melanie looked at him for a moment then spoke to the water and sky. "I'm much stronger."

It was true. Her body was strong again. She jogged and swam and the pain was almost gone and the weakness was vanquished. Her body *felt* fit, but she avoided looking at it. One day she caught her reflection in the mirror and noticed that a once dark-purple scar had faded into a pastel pink. Maybe, as promised, eventually the scars would all be fine white lines; it didn't matter.

"I saw your designs. They're wonderful."

"Thank you." Melanie smiled slightly. "I've even sold some at the boutique in Lorient."

"Melanie Chandler, New York's hottest fashion designer," Charles suggested carefully.

"Not Melanie Chandler." *And not New York.*

"No?" Melanie Sinclair?

"I don't want my success—if I have success— to be because of who I was."

"Who you *are*," Charles corrected swiftly. *Melanie, look at me.* "So, what label?"

Melanie smiled wistfully at a distant memory that lay beyond the azure horizon.

"I thought of it because of what you said once."

"Yes?"

Melanie nodded and whispered the name of the label that already appeared on the designs she had sold in St. Barts, "Cocoon."

"Melanie."

The softness of his voice filled her eyes with tears. Charles wanted to hold her and kiss away the sadness, but she was so far away.

"Melanie, I know I hurt you terribly And I know you wondered if—"

"No." She turned and spoke to the dark-brown eyes. "No, Charles, I never wondered that."

I never wondered if you were the Manhattan Ripper. I always believed in you, Melanie thought as she returned her gaze to the sea. *I always loved you.*

"I thought you wanted to try again." His voice was so gentle.

"Yes," she whispered just above the soft sea breeze.

"Then what happened, darling? Why did you leave?" *Tell me, please.*

Don't you know, Charles? Of course, you know. Why are you asking?

"Remember what you told me in Monte Carlo, that I would be better off without you?"

"Yes. I believed it then."

"Because you had deep flaws."

"Yes, and because I loved you so much."

"But you didn't really have deep flaws." Melanie smiled sadly "And now I really do."

"I don't understand."

"Charles, you've seen what I look like."

Hot tears spilled onto her cheeks. Charles moved in front of her, cupped her lovely, sad face in his strong hands, and made her eyes meet his.

Why are you looking at me like that, Charles? Why are you smiling? How can there be desire in your eyes?

"Melanie, is that all?"

"All?"

"Darling, I love *you*. I hate what he did to you, because he hurt you and frightened you, but it doesn't *matter.*"

"Charles, I . . ." Melanie's voice broke.

Charles rescued her with a kiss.

"I love you, Melanie," Charles whispered as his lips brushed against hers.

"I love you, Charles."

They made love on the white sand beach in their private cove on St. Barts. The tropical sun caressed their naked bodies with a gentle warmth and the sapphire-blue water lapped softly at their feet. They made love slowly and tenderly, leisurely savoring the magnificent joy of being together. This time their loving wasn't desperate. This time they knew they had forever.

IF YOU HAVE ENJOYED READING
THIS LARGE PRINT BOOK AND
YOU WOULD LIKE MORE
INFORMATION ON HOW TO
ORDER A WHEELER LARGE PRINT
BOOK, PLEASE WRITE TO:

WHEELER PUBLISHING, INC.
P.O. BOX 531
ACCORD, MA 02018-0531